DAGGER HILL

DAGGER HILL

DEVON TAYLOR

Swoon
READS

SWOON READS
NEW YORK

A Swoon Reads Book
An imprint of Feiwel and Friends and Macmillan Publishing Group, LLC
120 Broadway, New York, NY 10271
fiercereads.com

Our books may be purchased in bulk for promotional, educational, or business use. Please contact your local bookseller or the Macmillan Corporate and Premium Sales Department at (800) 221-7945 ext. 5442 or by email at MacmillanSpecialMarkets@macmillan.com.

Library of Congress Cataloging-in-Publication Data
Names: Taylor, Devon, author.
Title: Dagger Hill : a novel / by Devon Taylor.
Description: New York : Swoon Reads, 2021. | Audience: Ages 13–18. |
   Audience: Grades 10–12. | Summary: After a mysteriously catastrophic
   incident shakes up their sleepy hometown, seventeen-year-old best
   friends Gabe, Kimberly, Charlie, and Sonya discover they are being
   hunted by a sinister presence.
Identifiers: LCCN 2020038680 | ISBN 9781250763341 (hardcover)
Subjects: CYAC: Best friends—Fiction. | Friendship—Fiction. |
   Supernatural—Fiction.
Classification: LCC PZ7.1.T3844 Dag 2021 | DDC [Fic]—dc23
LC record available at https://lccn.loc.gov/2020038680

First edition, 2021
Book design by Trisha Previte
Printed in the United States of America

ISBN 978-1-250-76334-1 (hardcover)
1 3 5 7 9 10 8 6 4 2

For my brother, Shane,
whose love of pop culture and music
brightens my life and lives in these pages

A song sung one, the end of the line.
A song sung two, we'll be just fine.
A song sung three, dead is divine.
A song sung four, all outta time.

—*Unknown*

THE ALMOST NOBODIES

JUNE 16, 1989
WINDALE, PENNSYLVANIA

THERE'S NO TIME to think before it hits.

When the plane comes rushing out of the storm, trailing streamers of cloud and smoke, in my mind I see it as a bird of prey. A huge, screeching eagle maybe. Sleek and featherless. But then I see the turbine engines. One under each wing. Vicious, spinning fans sucking in stray leaves and bits of debris kicked up by the wind. It's coming in slightly lower than where the four of us are standing. Our clearing. Our escape through so many summers and weekends.

At the last second, the plane's nose tips up, angling in our direction. I catch a glimpse of the cockpit window, dark except for the vague shape of somebody in the pilot's seat. Or maybe I'm just imagining that.

Maybe I want to pretend that someone could have even a tiny bit of control over what's happening here, that they could pull up with inches to spare and go screaming right over us, the fuselage scraping along the treetops. Like something out of Top Gun.

But Windale isn't the kind of place where miracles happen.

1.

GABE

ON THE MORNING of the most disastrous day in Windale history, I'm in the passenger seat of my dad's patrol car, dripping sweat. The ailing Crown Vic hasn't had fully functioning AC since last summer, when Dad burned out the blower, and today is already one of the hottest days on record. I shift and squirm, trying to find some relief. But my clothes are glued to my skin and my bare arms are peeling off the leather like it's flypaper.

"Dad," I say, "are you ever going to take this thing in to the shop? I think I lost ten pounds just this morning."

Behind the wheel, Dad turns the patrol car off Route 24, onto Old Briar Lane. We were in the Triangle before this, sitting in the damp, stagnant air of the car, parked right in front of the air-conditioned police station. We were breathing in the reefer stink coming from Sid Porter's comic shop, and Dad was trying to decide whether he wanted to go in there and bust him for possession (again) while I was around. Then the voice of Rebecca Conner, Dad's top deputy and right-hand woman, crackled through on the radio, told Dad she needed him out at the Webber farm right away. And off we went.

Dad caresses the worn-out steering wheel and says, "Why would I take it to the shop"—I mouth the next part along with him—"when I can just fix it myself?"

He doesn't see me mocking him, so it's safe to keep jabbing. "Because you don't have *time* to fix it yourself. And if I'm going to ride around with you all summer, I can't keep sweating like this. It's going to totally screw me for football next year."

Dad's lips press together. He knows what I'm doing, trying to skip out on him. Not just today, but the rest of the summer. I told my dad I wanted to be a cop because I thought it was what he wanted to hear. I told him I wanted to play football for the same reason. Now I'm bartering with one to get out of the other. For now, at least. It's my last summer in Windale, before senior year, before graduation. I'd rather spend it with my friends than cruising around town in this piece-of-shit car, wasting away in the heat.

The Webber farm comes into view, a wide swath of flat, grassy fields surrounded by low hills and dense trees. Clark Webber runs a cattle farm, and his land is all pasture, but today there's not a cow in sight.

Dad angles the Crown Vic onto the property and parks behind his other two deputies' patrol cars. He shuts off the engine, and the car chuckles with relief.

"I thought you wanted to do this with me," he says, looking at me but also not. He's squinting at something just over my head. I'm forced to stare at either his mustache, coated in droplets of sweat, or the ring of damp fabric that's supposed to be his collar.

"I do," I lie. "Just, you know, not all the time. I've only got one summer left, Dad."

"And you'd rather spend it with your friends." There's color in his cheeks, and I can't tell if it's from the heat or from his rising anger. Maybe both. "Is that what you're doing this afternoon?"

Here we go. "Yeah. We're just getting together for lunch. Then maybe a movie at Sonya's place."

"Where's lunch? The diner?"

"Dad, why are you interrogating me?" I say, gesturing out the window at the farm. "Shouldn't we . . . ?"

"Just tell me where you're having lunch, son." Dad's tone is patient, but his words are exactly the opposite. This is a conversation that's nearly as old as I am.

I mumble the answer, because I shouldn't have to say it when he already knows.

"Come again?" he says, raising his eyebrows. He stops short of cupping his hand around his ear.

"Dagger Hill," I say, louder this time.

"There it is." Dad leans back, looking satisfied but also seething. Meanwhile, through the windshield, Rebecca Conner appears and waves, a little frantic, her brown skin shining with sweat. Dad gives her the "one second" finger, then cocks a thumb in my direction. Subtle.

Rebecca doesn't miss a beat, though. She nods, gives Dad a thumbs-up, then catches my eye and winks. *Hang in there, kid*, she likes to say when Dad is on one of his tirades. Melvin O'Connell, Dad's other deputy, is as good a guy as they come, but Rebecca is easily my favorite. She's exactly the kind of person you want on your side when the shit starts to hit. Usually, when it comes to arguments between me and Dad, she's on mine.

"Gabe, I've been telling you and your friends to stay off that hill since you were ten," Dad goes on. "It's not safe."

"Dad," I say, dropping my head back against the seat, "can we please talk about this later? Like, somewhere that's not five hundred degrees and smells like cow shit?"

"Language," Dad says, not with any conviction. Cussing apparently doesn't bother him as much as me and my friends hanging out in the only place we ever have to ourselves. "I really don't like it when you kids go up there, son."

"We're not kids, Dad. And we just go up there to . . . I don't know . . . get away. Everyone else from school is always down at the Heart-to-Heart Bridge, and I know you *definitely* don't want us hanging around *that* crowd. Dagger Hill is just the next best option."

Only some of that is true. Charlie, Sonya, Kimberly, and I—we couldn't show our faces at the Heart-to-Heart even if we wanted to. The four of us have been friends for so long, and we're so tightly knit that we've funneled ourselves into our own subcategory of the high school social hierarchy. They like to call us the Almost Nobodies.

Dagger Hill has been our escape for as long as I can remember.

Dad sighs, scratching at the scruff under his chin. It makes a sound like sandpaper. "We will table this conversation until later. But you're not off the hook, Gabe. Just because you're going to be a senior doesn't mean that the rules no longer apply to you. The same goes for your friends."

I don't say anything, just nod. With Chief Jack Albright, there's a good time to speak and a bad time to speak. Opening your mouth after he thinks he's had the final word falls under the latter.

We open our doors, step out into sweltering sunshine. It's hot and hazy, shimmering with the slow drip of summer. But a slight breeze makes it a little more bearable than the baking dish of Dad's patrol car, though there's a whiff of something unpleasant attached to it. Dad pulls his hat out from behind the driver's seat and screws it down on his head, shading his face. Then we crunch up the gravel driveway to where Rebecca and Mel are waiting.

Out here, the morning sun is already well above the horizon. Long golden streams of light reach out from between the trees at the edge of the farm, and the shadows are all strung out like dark caricatures of the objects casting them—the house, the barn, the fence, the herd.

The herd.

As we approach Deputies Conner and O'Connell, I only take a cursory glance at the property. Dad too. Thumbs stuck in his belt, aviator sunglasses on over his eyes, hiding his expression. If he were any more of a stereotype, he'd have on chaps and a cowhide vest with a gold star pinned to it.

But something about the herd of cattle inside the far fence makes us both do a double take. I look back, and my stride slows. Dad's jaw unhinges, dropping open. He stops completely, pulls the shades off his face. I feel my stomach churn as we stare.

"Hell of a sight, huh?" It's Rebecca, closing the distance between where Dad and I halted and where the others were waiting—her and Mel and Mr. Webber.

"I . . . ," Dad starts, but the words die in his throat. He smacks his lips together a couple of times, as if trying to get the motor running

4

again. "What the fffffuuuu . . ." Those words get lost, too, dissolving into a noisy exhalation.

"What . . . what happened?" I ask. My mouth feels very dry.

"Not a goddamn clue," Rebecca says, standing beside us now with her arms folded. Her thick black hair is pulled into a tight bun, and the creases in her uniform are all but perfect. She stands straight and tall, as always, never willing to take a single ounce of bullshit from anyone. Still, there's something in her voice today. A tremor that I've never heard before. I doubt Dad has, either.

The other two men begin stomping through the dirt toward us, led by the pulled-taffy shape of Clark Webber—tall, pale white, withering, and hunched over like he's got a crick in his back. He probably does.

I try not to, but I glance at the cattle again, really seeing them for the first time. Really *smelling* them, too.

A few yards into the pasture, piled into a mountainous heap, the herd lies dead. Their knobby limbs jut out this way and that, their heads—the ones that are still all the way intact—loll to one side or the other, tongues dripping from wide-open mouths like coagulated oil. Glassy, surprised-looking eyes stare out in every direction. Some of the animals have been shot, bullets shredded into meat, leaving flaps of shiny pink muscle dangling like gruesome Christmas tree ornaments. Deeper down in the pile, there are cows that appear to have died from being smothered or broken by the others. One poor heifer has another's entire leg shoved far back into its throat, a look of shock and horror on its face so real that it's almost comical.

The entire herd is like that—twisted and mangled, wrapped up in each other in a way that looks like they were trying to push themselves together, to merge into a single supercow. Already the flies have begun to swarm, buzzing in and out of the mass, creeping across the marbles of the cattle's eyes.

Mel and Mr. Webber join us, and our entire group of five can do nothing for a few moments but stare into the field, as if we're at one of the art shows Kimberly's always going on about, observing a sculpture that doesn't make any sense to us.

Dad is the first to break the silence. "Anyone care to take a crack at trying to explain just what in the absolute shit happened here?" His eyes fall on me for a moment, and when I look over at him, I feel like I might puke or pass out or both. Dad's face is hard as stone, but I can see that some of the color has drained out of it.

Mr. Webber steps forward then, breaking the moment. Dad takes the farmer's hand and shakes it, a strange formality given the circumstances.

"Jack," Webber says.

"Clark," Dad replies. "Feels like we haven't caught up in a while."

"Not since the last time yous were out here. Couple years ago, I think that was. When the Williams kid stole my tractor."

"Ah, you're right." Dad glances over at me with a slight smirk, drops a hand on my shoulder. "You remember my son, Gabe. He's riding along with me for the summer, getting a few internship hours under his belt before college."

"I'm sorry about your herd, Mr. Webber," I say, shaking his hand, then stuffing my fists into my pockets.

Webber sighs. "You and me both, kid. I don't . . ." The man falters, and he looks down at his feet, kicking at the earth with the toes of his boots. "I had to shoot some of them myself. Put them out of their goddamn misery. That's where the bullet wounds came from. I . . . I just didn't know what else to do."

"Clark says they went crazy," Mel interjects. It's the first time he's spoken, which is unusual, because Mel is my dad's version of my best friend, Charlie—a wisecracking, sarcastic son of a bitch who knows the exact wrong thing to say at exactly the wrong time.

Dad nods at his deputy, then turns back to Mr. Webber. "Can you tell it one more time, Clark? For my sake?"

Rebecca shifts uncomfortably on her feet, as if she doesn't really want to be around for this again. I glance over at her, offering what I hope is a comforting smile. *Hang in there, kid.* And she grins.

"I heard 'em before I saw . . . before I saw what was happening," Webber says, keeping his eyes fixed on any point that is not the dead cattle. "They weren't just out here making their usual noises. Sometimes at night, they would get a little spooked. They'd give a little holler now and then, maybe just talking to each other, making sure they're not alone. But this . . . Last night they weren't just talking. They were *screaming*."

I glance back into the pasture, eyeing the corpses again. I'm glad I haven't eaten anything yet today, otherwise my stomach would be doing a horrible song and dance.

Webber keeps going. "So I came out here. Something told me to grab my rifle on the way out. In all my time on this earth, I've never heard cattle make noises like that. I knew something was wrong. I knew something was scaring the shit out of them."

"And *was* something scaring the shit out of them?" Dad asks, keeping his voice firm, though I can hear the cracks underneath.

"That's just it," Webber says, "I never saw a damn thing. Not a raccoon or a fox or even a goddamned bear, which I know don't really live out here, but still. I just can't imagine what would have caused my herd to be so afraid."

"What was the herd doing when you came outside?" Dad says.

Still without actually looking at it, Mr. Webber tilts his head toward the hill of wrecked cattle, frozen in a state of violence the likes of which I didn't think these animals were capable of. "They were doing this. I . . . I think they were trying to huddle together, trying to protect one another. But they got so scared that they just . . . they just started climbing all over each other. They were scrambling and flailing. In the dark, it was hard to see. But I thought maybe there was something in the middle that they were . . . I don't know . . . *attacking.* Cows don't know how to defend themselves. You bump into one of 'em with the tractor, they just get out of the way like it was their fault. I just . . . I keep trying to come up with a rational explanation, and I can't do it."

After a beat, Mel asks, "When did you start shooting, Clark?"

The farmer doesn't hesitate. In a steady voice, he says, "When I started to hear their bones breaking."

Rebecca and I both wince.

"They went on like that for hours," Webber continues. "I yelled and screamed and threw shit at 'em, but nothing got them to stop. They were killing each other. Terrified enough to forget the herd and do whatever it took to survive. They just used their own kind to try to climb up and out, to try to get away from whatever it was that scared them. When the ones that made it to the top started crushing the ones on the bottom, that's when I fired my gun. I didn't know what else to do. Most of these cows were on their way to the slaughterhouse. They were as good as dead, anyway, ya know? But it's different like this. Whatever the fuck happened here, it isn't right. I couldn't let them suffer."

Dad grips the man's shoulder and squeezes. They're by no means friends, but they're neighbors—in that old-fashioned, small-town sense of the word, anyway. "You did the right thing, Clark."

Webber's eyes are wide and bloodshot. There's a weary rage in them that makes us all uneasy. "No offense, Chief, but it doesn't matter if it was right or wrong. When you don't have a choice, the ethics of a thing go right out the fucking window. This farm has been running for three generations. We raise the cattle, treat 'em right, feed 'em well, and make sure they meet the end as humanely as possible. This . . ." Finally, he looks at the mass of brutalized animals, *his* animals, and his eyes well with sudden tears. "This took all that out of my hands and left me with only one thing I could do."

"Let them kill each other," Dad says, "or kill them yourself."

Mr. Webber nods, sniffling. And again, our group is quiet.

I think for a second that we're done here. Dad didn't write anything down, but I notice a tiny notebook in Rebecca's hand, the fleshy pink of a pencil eraser sticking out from between the pages. I'm itching to check my watch, even though Dad would say it's impolite. I shove my hands deeper into my pockets to resist the urge. I'm not just anxious to get back to the Triangle and meet up with my friends—I'm also anxious to leave this horror show behind.

Clark Webber wipes his face with a dirty rag that came from his back pocket, and he looks at my dad, then at the rest of us—maybe to make sure we're paying attention—and nods at something over our heads, behind us to the west.

"This is all *their* doing," Webber says. His voice is empty of grief—there's only that exhausted fury left.

I know exactly what I'm going to see before I turn around, but I turn anyway, for the same reason that I didn't check my watch. Dad gives me a look as we turn, but I don't know what it means.

Out beyond the pasture, decorated now with the pile of mostly self-slaughtered cattle, is a stretch of tall trees that run the length of Mr. Webber's property. Thick branches, thicker trunks, a canopy of bright green leaves so dense that the shadows beneath it are almost black. With the perfect blue sky behind it, the whole scene could be a Bob Ross painting—except for the dead cows, of course, and the cluster of antennas and satellite dishes poking up from behind the tree line. From here, I can just barely see the gray concrete rooftop they're attached to.

"TerraCorp," Dad says.

"I don't know what kind of wacko science experiments they're up to in there," Mr. Webber says behind us, "but that place has been doing damage to this property for almost twenty years. Since before you were chief, Jack."

I continue to stare at the radio cluster on TerraCorp's roof even as Dad turns back around to face Webber. The biggest satellite dish is a shiny metal bowl, sparkling in the sunlight as if it were made of aluminum foil. After a few seconds, something else grabs my attention, taking shape in the sky to the northwest. At first, it's just a dark blip, an ink smudge, a "happy accident." But then it turns an olive shade of green, and it grows a pair of wings. It has a low belly and a couple of big turbine engines, one under each wing. I hear it before it comes all the way into view, a soft, coughing roar.

"Did anything strange happen out there last night?" Dad is asking Mr. Webber. "Something that might have startled your animals?"

"Startled?" Webber chuckles. "You call that startled, Jack? Really?"

"Uh, Dad?" I say over my shoulder, my eyes pinned to the incoming plane. It's clearly some kind of military cargo jet, and it's angled toward Windale, coming down steep, turning slightly. TerraCorp is a government installation, top secret. People in town whisper about what goes on there, our own personal Area 51. There are plenty of wild theories, but I've definitely never seen a plane coming in to land out there.

"You know what I mean, Clark," Dad says. "That was a poor choice of words. Did you see anything happening out at TerraCorp last night that we might be able to link with what happened to your herd?"

"Dad?" I try again, watching the plane descend even more, growing clearer, sharper. "Rebecca? Anyone?" The sound of the engines is building, swallowing up the buzz of the cicadas.

"Nobody's seen inside the walls of that place since they built it in '71. You should know that better than anybody," Webber says to Dad.

"*Dad!*" I yell. Everyone goes quiet behind me. Dad steps up to my side, mouth tucked tight under his mustache, his brow crushed into a knot.

The plane is louder than ever now. It pivots in the air, dropping lower and lower, swooping in like a hawk. It glides over the treetops, then disappears behind them. I brace for an impact—but it never comes. All the way out here, the record-scratch sound of tires touching down on tarmac carries.

"Since when does TerraCorp have a landing strip?" Rebecca asks.

"No idea," Dad says, distracted. But I can see his eyes drift over to me, casting the same look as before. I know what it means now.

"Bastards." Mr. Webber again, speaking through gritted teeth. "They killed my herd. Murdered 'em. What's next? Am I gonna open the henhouse and find all my chickens in a heap just like this one?"

I turn back around, now that the sky has gone quiet and empty, and find Mr. Webber shaking, fists clenched.

"Someone's gotta answer for this," the farmer says.

"Clark," Dad says with a warning in his tone, "don't do anything that's going to make me have to arrest you. You did the right thing by calling us. Let us take it from here."

Webber is still shaking, his eyes trained on the smooth, light-filled bowl of TerraCorp's main radio dish. "You've done enough," he says. "Thank you for coming. Now if you'll excuse me, I have a mess to clean up."

His head dips ever so slightly toward the mountainous tangle of cows, and I can't help but take in the sight one last time. A light breeze picks up the smell and drags it over to us. Heavy, coppery—ground beef and pennies. It's so overwhelming my eyes start to water. I have to fight to not gag.

I step up to Mr. Webber and put my hand on his shoulder. I squeeze gently but firmly, the way Coach Ferguson does to me on Friday nights before a game.

"I'm sorry for your loss, Mr. Webber," I say, trying to sound polite and comforting and probably coming off as neither. "Good luck with everything."

He seems startled for a second, both from my touch and my words. But it breaks the hold, and his eyes finally drift over to me. I've got a good few inches on him, but I'm tilted to the side so that we're almost eye to eye. His are bloodshot and wrapped in angry red rings.

"You too, kid," he says.

2.

SONYA

"ALMOST THERE?"

My voice rings down the hall, aimed at Dad's office. Leaning half in and half out of my bedroom, I can hear Dad tinkering around at the back of the house, through the open door of what my friends affectionately refer to as the "secret lair." I glance in at my vanity, an old family hand-me-down that Mom insisted I have, which is now overcome by a Commodore Amiga 500. There's a picture of the four of us—me, Charlie, Gabe, and Kimberly—tucked into the mirror frame. We're sitting together at a booth in the diner, a bunch of food between us, laughing about something. That was from last summer, and there's a weird, uncomfortable throb in my heart thinking about what this summer means, what's coming at the end of it.

"Got it!" Dad calls from the shadow of his open office door. "Are we on?"

On my vanity, the beige plastic hulk of a computer blinks to life. A big orange extension cord winds its way out my door and down the hall. Dad wanted to hook it up to the surge protector in his office so we don't trip any breakers.

I sit down at the stool in front of the vanity and brush my fingertips over the keyboard. "We're on," I say, not quite loud enough. But I'm too caught up in the crackly sound the thick keys make as I sweep a hand over them. I feel like a pianist getting acquainted with her instrument.

Dad either hears me or just has a little fatherly intuition, because his head pokes around the doorway. He's a quiet man. Kind, patient.

All those other things that First Corinthians says love is. He gets along with everyone in town. Well, everyone except Chief Albright. But according to Gabe, that's only because his dad has a natural distrust for anyone in a white coat. *My* dad happens to have one draped over his arm at this very moment. He's on his way to work. I can see the TerraCorp ID badge clipped to one lapel, flashing a picture of Dad that's as old as I am.

"What do you think?" he asks with a sideways grin.

"I . . ." I glance over at the computer, at the swampy screen and the green flashing cursor. "It's awesome, Dad. I can't wait to get to work."

"Good." His grin gets wider. "Getting into MIT isn't easy. You have to show them you really deserve to be there."

I nod, looking away. "I know. I'll make you proud. I promise."

Dad steps into the room, leans over my chair. I can smell the bland fragrance of the soap he always uses. I feel his lips press into my nest of curls. "You already have, little one," he says.

Down the hall, in the secret lair, Dad's private phone rings. The loud jangle of it startles us both, and we laugh as he ducks back into the hall and jogs for the office.

"Don't move!" he calls back to me. He promised to help me set up the computer before going in to the lab today, but I already know this phone call means our time is getting cut short. It doesn't bother me, really. Not anymore. Whatever work they do at TerraCorp is important enough that Dad is willing to drop everything to go do it. Either I've come to accept it or I'm just numb to it now. If my feelings got hurt every time Dad got called into the lab, I'd be a sulky, miserable wreck.

Normally, when his private line rings, Dad slips into the office and closes the door. The latch has a very distinctive click, and the door always thumps perfectly into its frame, cutting Dad off from the world, his own private isolation room. But today I don't hear the click or the thump. He must have pushed the door shut behind him but not hard enough for it to close all the way. I can hear his voice drifting down the hall to my room.

". . . the hell are you talking about?" Dad says, his voice hushed but urgent. "I did not authorize . . . Well, *who did?*" He sounds angry, which is not an emotion I usually associate with my father. I can't help myself; I get up and cross the room to my own door and lean against the frame so I can hear better. "You can tell Colonel Higgins that she has no business on TerraCorp property, and she is not to touch any part of our research. I . . . Yes, I know you're not in charge of the army, Claudia. Neither am I. But I will get President Bush on the phone if I have to."

Whoa. I've never heard that line before. TerraCorp is a government-contracted facility, which is pretty much all I know about it, but I didn't realize Dad had such high-level connections. Unless he's just bluffing for Claudia's sake.

". . . don't care what kind of paperwork she shows you. Higgins does not enter that lab until I get there. Do you understand me? She stays on that airstrip. And with any luck, once I arrive, she won't get past it. Keep stalling, Claudia. Give me twenty-five minutes at most."

I hear the clack of the phone being dropped into its cradle, and I rush back to my chair, padding across the carpet as quickly and quietly as I can. Dad's heavy footfalls shuffle across his office, pause at the entryway—maybe to inspect the door he left ajar—then come down the hall to my room again.

"Hey, little one," he says, a slight perplexity in his voice.

I pretend to be busy examining the Commodore. "Hey." *Everything all right at work?* almost slips out, but I catch it just in time. I don't want him to know I was eavesdropping.

"You didn't hear any of that, did you?"

"Hear any of what?" I say, not a beat missed.

He pauses. I can feel him watching me. Then: "You know what, never mind. I have to run, though. I'm sorry."

"Yeah, I kind of figured. It's okay, Dad."

"You sure?" He stares at me over his glasses.

"Of course," I reply. "The great Dr. Alvaro Gutierrez is needed at the lab. This can wait." It comes out sounding snarkier than I mean it to, but Dad knows I'm just jabbing him. The chime of his office phone has been a running joke in our family since I was a kid. While my friends call the office itself the secret lair, Mom and my little sister, Sophia, and I all refer to that phone as the "hotline."

He rolls his eyes and grins, readjusting the folded lab coat on his arm self-consciously. "I don't know when I'll be back," he says. "But as soon as I am, we'll finish getting that thing working, okay?"

"Deal," I say. I offer him a smile of my own, but it doesn't feel genuine. I've been faking smiles a lot lately, for a lot of reasons. This afternoon, I'll have to fake even more. These days, I dread spending time with my friends almost as much as I look forward to it.

Dad winks, pushes off my bedroom doorframe, and disappears down the other end of the hall. And then I'm alone.

3.
CHARLIE

CLICK.

The shutter in my head snaps, and there's a picture of Don Cranston, editor in chief of the *Windale Press*, looking through a stack of my photos. He's a wiry man with a bristly mustache, white skin, and an ever-widening bald spot on the very top of his head. The hair that rings it isn't quite brown, but it's not totally gray, either. It's the color of dead leaves in the fall.

Don is examining my photos with a level of scrutiny I would only associate with a jeweler peering through a loupe at the crystalline angles of a diamond. He's even got a magnifying glass nearby. There's a reason Chief Albright likes to refer to Don as "Mr. Junior Detective." Don lives and breathes with the tiny, intricate movements of our small town, stalking from corner to corner in a long tan trench coat, scribbling in his pocket notebook. The magnifying glass really puts that image over the top.

After a few minutes, Don finally sets down my stack of pictures. His oversized wooden desk stretches between us, and he watches me across it. His fingers are laced together over his mouth.

"You're friends with the chief's son, right?" he says finally.

"Yeah . . . ," I reply, readjusting my seat in the chair. "What does that have to do with anything?"

"It doesn't," Don says. "I just wanted to see if you'd ask that question. You're applying for the summer internship?"

"Uh . . . yes. Why else would I be here?" I cock my head at him, confused and weirdly uncomfortable.

"Another good question. You know you're one of many applicants for this program, right?"

"Wait, really?"

"Well . . . no. But it's still a tough program."

"I assumed so," I say, already regretting coming down here. "That's why I wanted to be a part of it. I'm trying to get into a good journalism school."

Don eyes me for a moment. "That's admirable. And I'm honored that you'd consider the *Press* to help you in that journey." For that split second, he almost sounds genuine. "But one thing they'll teach you in journalism school is what exactly assumptions are and whom exactly they make an ass out of." He waggles his bushy eyebrows in a very Groucho Marx kind of way, and I'm suddenly ready for this interview to be over. My friends are meeting up soon for lunch on Dagger Hill, and I can't think of a better way to spend my afternoon.

"Listen, Don—er, Mr. Cranston," I say. "I just need a few good internship hours for my college application. Can you help me or not?"

Don pauses, trying to look intimidating but failing. Eventually he sighs and removes his glasses. "Your pictures are really good, Mr. Bencroft," he says. "And I mean *really* good. Not only can you come in here whenever you want over the summer, but if for some reason the college thing doesn't pan out, I'll hire you the second you graduate high school. The *Press* could use a photographer like you."

I emerge from the *Windale Press* office a few minutes later. It's an old, tilted building at the corner of King Street and Perkiomen Avenue, only about two miles west of the Triangle. The sky is bright and blue and full of possibility. It's going to be a hot one today, but I've got my red puffer vest and my dad's hat on. Not to mention his old Polaroid Sun 600 draped over my shoulders. I take a big whiff of premium summer air and let it out in a long whistle.

Up the street, some kids are playing hopscotch along the sidewalk. It's extra hard because the concrete is broken and buckled, lifted by old tree roots. I stop, aim my camera, snap the shot. The picture comes sliding out the front, a gray square. I won't know if it's a decent shot until it's fully developed, but that's part of the fun. Risking what feels most precious—in this case, a piece of film that may or may not have been wasted—and taking the chance anyway, waiting to see how it all turns out, being okay with the outcome no matter what . . .

My friend Kimberly would call that blind optimism. I just think of it as hope.

Thinking of Kim, I check my watch. Her shift is almost up at the diner. Gabe and Sonya are supposed to meet us outside, then we're going up to Dagger Hill for lunch. After that, it's back to Sonya's place for a while, then on to the premiere of *Ghostbusters II* tonight.

As I head east on King Street, flapping the undeveloped photo at my side, I notice a dense knot of black clouds to the north. Right now they're just a single blemish on a smooth, perfect sky. I'm sure if there is a storm, it won't interrupt our lunch.

I hope.

4.

KIMBERLY

THE BELL DINGS, and I swirl away from the counter with a hot pot of coffee in my hand. With the empty one, I scoop up Mr. Halvorson's short stack and eggs. I carry it down the line, swirl again, and bring the plate in for a landing. Mr. Halvorson doesn't notice until the glassy *thunk* against the countertop. He lowers his paper, offers me a toothless smile as I top off his mug.

"Thanks, Kimberly," he says. "Too bad I can't take you home with me. You're a helluva better waitress than the old ball and chain, if you know what I mean." And then he winks.

I can't think of an adequate response that won't get me fired, so I just smile and say, "Let me know if you need anything else, Mr. Halvorson."

I retreat. Quickly. Dropping the coffeepot back into its cradle, I take a second to stretch and check the clock over the kitchen window. Only five more minutes to go. Breakfast rush is the busiest shift, but it's also the fastest. It forces me to get out of bed at a decent hour even though there's no school, and I have the whole afternoon to do as I please. It's not the greatest gig in the world—especially when you have people like "Handsy Halvorson" to deal with—but this'll probably be my last summer doing it.

After that? Not a single goddamn clue.

"Hey, Kimberly."

I smell a stale cigar before I see Harry Kunz, owner of this fine establishment known as the King Street Diner. He's getting up there in age, has to walk with a cane to keep his bad hip from giving out, and the lenses of his bifocals are so thick they make his eyes look as if they're inflating out of his skull. He should be scary—not just because he's my boss—but he's one of the kindest people in Windale.

"Hey, Harry," I say. I try to smile, but the muscle groups required to do so are all worn out. I'm not sure they were working properly this morning to begin with. I've been off all morning, feeling drowsy and cold even as fine droplets of sweat slither down my back. Bad dreams. Night sweats. Waking in a fit, tangled in my bedsheets, struggling to breathe.

I'm one of the Almost Nobodies, a moniker we picked up somewhere in middle school when we were already too attached to each other to make different friends. But even among our little group, I'm kind of known as the downer, the black cloud that sometimes hovers over the sunshiny day. Sonya is always quick to defend me, calls me a realist, which is only sometimes true. Other times, I'm just . . . sad. For no reason. My body feels like it's full of sand, my brain feels like it's turned into the scrambled eggs that Mr. Halvorson is currently sucking up like spaghetti.

Today is one of those days. In fact, today might be *worse* than one of those days.

"Yous doin' okay, hon?" Harry asks. I already forgot he was standing there.

I blink a few times. "Um. Yeah. You know. Just trying to shake off the last of the school year. Those final exams are killer."

"Yeah" is all he says, watching me with those buggy eyes. "How about yous take off early?"

"That's okay, Harry," I say. "Really. I've only got a few minutes left anyway."

"Except you and I both know it won't just be a few minutes." Harry raises his eyebrows, leans toward me. "Right? Yous'll get sucked into grabbing a few more tables because you're a good worker and you're trying to help out, and your friends'll be waiting outside for the next half hour while you finish up. Am I right or am I right?"

That drags a dusty laugh out of me. And before I can protest further, Harry presses a wad of cash into my hand—today's tips.

"Are you sure?" I ask. I glance over his shoulder at Mr. Halvorson, who's only half preoccupied with his breakfast. He likes to eat slow.

Harry follows my gaze, chuckling. "I'm sure," he says. "Get out of here. Yous look like you could use an extra few minutes to yourself. I'll go see if old Handsy has a thing for mostly blind old coots." He waggles his eyebrows, and like some kind of magic, I feel myself laughing again.

"Thanks, Harry," I say, trying to hold on to that bubbly feeling. It fades too quickly.

Outside, the day is thick and muggy, alive with insects and people tooling around the Triangle. The King Street Diner is on the northwestern corner of the intersections of King, Spruce, and Main. Lining the sides of the small triangle formed by these intersections are rows of local businesses and official buildings. Sid's Comic Emporium, Miles of Styles hair salon, East Capital Bank, the police station, the library, the Stuck Pig tavern, and the Sunrise movie theater, to name a few. In the middle is a small, triangular courtyard dotted with a few trees and boxy hedges, and some benches that sit around a simple fountain. The fountain, for some reason, is in the shape of a circle.

I cross King Street to the courtyard and do a quick turn on the sidewalk opposite the diner. I'm scanning for my friends—Charlie sidling in from whichever direction, Sonya on her bike, Gabe in the Chevelle he recently inherited from his dad. The Chevelle is here, parked in front of the police station, but the chief's patrol car is missing, and so are my friends. It's strange to be out here on my own, waiting for them—normally, I'm the holdup.

Looking around, I spot Mrs. Rapaport and her boom box perched on one of the courtyard benches. Mrs. Rapaport is a bizarre combination of town gossip and town witch. At least, that's what Charlie and I think. Sonya has too much faith in science to think that far outside the box, and Gabe has remained mostly silent on the subject over the years but more recently seems to have an unspoken alliance with Sonya. Of course.

Mrs. Rapaport looks as if she should be feeding bread crumbs to pigeons out of a brown paper bag. But there's no bag and no pigeons. She has silver hair that gets a dye treatment regularly from Maureen Newcomb at Miles of Styles—it's supposed to be brown, but today her roots catch the sunlight. She sits with her pale, papery hands folded neatly in her lap, rocking forward slowly, then settling back against the bench. An old, stretched afghan is draped over her shoulders despite the heat. And the boom box plays long, uninterrupted hours of static. Mrs. Rapaport watches the Triangle with milky eyes and a contented smile.

I struggled for a long time to find a good way to describe Mrs. Rapaport. (I guess, because both of my parents are writers, I picked up a talent for it myself, scribbling notes and poems in the margins of the books I read.) Until a couple of months ago, when this movie *Teen Witch* came out, and I realized that maybe Windale has its very own version of Madame Serena.

"Morning, Mrs. Rapaport," I say, idling on one of the small pathways cutting across the courtyard. I fidget with my hair—it's frizzed and frayed from work—slide my favorite blue scrunchie out, let the hair fall around my shoulders in sandy blond waves until I feel like it's stifling me, and then gather it all up again, lock it in place with the scrunchie.

"You don't have to worry, dear," Mrs. Rapaport says. There's a bray of something that sounds like a distant, fuzzy talk show on her boom box, then it's back to the steady white noise.

That's a funny way of saying good morning, I think. I have to clamp my mouth shut to keep it from spilling out.

"Worry about what?" I ask instead. But her words are kind of chilling. I live with a constant knot of anxiety in my gut, pulled taut by nagging fears and self-consciousness, and weighed down by a thick, dark cloud of dread. I've said a thousand good mornings to this woman, but nothing really beyond that. My friends don't even know how desperate my mind can get; why would Mrs. Rapaport?

"The sleep is safe," she says. Her head swivels around, tilts back so her faded eyes can look at mine. "Whatever you do, don't wake up." Another sputter of half-coherent garble from the boom box, loud enough this time to startle me.

"But I am awake," I say, my voice barely there.

Mrs. Rapaport looks away. "For now."

The boom box cuts to a crystal-clear snippet of music, somebody playing saxophone. I recognize it immediately as "In Your Arms" by Richard Elliot. The song at the end of *Teen Witch*.

"Hey, Kim!"

I jump at the sound of my name, and Mrs. Rapaport's stereo snaps back to static. But there's a coy smile lingering on her lips as she watches the arcs of the fountain.

Charlie comes up beside me, hands stuffed into the pockets of his puffer vest. His horn-rimmed glasses catch the sun as he smiles down at me, and of course his Polaroid is knocking against his chest.

"Hey," he says, almost breathless. "You're out here early. Did Harry fire you or . . ." He scrunches his eyebrows, tilting his head. "You okay?" He must see the look on my face.

"I . . . don't know," I say.

Through the corner of my eye, I can see Charlie following my gaze. When he spots Mrs. Rapaport sitting there, he says, "Ah. I see."

Without another word, he lifts his camera, aims it at the old woman, and snaps her picture.

5.

GABE

MY FRIENDS—SONYA, CHARLIE, Kimberly—are all waiting in the Triangle courtyard when Dad and I pull up in the Crown Vic. Dad slides it into the spot with a rusted-over sign that says RESERVED FOR CHIEF. He cuts the engine, and the old boat dies with a croak and a wheeze.

I move to open my door, but Dad catches my arm. He's never laid a finger on me in anger; he just gets loud, like a tornado siren, revving up and reeling in at equal bursts. But I'm more afraid of these moments right here, quiet and tense, thick with all the words we wish we could say out loud.

"You're still going up to the Hill for lunch?" Dad asks. He's not looking at me. His eyes are fixed on the useless AC dial.

"Yes . . . ?" There's already a whisper of attitude in my voice. *Like, of course we're going up to the Hill, Dad. We've been hanging out up there since we were in fifth grade, and none of your old stories about ghosts or mysterious deaths or serial killers or whatever are going to make us afraid. So please don't waste my time with another one.*

I swallow it all back down.

"I wish you wouldn't," Dad says.

"I know, Dad. I promise we'll be careful, though, okay?"

"You can promise whatever you want, son." His mustache quirks as he presses his lips together. Holding back his own tirade, maybe. "It doesn't change the history that Dagger Hill has with this town. And none of it is good. I just don't want to see you or the other kids become a part of that history."

"We're not kids anymore, Dad. We're going to graduate next year, and then . . ." I trail off because I don't know what happens after that. College, I guess. The four of us jettisoned to random parts of the country. I glance in the rearview at the others, standing around, laughing, that weird apprehension in their eyes that wasn't there before. The Almost Nobodies are almost nothing, and I have no idea how to stop it. Maybe I'm not supposed to.

"Gotta go, Dad," I say, and yank the door handle before he can protest.

"Gabe, wait a second—" The rest is cut off by my door slamming.

I hurry away from the chief's patrol car, snapping on my best smile, patting my jeans to make sure I've still got my keys—thank god I didn't leave them in Dad's car. I throw my hands in the air when the others see me and yell, "Heeeeyyyy! What's happening, Nobodies?"

Kimberly rolls her eyes, but Charlie and Sonya laugh.

"Hey, dick," Charlie says as he slaps me five. "I thought part of acquiring a nasty nickname in high school was never calling yourself by that nickname." He's grinning as he says it, though, because if anyone knows how to embrace the suck, it's Charlie Bencroft.

"It's not a nickname," Sonya says, draping an arm over Charlie's shoulders. "It's a club. And we're its only members."

"Aha." I point a finger at Sonya. "That's why nobody likes us." We all laugh, even Kim, who seems more melancholy than usual today. I nudge her with my elbow. "You good?"

She looks at me, a little startled. "Yeah. Yeah, sure. Just got off work. You know." She shrugs.

I glance back at the police station. Dad's no longer sitting in his patrol car, and he's not outside anywhere. He must have retreated back to the sanctuary of his office and his secretary Alice's terrible coffee. For an instant, an image of Clark Webber's cattle farm blips across my vision, and all I see are dead cow eyes watching me.

"Yeah," I say, blinking myself back into focus. "Yeah, I know. Who's ready for lunch?"

We all climb into the Chevelle, a gift from Dad earlier this year, which leaves me feeling especially guilty as I drive it up Main Street, out of the main part of town and across the Hill-to-Hill Bridge, which stretches across the widest segment of the canal. On the other side, Main Street turns back into Route 24 and takes us past Franklin Road, which leads to both the Dagger Hill Mobile Home Park (where Charlie lives) and the massive waterfront house (where Sonya lives) that sits by one of the narrowest, shallowest segments of the canal.

Route 24 cuts across the train tracks, then begins to wind upward and around Dagger Hill. There's a dusty, rutted road branching off 24 that takes us higher, to a washed-out pile of splinters in the shape of a picnic table. It's an old lookout spot from back in the days when people actually hiked up here. This is where we park the Chevelle.

Sonya grabs the cooler she brought out of the trunk, and instead of stopping here to eat, we go deeper into the trees, climb up using an overgrown strip of dirt that, according to my dad, was once referred to as Whisper Trail. We found it by accident one day almost seven years ago, riding our bikes and looking for an adventure. When I told Dad where we'd been, he completely wigged out, told us over and over again that Dagger Hill is dangerous, that people have died up there, that there's something not right about it. But we kept coming. Who knows why. It's just our spot now, a little clearing at the end of Whisper Trail, where nobody can find us, nobody can call us nobodies, nobody can tell us who we are or who we're supposed to be.

Before we get there today, though, Charlie stops. He pulls his Polaroid over his head and tosses the camera to me. I catch it deftly, almost subconsciously. I don't even know what he's going to do until he's doing it. There's a huge boulder alongside the trail, as tall as I am now. Back when we were ten, it felt enormous. Charlie is pulling himself up onto it, the bottoms of his high-tops sliding and skittering.

As he climbs, Kimberly presses her hand against the surface of the rock, smooth and rough at the same time. "You remember when we used to play pirates?" she asks. She's smiling, petting the boulder like it's a stray dog.

"Oh yeah," I say with a laugh. "This boulder was a lot of things when we were kids, but who could forget the SS *Daggerwhisp*? We thought we were very clever coming up with that name."

"Hey," Sonya says beside us. "*I* came up with that name, and I happen to think it was *very* clever. Albeit a little silly."

"It was an awesome name, Sone," I say, backpedaling. My heart begins to race, and my face grows hot.

Sonya looks away quickly, and I can't tell if she's actually hurt or just uncomfortable. It's been weird territory between us lately.

"Aren't we still, though?" Kim asks. Her focus remains on the boulder, which Charlie has nearly conquered once again.

"Aren't we still what?" I ask.

"Kids. Technically, I mean. We *are* still kids. Right?" There's a distressed, pleading look on her face as she says it.

"I don't . . . I don't know." It's the truth. Really, it's been weird territory between all *four* of us lately. "I just got done telling my dad off about how we aren't kids, but . . . I don't know. Some days it's hard to tell. Some days it just feels easier to pretend we are."

Kimberly doesn't say anything for a long moment. Then: "Yeah." And that's all.

Up on top of the boulder, Charlie clears his throat, spreads his arms out wide, letting beams of sun fall down through the treetops and across his shoulders. "I need you guys to do something for me," he says, growing suddenly serious. "Promise me we'll always be there."

He's addressing us the way a king might address a battalion of knights. It's his way, I guess. Charlie is long and lanky—if he turns a certain way, he all but disappears. But his voice carries. There's a richness in how he speaks. The only way I've ever been able to describe it is that Charlie Bencroft is *full*. Of spirit, of heart, of passion . . . I don't really know. But whatever it is, it makes us full, too.

Still, I cut him down. Maybe that's my way.

"Ah Jesus, Charlie," I say. "Don't get all squishy on the insides. School only let out a day ago." Even as the words leave my lips, my fingers twitch to the camera in my hands, Charlie's Polaroid Sun, which he carries with him everywhere. I should capture this moment. I should put Charlie as he is now inside the white borders of an instant film picture. Preserve him somehow. But I don't do it. I leave the camera dangling against my chest.

On my left, Kimberly digs her elbow into my ribs. When I look at her, she shoots me a glare that by now only makes me grin. The stink eye is worse than my mom's, and my mom's makes my stomach hurt from trying not to laugh.

To my right, Sonya barely notices that I've spoken, or that Kim is mothering me. She just stands there, arms crossed, watching Charlie with rapt attention. There are strings of fire in her hair from the midday sun. It's catching in her eyes and along the glossy curves of her lips. Her skin is a deep auburn color that carries its own light. To me, she stands out as something separate from the rest of the world.

Kim elbows me a second time, crossing her own arms. She rolls her eyes, and I can see the genuine annoyance in them. I must have been gawking again.

Meanwhile, Charlie carries on, unhindered by his three friends, who, despite the naggings we all give each other, are something closer, more powerful than family. It's not like we ever have to say it to each other—there's no time for that when one of us is always on another's case. We just know it.

"Promise me we'll always be there," Charlie says again, looking right at me. "For each other, for ourselves. For our parents, who will never, ever leave this shitty, nowhere town. Promise me that no matter how old we get, or how far away from here we go, we'll always find our way home."

That's what we are. The four of us together. We're home.

"I promise," Sonya says. She doesn't even hesitate. There's this goofy smile on her face, and she's squinting up at Charlie, one eye squeezed shut against the sun. When she turns to look at me, I'm not prepared for it. For the way her smile hits me right in the chest.

I can't help but smile back. "Yeah. Me too."

"Agreed," Kim says with a sigh. There's a strange edge in her voice. "Can we please have lunch now?"

My eyes shift to Charlie, still standing on his rock, hands on his hips. He's wearing a battered trucker hat of his dad's and a red Marty McFly puffer vest. Charlie says he's going to wear that thing every day until *Back to the Future III* comes out. Kim and Sonya and I all have a bet going for how long he actually makes it. Today it's eighty-seven degrees with 90 percent humidity, and Charlie's brow is already shiny with sweat. But he couldn't look any happier. He's watching the three of us from his perch with something like pride.

"Yeah," Charlie says finally, smiling wide. "Let's eat." When his gaze moves from my face to over my shoulder, the smile falters. "Better do it quick, too. Looks like there's a storm on the way." He pushes his horn-rimmed glasses up on his nose and blinks a few times.

I turn and look in the same direction. Charlie's right. Windale sits down in the middle of the valley, a rolling jumble of shimmering glass and church spires and pointed row-home rooftops. Past the pale blue water tower, along the top of Sunrise Hill and to the north, a mass of black clouds is pushing toward us.

As we watch, a shadow starts to unroll over town.

6.

SONYA

I CAN'T LOOK at her.

And I can't look at Gabe, either. He's got those big goo-goo eyes like E.T. It's so pathetic it's almost cute. I'm watching Charlie as he makes his speech. It really is heartfelt. And by the time he's done, I'm close to forgetting about everything. I'm close to feeling like I can breathe again.

Unable to help myself, I look at Gabe. The smile on my face is real. I love these guys. I love Gabe, even if it's not the way he wants me to love him. Charlie's been my closest friend since we were in diapers. And Kim . . . well, that's where it gets complicated.

"Who's hungry?" I ask. I have the plastic cooler hooked on my elbow. Inside, the Coke bottles clink together.

"What do you got?" Charlie hops down from what was once the SS *Daggerwhisp*. Finally. That whole moment was sweet, but . . .

I don't know. I'm starting to realize that maybe this won't last forever. We have one more year of high school together, and after that we're all taking off in different directions for college. I'm going to MIT. I have to. My mind is already wandering back to my house, to my newly installed computer and the software coding I want to be working on. How am I supposed to prepare myself for that future when Charlie is trying to anchor us all to Windale? How do I move away and stay here at the same time?

"Sone?" Charlie says. He's beside me, bumping his shoulder into mine. The sun flashes across the lenses of his glasses and hides his eyes. But I can see the concern in his frown, the way he digs his hands down into the pockets of his ridiculous vest. "You okay?"

"Uh . . . yeah," I lie. The four of us are walking now, leaving the trail behind. At the end of it, the old Chevelle that used to belong to Gabe's dad is parked near the picnic table, where we're *actually* supposed to eat. But we know this hill and the forest that creeps up the side of it like no one else in Windale. Even though Gabe got his license last year and is perfectly willing to cart us all wherever we want to go, we always find ourselves up here anyway. There's comfort in the familiar, I guess.

"Good," Charlie says. "You gonna tell me what's on the menu or is it supposed to be a surprise?"

"Like Mystery Meat Monday at school?" Gabe says over his shoulder. That coaxes a laugh out of me, but I keep my eyes pinned to the back of his striped polo shirt so I don't have to see how proud of himself he is. My cheeks burn under his gaze until he finally looks away, trudging ahead with Kim at his side.

"It's not Mystery Meat Monday," I say, brightening as best I can. I shoot Charlie a playful grin. "It's Fancy Feast Friday. Mrs. Garber gave me her best cans of paté, just for you, Charlie."

"That's not even funny," Kimberly says, giggling for probably the first time all day. "I'm positive there really is cat food in some of her recipes."

"The meatloaf," Charlie muses.

"The beef nuggets," I add, cringing.

"The lasagna," Gabe says.

"The *lasagna*," we all groan together. And then we're laughing. It feels easy and real because it is. Then I have to go and ruin it.

"Well, at least we only have to endure one more year of the cafeteria food," I say, almost naturally.

Just like that, the laughter dies. I feel my heart squeeze, and it really hurts. These are my best friends in the world. I'd do anything for them, and I know they'd do anything for me. We've all lived in

Windale our entire lives, stuck at the bottom of this sinkhole of a town because the world beyond it just seems too far away to reach. I'm the only one of us who has ever been outside of Pennsylvania, and that's just because my parents are rich and like to travel. If I could have taken Gabe and Charlie and Kim with me on those trips instead of my parents and my little sister, I would have done it in a heartbeat. Leaving my friends behind after we graduate is going to be the hardest thing I'll ever have to do.

But I also can't wait.

I can't wait for a fresh start. To have the freedom to explore parts of myself that I'm only now beginning to understand. There's a whole other version of Sonya Gutierrez waiting in a dorm room at MIT. She's a person my friends here would never relate to, would never be able to comprehend. She doesn't keep secrets from the people who are closest to her. She doesn't keep secrets from herself by pretending they don't exist. And she sure as hell wouldn't be deliberately pushing her best friends away because it's just easier to give up and move on than it is to keep clinging to the only life she's ever known.

This thing with Kimberly is only part of it, but it's a big part. How do I explain who I'm capable of loving? To Gabe, to my parents. To anyone. How do I tell them that whoever I'm into doesn't necessarily have to be a guy? They don't have to be a girl, either. They don't *have* to be anything. It doesn't matter what they look like or where they're from. The only thing that matters is their heart and the way it speaks to mine.

She glances back, flashing a tiny smile, right as I'm thinking about her. Of course. Every time she looks at me, I can feel Kimberly's heart talking.

When we cross into the clearing, the sun is still shining. Dapples of light drop down through the trees and ripple across the brush, in sync with the hot breeze. We scatter and sit. I open the cooler, pull out the Cokes and sandwiches. Charlie sets his Walkman down in the grass. When he flicks it on, Axl Rose is yelping the last few lines of "Patience" on WKED ("The Wickedest Rock Radio in the Commonwealth"). Kimberly sinks down and puts her back against a tree at the edge of the clearing. Gabe hunkers next to Charlie, and they start talking about *Ghostbusters II* tonight.

"You guys are nerds," I jab, tossing each of them a sandwich.

The boys laugh.

"Yeah, right," Gabe says. "Because you totally didn't buy your ticket this morning."

I laugh, too, because he's right. I stopped at the Sunrise before we met up at the diner. My ticket is in my pocket as we speak.

With the other two baggies and bottles of Coke in hand, I leave Gabe and Charlie to discuss whether Sigourney Weaver and Bill Murray will finally hook up in this one, and I go to Kim.

She's not paying attention. Her knees are up against her chest, arms wrapped around her legs, hugging herself. She's watching the storm clouds sweep over the valley. They're heading our way for sure. But it's not like we've never been caught out here in the rain before.

"Hey," I nearly whisper. I squat down in front of her and offer one of the sodas. "You with us?"

"Huh?" she replies, blinking. "Oh. Yeah. Sorry." She smiles in a sad way that I can't quite pin down, but she takes a bottle and pops it open with a hiss.

"You sure? You seem like you're not really here today." I'm pressing, which I know she hates, but I can't help it.

She finally looks me in the eye, and there's a hint of a real smile at the corners of her lips. "I'm good," she says. "Promise." Her eyes tick down, looking away. My cue to leave her alone.

"Okay" is all I say. I start to stand.

She surprises me, though, reaching out to grab my hand before I get all the way up. "But," she starts, then pauses, glancing over at Gabe and Charlie, who are in their own little world. "Maybe we can talk later?"

My smile is automatic. "Of course."

"Okay," she sighs, almost relieved. "Okay, awesome."

When I stand up, taking a bite of turkey and swiss on wheat, I feel a little lighter. There are all these unspoken lines of communication between the four of us, like a network of information that's been built up over so many years. Nothing is ever fully resolved. It's just covered up with a new layer of something else. We're always checking in, trying to figure each other out even though we already know so much. It's both beautiful and terrifying at the same time.

It makes me think of something my dad was talking about a couple of months ago. His own job is very private, but he loves to bring home bits of information he's picked up from across the scientific community, as if that's something all families talk about over their TV dinners. He said some scientist in Switzerland was proposing a global space for shared information. Something called the World Wide Web. I still don't really understand what it is, but I know I want to be a part of it. Especially if it turns out to be anywhere near as lovely and complicated as this friendship has been.

Has been. There I go again thinking it's over between the four of us.

We eat our lunch together and talk about nerd stuff, the same as we've done for years. Only a mile or so to the northwest, thunder is rumbling closer.

7.
CHARLIE

I HEAR IT before the other three do. My eyes might be bad, but my ears work just fine.

By now, the sky's gone dark above us. The wind's picking up. Pine needles twirl around my ankles, and the young leaves above us are turning over, showing us their palms. Waving at us in warning.

The black mass of clouds is strung out low between both hills like a canopy. It obscures the gridwork of Windale down on the other side of the canal. From inside that mass, thunder cracks like a whip, and blue lightning flickers. It's still a mile or so west of us, but it's moving quickly.

And there's that noise I can't describe. It starts off as a whistle, low and steady. Then it builds. Getting louder, getting higher.

Gabe, Kim, and Sonya don't seem to notice. Sonya's busy chasing Coke bottles and empty Ziploc bags around the clearing, trying to stuff them haphazardly back into the cooler. Gabe has the Polaroid, which has been around his neck since I tossed it to him at the boulder. He's snapping photos of the storm. I watch the film spit out from the front of the camera like white square tongues. He plucks each one without taking his eye away from the viewfinder. The stack collects in his hand, all the images gray, underdeveloped.

"This is so cool," I hear him mutter.

"It won't be very cool when a bolt of lightning turns you into Gabe-bacon," I say, bending down to snatch a baggie before it can slip between my legs. "And don't waste all my film!"

He lowers the camera, thinking about it. "Gabe-bacon," he repeats, wrinkling his nose. "Gnarly." But then there's a flash behind me, and he points, clicks, waits.

I roll my eyes at him but can't help feeling that flutter in my gut. This is an adventure. With my best friends. We've had so many over the years that it's hard not to blur them all into a single bright image. There are pictures I've taken all over my bedroom wall at home. Us out here on Dagger Hill, dicking around for hours on end, spread out in this very clearing with comic books and magazines and maybe sometimes a stolen six-pack of my stepdad Chet's PBR. Us in front of the Sunrise Theater in the Triangle, the marquee ringed in bright neon behind us, the movie of the week spelled out in black letters over our heads. Us in one of our bedrooms (usually Sonya's, because her parents buy her all the coolest stuff), playing Nintendo or watching tapes on the VCR or listening to a stack of cassettes that Kimberly brought over. Us in a booth at the King Street Diner with plates of pancakes and home fries laid out between us. It's a mosaic of memories that I put up to cover the water stains across the wall-paper, to add a layer of something happy between me and the not-so-muffled screams coming from my mom and stepdad's bedroom. It's a road map of my favorite moments with my favorite people at our favorite places.

And in less than a year, we're going to hit the end of the road.

We've been talking for weeks about how incredible this summer is going to be. Now that Gabe has a car, we're going to get out of town, go sightseeing. My mom and stepdad don't give a shit what I do. For me, this summer is going to be fearless. *Reckless.* My friends and I are going to take these sweltering months and wring them out until not a single drop of adventure is left. This summer, if it really is our last one together, is going to be the one we remember for the rest of our lives.

Another blast of thunder snaps me back to reality. I can feel this one in my bones. An accompanying flash of lightning turns the clearing into a negative image. For a moment, I see all my friends' faces with white lines where shadows should be, their teeth standing out stark against the blue skin of their lips. They look sickly, alien. They look like people I don't recognize.

In the same instant, my eyesight goes back to normal, if a little spotty. But the wind is stronger than ever, gusting into my shoulders, pushing me over. I have to put my hand on top of my dad's hat to keep it in place.

Sonya has everything in the cooler, and Gabe seems like he's done giving the storm clouds a photo shoot. A few feet away, Kim is on her feet, staring at the darkness as it approaches. The wind blows the stray curls of her sandy blond hair around her cheeks and ears. The rest is up in a messy ponytail, held tight with her favorite blue scrunchie. There's a weird serenity in the way she's staring down the storm. As if it's calming her.

More thunder rips across the sky right above us. We all flinch.

"Okay," Gabe says. "It might be time to get back to the car."

"You think?" Sonya asks, looking up.

But nobody moves. My feet are fused to the ground. I can't even turn and face the storm head-on. I realize it's because I'm afraid. Apart from the thunder and the lightning—which aren't my favorite to begin with—there's that other thing. That hum that keeps getting louder, almost lost in the rustle of the leaves and the howl of the wind. Almost, but not quite.

It's building.

Finally, I manage to get my legs working. I turn and see curtains of rain sweeping over Windale like broom bristles. Currents of white lightning connect the sky to the buildings and roads of town. I think of *Back to the Future*, still the best movie I've seen this decade, even after almost four years. Down in Windale, there's a clock fixed at the top of Town Hall. I imagine it being struck by lightning, frying it in place, stopping time in Windale forever. Maybe then senior year won't come, and graduation after that.

Maybe then I won't have to watch my friends leave.

It's only a fleeting wish. There and gone again. I regain focus when the sound of squawking birds and flapping wings fills the air somewhere above us. I look up, peering into the cloud cover, and all I see are tiny dark shapes moving in the gloom. Hundreds of them, heading east, racing away from the storm.

Or from something else.

Then that whine becomes a moan becomes a screech becomes a scream becomes a roar. The dark shape of something way bigger than a frightened bird appears within the storm clouds, backlit by blue stutters of lightning. It's only a shadow for a moment before it bursts out of the mist, real and tangible, barreling right at us. The sound of it swallows up all other sounds. The storm is a far-flung memory. So is our summer.

This is when everything changes.

8.
KIMBERLY

THE STORM CAME like a fist, shattering a perfect blue sky and replacing it with frothing black clouds. It was beautiful, but now it's terrifying. I'm afraid it might shatter us, too.

"Guys!" I yell over the rush of the wind and the howl of . . . something else. "We need to get the hell out of here!"

Sonya's hand is in mine, warm and soothing. "It's okay," she says. Quiet, just for me. "I've got you. Let's go before this gets any worse." Then, to the guys: "Gabe! Charlie! *Let's go!*"

"We're coming!" Gabe calls over his shoulder. But he's kind of mesmerized, watching the storm through the viewfinder, a poker hand of still-gray Polaroids fanned out between his fingers.

I follow his sight line, out across the misted-over shadows of Windale. From here, I can just barely make out the silhouette of the water tower. There's something else, too. In the growing dimness, it looks like a giant mushroom plummeting from the sky, swaying like a pendulum in midair. I squint, leaning forward.

"What the . . . ?" Sonya says beside me, echoing my exact thought.

The thing in the sky isn't a mushroom; it's a parachute. A bubble of faded green fabric drifting out of the storm, down to the streets of Windale. I can just barely make out the flailing shape of a man below the parachute, kicking his legs and yanking desperately at the guide strings as the wind rips and tears at him.

Another flash across my vision, this one less intense. Because it wasn't lightning this time; it was Gabe snapping yet another photo.

I wrench my eyes away from the man and his parachute and turn to look at Gabe. His head swivels back, and his gaze finds mine.

"Did you see that?" he asks.

I look at Sonya, who's still watching the man descend from the unruly sky.

"Holy shit, holy shit, holy *shit.*" That's Charlie—he's scrambling backward, his attention fixed on something else in the sky, higher above the parachute. Charlie hits the dirt, hard. But that doesn't stop him from retreating. He kicks and pushes himself away, digging his heels into the grass, tossing clods of dirt and dust into the air. "Guys, go!" His scream turns his voice ragged. *"Get away! NOW!"*

But none of us moves. Maybe there's just too much happening. Maybe our minds can't keep up with what is obviously a nightmare. Mrs. Rapaport's voice floats into my mind. *Whatever you do, don't wake up.*

It's only a span of a few seconds after we see the man parachuting before I think, *If somebody jumped out of a plane, where's the plane?*

It crashes down on top of us a few seconds after that, and my mind is consumed by fire.

9.

GABE

THERE'S NO TIME to think before it hits.

When the plane comes rushing out of the storm, trailing streamers of cloud and smoke, in my mind I see it as a bird of prey. A huge, screeching eagle maybe. Sleek and green and featherless. But then I see the turbine engines, one under each wing. Vicious, spinning fans sucking in stray leaves and bits of debris kicked up by the wind. It's coming in slightly lower than where the four of us are standing. Our clearing. Our escape through so many summers and weekends.

At the last second, the plane's nose tips up, angling in our direction. I catch a glimpse of the cockpit window, dark except for the vague shape of somebody in the pilot's seat. Or maybe I'm just imagining that.

Maybe I want to pretend that someone could have even a tiny bit of control over what's happening here, that they could pull up with inches to spare and go screaming right over us, the fuselage scraping along the treetops. Like something out of *Top Gun*.

But Windale isn't the kind of place where miracles happen.

We have zero time to react. I can see Charlie in front of me, frozen in place, still sitting in the grass as if he's been there all day. I flick my eyes toward Sonya, who dropped the cooler, letting it tip and spill all the trash she worked so hard to pick up, the detritus of our last lunch together. Her dark hair sweeps around her head, showing off the line of her jaw, the dimple in her left cheek, the curve of her neck down to her shoulder. Her eyes are wide and full of terror.

She's as beautiful as ever. I wish I had time to go to her, to tell her how I feel. I wish I had time to reach all three of them, pull them out of harm's way just before the plane hits. But I can't even pull myself out of the way.

"Guys, what do we do?" Charlie screams. I can barely hear him over the mechanical scream of the plane's engines, only feet away. I reach out to Charlie, but the plane is behind him, low and heavy, and it hits me that I've seen this plane before, only a couple of hours earlier. I watched this plane disappear into the TerraCorp compound from Mr. Webber's farm.

"Charlie! Get your ass up and run!" I shout. I scream so hard it feels like my lungs are going to come flying out through my throat. He listens, though, stumbling to his feet, running toward me with the hulk of the machine chasing behind him.

The plane's downward momentum is too much. Even as its nose is lifting up, matching the slope of the hillside, the rest of it is still racing toward the ground. It's so close I can smell jet fuel and metal. I can see slivers of light shifting across its smooth surface.

And then it punches into the side of Dagger Hill and shatters.

Hundreds, thousands, maybe millions of pieces are ripping off and flipping away from the point of impact, maybe twenty yards from where my friends and I stand. The ground under my feet lurches, as if the whole hill shifts from the force of the crash. I watch the plane come apart like one of my old Lego sets, snapping into individual components that spin outward in every direction. One of them whizzes right past my head. Another, much bigger piece hits Charlie in his legs and sends him sprawling. I watch him go down. The angle in one of his knees is all wrong.

But then there's a turbine engine, tumbling through the air like a tossed beer can, still whirring and groaning. It comes down only a few feet to my left, just outside of the clearing. It eats up tree branches and leaves and loose grass before it locks up. The machinery inside starts to whine and clang. The back end of it begins to shoot out plumes of acrid smoke.

"RUN! GET OUT OF HERE!" I scream, turning to Sonya and Kim. I flail my arm at them. But Kimberly's watching the engine that's about to explode behind me. And Sonya is staring at Charlie, who's doing his own screaming from his spot on the ground.

"Oh god! Oh my god, my leg! My fucking leg!"

I can feel the sound of it burrowing into my head, ready to haunt me forever if I make it out of this alive.

Down below where Charlie is, the barely intact fuselage of the plane is still skidding upward, turning as it goes. It's swallowing trees like a wood chipper, its own integrity collapsing with every small impact. The woods are tearing it apart even as *it's* tearing the *woods* apart. Only a handful of yards are keeping it from rolling right over top of us.

It takes me forever to close the distance between Charlie and me. I go to him, kneeling down next to where he's twisting and wailing. His arms and torso jerk back and forth. His legs don't move at all. The one is buckled in a way that makes my stomach clench.

"Charlie," I say. "Charlie, we have to go. I'm going to get you up, okay?"

"Me too."

Sonya is beside us, glancing at me sidelong. There's a cut along her cheek.

"You get one arm, I'll get the other," she says.

There's no time to argue.

"No," Charlie pants. "Please. It hurts so bad, you guys. I . . . I can't." His glasses are askew, and the eyes behind them are wide, panic-filled saucers.

"Yes, you can," I say. "We're not leaving you, Charlie. So let's get you on your goddamn feet."

"Guys?"

Kim's voice this time, from somewhere far away. She sounds small and confused. For the first time, there might be a touch of fear in her. But I don't respond. There's no time for that, either.

As I hook an arm under Charlie, I glance back at the engine, which is choking on the forest beneath it. The pained sound coming from inside is ramping up.

On Charlie's other side, Sonya is preparing to lift. We each grab one of Charlie's arms and drape it over our shoulders. Even that tiny movement is enough to make him cry out.

"Please just leave me," he begs. "Don't move me any more. Please. *Please.*"

We ignore him. I look at Sonya and she looks at me.

"One, two, three," I count. *"Go!"*

Together we haul Charlie up off the ground, his broken leg dangling under him. He screams like I've never heard him scream before. Raw, anguished, desperate. I look at his face and see it folded into sobs, tears spilling across his cheeks. I don't know if I can put him through any more pain. But I can't just leave him here to die, either.

My pulse is hammering in my ears. My arms and legs are shaking, nerves rattling with terror. Everything around me is a blur of toxic smoke and blackened trees and splintered metal. Hunks of the plane are scattered everywhere, and little fires are starting to crop up in places. Metal screeches; thunder rumbles across the sky. Charlie whimpers in my ear.

Then the engine explodes.

10.
SONYA

THERE'S A RUSH of heat. The skin on the back of my neck singes. I smell something that can only be burning hair. Charlie, Gabe, and I are thrown forward, more shrapnel zipping over and around us. A piece of something slices across my calf, splitting it open. I feel liquid rolling down my ankle that feels cool compared to the heat of the explosion. But I know what it is, and I know what'll happen if I look at it. I can't do that. I can't leave my friends alone while I'm crashed out in the dirt, fainted from the sight of my own blood.

Fire crackles all around me now. There's a new kind of heat pulsing through the clearing. Not the sun, but the plane, the trees, the grass. I'm flat on my face, my body still reeling from the blast. I'm trying to get my legs under me, but they're so shaky. And my calf is burning where it was cut. When I suck in a breath, my lungs fill with something harsh and choking. It stings along the inside of my chest until I start hacking it back up.

"Charlie," I say in a gasp between coughs. "Gabe. Kim?"

I'm answered by the snap of a tree coming down nearby, accompanied by the moan of twisting metal. Flames pop and sizzle all around the clearing. My eyes are watering, my lungs burning. I can't get my bearings.

At this point, I'm just waiting for the moment when I get to wake up and realize this was all some horrible nightmare.

"Sone?"

It's Charlie. To my left. When I glance that way, though, I can't see him. There's too much smoke swirling through the clearing, blown by the wind of the storm that's still lashing across the sky above Dagger Hill. It's going to start raining any minute now. The fires will go out. The smoke will die down. As long as nothing else explodes, we might just be able to stay put and ride it out. Wait for help to get here. Already, from down in Windale, I can hear the sirens at the firehouse wailing.

"Charlie," I say, reaching out for him. "Charlie, I'm right here. Can you hear me? Follow my voice."

"I . . . I can't see you." His voice is full of so much pain, so much fear. He sounds so different from the Charlie who was standing on top of his boulder only half an hour ago, making us promise not to forget about each other. "Sone, where are you?" He coughs. "I can't find you—"

"I'm here, I'm here—"

"Guys?" Gabe's voice floats out of the smoke toward me, a blistered wheeze. "Sonya? Tell me you guys are okay—"

"Kimberly?" I hear myself cry, yelling as much as I can. "Kimberly?" Nothing.

I blink back tears. All I can see through the stinging smoke are hazes of orange light, cut every so often by flickers of blue. If my eyes and chest and leg didn't hurt so bad, if I didn't think I might die in the next few minutes, the blur of colors might be beautiful. Instead, it's disorienting, and I can feel the cold grip of panic closing around my throat. Afraid to move. Afraid to breathe. Afraid to see the wreck of the plane or what it's done to my friends.

Don't think about it. Don't think about her.

It's the mantra I've been repeating to myself for months, trying and failing to push all the inevitability of this last summer out of my head. College is the furthest thing from my mind right now, but the same rules still apply. If I keep pretending it's not real, then it's not.

"We have to—" Gabe stops to cough, a dense, mucus-filled sound—he could be drowning out there in the haze. "—get back to the car."

He's so far away, and it feels like he just keeps going farther.

"You're right," I say to the ground. I'm on my hands and knees. The grass is poking up between my fingers in vivid tufts. My arms are heavy. I try to lift one, try to pull myself up onto my feet. I'm full of cement. The curls of smoke billowing around my head are getting thicker, darker. Or maybe that's just my vision.

"Sone," Charlie whimpers from a place right next to me and a thousand miles away. "Please don't leave me. Please."

My voice erupts like thunder in my ears when I yell back. Who knows if he understands what I'm saying. With a massive effort, I lift my head, lift my arm, lift my knee. I take one shaking, wobbly lurch forward. Then another. Along the edges of the clearing, I can make out gnarled chunks of the aircraft. Burning, smoldering, hissing with steam. Something pops nearby, and hot red sparks rain across the grass.

I'm fading even as I'm crawling in the direction of Charlie's voice. Or what I hope is the right direction. Every movement is a battle against myself. My muscles are shivering, the cut on my leg throbs, my head is beating like a heart.

Something shifts behind me. A scraping metal sound. I fight against the throb in my shoulders to turn my head and look back, hoping to see Gabe or Kimberly. *Oh please god let it be Kimberly. Let her be all right.*

At first, I see nothing. Just that constant, smoggy curtain. But then there's a figure. The shape of a man stalking through the new terrain of debris. He looks too tall and hunched to be Gabe. In fact, he looks too tall to be human.

I think of Gabe's dad, the chief, and all his stories about Dagger Hill. Legends mostly. Folktales about murders and ghosts and monsters. As I watch the man take one long-reaching step after another, I also watch him shift before my eyes, shrinking to a reasonable six-foot height, with broad shoulders and a longish neck. He's still just a silhouette, backlit by fire and obscured by smoke, but it's definitely not Gabe. Not Kimberly, either. Maybe my eyes are just going funny, and it's help, here to rescue us.

I slump down to my elbows, then tip over onto my side. I can't go for Charlie, and I can't call out to the person crossing the clearing, moving through the flames in gangly strides. The last of my vision is falling down a deep well, collapsing into blackness. The volume in my ears goes all the way down, replaced by a thin ringing. I can't hear, can't see, can't breathe.

Then my entire world is smudged out.

11.
CHARLIE

WHERE ARE MY GLASSES? *Where are my* legs?

I'm on fire from the waist down. Not literally. I don't think. But I might as well be. There's no way my legs could hurt this bad without them being either wrapped in flames or gone completely. Even if I could see them without my glasses, without the stinging smoke obscuring everything, I'm too afraid to look. Whatever it was that hit my knee, it snapped my leg apart like a dry twig. The pain filled me up so completely that I was sure I'd never feel anything else again. Just the agony, flowing through me, becoming me. Constant. Total.

Now, I'm just floating around inside a black cloud. My legs are still full of that white-hot ache, but I feel it somewhere beneath the rest of my senses. Background noise, like the feedback from my stepdad's Fender when he plays his shitty folk-rock songs.

Speaking of my stepdad, where is he right now? Shouldn't he be home already? Actually . . . where am *I*?

I'm so hot, my shirt is pasted to my body like a strip of sweaty papier-mâché. I can barely catch my breath. Every small, labored hitch that I manage to pull in brings very little oxygen with it. The gray world that surrounds me gets darker by the second.

I think I'm going into shock.

"Charlie?"

Is that Sonya?

"Charlie, if you can hear me, don't move!"

Why is she yelling?

"I'm coming to you!"

We never hang out at my place. Mostly because my stepdad is a disgusting prick who likes to ask Sonya and Kimberly how many days are left until their eighteenth birthdays. But since Chet clearly isn't here, maybe she decided to stop by. Maybe . . .

Then there's the grass brushing against the back of my neck. Embers tickling my cheeks and arms with scalding fingers. Crackling flames pushing nauseating heat across the clearing. There are metal sounds—clanking, rattling, groaning. Somewhere way above it all, thunder smacks its hands together. It's like being inside a car engine just before someone shuts it off. Hot and loud and dangerous.

I feel one raindrop smack into my forehead. Another one hits the back of my hand. *Here it comes*, I think, remembering the curtains of rain that fell over Windale just before the plane crashed.

Plane crash? Is that really what happened?

My body is still shaken from the shock waves of the explosion. My ears are still ringing, my head still thumping. Yeah, that's really what happened.

The rain starts as a whisper, then builds into the hollering crowd at a Phillies game. It shushes through the trees, and the sound is so soothing that for a moment I don't even realize I'm being drowned. Fat drops are pummeling my face, soaking my already soaked clothes, pooling in my open mouth until I'm practically gargling rainwater.

Finally, I manage to roll over, sputtering and choking. At least it's not on smoke this time. The cool water feels good on my face. It clears my senses a little bit, allows me to refocus. To *remember*. I think of Gabe and Kimberly and Sonya. My friends. My home.

Speaking of Sonya—where is she? Wasn't she coming? I thought I heard her moving. I squint past my shitty vision and the relentless rain and the smoke that's only just breaking apart from the downpour. There are so many stuttering fires and bulky shapes of ruined plane parts. I can't make anything out. There's a lump of something on the ground a few feet away that might be Sonya. But it's not moving. *She's* not moving.

"Sonya," I say. "*Sonya!*"

I reach for her, but each time I twitch a muscle, my leg sings me a song of torture and misery. I bite down against the pain, try to drag myself across the grass. The ground under me is softening; I feel like I'm sinking. And my body is giving up.

In the distance, past the thing that might be Sonya, amid crooked, towering hunks of the plane, I see a dark, narrow line moving through the mess. A person? Gabe, maybe? Kimberly? I don't know.

"*Hey!*" I scream, mustering the last of my strength. I break out into a coughing fit, my throat burning all the way down into my lungs. When I try to scream again, I sound like a broken kazoo. "Hey. We're here. Please. Help us."

The stringy shadow stops. Maybe it turns to look at me. Maybe it doesn't. Did it hear me? It had to. It responded to my voice. *They*, I mean. Whoever they are.

But then the shadow resumes its stroll through the crash site, heading toward the northern edge of the clearing, away from the wreck, away from Whisper Trail leading back to the lookout and Gabe's car.

I can still see the four of us a couple of days ago, crammed into that olive-green monstrosity, listening to "Batdance," the most ridiculous and hilarious song ever, on the radio. We almost didn't come up here today. Gabe was talking about driving to Pittsburgh. He almost turned down King Street instead of Main, almost drove us right out of town in the opposite direction of Dagger Hill. We almost let him. But Kimberly said no; she didn't want to be in the car for that long, just to have to turn back and come home right away. We settled on the Hill then, like we always do when we can't agree on where to go or what to do, which is pretty much all the time.

What did it matter, though? We had the car, we had food, we had music, we had each other. It didn't have to be Pittsburgh. It could have been Philly or New York or Atlantic City. It could have been an open road with no destination at all. The only thing we had to do was drive. But we didn't.

And now we're here.

"Sone . . . ," I say, trying again, pleading. My voice is gravel and nails. "Sonya. Gabe. Kimberly. Anybody." I'm talking through dribbling rainwater to no one. The firehouse siren is crying out through all the chaos.

Someone will come for us, I think. *Yeah. Someone will come.*

I shut my eyes and put my head down on the grass. It's cool and wet, and I think I might just lie here forever.

12.

GABE

THE EXPLOSION KNOCKED me out of the clearing. I fell through branches and bushes, all of them grabbing at my clothes and skin, tearing into both. When I hit the ground, there was a crunch under me. Charlie's Polaroid. I don't know how broken it is. There are shards of black plastic everywhere. Who knows if the film is even good anymore? Weirdly, my first reaction after I get my bearings is to reach for the snapshots in my pocket, the ones I took of the storm and maybe of the plane coming out of it. Also, the other thing—the man floating down to Windale on a parachute.

The photos are still there, still intact if a little crumpled. I don't have time to look at them, though. Not when there's a pillar of smoke rushing up out of the clearing and into the sky. One dark mass merges with another, and in a single confused moment, I swear the storm is reaching down, punching into the earth.

It starts to rain, and some of the smoke begins to clear. Through the trees, I can see misshapen hunks of the thing that used to be a plane. Some of the metal looks molten where it's been torn apart. Glowing red teeth biting into nothing.

Beyond the mist and the smoke, Windale is just a dark splotch in the distance. But along the county road that winds up Dagger Hill, I can see pulsing red lights moving toward us. I can hear sirens getting louder, getting closer. Help is coming. If I can just get to the others, we might make it out of this.

Charlie and Sonya are still somewhere in the clearing. For a moment, I think I can hear Sonya calling for Charlie, but then her voice fades.

Or what I think is her voice, anyway. My head could just be making shit up, trying to convince me that all this will somehow turn out okay. Even though it's already so, *so* far from being okay.

I get myself up. My balance is wonky from being tossed like a Raggedy Ann doll, but I manage to stay on my feet. I put my back against a tree, waiting for the world to stop tilting. Across my body, I can feel burns and cuts and aches. And, I realize, a place on the back of my head that's pulsing with its own special kind of agony. My left shoulder doesn't feel right at all, and if I move it more than I have to, searing pain shoots down to my fingertips, up into my neck.

It takes me a minute, but eventually I build up the confidence to push off one tree, clutching my bad arm against my chest as I stumble over gnarled roots and wet, tangled brush, then fall back into another tree. With the rough bark and sturdy support of the trunk behind me, I fight back a wave of nausea—from the pain, from the panic, from my equilibrium, which is so fucked at this point that I can't even believe it.

How did this happen?

I circle the tree trunk, keeping my back to the clearing and the wreck, afraid that other parts of the plane might decide to explode. If I can work my way around the clearing like this, slowly (*very* slowly) but surely, I can get back to the hiking trail, back to my car, where the first responders will hopefully be gathering, and I can lead them back to Charlie, Sonya, and Kim.

Focus, I tell myself, reciting my pregame mantra. *Take it one yard at a time.* I close my eyes, take a deep breath.

When I open them again, I see Kimberly. She's on her back, arms splayed, thrown from the clearing just like I was. Her face is smeared with soot and blood. The scrunchie in her hair is loose, barely staying in place. Her curls have fallen in every direction, matted and clinging to her forehead in the rain.

"*Kim!*" I yell. Part of me can't believe I'm actually looking at her. "*Kimberly!*"

She doesn't move. Through the pouring rain, I can't tell if she's breathing. She's perfectly still, eyes closed, not even a twitch in her fingers. I've seen her sleep before—we've all spent the night at Sonya's house together more times than I can count—and Kimberly's never looked like this.

My stomach drops. A lump pushes up into my throat. There's a pressure behind my eyes that threatens to break, to form tears that will only get lost in all the rain that's dripping down my cheeks.

It's hardly a whisper when I say her name this time.

She's not that far away—a few feet maybe. I could reach her if I tried. But then what? With my dizziness and my popped arm, all I could do is lie there with her. Maybe that's enough. For at least two of us to be together when whatever's going to happen happens.

So I push back against the tree trunk and take a step forward, ignoring the way the world dips to one side like an imbalanced scale. Immediately, my foot gets hooked under a thick root, and I pitch forward, splashing to the ground in a pool of soupy mud. My left arm shoots out instinctively to help brace for the fall, and fresh pain rockets through me. I try to bite back a scream, but it gets loose anyway.

I'm soaked down to my very core, my lungs still aching from all the smoke I inhaled, my arm throbbing, my head swirling. My drenched clothes are weighing me down. I feel like I'm being battered by the downpour. Charlie would be quoting Marty McFly right about now: *This is* heavy, *man.*

Kimberly hasn't moved. I look up at her, only a foot or so closer now, wishing that the rain would stop so I could see if her chest is rising and falling. She's a fallen statue, left to the elements. And I'm a weeping teenager, too afraid to be anything else, staring at my friend who might be dead.

Something moves between the trees behind where Kimberly is lying. A figure . . . a *person.* They're coming this way, materializing out of the sweeping fog that's a mixture of spattering rain and drifting smoke.

At first, they're just a dark silhouette, a human-shaped gap in reality. But then their features start to come into focus—tall, slender form; black boots and black pants and a black leather jacket, shiny and slick from the rain; dark gloves worn over long fingers that are squeezed into vicious-looking fists; a black cap hiding their hair; and the last thing, covering their face, is a gas mask, black like everything else, with dark, bug-eyed lenses and a metal canister screwed on where the mouth is.

Whoever they are, they look more like an insect in that getup than anything else. But they have to be here to help. They must be one of the volunteer firefighters, wearing their own gear. Or maybe just a Good Samaritan from town who saw the crash and came up here on instinct. I know plenty of people in Windale who would do something like that.

As I watch them approach, boots squelching through the muck, I notice broad shoulders and dense, muscular legs underneath the metalhead outfit. There's still a chance they could be a woman, but they're probably a man.

A bug man, I think, watching those big gas mask lenses watch me.

The Bug Man steps up beside Kimberly, staring at me for a moment. I can see the clearing and the ruined, burning plane reflected in his creepy insect eyes. Then he looks down at Kim, seeming to assess the damage.

"Help her!" I call weakly. "Please help her first! Get her out of here!"

He doesn't look up, but he does squat down next to her, casually resting his arms on his knees, letting the rain spill over him.

"Please," I say again. My head is starting to spin, and my one good arm is weak from holding myself up. I don't know how much longer I can keep it together.

The Bug Man tilts his head back up and locks on to me with his wide stare. He doesn't stand, doesn't move any other part of his body. But with one gloved hand, he gives me a thumbs-up. If not for the weather and the burning aircraft behind me, I'd probably be able to hear the creak of the leather covering his hands.

Then he puts his arms under Kimberly and scoops her up. She's sopping wet, covered in grime. Her limbs just hang there, dangling like lengths of thick, pale rope. I can't tell for sure, but I think I see her turn her face into the crook of the Bug Man's elbow. A burst of relief falls over me, and my arm finally gives out. I tip over onto my side and lay in the mud, letting the world go fuzzy and dim. I can't remember if you're supposed to go to sleep if you have a concussion. Probably not. I can't help it, though. I'm just so tired.

I watch the Bug Man take a step back, his glass eyes watching the clearing behind me, surveying the destruction. Then he turns, with Kimberly still in his arms, and walks deeper into the woods. He's doing what I asked, getting her out of here, getting her to safety. I can only assume that others are doing the same for Charlie and Sonya, and that sense of relief gets stronger.

The tall shape of the Bug Man morphs into the trees and the trees morph into blurry gray lines and those morph into solid black nothing. Before I let myself go, I see Sonya's face, the way it was lit up by the sun earlier today. Her eyes are a couple of brilliant sparks that light my way through the darkness.

And then I'm gone.

13.

"DISASTER ON DAGGER HILL"

WINDALE, Pa.—Early in the afternoon on Friday, a United States Army cargo plane crashed into the side of Dagger Hill. The incident occurred during a heavy thunderstorm that swept through the area only moments before the plane fell out of the sky, which made rescue efforts even more difficult.

The crash caused extensive damage to trees and surrounding forest area along the side of Dagger Hill, about a quarter mile from the hiking trail that winds its way up the west-facing side. Though heavy rains reduced the potential for wildfire, volunteers of the Windale Fire Department were still putting out brushfires late Friday night.

The U.S. Army arrived in Windale less than two hours after the incident. Besides taking over the investigation of the crash from the Windale Police Department, army officials closed all roads leading into and out of Windale and have not given any indication as to when residents can expect them to be reopened.

In a tragic turn of events, four students from Windale High School were having lunch on Dagger Hill when the crash occurred. Gabriel Albright, Sonya Gutierrez, Charlie Bencroft, and Kimberly Dowd are the only individuals involved in the crash that have been identified. Officials declined to comment on their condition. Any crew or passengers aboard the aircraft have yet to be named.

Chief of Police Jack Albright, father of Gabriel Albright, stated that, despite the army presence in town, the Windale PD is still actively investigating the case. He also said that three of the four Windale teenagers have been accounted for. Kimberly Dowd, as of Saturday morning, is still missing . . .

BE KIND, REWIND

ON THE WEST side of town, in the strip mall that was built just last year, Ricky Montoya, owner of Ricky's Video Rentals, is opening up shop for the day. His key slides into the lock and turns with that satisfying click, the soundtrack of small-business entrepreneurism. The hydraulic hinge sighs pleasantly as the door swings open, and the electronic bell sounds from deep in the throat of the store.

Ricky's only twenty-one. Wasn't even a sophomore at Penn State before he saw the opportunities in his hometown. VHS rentals are good business, big business. While he was at college (for business, of course), Ricky kept hearing about this place called Blockbuster Video. Sprung up out of Dallas, Texas, taking over the world like a blue-and-yellow plague, opening a new store every twenty-four hours or some such bullshit.

Not in Windale, they're not.

In Windale, PA, Ricky Montoya is the video-rental king. In twenty, maybe thirty, years, when the industry is at its peak, rolling along like a high-functioning tape rewinder, Ricky will finally cave and sell his place to those Blockbuster assholes. He'll retire early, kick back in his La-Z-Boy made of fresh stacks of Benjamins, and catch up on all the daytime soap operas he missed while running this joint.

When the door swings shut behind him, cutting off the bird chatter from outside, Ricky hears it. His eyes adjust to the dim light—the switches are in the office, the fluorescent bars overhead remaining dark until he gets back there to flip them on. Floating amid the shadows is Ricky's kingdom. White particleboard shelves crammed with empty cardboard sleeves (he'd figured out early on that keeping the actual tapes in the back was the best way to keep them at all), more of the same along one wall, each shelf categorized by its own genre, *every title organized alphabetically—tedious work that Ricky doesn't plan on doing himself for long.*

Stretching across the other wall are more shelves, these ones thicker, stronger, bowing slightly under the weight of at least a dozen brand-new(ish) TVs. Ricky picked up the sets for a steal at a place he'd only kind of heard of—Best Buy Superstore—out in Philly. He has them on sale here for twice what he paid, which is still a good deal, if you ask him.

But the price tags dangling below each of the TVs—some of them twirling and dancing in the breeze made by the AC vents—aren't what caught Ricky's attention.

Normally, when he comes in, Ricky heads straight for the office, flips the lights on, gets the coffee maker going, and comes back out to what he thinks of as the "sales floor" to turn on all the TVs. It's a much more impressive display when they're all playing a different movie pulled straight out of Ricky's stock. He keeps the volume low and the brightness high, and it's like a beacon of sanctuary to all the dads and teens who roll in here with their families on a Friday night—they swarm to the light like mosquitoes to a bug-zapper.

Every morning, the TVs are dark, staring out at Ricky's self-built kingdom with curved glass eyes. Spider eyes, Ricky sometimes thinks, before he's had his caffeine fix and sees them in his periphery, watching them watch him.

Today, the screens are already lit, all of them playing a blizzard of static.

Ricky's only a little startled when he realizes that's what he's hearing—the soft shush of black-and-white fuzz coming from the display. He doesn't remember leaving the TVs on last night after he closed up, but there was a lot of excitement yesterday with the plane crash and all—Ricky heard the explosion all the way from here.

He approaches the shelves lined with glowing TV screens, weirdly planning to switch them all off, even though he's about to open up shop. Weirder still is that his arms are crawling with goose bumps, the hairs on the back of his neck lifting. Is he nervous? Why would he be nervous?

Together, the various TV sets—crammed on their shelves, some of them smaller, some of them bigger—almost form one giant screen. Ricky never noticed it until now, seeing the same blur of static across each individual segment. It's like one of those big billboards in Times Square, all the smaller components lighting a different part of a single image.

This morning, in the confines of his video-rental store, Ricky Montoya is sure he sees a face.

Lines of shadow move along the TV screens, cutting through the static. Deep, dark curves amid the avalanche of light that, in staring at only a single square, one might simply see as a visual anomaly. But Ricky, as always, is looking at the bigger picture.

There: a fuzzy dimple at the corner of a smirking mouth.

There: the defining lines of pointed cheekbones, shadowy, sunken cavities below.

There: blackened pits for eyes, bathed in darkness, watching without being seen.

Watching Ricky watch them.

He feels his fingers trembling. He feels his knees shaking ever so slightly. If he tries to move, tries to take even a single step, he knows they'll give out and he'll be sprawled on the cheap, ugly carpet, spirals and whorls of color turning out from under him like rivers of body fluid. He purposely picked out a pattern that had all the pop and funk of the MTV logo, thought it was a good business choice. But now, as it warbles along the bottom of his vision, it only makes him dizzy.

A healthy dose of sunlight spills into the store through the front windows, but Ricky still feels like he's alone in the dark. Cold, shivering, afraid—all the things the dark somehow makes you feel even when you're grown.

Faulty tubes, *he tries to think. A last-ditch effort to rationalize, to* make the face a product of his tired mind and crappy televisions. His whole body shivers now.

The face seems to sharpen, the lines of its features getting stronger even within the limitations of its staticky canvas.

And it winks.

14.
GABE

WHEN AM I allowed to wake up?

I feel like I've been swimming through unconsciousness for a long time, caught in a riptide of images churning behind my eyes. Charlie in his vest, making us promise that we'll always be there. Sonya, with her hair glowing in the afternoon sun. Storm clouds over Windale, pulled across the sky, dark and gnarled. The big, winged thing plummeting out of that storm, a movie prop gone horribly wrong. Pieces of it snapping and splintering and *bursting*. In my mind, the explosions are more like bubbles popping, only instead of water, they splash heat and fire across the clearing. *Our* clearing.

That nauseating roll of mental pictures flips over again, and I'm on the ground, in the mud, drowning in the rain. There's Kimberly, looking pale and waterlogged, looking dead. I'm certain she's dead; there's no way she's not dead, oh god oh god oh god—

Then I see the guy in the gas mask—*the Bug Man*—and he's bending down, lifting Kim in his arms, and she's turning in to the safety of his embrace. I'm sure of it. Her head shifts, the gentle movement of a deep sleeper only a little perturbed by the carnage happening around her.

Please let it be true, I think. *Please let her be okay.*

My brain is out of film after that, I guess. Because it gets quiet, and I'm just floating now, lifting toward the surface that exists some unknowable distance away. Maybe *I'm* the one who's dead. I've got a whole list of *maybes* like that, most of which I don't even want to begin to think about.

Gabe, a voice in my head says. *Gabe, honey.*

Honey?

That voice isn't mine. And the more it speaks, the more I begin to recognize it as my mother's. Soft and soothing as always, never laced with anger. Sarcasm, sometimes, but never anger. She and my dad are polar opposites that way. She says that my dad only knows how to speak in the language of the brutes but that, luckily, she knows just how to translate.

It's okay, honey, she goes on. *Everything's okay.* You're *okay.*

Am I, though?

Please, baby boy. Please wake up.

And then I'm breaking the surface, startling up out of sleep not gradually but all at once, finally coming up for air. I see nothing but bright pastel smears until my eyes begin to focus.

"Oh, thank you, god." It's my mom, live and in person this time. I feel her hand on my chest, pushing me back against a pillow as I try to clamber to my feet. "Shhhh. Gabe, honey, shhhh. It's okay. You're safe. You're safe now. Just lie back. Relax."

I realize that I'm flailing, grabbing the side railing of what must be a hospital bed and fighting to get up out of it. There are wires taped all over my body, though, like weeds that have grown across my motionless limbs while I slept. I feel the pinch of an IV in my right forearm, too. My left arm feels heavy and sore, wrapped up in a sling and pulled close to my ribs. There's also an oxygen mask over my face.

An image of the man in the gas mask (*The Bug Man. You called him the Bug Man, remember?*) lifting Kimberly off the ground flashes across my vision.

With my right hand, I grab the rubber mask, held over my face by a couple of elastic straps, and tear it off. The straps come loose, and the mask falls away, and for a few seconds, I feel relief, like I've just been let out of a locked closet. But when I try to inhale, my chest tightens. It *burns.* Instead of a great big gulp of air, I get a thin trickle of oxygen that sets my lungs on fire.

Mom is frantic now. I can see tears dribbling down her cheeks as she scrambles to get the straps reattached to the oxygen mask. I've given up on trying to get out of bed; I'm too busy lying here, focusing on breathing, which hurts worse with every small wheeze. The diameter of my throat feels like it's been reduced to the size of a pinhole. I might as well be sucking air into my body through a straw.

"*Mom,*" I croak, thinking of the plane crash, thinking of the fire, thinking of the smoke, thinking of my friends. "*Help.*"

She says, "I'm trying, baby. I'm *trying*. But you broke the straps on this . . . I . . . I can't . . . *Jack!* We need you! *Quick!*"

Charcoal shadows are smudging the edges of my vision. My skull feels like my brain is kicking it from the inside. I might pass out again, I think. And what happens then? Maybe I don't wake up this time. Maybe, after dropping a goddamn plane on my head, the universe decided to let me see my mom one last time before pulling the plug for good.

Where are my friends?

I need to know if they're all right, and I need to know *now*.

Dad charges into the room. Behind him are another man and woman in some kind of uniform. The fabric is green, like the uniforms on my old G.I. Joe action figures. Are they with the *army*?

But then, of course, they would be. The plane that crashed is the same plane that Dad and I saw land at TerraCorp . . . whenever that was. Maybe it was hours ago; maybe it was days. Either way, the army wasn't called in to investigate the crash. They were already here.

Dad, still dressed in his own uniform, takes two long strides across the room and yanks the oxygen mask out of Mom's hands. He doesn't bother fiddling with the straps; he just leans down and cups one of his hands behind my head, lifting me off the pillow slightly as I continue to struggle to suck air into my stubborn, aching lungs. With his other hand, Dad presses the mask gently but firmly to my face.

"Breathe, son," he says. "Just breathe."

The man and woman who came in with him are polite enough to stay back a few steps, but they're staring at me, staring at Dad, like a couple of scientists observing lab rats—not concerned, not willing to help, just curious. The walls behind them are textured and gray. They belong to the Windale Medical Center—I've been in here with enough sore throats and colds to recognize the place. But why are *they* here?

As if seeing all this registering in my eyes, my dad leans in closer, pushing the mask a little tighter, his other hand still bracing the back of my head in a way that he probably hasn't done since I was a baby. Even through the thick rubber of the respirator, I can smell his aftershave (this stuff called Chaz that Mom buys him every year for Christmas). I can see the tiny scar at the corner of his jaw where he got socked in the face by some dillhole who was pushing his little brother, my uncle Hank, around when they were kids. *Just stupid kid shit*, my dad says sometimes, chuckling from behind the morning paper.

Is this stupid kid shit that we're in now?

For a moment, I'm not sure. But then Dad answers the unasked question by putting his cheek to mine, on the right side of my face where the man and woman in the green duds can't see what he's doing. His breath is warm on my ear, and all I want to do is hug him, let him anchor me to something that feels like reality for just a little bit.

"Whatever you do," he says, barely whispering, "don't say *anything* to these people until you get a chance to talk to me first. Cough if you understand."

He pulls away and locks eyes with me, reinforcing his words with that stare that tells me he means business. The words take a second to register, and when they do, they bring about a whole new wave of panic and disorientation. But I trust my dad to protect me—to do the right thing not just by his family, but also by his town. Windale is his to protect, and these other people, the man and woman who keep watching us like we're something they might want to dissect with sharp, pointy things, they're strangers here. And they don't look friendly.

Without taking my eyes off Dad's, I cough once.

"He's okay," Dad says, looking over his shoulder at Mom. He straightens slightly when I take over holding the mask for myself. "He just needs to keep the oxygen flowing until his airway opens up a little more."

"You inhaled a lot of smoke." That's the man in uniform, finally stepping over to the bed I feel trapped in and giving me something that is probably supposed to be a smile . . . but isn't.

"Gabe, this is Sergeant Hollis," my mom says, ever the trusting one of our trio. "He's the doctor who's been taking care of you. These folks are with the army." She gives the whole group an uneasy glance but settles on the woman still standing away from us. "They're here to help." The edge in her voice makes it sound like she's not so sure that's true. I'm not so sure it is, either.

"As far as we can tell," Sergeant Hollis continues, "your lungs aren't permanently damaged, but it'll take some time before you can breathe on your own without the help of oxygen. After that, you might feel some pressure in your chest that will make it hard to do things like run or exercise. You have a mild concussion, as well, so there may be some disorientation, some trouble with your memory in the short term. But as your head heals, so will your mental faculties. You should be fine, otherwise. Aside from a few scrapes and bruises, of course. Oh, and that left shoulder, which was a bear to pop back in. You might be feeling that for a while." He grins at that, as if he's said something funny.

I nod, because if my parents did nothing else, they raised me to be polite, which is sometimes a real pain in the ass.

Dad looks at the woman in the corner, piercing her with that same deadly look. She levels one of her own at him, not hesitating to meet his gaze, and I feel goose bumps ripple over my skin.

"Colonel Higgins," Dad says, his voice razor-sharp, "can I ask again why we weren't allowed to see our son until now?"

The woman takes a single step forward, her arms locked at perfect angles behind her back. She's about as tall as my dad, white with dark hair pulled into a tight bun. Her features are daggerlike and a little frightening, mostly because everything about her seems to lack any kind of personality. She's cold and pointed, the empathy drained out of her, probably by some ungodly experience she went through while serving her country.

"You can ask, Mr. Albright," Colonel Higgins says, "but the answer will be the same. Your son is under the care of the United States Army. He's here because our job is to deconstruct the incident and figure out just what the hell happened. He needs to be kept under our supervision so that when he's ready, he can be debriefed. And up until a little while ago, we had not determined that it was safe for your son to have any visitors." Her eyes tick over to my mom. "I understand this is difficult."

Dad steps in front of Mom, as if trying to protect her. "First of all, in this town, it's *Chief* Albright. And second, whose safety are we talking about here? Gabe's? Or ours?"

At that, Mom makes a little whimpering noise. Higgins says nothing at all.

"What exactly was the army transporting on that plane, Colonel?" Dad asks. He raises his eyebrows at Sergeant Hollis. "Sergeant? *Anybody?*"

Higgins and Hollis are silent. Only Hollis seems slightly intimidated by Dad's glare—he stares down at his boots, which are reflecting pale rectangles of fluorescent light back at him.

"My son's testimony isn't going to help you figure out why that plane fell out of the sky," Dad continues. "It's just going to make him relive the whole thing. And I won't allow it."

Higgins looks down at her own boots and actually laughs. It's not a sound that has any joy in it, though, and her lips don't smile. When she glances up again, she looks as menacing as ever. I can see the smallest falter in my dad's resolution. He may have finally met his match, which would be funny under different circumstances.

"I like you," Higgins says. Her voice sounds the way a cobra looks when it's coiling, preparing to strike. "And for that reason, I will grant you one small courtesy. But let me make something very clear, *Chief* Albright. The fact that Gabriel is here, that he was part of the incident, is the only thing keeping me from putting you back behind the civilian line. Your son is going to receive the best care this country has to offer, by one of its best doctors." Her elbow moves just slightly, pointed at Hollis, who's trying to look busy writing something down on a clipboard. "But this is *my* investigation, and I will run it as I see fit. And you will not get in the way again. Do I make myself clear?"

Oh god, lady, I think. *You just made a very big mistake.* If there's one thing my dad can't stand, it's when somebody talks down to him.

But with his jaw clenched and the tendons in his neck standing out, Dad says, "Yes."

"Good." Higgins turns to Hollis. "Come find me when he's ready to be interviewed." And with that, she turns on her heel and steps out the door. The air seems to shift around the room, as if it's relaxing now that she's gone.

Sergeant Hollis does his best to offer a reassuring look.

"I want continuous updates on the progress of the investigation," Dad says, trying to reassert his own ability to intimidate. "That might have been your plane, but Windale is still in *my* jurisdiction. I have a right to know what the hell happened yesterday."

Yesterday. Sunlight is coming in through the gaps in the blinds on the window, which means I've been out for almost a full day. Jesus.

"I understand, Mr.—I mean, Chief Albright," Hollis says. "But with all due respect, your jurisdiction doesn't mean jack now that the army is here. The investigation is classified."

"Why?" Dad presses, his face turning a tomato-y shade of red, voice rising. "Because you asshats don't want us to know what happened? Because it might have something to do with whatever bullshit you have going on at TerraCorp?"

"Jack," Mom says. She sounds tired; her eyes are puffy from crying.

Hollis glances down at his clipboard again, as if he's going to find some kind of help from it. *Sorry, buddy. No getting out now. Once he's on a roll, he's on a roll.* Usually, for me, the roll ends with my being grounded. I don't think Dad can ground an army doctor, but he's sure as hell going to try.

I think Hollis might cave, tell Dad what he wants to know. But then his face hardens, and he locks his arms behind his back, clipboard still in hand, stands up straight. "I'm sorry," he says, not sounding sorry at all. "I understand this is difficult."

Before he steps out, Hollis fixes the straps on the oxygen mask so that it stays on my face without having to be held there. Then he's gone, leaving Dad standing beside the bed like a volcano about to erupt.

"Jack, it's okay," Mom says, putting a hand on his arm placatingly. She's good at talking him down, probably the only person who can. "Our son is alive. He's here. Can we just focus on that for a second?"

With a great whoosh of air, Dad relaxes, shoulders drooping. He glances at me, and I'm shocked to see his eyes red and swimming, tears on the verge of spilling over. "I thought we lost you there for a second, kid," he says.

"Everything's going to be fine," Mom adds. She takes my hand and squeezes it.

"What . . . ," I start with a voice that cracks like dry skin. It hurts to speak, but I have to ask the question. I have to know. "What . . . about . . . the others?"

They don't need to ask who I'm referring to.

"Sonya is in a room a few doors down," Dad says. "She's still out, but her parents are here. Charlie's in surgery."

"*What?*" I croak.

"He's in pretty rough shape, Gabe," Dad goes on.

I look away, squeezing my eyes shut, fighting against my own tears. How could things have gone so wrong so fast? When I turn my head back, I'm only slightly more composed. I don't think I can handle any more bad news. I think of Kimberly being lifted off the ground by whoever that was (*the Bug Man, damn it, the Bug Man*) and seeing him give me the thumbs-up when I told him to help her. There's a little spark of hope in my chest, ready to ignite into full-blown relief.

"And . . . Kim?" I ask, ignoring the steady burn in my esophagus.

But my heart sinks down through the bed when I see Mom and Dad exchange a look. Mom lowers her head, fingers working at her temples, as if she can't even look at me. Dad puts his hand on my shoulder.

"Gabe," he says, voice cinched tight. "Son, we don't know where Kimberly is. Nobody does."

15.

SONYA

"WHAT THE HELL do you mean they still don't know where she is?"

My voice is scratchy, my throat as dry and crackly as a brown paper bag. My arms and legs look like they were used as targets for archery practice, crisscrossed with slashes and gashes. Most of them are superficial, some of them have been hidden away by a few layers of gauze. The rest of me feels intact.

Except for my heart, which might be collapsing in on itself.

"Sonya, please," my mother says from the corner of the room. "Watch your language."

"Really, Mom?" It's hard to sound like a teenager when my voice rasps like I've been smoking two packs of cigarettes a day for decades, but I give it a go anyway. "I almost died and you're still more concerned about my cursing? Can you even call that cursing?"

Mom's mouth pinches into a tight, frightened line, with tiny wrinkles appearing to slash through her lips. When she makes that face, it looks as if her mouth has been sewn shut. Though I would never wish that was true, I could sometimes do without my mother's opinion.

But I suppress those feelings today. My ongoing struggle to get along with my mom is not what I should be focusing on right now. I sat here for two, maybe three, hours with my parents watching and waiting in silence for my voice to level out at least to the point where I could speak. (Thank god they left my little sister, Sophia, at home—she would have made cackling remarks about my "robot voice" the whole time.) I ditched the oxygen mask about twenty minutes ago, and even though my chest is still tight and my throat is still sore, I can breathe just fine on my own. Sure, it hurts, but it hurts the way popping a particularly stubborn zit hurts—it's a painful relief. Because that ache in my lungs is proof that I survived yesterday, even though yesterday tried to squash me like a spider in the bathroom sink.

Then they told me about my friends. Gabe, and Charlie, who needs some kind of surgery. And Kim. Oh god, Kim . . .

My dad is standing on the opposite side of the room from my mom. His white lab coat is draped over his arm again, and he's wearing the same shirt and tie from yesterday, only now the tie is loosened and the top button of the shirt is undone. It's almost like we're still in my bedroom, setting up my computer. That would be far preferable to this disaster.

"Sweetheart," he says to me. "I know this is scary—"

"*Scary?* Dad, she's . . ." So many words come to mind, fighting to get out. Some of them are true. Some of them I only *wish* were true. I settle for the only thing that makes sense right now: "She's my best friend."

Dad sighs, takes off his glasses, pinches the bridge of his nose, the only way he ever expresses frustration. Now I can see the strain pulling at the corners of my father's features, creasing his skin right before my eyes. He looks older now than he did yesterday morning. And somehow that's almost as frightening as the fact that Kimberly is missing.

Mom goes over to him, her shoes clicking on the tacky linoleum, and she hooks an arm around his elbow, finds his hand, laces her fingers in his. She puts her head down on his shoulder, and together they both seem to relax. I watch the tension drain from their bodies a little at a time. It makes me ache.

At home, stuck to the corkboard in my bedroom, is a strip of pictures that Kim and I took together in a photo booth at the county fair a couple of years ago. One of those stills is of us in almost the exact same pose that my parents are in now. Shoulders together, my head tilted onto Kim's shoulder, her head resting on top of mine. We're smiling, but we're also content. At least, I was. And she looks it in the picture. That was the night that I realized how I felt about her, and her heart wasn't just talking to mine then. It was singing.

"Listen, little one," Dad finally says. "I know you're afraid for Kim. We all are. But there's not a lot we can do right now. You have to worry about your own health first. You're no good to anyone if you go into cardiac arrest while you're out looking for her."

"But, Dad, we have to do *something*." I'm pleading now, which I haven't done in years. Not since I was in grade school, I think. I know he can see the pain in my eyes. If it looks anywhere near as bad as what I feel in my heart, then he'll know that I won't just let this go. I can't.

Dad shifts on his feet for a second, seeming to examine the water-stained ceiling.

Then he says, "Okay. Let me see what I can find out. The army people haven't exactly been forthcoming with information. Especially the one in charge, Colonel Higgins. But Jack and Valerie Albright are with Gabe a few doors down—"

"Wait," I cut him off, my heart pumping blood in my ears. "Colonel *who*?"

Dad slowly rests his glasses back on his nose, watching me carefully through the lenses. "Higgins," he says. "Colonel Audrey Higgins."

"Oh." It's all I can manage. I swallow hard, listening to Dad's voice replay in my head, the conversation he had yesterday morning in his office, the one he didn't know I was listening to. "Okay," I finally squeak. "That's what I thought you said."

"Uh-huh." He tilts his head back, squinting at me. Mom is watching us both, confused. "Anyway," Dad goes on, "I think we should wait it out a little longer, see what they want to do with you guys next. And if I get a chance, I'll talk to the chief and see if he knows anything more than we do. We aren't exactly friends, but he'll be just as anxious for answers as we are."

"Gabe will be, too," I say, thinking that only part of my dad's statement was true. The Albrights will definitely be itching to get some info, especially if the chief has been kept in the dark even a little bit. But there's no way Chief Albright knows more about the crash than Dad does. In fact, I'm pretty sure the only other person in this building who knows as much as Colonel Higgins does is Dr. Alvaro Gutierrez.

16.

CHARLIE

IT ISN'T THE noise that wakes me. It's the silence.

I live in the trailer park on the Dagger Hill side of the canal. There's a railroad track that cuts through town going north to south. An iron trestle just north of the Hill-to-Hill Bridge brings the route across the canal and down, cutting almost right through my backyard. Once or twice a night, a train comes whistling through, wheels singing across the rails, rumbling the entire trailer. The lonely sound of the horn blasting into the night usually startles me out of sleep, but the steady *ka-chick, ka-chick, ka-chick* of the cars rattling along the tracks will lull me back into it. It's a cruel game we play, night after night. But I'm so used to it that after a few hours here, in a strange room, in a strange bed, I jerk awake in a panic.

My body shifts, stiffening with the fear of realizing that I have no fucking clue where I am, and pain explodes in my legs. It's so bad that I feel it in my groin, deep in the bottom of my gut. It takes my breath away, as thin as it was to begin with, helped along by an oxygen mask strapped over my face.

I try to roll onto my side, try to curl into a ball. But I'm too bogged down by wires and tubes, all of which wind their way back to various machines circling my bed. Not to mention that one of my legs is wrapped in a full-length cast, as solid and unmoving as concrete. The white plaster material starts at my ankle and encircles my left leg all the way up to the thigh. And I can only really make out the hazy impressions of what I'm looking at because I don't have my glasses.

I don't even want to know what kind of Frankenstein bullshit this will look like when I can fully see again.

My body wants me to hyperventilate now. My lungs are gearing up for it. My nerves are frayed wires whipping and snapping and sparking along the surface of my skin. But my chest hurts. My throat, too. Each breath I take is only managed with the push of the oxygen tank, shoving air down into my lungs. I've seen enough movies to know that I must have inhaled a bunch of smoke. If it hadn't started raining, cutting through some of that fire, we might have died up on Dagger Hill . . . when? Today? Yesterday?

We.

I realize with another start that I'm alone. I have no idea where Gabe and Sonya and Kim are. Or if . . .

For a minute, my vision is blinded by a scene from earlier yesterday: the storm unfurling over Windale like a black, gnarled balloon; the rain and the thunder and the lightning accompanying it; the dark shape of the plane barreling out of the clouds, first just a vague outline, then a full-on monstrosity plummeting toward us like one of the freight trains that rocket past my house every night.

"Ah, you're awake!"

The sound of another person's voice in the room startles me out of the vision. And even though the images fade, they leave behind a ripple of goose bumps down my arms.

There's a doctor in the doorway, white coat standing out a little too white against the patterned, textured walls of the room. Even though I'm pretty sure this is the Windale Medical Center I'm in, I don't recognize her. She's got one hand in the pocket of her slacks and the other gripping a clipboard. Trying to look casual, I guess? I don't know; but whatever it is, she looks stiff and robotic. Uncomfortable in her own skin.

"How are you feeling?" the doctor asks. She doesn't check the clipboard. Keeps her eyes on me. Sapphire blue under a nest of hair that's almost entirely gray. It's kind of creepy to be watched like that.

But the adrenaline from my initial burst of panic is starting to wear off. The agony in my legs is tuning up for a Metallica guitar solo of pain. It feels like something is trying to rip them off. Maybe I'd be better off that way.

I just shake my head at the doc and look down at the cast.

"I won't lie to you, Charlie," she says. "You're lucky to be alive." Her eyes are still locked on mine as she says it. There's a sympathetic grimace on her lips, but it doesn't quite make it to those perfect blue orbs. They're pretty eyes—they just don't look very alive.

She steps farther into the room. Right behind her, to my immense dismay, I see my stepdad, Chet. He's even skinnier than I am, with bones and tendons standing out at every joint. His eyes are always sunken and purple, his hair a thinning puff of smoke. It's pretty clear that he needs some kind of fix—a smoke, a drink, a snort. His eyes dart from side to side, looking up and down the medical center hallway with his hands jammed down in the pockets of his ratty jeans.

The doctor sees me watching him and says, "Your dad can come in if you want."

"He's not my dad," I say instinctively. Through the rasp of my voice and the muffling of the rubber mask, it comes out garbled. It also hurts to speak, so I don't think I'll be doing that again for a while.

Chet comes in anyway, looking relieved to be out of the open sight lines of the hallway. He takes one last nervous glance over his shoulder, and then he turns the hate on, laser-focused, and aims it right at me.

Dr. Blue Eyes doesn't seem to notice. She plows ahead, finally lifting the clipboard to examine it. "I'm Dr. Claudia Reed, by the way," she says. "I'm a doctor with the United States Army."

The army? Jesus, no wonder Chet's so paranoid.

"There was some pretty severe damage to your legs, Charlie," Dr. Reed continues. She lowers the clipboard and looks at me gravely. "We were very nearly forced to amputate one of them. I'm sure you can guess which one." She glances at my left leg as if it's a piece of art. "Let's just say that you've got most of the nuts and bolts aisle of a hardware store in your leg. Getting back to normal is going to take a lot of time and a lot of work. A lot of pain."

I don't have a response for that. The pain she's talking about already outweighs the anxiety of what my future looks like. I just don't want it to hurt anymore.

"The commanding officer here in Windale, Colonel Higgins, will arrive later this evening to get a statement from you about what happened. Leave that respirator on. It'll help with the smoke inhalation and make it easier for you to talk when the time comes. We've got you on a shallow morphine drip right now for the pain in your legs. Just enough to take the edge off. Once Colonel Higgins gets her testimony from you, we can amp up the meds to make you more comfortable if you need it. Okay?"

Her voice is kind enough but also sort of robotic. Like her eyes, it doesn't have a whole lot of life in it.

Dr. Reed gives Chet a look. "If this isn't your dad," she says, "then are your parents around?" I guess she understood me after all. It's the first time that she sounds genuinely interested.

Chet speaks up first. "I'm . . . uh . . . Charlie's stepdad, Chet Landry. Charlie's dad . . . he, uh . . . he passed away a while ago. Big truck accident on the highway. Real shame. The kid's mom . . . uh, my wife, I mean. Samantha. Sammy. Everybody calls her Sammy. She got caught outside of town when your guys closed the roads. She works at Martin Guitars over in Nazareth. Kind of a hike, so she doesn't get home until late usually."

Oh god. They closed the roads?

And of course Mom is stuck outside the barricade. That thing about her working at Martin would have been true ten, maybe eleven, years ago. She used to come home smelling like sawdust and lacquer, whistling some Johnny Cash song or other, her fingertips stained black with ebony. It was a good job, and she loved working it. But after she met Chet, her interests followed his into things that seemed a little more worthy of their time. Cocaine, mostly. Which is why Mom's not here and Chet looks nervous as hell.

"Well, then," Dr. Reed says, addressing Chet directly for the first time. "I guess that makes you Charlie's legal guardian for the time being." Talking to me again, she says: "I'll be back shortly, probably when the colonel shows up. Don't go walking off on me now." Then she winks.

When Dr. Reed is gone, Chet turns to me. His eyes are boiling over with a slow-burn rage that I know all too well. Behind them, though, I see a hint of something else. Panic, maybe. If Mom was out on a drug run, and with the army skulking around town, there's no telling when Chet will get his next line. He's already fidgety and anxious. I have so many questions I want to ask. Mostly, they're about my friends. But Chet won't know anything. Even if he does know, he won't tell me. Every little torture is a new kind of treasure to him. And right now, he's got me all to himself. Even the fresh, vivid memory of a plane falling out of the sky on top of me and my friends—the pain in my legs a constant, throbbing reminder—can't rival how terrifying that is.

Chet shows his crooked, browning teeth in a grin that's even more lifeless than Dr. Reed's eyes. "Guess it's just you and me, kid," he says.

17.

OFFICIAL TRANSCRIPT

SATURDAY, JUNE 17, 1989—WINDALE, PA

EYEWITNESS TESTIMONY OF INCIDENT OCCURRING JUNE 16, 1989

INTERVIEW CONDUCTED BY COLONEL AUDREY S. HIGGINS

INTERVIEWEE: MS. SONYA GUTIERREZ—STUDENT, WINDALE HIGH SCHOOL—*ON SITE WHEN INCIDENT OCCURRED*

COL. HIGGINS: How are you feeling, Sonya? May I call you Sonya?

GUTIERREZ: It doesn't matter. Call me . . . whatever you want.

HIGGINS: Throat still bothering you? I apologize that we're doing this so suddenly. It's very important that we get as many details from you as we can while they're still fresh in your memory.

GUTIERREZ: It's fine. Can I see . . . Gabe and Charlie . . . after?

HIGGINS: We might be able to arrange for you to see Mr. Albright— as long as everyone's cooperative, of course. But Mr. Bencroft is probably just waking up from surgery. He'll need as much time and space to recover as possible, I'm sure. I'm going to see him right after we're done here. I can say hi for you. Let him know you're okay.

GUTIERREZ: Yeah, I guess . . .

HIGGINS: I understand this is difficult. You're worried about him. That's sweet. You two aren't . . . ?

GUTIERREZ: No. It's not . . . like that. We've been friends forever.

HIGGINS: I see. Maybe you and Mr. Albright then? He's a very handsome young man.

GUTIERREZ: We're just friends.

HIGGINS: Right. Best friends, correct? Just like you and Ms. Dowd?

GUTIERREZ: Yeah . . . right.

HIGGINS: Ah.

GUTIERREZ: Do you have . . . any idea where she is?

HIGGINS: Unfortunately, no. There are volunteers up on the Hill searching in and around the crash site. If something turns up, they're to report it to one of the MPs guarding the town line.

GUTIERREZ: Volunteers? Like, from Windale?

HIGGINS: Yes.

GUTIERREZ: Why do you need volunteers when you've got the whole army out here?

HIGGINS: My personnel are busy with more important tasks at the moment.

GUTIERREZ: But she could be <u>dead</u> out there! She could be . . .

[PAUSE WHILE MS. GUTIERREZ COUGHS SEVERAL TIMES]

HIGGINS: Try some water.

[GUTIERREZ COUGHS SEVERAL MORE TIMES]

HIGGINS: Better?

GUTIERREZ: Sure.

HIGGINS: Listen, Sonya. I know this is a hard situation to be in. Especially given your relationship with Ms. Dowd. Can you please describe what you saw yesterday?

GUTIERREZ: You mean other than the army plane that fell out of the sky on top of me and my friends? Why don't you tell me what you already know, and I'll help you fill in the parts that you don't. Which probably isn't a lot.

HIGGINS: Ms. Gutierrez, I know you think that because of your father's position at TerraCorp, you may have some kind of authority here, or any right at all to speak to an officer of the United States Army in that manner. But let me assure you that you are incorrect.

GUTIERREZ: My father has nothing to do with this. Or . . . does he?

HIGGINS: I'm going to move on. What we know so far is that the plane came down in the storm shortly after taking off.

GUTIERREZ: From where?

HIGGINS: That's not important. What is important is that it crashed into what is known locally as Dagger Hill shortly after one in the afternoon yesterday. It broke apart, catching you and your friends in the middle of its debris field. You, Mr. Albright, and Mr. Bencroft are the only survivors of the incident that we know of so far. We have not yet recovered the bodies of the pilots, nor have we located Ms. Dowd. Understanding what happened between the time of the crash and the time of your rescue is critical to helping us find her.

GUTIERREZ: Well, all I can say is that there was a bunch of smoke. The plane just dropped right out of the sky, like the storm had chewed it up and spit it out. After it hit, we all got separated.

I got these cuts on my legs. I couldn't see anything through all the smoke. I tried to help Charlie, but . . . but I just couldn't get to him. I passed out after that.

HIGGINS: You didn't see where Ms. Dowd might have gone? She could have wandered into the woods. Disoriented by the crash, maybe.

GUTIERREZ: The last time I saw her was right before the crash, when we were all watching the storm come in and . . . Wait. You said you haven't found the bodies of the pilots?

HIGGINS: That's correct.

GUTIERREZ: What about the man who parachuted into town?

HIGGINS: What man?

18.

OFFICIAL TRANSCRIPT

SATURDAY, JUNE 17, 1989—WINDALE, PA

EYEWITNESS TESTIMONY OF INCIDENT OCCURRING JUNE 16, 1989

INTERVIEW CONDUCTED BY COLONEL AUDREY S. HIGGINS

INTERVIEWEE: MR. CHARLES BENCROFT—STUDENT, WINDALE HIGH SCHOOL—*ON SITE WHEN INCIDENT OCCURRED*

BENCROFT: Why did you close the roads into town?

COL. HIGGINS: You're awfully spry for someone with a shattered leg, Charlie. It is Charlie, right?

BENCROFT: Only to my friends.

HIGGINS: Uh-huh. And you're aware of what's happening with one of those friends in particular?

BENCROFT: I know Kimberly's missing. My mom's husband told me.

HIGGINS: Mr. Landry?

BENCROFT: Yes.

HIGGINS: Whoever runs your local paper makes quick work of big news.

BENCROFT: If you didn't want anyone to know, maybe you should keep a tighter leash on your people.

HIGGINS: Hmmmm. I very much doubt that it's my people I have to worry about, Mr. Bencroft. Windale, for as quaint and quiet as it may appear to be, seems like a very gossipy place to live. Would you say that's true?

BENCROFT: I don't know what to tell you. Mostly I think we're just not fond of people who shut down our roads and take over our town.

HIGGINS: Nobody's here to take over your town, Charlie. There was an accident. A terrible one. And now there's a missing person, who happens to be one of your closest friends. We're here to figure out what happened to her.

BENCROFT: Let me guess. The more cooperative I am, the faster that happens.

HIGGINS: Precisely.

BENCROFT: Can I make one request?

HIGGINS: That depends on what the request is.

BENCROFT: Can you make sure my mom gets let back into town?

HIGGINS: Ah. She got stuck on the outside when the lockdown went into place?

BENCROFT: Something like that. I'm not even sure what the lockdown is for.

HIGGINS: It's for the protection of government property that might have been on board that plane when it crashed. And unfortunately, the lockdown cannot be lifted until we've taken inventory of the crash site.

BENCROFT: Inventory of what? The plane blew up. On top of us.

Trust me, if there was anything valuable on board, it's in a bunch of pieces out on Dagger Hill right now.

HIGGINS: Charlie, I understand you're upset about your mother. The best I can do is send somebody out to make sure she's okay, which I'm sure she is. The person you should be most concerned about right now is Kimberly.

BENCROFT: I . . . guess. I mean, yes. Yes, of course. Kimberly is missing, maybe even hurt. I'll do whatever I can to help find her.

HIGGINS: Good. You can start by telling me about the man you kids saw parachuting into town.

BENCROFT: Oh. Shit. That's right. I . . . I only caught a glimpse of him just before . . . everything. But it was a green parachute, so I guess maybe it was one of the pilots jumping before the crash?

HIGGINS: You didn't make out any other details? A description of the man, maybe? Or which part of town he was descending toward?

BENCROFT: He was too far away and too high up to make out anything specific. Nobody else in town saw him?

HIGGINS: Let's move on. After the crash, before you were rescued, did you see or hear anything out of the ordinary?

BENCROFT: Something that might help us figure out where Kimberly is, you mean?

HIGGINS: Of course.

BENCROFT: No. A bunch of debris snapped my leg apart, which hurts like an absolute motherfucker, by the way. I blacked out.

HIGGINS: I see.

BENCROFT: I'm sorry I can't be more helpful. Will you keep us updated on what's happening with Kim?

HIGGINS: As best we can, yes. There are a lot of variables to juggle with this, so some information might be delayed.

BENCROFT: Okay . . .

HIGGINS: One more thing, Charlie. You've spent a lot of time with Ms. Gutierrez, correct?

BENCROFT: Yeah, we've been best friends since we were kids. Or . . . younger kids. Whatever.

HIGGINS: What do you know about Sonya's relationship with her father? How close are they?

BENCROFT: Super close. They're even nerdier than I am.

HIGGINS: Would you say they're close enough that Dr. Gutierrez might be compelled to share certain kinds of information with his daughter? Things related to work, perhaps?

BENCROFT: I . . . don't know. Dr. G has always been really secretive about his job. Keeps everything locked up in his office at their house. Why? Does this have something to do with TerraCorp?

HIGGINS: Thank you for your time, Charlie. I wish you a speedy recovery.

19.

OFFICIAL TRANSCRIPT

SATURDAY, JUNE 17, 1989—WINDALE, PA

EYEWITNESS TESTIMONY OF INCIDENT OCCURRING JUNE 16, 1989

INTERVIEW CONDUCTED BY COLONEL AUDREY S. HIGGINS

INTERVIEWEE: MR. GABRIEL ALBRIGHT—STUDENT, WINDALE HIGH SCHOOL—*ON SITE WHEN INCIDENT OCCURRED*

COL. HIGGINS: I'm afraid your father and I may have gotten off on the wrong foot, Mr. Albright. Hopefully we won't do the same.

ALBRIGHT: I think that ship might have already sailed, Colonel. But what goes on between you and my dad isn't really my problem. I just want to see my friends. And I want to find Kimberly.

HIGGINS: Well, maybe you can help us do that. I just need some information about what happened yesterday, and then you're free to see Mr. Bencroft and Ms. Gutierrez.

ALBRIGHT: I . . . I'll tell you what I can.

HIGGINS: I hope so, Mr. Albright. For Kimberly's sake. Let's start with the crash itself. What do you remember? What did you see?

ALBRIGHT: Nothing until it was too late. There was just the storm. And then the plane was falling right on top of us and . . .

HIGGINS: I understand this is difficult.

ALBRIGHT: With all due respect, I don't think you have any idea what this is like.

HIGGINS: Maybe not. But I've been through my share of trauma, I assure you. It's hard to get over. It's harder still when you're not completely honest. With yourself. With those you care about.

ALBRIGHT: Okay. Well, I don't have anything to hide, if that's what you're saying. This whole thing was a freak accident. Right?

HIGGINS: There's no need to be hostile, Mr. Albright.

ALBRIGHT: I'm being hostile?

HIGGINS: You're being defensive. Which is usually a sign that somebody knows more than they're letting on. Or that they're scared. Or both. So which is it?

ALBRIGHT: It's neither.

HIGGINS: If you say so. I've already established with Mr. Bencroft and Ms. Gutierrez that the four of you witnessed a man parachuting into Windale, presumably a pilot escaping the plane before the crash. We're investigating that claim as we speak.

ALBRIGHT: Oh. Okay. Right.

HIGGINS: What I need to know from you is if you saw anything out of the ordinary before, during, or after the crash that might somehow be connected to Kimberly Dowd's disappearance.

ALBRIGHT: I . . . didn't. After the plane came down, I lost track of the others. I tried to crawl away to safety, but I banged my head and dislocated my shoulder. I passed out on the ground and woke up here in the medical center. That's all I know.

HIGGINS: . . . All right then. I guess we're done here.

20.
GABE

HIGGINS TELLS ME I can go.

"Just like that?" I ask. We're in my room at the WMC. There are paper ribbons taped to the air vent above my bed. They sway gently, but I don't feel any breeze. Outside, the sky is already creeping toward evening, turning the milky gray of summer dusk. I feel sweat sliding down the back of my neck, dripping between my shoulder blades.

"You don't have anything else you'd like to share, do you?" Higgins says. She has a folder on her lap. Beside her, on the room's only table, is the tape recorder—a thing the size of a VCR, with wide buttons that she presses so hard her finger bends backward. She hasn't opened the folder once. It's so thin I'm not even sure there's anything inside it. Would it matter if there was? She gives me the feeling that she already knows everything she wants to know; she just wants to hear me say it.

But what is there to say? I could have told her about the man on the Hill. The . . . the Bug Man—my brain won't stop calling him that. I just haven't figured out for myself yet if he really exists. That memory is fuzzy, blurred by rain and smoke and a concussion. I don't even know if I really saw Kimberly out there. My mind could have made the whole thing up.

If he is real, though . . . if I did see him scoop Kim up and carry her off into the woods . . . then I have to tell someone. It just can't be Higgins. It's clear that she's only here to tie up loose ends. That plane landed at TerraCorp yesterday morning. Dad and I watched it.

And then I watched it crash. The one and only time there's ever been a plane landing at that compound, and it gets knocked out of the sky less than six hours later, before it can make it back out of Windale airspace. But Colonel Higgins doesn't know that I know that part. She just knows that whatever the reason was for bringing that plane into Windale, it was a mistake. If she really does want to help us find Kimberly, it's only because Kim's a witness, a *victim*, just like me and Charlie and Sonya. And she has to make sure we won't go spinning this the wrong way.

Maybe she doesn't want anyone to know that the plane was ever at TerraCorp.

"Gabe?" Higgins is standing near the door, folder and tape recorder in hand, carrying them like a briefcase. The reels are still turning, like fast-moving clocks.

Finally, I look at her. "No. I don't have anything else I want to share."

"Okay then. Sergeant Hollis has one more test to run, and then you're free to go home with your parents." She smashes the STOP button on the recorder, and it's suddenly a lot quieter without the steady whir of the winding tape. "Please know that we're very sorry that this happened to you. And about your friend. I'm going to do everything in my power to rectify this situation."

"I'm sure you are," I say. There's a bitterness in my voice that I can't help. A vision of Kimberly being picked up and carried off by a black-clad stranger distracts me.

I can feel Higgins watching me for a moment. Then the door groans softly, and it's the creaking leather of the Bug Man's gloves, giving me a thumbs-up.

Sergeant Hollis comes in. Higgins nods at him before she steps out, lugging our conversation with her. I can only stare at my feet, dangling off the side of the bed.

"How are you feeling, Gabe?" Hollis asks. He sets a small plastic case on the table where the tape recorder was.

"It still hurts to breathe," I reply. Every breath rakes hot coals down my throat and into my lungs. But my airway feels a lot wider than it did earlier today, and despite the pain, I can breathe without the oxygen.

"It'll be a while before that part gets better, unfortunately," Hollis says. "How about the arm?"

My left arm is tucked against my body, held by a sling. My shoulder is sore, and my fingertips still feel somewhat tingly, but it's no worse than my lungs. Or my head, which is heavy and aching and filled with a bunch of scary thoughts.

"It's okay" is all I say to Sergeant Hollis.

He nods, opens the case he brought in with him. The lid swings up toward me, so I can't see what's inside. He's fiddling with something, though. "I have a teenager, you know," he says. "She's a little younger than you. A sophomore, back home in Lexington."

"Kentucky?"

Inside the case, Hollis's hands move, and something metallic clicks together.

"Unless there's another Lexington that I don't know about." Hollis grins. His arm is gyrating, twisting something out of sight. Screwing something into place, maybe. "She can be kind of a handful." For the first time, I notice the subtle Southern lilt in Hollis's voice. "Anytime she says that something is just *okay*, I have to really dig down deep to get the truth. You know?"

Hollis's arm swings up from behind the top of the case. In his hand is a shining steel syringe about the size of a baby's arm. At the end of it is a needle as long as a pencil and as thick as the spokes on a bike wheel.

"Whoa," I say, breathless.

"I know," Hollis says, coming around the table to the bed. "It's kind of intimidating. But I promise it'll be painless."

"What . . . what's it for?"

He pulls back on a peg that's jutting from one side of the syringe. A slot opens along the tube, and Hollis peers inside for a moment before twisting the peg and sliding the slot back into place in one precise, fluid movement. Like he's loading a rifle. Even the way the metal pieces lock home sounds the same.

"I'm going to put this little guy in your arm," Hollis says. His voice is smooth and chipper. He's a new man now that Higgins isn't here to make him nervous. "It's going to inject a small vial, kind of like a pill. The outer shell of the vial will dissolve and release a chemical into your bloodstream. If you or your friends were exposed to any kind of radiation or harmful biowaste during the crash, this chemical will react with that stuff."

"Radiation?" I ask. My heart is kicking up. "Why would there be any radiation?"

Hollis smiles indulgently, but this close, I can see one of his eyelids twitch. "The plane that crashed was coming from an army base in Washington State where some, uh . . . *unique* scientific studies were being done."

"Kind of like TerraCorp?" I say, trying to keep my voice level.

"Right." Hollis's smile turns icy in a second. "But in Washington State. According to the manifest, there wasn't anything on board the plane that you should worry about. But the plane itself, or even the pilots, may have been exposed. So as a precaution . . ." He waves the enormous needle, showing perfect rows of teeth in a smile that does nothing to make me feel better.

Not to mention that he's lying right to my face. Which seems totally pointless because plenty of other people in Windale must have seen that plane land at TerraCorp yesterday. I can name one right this second: Clark Webber. Two more: Rebecca Conner and Mel O'Connell, my dad's deputies. What are they going to do? Convince the entire town to lie for them? To pretend that none of this happened, even when Kimberly is still missing?

Hollis wobbles the syringe again. "In a couple days, you'll have to come back and do a urine test. If the chemical in this vial reacted to anything in your body that doesn't belong there, we'll be able to see it and get you the proper treatment. Like I said, though. Just a precautionary measure." He shrugs and takes a last step toward me, until his knees are almost touching mine.

On instinct, I scooch back farther on the bed. "C-Can't you just use a Geiger counter or something?" The panic is back in full force. Suddenly, I couldn't care less about where the plane came from or where it was going. I'm too focused on the needle.

"Not exactly," Hollis says with a dry laugh. "Not for what we're looking for. Now do me a solid and stay very still. Okay?"

"Did, uh . . . did you ask my parents about this?" I'm stalling. The scratchy hospital blanket under me is balled up in my good fist, the one that's not dangling from a sling.

"We did. Your dad signed off on it."

Bullshit, I think.

"Sonya's dad, too?" Even though Dr. Gutierrez works at TerraCorp, and maybe knows more about what's going on here than any of us, there's not a chance he'd put Sonya through something like this.

"I'm not sure I'm allowed to share that information with you," Hollis says, getting impatient, his arms dropping to his sides, the needle waving around in his hand like he forgot it was there. "But if it makes you feel better, then yes, Dr. Gutierrez signed an authorization form for his daughter as well. In fact, this test was his idea."

I go still. "Really?"

He nods. "He wanted every box checked in regard to the safety of you kids."

I don't know what to say to that. My chest is still heaving, fanning the flames in my lungs, and my heart is racing. But I've known Sonya's dad almost as long as I've known Sonya. Charlie and I jokingly call him the mad scientist from time to time, even though he's quiet and caring and has always been around to help the four of us out if we need it.

"Okay," I say. I hold my right arm out to Hollis. The fingers on the end of it are trembling.

"Great," he says.

When the needle goes in, I can feel the cold metal inching up the inside of my arm, almost all the way up to my elbow. Sergeant Hollis squeezes a trigger at the bottom of the syringe. The tube shutters and hisses, then the mechanism inside it retracts. Hollis pulls the needle out of my arm, a sword withdrawing from a fleshy sheath, and covers the puncture wound with a cotton ball and tape.

"All set," he says.

21.
SONYA

MOM WENT HOME to get Sophia some dinner, so Dad's in the room with me when Sergeant Hollis and another woman, Dr. Reed, administer the roadside attraction known as the World's Biggest Fucking Needle. Before they come in, Dad assures me it's a routine test, something they do at work sometimes to make sure no one has been exposed to anything unsafe. He's quieter than usual as he says it, disconnected somehow. And when I hiss in a sharp, frightened breath after Hollis opens his case and shows me the needle, Dad just stands in the corner, arms crossed, head down, fingers pinching his nose. He told me this was his idea, but he doesn't look happy about it. I'm sure I look even worse.

Hollis seems a little too excited as he pushes the needle under my skin. And Reed's hand is ice-cold when she lets me squeeze it, turning my face to my shoulder, shutting my eyes. After the needle is out, I can feel the pressure of the "vial," as Hollis called it, lodged in the crook of my arm. It's wigging me out.

When the two doctors finally leave, they don't shut the door behind them.

"Time to go," Dad says. He sounds empty, and his eyes look the same way.

"Dad." I grab his arm before he can lead me out into the hall. My voice is scratchy and burnt. "Are you okay?"

He doesn't look at me. His tie is in his hand now, and he keeps wrapping it around his knuckles, like a boxer taping up before a match. "Yes. Let's just go home, okay?" He tugs his arm out of my hand, walks out the door without a look back.

I have to take a second to regain my composure before I follow him, pushing down tears that threaten to spill. I feel stupid for wanting to cry. Mom says that crying does nothing to solve your problems. I guess she's right, but sometimes it just can't be helped. Sometimes the only thing left to do is cry.

But I blink away the tears for now—I'll save them for later, at home, in the confines of my bedroom, where I can muffle the sounds with a pillow. I step out into the hall and spot Gabe and his parents a few doors down. I can't help myself. I run as fast as I can and throw my arms around Gabe, and suddenly the tears can't wait. Some of them escape anyway, which is fine, because these, at least, are happy tears.

Gabe and I are locked tight. He's hugging me as hard as he can with one arm in a sling. I bury my face in his good shoulder. For a few seconds, I'm holding my friend and it's just us; the rest of this bullshit nightmare falls away.

"Are you okay?" Gabe says quietly. "I was so worried."

He tries to pull me closer, and that's exactly when I pull away. Smiling a little awkwardly up at him, wiping a stray tear off my cheek with a thumb, I step back, realizing the implications that hug might have had. The look on Gabe's face kills me a little, but I don't want to give him the wrong idea. The plane crash hasn't changed my feelings for anyone. If anything, it's only made my feelings for Kimberly clearer. Because she's not here, and I need her.

"I'm fine," I say. "You?"

"Yeah," he says. He slides his hand into his pocket. "As good as I can be, anyway."

"Did you get . . . ?" I turn my thumb and index finger into a gun and aim it at the inside of my elbow, where the ball of gauze is taped.

He nods, turning his right arm out to show me his. "Did it hurt?"

"Not really." I shrug. "Kind of. I wonder if they gave Charlie the same thing."

"I'm sure they did." Gabe turns to Chief Albright, waiting with his wife a few feet away. His arms are folded, and the perpetual scowl on his face has deepened to the point of almost being funny. "Dad, we're going to go see Charlie, okay?" Gabe asks.

I turn to find my own dad all the way at the other end of the hall, not looking at anyone, either. Dad and Chief Albright have never really gotten along, but they've at least been amicable. This doesn't feel even remotely close to that. This feels like something closer to outright hatred.

"Dad?" I say, raising my voice so he can hear.

Finally, he glances at me and says, "Go ahead, Sonya. I'll wait in the car." Before I can say anything else, Dad disappears around the corner.

When I turn back to Gabe, he's watching the spot over my shoulder where Dad was standing. "Is he okay?" he asks.

"Honestly? I have no idea." I take one last look at the empty hall, willing my father to come back and be himself again. But it doesn't happen. "Let's go see Charlie."

As we step past Gabe's parents, his mom says, "Wish him well for us, okay?"

"We will," I say, trying on a smile. It doesn't feel quite right.

"We'll wait out in the lobby," Chief Albright says. We're walking farther on now, but the chief isn't done. "And Gabe!" His voice is hard, loud, suddenly explosive. It startles Gabe and me both into turning and looking back at his dad. "When you're done, I want you in the car. You're going to be home for a few days."

"Wait, what?" Gabe says. "Why?"

Chief Albright gives me a strange look that I can't decipher, then, to Gabe, says, "We'll talk about it when we're home. Go make sure Charlie's okay."

"But, Dad—"

"I said go, son. Before I change my mind."

Beside him, Mrs. Albright looks concerned but doesn't protest. And she definitely doesn't look at me, which is weird. "See you in a minute, sweetie," she says. Then they're walking away.

"C'mon," Gabe says to me. He sounds confused and angry, the same way I feel. "Charlie's over in CCU."

The Windale Medical Center is a one-story building, stretched out over a few dozen acres. It's where people come for annual check-ups, get treated for common stuff, do bloodwork, get the occasional X-ray, and, in extremely dire circumstances, have a baby. The WMC isn't really equipped to deal with major trauma, which is why it's odd that Charlie is still here. I would have thought that he'd be transferred to a bigger hospital, especially if he needed surgery. I say all this out loud to Gabe.

"I don't know what the story is," he says. "If they really don't want anyone going into or out of town, then one of the army doctors must have done the surgery."

"I bet it was Hollis."

"Yeah, that guy gives me the willies." He chuckles, and so do I. "Listen," Gabe goes on, stopping just outside the door to the critical care unit, which is only two rooms deep. "Don't worry about . . ." He paddles his hand between us, gesturing to me, then to himself, then to me again. His face is pinched, like he's searching for the right words. ". . . anything. You know? I'm—*we're* fine. I'm just glad you're okay."

My heart sinks in a whole new way. This is not the conversation I wanted to have right now. "Gabe. Don't get me wrong. I really—"

I'm saved by Charlie's voice, echoing out of one of the rooms: "Is that my main man, Gabriel, and my Wonder Twin forever, Sonya G?"

Gabe and I exchange a look.

"Uh . . ." Gabe cocks his head to the side, confused. "Yes?"

"Get your asses in here! What are you waiting for?" Charlie calls.

"What did *his* needle have in it?" I mutter.

"Something way better than what they gave us," Gabe says under his breath.

We poke our heads in the doorway to Charlie's room. He's on the bed, alone. There's a TV on a shelf high up in one corner. It's tuned to *The Golden Girls*, but the volume is turned all the way down.

"Guys!" Charlie yells. Gabe and I both jump. "How's it hanging? Come on in to my luxury suite!" He says the last part in a terrible French accent.

"Hey, buddy," Gabe says tentatively. "You doing okay?"

Charlie looks strange without his glasses. I can't imagine why his mom wouldn't have brought his backup pair. But I'm less worried about his eyesight than I am about the cast that's swallowed his entire left leg.

He sees me staring, even in his bleary-eyed delirium, and says, "Ah, don't worry about me, Sone. This? This is nothin'. They patched me up just fine. Gave me some good stuff for the pain, too."

Charlie winks at us. Gabe and I give each other a knowing look.

"Ah," I say.

"He did get a different needle," Gabe says.

"Actually, I got two," Charlie says, puckering his lips and holding up three fingers.

"Listen, pal, we just wanted to come check on you," Gabe tells him. He sits down on Charlie's bed, careful not to bump his leg, and nudges Charlie with his elbow. "Did they tell you about Kimberly?"

I have to swallow a lump in my throat, and Charlie's face changes, slipping into shadow. "Yeah," he says. "I . . . I don't know . . . what happened." He's struggling for clarity, fighting past the meds. His face is all scrunched together in concentration.

"It's okay, Charlie," I say. I step closer to the bed and squeeze his shoulder. "We're gonna figure this out, all right? If not them . . ." I tilt my head to the door, looking at Gabe. He nods.

"Then us," he finishes for me.

Charlie's face brightens, like a child's. "Good. That's good. Kimberly's probably fine." He waves a hand, like it's no big deal.

Gabe, meanwhile, is chewing on his bottom lip, staring down at squares of linoleum. He glances up at me, catches me watching him, and looks away.

"I wonder if the man with the parachute is here," Charlie blurts out. "It looked like he was having a *lot* more fun than we were."

"They don't know where he is," I tell him.

Gabe's head snaps up. "What?"

"They didn't even know he jumped," I say. "Somebody in town had to have seen him, but they must not have gotten that far yet, because Higgins looked surprised when I told her. Like, *really* surprised."

"Holy shit," Gabe says. His mouth is working again, muscles in his jaw clenching.

"Gabe?" I have a question on the tip of my tongue, but, as if summoned by the very mention of her name, Colonel Higgins strides in before I can ask it. There's another soldier with her, carrying an armload of what looks like our clothes from yesterday. The ones we're wearing now were brought to us by our parents. Except for Charlie, who's still in his hospital gown.

"Before you kids go," Higgins says without any preamble, "I wanted to return some items to you. We had to comb through them, just to make sure there weren't any clues that could lead to Ms. Dowd."

Defiance leaps up in me like an uncaged lion. I can't tamp it down anymore. "Why? It's not like *we* did anything to her," I say.

"Nobody thought so," Higgins continues calmly. "But since none of you were very forthcoming with information during our conversations, we wanted to double-check to make sure you weren't carrying any clues that you might not have known were clues."

She picks something off the top of the pile that the private is holding for her—tiny slips of paper, it looks like. She holds them out to us between her fingers, like a magician doing a card trick. "We found these in each of your pockets. They're no good to you now, but I figured since you paid for them, you might want them back."

Gabe takes the slips of paper from Higgins, then hands me one of them. It's smudged, darkened and curling around the edges, but the words printed on it are still legible: **GHOSTBUSTERS II—6/16/89—7:15PM**. My movie ticket from the night before.

Charlie reaches out and plucks the last ticket out of Gabe's hand, reads it, and grins. "*Gah!* This was such a good movie."

Gabe pats Charlie's hand. "Sure it was, buddy."

Higgins glances at the private and tilts her head toward us. The soldier puts the stack of clothes in my arms, topped off by Charlie's Marty McFly puffer vest, the slippery red fabric burned black in spots, with tufts of down poking out.

"We would have passed this stuff along to your parents, but it seems they already left." Higgins shrugs, turning to go. But then she stops. She looks at Gabe with something like curiosity, like he's a puzzle she's trying to figure out. "There's one more thing. We found this near the spot where we found you, Mr. Albright. I would have returned it to Ms. Dowd's parents, but . . ." She stops, the very corners of her lips turning up in a pointed, secretive smile. ". . . maybe you want to take it back to them yourself."

She holds the item out; it's small enough to fit in the palm of Higgins's hand. The last of my tears finally let go when I realize what it is. The thing is blue and smudged with soot, coated in bits of grass and pine needles. Kimberly's scrunchie.

Gabe doesn't take it right away. He only stares at it, mouth wobbling, eyes wet. Not even Charlie is immune to it. Like some kind of talisman, the scrunchie washes away his dazedness. All that's left behind is grief, stark and pained on his face. "Shit," he whispers just before his face crumples and he breaks down into sobs.

"It's okay," Higgins says to Gabe. "Take it. It might make you feel better." She says it slowly, breaking down the words into sharp, distinct syllables.

With a shaking hand, Gabe takes the scrunchie. It releases some of the grass and needles as it moves from her hand to his. I watch them twirl to the ground.

"Have a good evening, kids." Higgins specifically emphasizes the word *kids*. "We'll be in touch."

She and the private march from the room. It feels like a long time before the thumping of their boots goes quiet.

The three of us are left in silence. Gabe stares down at the scrunchie in his hand. I can't bear to look at it. Or him, for that matter. He knows something. I can feel it. Something he doesn't want anyone else to know. But why? If it could help us find Kimberly, why wouldn't he want to tell whoever he could?

For the same reason you didn't tell Dad about eavesdropping on his phone call, maybe? Or the same reason you haven't told anyone that you knew Higgins was already here in Windale yesterday, presumably arriving on the very plane that caused this mess in the first place?

"Are you guys hungry?" Charlie says out of nowhere. "I'm hungry. Like, *starving*. Like, I'm so hungry that I could eat both of you guys right now and not even feel bad about it. Well, that's not true. I'd feel kinda bad. No, really bad. But I wouldn't be hungry anymore, so—"

I put a hand over his mouth. "Charlie. Dude. We get it. You're hungry. Let me go see if I can find someone to bring you dinner. Where's your mom? Or Chet?"

"Mom's not here," he says, getting sad again. "They locked her out."

"Out of the *building*?"

"Out of town."

"Oh. Shit. So your mom's not in Windale at all?"

He shakes his head, and my heart twists into a knot.

"What about Chet?" I ask, afraid of the answer. Chet has a colorful history in our little group, and by colorful, I mean crimson. We've had to get Gabe's dad out to Charlie's house on more than one occasion. He even threw Chet in lockup overnight once. It wasn't a good night. Usually, the only thing standing between Chet and Charlie is Charlie's mom. If she's not around to keep the peace . . .

"He was here," Charlie says, staring up at Betty White on the TV screen. "But then he left. I don't know if he's coming back." His eyes start to droop. The painkillers are putting him under.

"Charlie, we're gonna go," I whisper. "But I'll be back tomorrow to check on you, okay?"

He just nods sleepily, smacking his lips and sinking deeper into his pillow.

I nudge Gabe's arm, breaking him out of whatever trance he was in, and nod toward the door. He looks at Charlie, gives his hand one last squeeze, then we sneak out as quietly as we can, taking our ruined clothes with us.

We're down the hall, away from the CCU, before either of us says anything. I'm walking with my arms wrapped around my outfit from yesterday like it's a stack of books at school, thankful that somebody had the decency to tuck my underwear inside my shorts.

It's Gabe who says something, mumbling under his breath.

"Huh?"

He stops, looking up and down the hall, maybe to make sure nobody is around. "What happened to the camera?"

"What camera?" I ask. But then it hits me. Of course. Charlie's Polaroid. Gabe was snapping pictures of the storm with it just before the crash. My eyes go wide. "Did you get a picture of . . ." I look around myself now, making sure there aren't any soldiers lurking around the corners. Instead of speaking, I put my clothes over my head and sway from side to side, trying to mimic somebody falling through the sky with a parachute.

Gabe understands, nodding. "I think I did."

"Maybe they found the photos? Kept them for evidence?" I'm whispering and I have no idea why.

"Higgins said you and Charlie told her about . . ." He puts his own clothes over his head with his good arm and impersonates the parachuting man.

"If they'd found the photos, they would have known already that he jumped."

He nods.

"Why are we whispering about this?"

"Because I don't know about you," Gabe replies, "but I don't think Higgins is here to help anyone but herself."

I think of Dad's phone call yesterday. Him telling Claudia not to let Higgins inside the lab at TerraCorp. Telling her to make sure that

Higgins never made it past the runway. Not even Dad wanted the colonel here, and that was before her plane crashed on top of his kid.

"So then . . . what? They're trying to cover up the plane crash?"

"I don't know," he says. "But why hasn't the pilot—or whoever he is, the guy who jumped out of the plane—why hasn't he turned up yet? If he's dead, somebody would have noticed."

"And if he's alive, he would have linked back up with the army, and Higgins wouldn't have been so caught off guard. So . . . what? He just disappeared?"

Gabe nods slowly. "Maybe on purpose. Maybe he's hiding from something."

"But why?"

Gabe's face goes white, and in the corner of my eye I see him squeeze Kimberly's scrunchie. "I don't know," he repeats, too quickly this time.

"Gabe, listen to me, if you saw something—" I point a shaking finger at his face, more out of fear than anger.

"*Gabe!*" We're interrupted a second time by Chief Albright, who comes barreling around a corner at the end of the hall, face the color of a freshly picked apple. "What's the holdup?" The chief lifts his arms in a *what the hell* gesture. He gives me another one of those looks that I can't figure out.

"I'm coming, Dad," Gabe says, rolling his eyes.

"Now." Chief Albright puts his hands on his hips and waits, and suddenly we're thirteen again, playing video games at the old arcade a few minutes outside of town, before it moved to the strip mall, Gabe's dad is chaperoning, and he's had plenty for one day, but Gabe just won't quit. One more quarter.

"Take this," Gabe says. He puts Kim's scrunchie in my hand. "I think she'd want you to have it."

"I'll take it, but I'm not keeping it," I say. "She'll take it back when we find her." He's walking away. *Running* away, it feels like. He reaches his dad where he's waiting, and they both turn to go.

"You hear me, Gabe?" I shout. The halls are empty, and my voice echoes. "She'll take it back when we find her!"

But there's no one there to listen. Gabe and his dad are already gone.

BANSHEE PALACE

RICKY MONTOYA DOESN'T feel like himself. In fact, he doesn't feel right at all. As Sonya Gutierrez and Gabe Albright are leaving the Windale Medical Center with their parents, and Charlie Bencroft is settling in for a night alone, Ricky is perched atop his own personal kingdom.

On the roof of his video-rental store, he shoves cardboard boxes full of unassembled electronics and cables across the gravel. There are two short brick barriers separating the roof of his establishment from those of the other businesses squeezed into the strip mall. Nestled along the inside of one of those barriers are various electrical panels, all of them open, all of them spewing wires and connectors. Behind the strip mall, Sunrise Hill looms in the gathering darkness. In the opposite direction, the lights of Windale are just coming on, twinkling to life in company with the stars. The high school football field is out there, the bright rectangles of arc sodium lights glaring down on the new army encampment that sprouted there like a fungus overnight. There's a separate set of lights across the canal illuminating a blackened scar cut into the side of Dagger Hill.

Ricky is mostly unbothered by all this. He's busy fiddling with the contraption he's putting together. Tightening bolts, screwing in cords, aligning splayed fingers of antennas.

"Gotta boost the signal," he mumbles to himself as he works. Absently, he scratches at an itch on the back of his head. It feels like there's something crawling there, but maybe it's just his skin. When he blinks, he sees the face in the TV screen, smeared with static, winking at him. "Gotta . . . gotta boost it. Boost the signal. Boost the signal."

The face was just the beginning of a very awful day. It was enough that Ricky had to close the sales floor, posting some stupid excuse on *a sign that he taped to the door. The face in the TV told him to do it. It didn't speak, didn't even have a mouth, not really. It just told him. Ricky felt it creep into his brain the same way he felt that itch on the back of his head. The face gave him other instructions, too, and he scribbled them down on the insides of VHS slip covers that he pulled from his shelves and tore apart, sitting cross-legged in front of his magnificent display. That was all fine and terrifying.*

But then the man in the gas mask showed up.

He just stood there, in a shadowy corner of Ricky's store, watching through the smoky lenses of the mask. That guy doesn't talk, either, Ricky discovered. And when you try to argue with him, try to kick him out of what's rightfully yours? Well, then he takes off the mask.

Ricky shivers and keeps working.

He moves with an almost frantic urgency, fingers shaking. His stomach grumbles, but Ricky hardly notices, can't remember when he last ate. He's been at this since this morning. If anyone has approached the store—looking to rent a copy of The 'Burbs, *perhaps—the video-rental king of Windale hasn't seen or heard them. They've only been met with the* SORRY, WE'RE CLOSED *sign hanging on the door.*

That's okay. Ricky has a new passion now. Or maybe the better word is obsession. *His new invention, something he may or may not have been able to come up with all on his own, stands like an aluminum alloy skeleton before him. A satellite of sorts. A radio broadcast tower built for something a lot more powerful than transmitting "Baby Don't Forget My Number" through the airwaves.*

A reckoning has come to Windale, a message of doom for some but salvation for many more, and Ricky Montoya is helping to spread it.

22.

CHARLIE

CHET LEAVES ME by myself at the medical center, goes home so nobody can see the twitch in his fingers. Not that the army much cares about an unemployed junkie, I'm sure. But paranoia just comes with the territory—I've lived down the hall from it long enough to know.

I don't remember when Gabe and Sonya left. I know they were here, and I know that Colonel Hellraiser Higgins was, too. Hopefully not with her monster tape recorder, because I'm sure I was a hoot and a half. Beyond that, my mind is a fog.

The TV is playing reruns of *Charles in Charge*. I'm only half paying attention to it, can't even really *see* it without my glasses. The other half of me is fighting off the drowsiness brought on by the pain meds the docs keep pumping in through my IV. I enjoy not feeling the throb of my leg, but I'm not really a fan of not feeling like myself.

The lights are off; the halls are quiet. I might be the only patient the WMC has tonight. There's supposed to be a soldier posted outside my door, but I haven't heard him out there in hours. He probably walked away for coffee and ended up talking to the nurse on duty, Louise Engleton, who graduated the same year I and the others moved from middle school to high school. Aside from the TV, the only light is a thin rectangle around the door, illuminated by the fluorescents out in the hall.

The shadow of the door itself is blacker than the night sky outside my window. And as my eyes flutter and sleep begins to crash over me in slow waves, I see the outline of something else inside that darkness. A silhouette—a person standing in the room with me. Even the blue flicker spilling across the room from the little Emerson set perched in the corner isn't bright enough to reach into that eerie, inky space.

Suddenly, sleep seems both immediately present and desperately far away. I try to focus on Scott Baio and his predictable hijinks or to let the exhaustion I feel down into my bone marrow knock me out for the night.

But it's watching me. I can feel it (feel *them*?). I don't know who it is or when they came in, but they're not moving. They're not even breathing, I don't think. Through the corner of my eye, I see the dark slopes of shoulders, a slender neck, and a head that turns, ever so slightly, to watch me. There's a soft reflection where the eyes should be, and I can see a distorted, transparent version of the TV flashing in one of those . . . what? Lenses? Is someone in here in the dark, wearing sunglasses?

Goose bumps creep across my forearms, up my back, around my neck. All the little hairs on my body stand at attention.

There's a weird creaking noise from that side of the room, like old wood or . . . or maybe leather. The silhouette shifts, the reflective eyes—big and oblong—turn sideways in an almost inquisitive way. *Insect eyes*, I think on impulse, a thought that doesn't so much feel like my own but one that was put inside my head.

"Chet?" I say. My voice sounds faint and groggy through the veil of medicated sleep. I lift my arm to find the remote that controls the TV and lights and, most important, calls nurse Louise. But my limbs are clumsy. Not fast enough. Not fast enough at all.

Then the thing (person? whatever it is?) is standing in the shifting light of the TV screen, moving from the door to inches away from my bed in a blink. A human-size fly dressed in all black, with wide, shining eyes and a strange protrusion at its mouth. Arms outstretched, fingers reaching.

I think of that movie from a couple of years ago, *The Fly*, with Jeff Goldblum, and Geena Davis saying, *Be afraid. Be very afraid.*

I'm so afraid I might piss myself. More afraid, I think, than I was yesterday afternoon, lying on the ground with a shattered leg and rain pouring down on me, surrounded by fire and the shredded remnants of an airplane. At least then I had Sonya's voice to keep me company.

Now I'm alone, and this bug thing is moving through the stuttering shadows toward me. Skittering across the room, the edges of its body flickering.

I squeeze my eyes shut, waiting for whatever happens next . . .

But nothing does.

A bray of laughter on the TV cuts through the silence. When I open my eyes, I see that *Charles in Charge* has been replaced by *Night Court*, and the clock on the wall, ticking dutifully, says that it's a quarter after three in the morning.

I've been sleeping this whole time.

It didn't feel like sleeping, though. Not even close.

Groggily, I pat around until I find the remote and switch the lights on. There's nobody else in the room, not even a sweater hanging off the back of the door that I might have mistaken for a person. Just me and the sanitized grayness of the room and Judge Harry Stone presiding.

Try as I might to shake the jitters away, I'm still creeped out. And the pain in my leg has cranked itself back up to a gnarly roar. I hit the button for nurse Louise and hope that when she doses me again, the sleep it brings is peaceful.

Before she arrives, though, I realize that there's something crumpled in the fist of my free hand. A piece of paper ripped from the notepad on the table beside the bed. I unfurl it with pale, shaking hands. There are a few words scribbled on the page, in handwriting that I know isn't mine. It looks almost like a child wrote it:

YOUR FRIEND SLEEPS LIKE YOU DO.
SWEET DREAMS, CHARLIE.

23.
GABE

ON SUNDAY MORNING, I struggle to get downstairs to the kitchen, feeling heavy and sore. After a night of blinking in and out of sleep, snapping between the warm, heavy dark of my room and the fretful, terrible dreams of the plane crash and the Bug Man and other horrible inventions of my mind—mostly related to what might have happened to Kimberly—I'm bone-tired.

Mom finds me sitting at the table. She gives me a long look, taking me in fully. After a minute, she crosses the kitchen and pours a cup of coffee from the pot. She doesn't add any cream or sugar.

"Here, kiddo," she says, setting the mug down in front of me. "My rule of thumb is that the coffee needs to be as black as the bags under your eyes in order to be effective."

I glance down at the tar-colored liquid in the cup through uncoiling ribbons of steam. "That bad, huh?"

Mom nods.

I take a sip of the coffee and cringe, but the bitter jolt does wake me up a little. Mom's got some casserole baking in the oven, the smell of which is making me nauseous, and I can guess who it's meant for. I just hope she doesn't make me deliver it to the Dowds myself. The portable radio on the kitchen island is tuned to WINK 104 in Harrisburg. That Richard Marx song is playing, the one where he'll be right here waiting for you. The music is cutting into my brain like a saw blade.

"Where's Dad?" I ask.

"Work," Mom says. "He didn't think it was a good idea for you to go out today. Or tomorrow, probably. Not until that . . . doohickey they put in you runs its course."

I roll my eyes. "I know what he thought, Mom. And it wasn't that. Did he tell you what we saw? At the Webber farm?"

Mom sighs, long and deep. "Yes. But that has nothing to do with your father and me deciding to keep you home for a while."

"No? It's not because Dad thinks that I'll tell Sonya and she'll tell *her* dad and then the government will . . . I don't know . . . erase our memories or whatever?"

"Geeze Louise," Mom says, laughing. "Remind me not to let you watch any more science fiction movies." She brushes a piece of my hair out of my face. She hasn't done that in a few years—I forgot how comforting it is. "Gabe, honey, you and your father have nothing to hide. The army, Colonel Higgins, they know what they're doing. Lots of people in town must have seen that plane land Friday morning."

"Did you?"

She pauses, blinks. "Well . . . no. But that doesn't mean anything."

"The Webber farm is on the edge of town, Mom. People might have heard it flying around, but how many do you think actually *saw* it? Not to mention what happened to Mr. Webber's cattle." I'd almost forgotten about that until now. But the images of the mangled cows come swirling back. "What if they're doing some kind of experiments out at TerraCorp that they shouldn't be? What if the plane really was carrying something dangerous, and after the crash, it got released? What if they're trying to contain it?"

"God, you sound just like your father. I don't know what happened to Clark Webber's cows. And I don't know that it matters whether people know that the plane was leaving Windale when it crashed. What you should focus on right now is Kimberly. I think you'll feel a lot better when she's home safe."

"But they lied to us, Mom," I say, replaying that conversation with Sergeant Hollis in my head, his story about the plane coming from some base in . . . where was it? Washington State? "Hollis told me point-blank that the plane was flying over from somewhere else."

She blinks at me, searching my face, and there's the tiniest bit of hesitation in her eyes. "You've been through a lot, Gabe. Maybe you just misheard him." She leans in. "Focus your worries on your friend, okay? Maybe you can go with me to drop this casserole off at the Dowds' later."

I pause, scrubbing my face with my hand. "Yeah. I guess."

I glance across the kitchen, and the Bug Man is watching me from the other side of the counter. In the skewed reflection caught in the gas mask lenses, I can see Mom and myself at the dinner table, my steaming coffee mug in front of me, Mom's hand over mine. Richard Marx is singing, *I hear the laughter, I taste the tears, but I can't get near you now.*

I blink, and the Bug Man's gone; the kitchen is empty. But the radio suddenly squawks, as if the antenna got bumped. It screeches through my head, making me wince.

"Sweetheart, what is it?" Mom asks. "Your head?" She gets up, snaps off the radio, and the silence washes over me, a cool, refreshing tide. I didn't realize how tense the music was making me. Now that it's off, my entire body relaxes. I lean back in my chair, relieved.

"Thanks, Mom."

"Is there anything else you need to get off your chest, honey?" Mom's voice is quiet, concerned. "You know I'm always here to listen."

I hesitate. "I know, Mom. And I appreciate it. I just . . . I really think I need to talk to Dad first. He'll . . . he'll know what to do."

"About what?"

I stand, leaving my unfinished coffee behind. My first intention is to just hide out in my room and wait for Dad to get home. But I can't be cooped up in there all day. Not by myself. I need to talk to Charlie.

"Gabe," Mom says. It's her *putting my foot down* voice, and it halts me in my tracks. But then she gets quiet again. "What else did you see out there?"

The question sends a rush of panic through me. I have to squeeze my sweaty hands into fists. I can't answer, can't look at her.

"Sweetheart, if you know something that can help them find Kimberly, you should—"

"I know, Mom." The words come out harsher than I mean them to, but I don't regret saying them. My gut is telling me that the more people I talk about this with, the more people I'm putting at risk. I don't trust Higgins. I still don't know if I can even trust Sonya's dad, and until I do, I can't put Sonya in harm's way. Talking to Charlie might be dangerous also, but I have to talk to *someone*. And maybe he can help me work through it before I try to explain it all to Dad. "I understand what you're saying," I tell Mom. "I'll figure it out."

I leave her in the kitchen. She watches me go up the stairs with a wide, worried look.

I go to my room, shut the door, and slip out of the shirt and shorts I slept in. I pull on jeans from yesterday and a fresh T-shirt, socks, and shoes. Then I gingerly slide my window up, trying not to make too much noise. I took the sling off my left arm this morning, and even though that shoulder is lowly humming with pain, I don't have any intention of putting it back on.

Sneaking out of the house is going to be a lot easier without it.

24.
SONYA

I DON'T SLEEP that first night home. It just doesn't happen. I lay there in the dark, eyes wide, listening to the tick of the alarm clock on my nightstand count down the seconds to daybreak.

The next morning—Sunday—I find myself on the couch, with the TV on in the background, only partially focusing on a book about software coding. Kimberly thinks the technology and engineering stuff is boring, but she always listens to me ramble on about it anyway. I can practically see her on the love seat now, sitting with her head propped up in her hand, her eyelids opening and closing lazily.

After a while, not long before lunch, I get restless and wander around the house, through the warmth brought on by the floor-to-ceiling windows looking out at the canal. It's not much as far as waterways go, but the view is still nice to look at, especially now, when the pines are full and green and the rhododendron are huge pink clouds, like cotton candy growing right in my backyard.

I stare out for a while, thankful that even though we're on the Dagger Hill side of the canal, we can only really see Windale proper from the windows, which primarily face west. If we had big windows like these facing east, I'd have a lovely view of the crash site up on the Hill, the deep, charred wound cut into the trees and the earth. I don't think I'd ever be able to look away.

Mom took Sophia into town for groceries, and Dad left for Terra-Corp before anyone else was awake—I heard him shuffling around at four this morning, then I heard the front door open and shut. I have the house to myself, and it's just too quiet. I plan to see Charlie after noon, but I have no idea what to do with myself until then. I'd go up to Dagger Hill and help the volunteers search for Kimberly, but Mom said I should take it easy at least for a day, let my body rest. This just doesn't feel like resting, though. My mind is like the spinning ball basket they show on TV when they draw numbers for the lottery.

Eventually, I drag myself up to my bedroom and collapse onto the comforter, facedown, breathing in the scent of the Radion laundry detergent my mom likes to use. It smells like home, but it doesn't feel like that. I feel like a stranger here, like a fictional character who wandered out of a movie and into real life, panicked and unsure about everything. Across the room, my new-used computer is sitting, plugged in, powered on. There's a low-frequency whine coming from it that sounds like a tuneless violin string.

I scream the word *fuck* into the mattress as many times, and as loudly, as I can.

When I pick my head up again to readjust myself, the comforter is no longer a quilted, floral-printed cloud. It's been replaced by a blanket of crawling, squirming thousand-leggers. Narrow, centipede-like insects with long, arching legs and searching antennae. They're surging under my body, tickling the bare skin on my arms. I can *hear* them, there are so many. An itchy, rasping sound as they claw and scrape over top of one another.

I scream, flinging myself up off the bed. A few of the bugs come with me, slinking across my hands and my arms and my shoulders. Flailing, I throw them off me, bouncing up and down, screaming some more because I don't know what else to do. The sound of it feels hollow all of a sudden, as if somebody else is doing the screaming.

Thousand-leggers. Real name: *Scutigera coleoptrata*. We did a research project on them when I was in seventh grade. They're gray and yellow and vile. They move in wiggling strides, clambering across walls and ceilings, bathroom vents, kitchen cabinets. Wherever it's dark and hidden. Or, in this case, *my fucking bed*.

But when I look back, the comforter is just the comforter again.

No pulsing, fidgeting insects. My whole body is covered in goose bumps, and I can't shake the feeling that more are crawling on me.

"Holy shit," I breathe. "What the . . ."

I trail off, my eyes shifting from the bed to the window. The bright early-morning light that was baking behind the curtains when I came in is now a grayish-bluish glow. It reminds me of the light on a crisp, snowy winter morning.

Trying not to look at the bed again, I move across the room and push open the curtains. My breath, already stuttering and burning from the panic the thousand-leggers caused, catches in my throat.

There's a bolt of lightning frozen across the sky. A rough, many-pointed dagger coming down out of slow-churning black clouds. It's not frozen exactly, just moving very, very slowly. I can see currents of electricity tracing lines, inch by inch, down to the ground. Beneath that slow-motion sky, Windale sits flat and pretty, awash in the cold ether of the storm.

I realize then, backing away from the window, unbelieving, that there are dust motes hovering in the air around me. Not twirling and falling in that snowflake way of theirs, but caught in time just like the world outside is. I can reach out and nudge one across space with my finger.

"What is happening?" I whisper. Hot tears sting my eyes. My lower lip quivers like I'm a kid again, caught scribbling crayon art on the walls.

Someone knocks on the front door.

The sound startles me, and a little yelp escapes my lips. I'm all the way up on the second floor, but the knock reverberates through the walls and doorframes, buzzing under my feet.

Now the tears are spilling down my cheeks because even though I clearly fell asleep, drooling into my comforter, and now I'm having some kind of bizarre nightmare, it doesn't feel like that. When I pinch my own cheek, I can feel the bite of it, but it doesn't wake me up.

Outside, the lightning continues its agonizing crawl through the atmosphere. The slowly bubbling clouds glow blue in places where more static charge is building. There's a deep, gurgling growl coming from somewhere. Not just from inside the house, from *everywhere*. It's thunder, I realize. Thunder rumbling in slo-mo, creating a constant, ear-aching thrum.

Another knock. This time it's more urgent. More like a bang.

Something tells me that staying here and ignoring the sound of whoever's at the front door is not an option. I don't know if I'm awake or asleep or . . . something else. It doesn't matter. Whatever this is, my own bedroom is not immune to it, which means that it's not safe. Which means nowhere is.

That thought is mostly terrifying. But it's also a bit freeing.

With only a little hesitation slowing me down, I open my bedroom door.

25.
GABE

THE WINDALE MEDICAL CENTER is in the northwest part of town, on Raspberry Street. It's only a few blocks from my house, and I'm nearly there when I hear the familiar *yawp* of a patrol car siren behind me. The whole way here, I walked with my head down and my hands in my pockets, took side streets and alleys where I could. Didn't matter.

It's Dad, I think, turning with my eyes squeezed shut and my shoulders up by my ears. *It's definitely Dad. There's no way it's not Dad.*

It's not Dad.

Rebecca Conner steps out of Car Two. She leaves the bubble lights flashing and the door ajar so she can hear the radio. It's silent for now. She starts to close the distance between us, hands on her gun belt like an Old West sheriff, and I decide to meet her halfway. She's going to take me home anyway, so I might as well make it less work for her.

"What's going on, kid?" She says it casually, as if she doesn't already know exactly what's going on.

But this is our banter, so I play along. "Not a lot," I say. "Just the usual." My voice breaks a little at the end.

She nods heavily, as if it's a struggle just to keep her head up. "Yeah. The usual. I think we left that behind a while ago. Right about the time I got the call from Clark Webber about his cattle." She's looking off to the east, toward Dagger Hill, even though most of it is obscured by the stretch of row homes we're stopped in front of.

"What's happening over there?" I say, daring to ask the question.

"Nonsense," Rebecca replies. "A whole bunch of nonsense, that's what's happening. The Triangle is crawling with MPs taking witness reports from everyone. And that colonel . . ." She trails off, shivering despite the heat.

"Yeah, you're telling me." I pause, waiting to see if she's going to jump right into her reason for stopping me. When she doesn't, I ask, "What have they said about the plane?"

Rebecca levels a serious stare at me. "You want to be careful about what you say and how loudly you say it." It's not a request.

I swallow hard. "Rebecca, they lied to me. I didn't even ask about the plane, and they just voluntarily told me that it came from some base in Washington where they do scientific experiments. Why wouldn't something like that be confidential?"

"It should be," Rebecca says, her voice low. "Your dad confronted Higgins about the plane, and she fed him the same half-baked line. She threatened to have him thrown in jail if he questioned her authority again."

"Bet that went over really well," I scoff.

"It's been a long morning, let's just say that. But my point is that Higgins is off the rails. That plane was at TerraCorp Friday morning. We all saw it. And I don't know what it was carrying, but there's no way it was anything good with the way they've put a gag on this town. We—" She stops, shuts her eyes for a moment, then goes on. "We could be in some serious trouble here."

"And what about Kimberly?" I can barely bring myself to say her name. Because if anyone is in real trouble right now, it's her.

Rebecca shakes her head. "Nothing yet. This morning, though, it was all Higgins could talk about."

"Really? She didn't seem all that interested yesterday."

"Well, she should be. If this is really some kind of . . . I don't know . . . cover-up, then Kimberly is a loose thread. And they won't stop until they make sure it's tied."

Except they might not get the chance, I think. *Somebody else already has her.*

"Now," Rebecca goes on, straightening up, adjusting her belt. Her voice is back to its normal, authoritative volume. "Am I taking you back to your house or back to the station to see the chief?" She only ever calls him *the chief* to me when I'm in trouble.

"Uh . . . neither?" I raise my eyebrows and put on an innocent face. "I was just going to see Charlie."

"But your dad told Mel and me that you were on lockdown. Not to leave the house until further notice." She gestures to the open world around us. "This is not the house."

"You're right."

"And don't tell me you asked your mom, because I know she wouldn't have given you permission, either."

"I won't," I say, feeling the defeat rise in me.

"Good," she says. "Thank you for not lying." Then she turns and heads back to the patrol car. "I'm heading over to the video store to check out a weird call. I'm going to pretend that I didn't see you. Don't make me regret it."

With that, she swings her legs back inside the car, revs the engine, and drives away. All I can do is watch her with a goofy smile as she goes.

26.
SONYA

I WOULD BE less afraid if I had some scientific way to explain what's happening to me. The best I can come up with is that I'm experiencing a kind of psychological break from reality. Tied to the trauma of the plane crash, of possibly losing Kimberly forever.

It makes at least a little bit of sense. I've read all about these episodes in the medical journals my dad has lying around. For a man who supposedly works in R&D at a company devoted to meteorological science, Dad has always had a persistent fascination with the human brain.

But this doesn't feel like psychosis. It feels like a hot, rancid sweat breaking out under my arms and at the small of my back. It feels like the sluggish roar of time-frozen thunder in my ears, like the sound of plunging into deep, crushing water. It feels like being caught in the static crackle of a lightning strike for minutes, not seconds, every hair and nerve on my body in a constant state of frayed tension. It feels real and immediate.

It feels like I'm *here*, wherever "here" is.

I make it downstairs to the foyer. I'm standing alone, watching the front door. The dead bolt is latched, as if that makes a difference. Through the sidelights, there is only the bluish-gray brilliance of the storm. No shadows from someone who might be waiting on the front stoop.

All the same, the knock comes again, louder than ever. Harder, too. Hard enough to rock the door in its frame. Three quick booms, each accompanied by a shudder of the door. *Bang-bang-bang!*

I flinch back, another startled scream bursting up from my throat. The sound of it scares me almost as badly as the knock did, and I cover my mouth with a trembling hand.

The pause that comes after the knock stretches out. My eyes are locked on the peephole in the middle of the front door, a glassy eye that stares back, watching me through constellations of dust motes that are perpetually caught in midair.

Another knock, only this time more subdued. Quieter, softer. And even though my body tenses instinctively, this version of the knock doesn't sound like a threat, doesn't sound like violence about to erupt from the other side. If anything, it sounds like an invitation.

Clack-clack-clack. Gentle raps against the wood. *Please*, it says. *Come.*

I can't explain why, but my feet propel me forward, toward the door and whoever is waiting behind it. My sneakers squeak noisily against the stonework floor of the foyer. I keep waiting to hear my parents whispering from the kitchen. Or my sister watching *Looney Tunes* in the living room. I know better, though. I'm alone here.

The distance between me and the door shrinks, and I have the dead bolt latch between my fingers, turning it. It cracks like a knuckle. The doorknob is in my hand, a big, gold-plated bulb that feels thicker and heavier than usual. It turns easy enough, though, and all of a sudden the front door is swinging open, like it's done a million times . . .

And I'm looking at an empty stoop. There's no one there.

On shaky legs, I step outside. The air feels charged and alive. The sky is a wavering terrain of light and shadows, inflamed red in some places, sterile blue in others, all of it paused like a videotape. As I move out from under the awning, onto the path that leads around to the driveway, something ignites behind the storm clouds, popping like a firecracker and sending a ripple of light out around it. There's a sound that goes with it, a deep, almost metallic rumble, like the workings of some faraway machine.

Alone in front of my house, I spin around, searching for any sign that someone has been there, searching for *anyone* in general. But it's quiet, except for that low, constant growl of thunder.

I come off the path, wade through the landscaping that my parents pay Mitch Henderson to do every year. It's still summer, and it's still hot, but there's a stagnant quality to the atmosphere. Leaves and twigs are caught in the act of tumbling from trees to the ground. As I move around to the back of the house, I can see the canal, a clear string of glass, streaked with frosty white shimmers. It's almost as if the water is frozen in midwinter, but the water never freezes, and it's not winter.

On the other side of the canal, Windale rises and falls in peaks of shingles and stone, creeping up the side of Sunrise Hill. Everything over there is as still and soundless as it is over here. Just as empty, too. But something wants me to go over to the town proper. It's a weird sort of instinct, the same guiding energy that produced the knock that got me out the front door. Not a thing that exists in this halted version of Windale, but a thing that exists inside *me*.

Maybe. I don't know. I'm scared and curious at the same time, my nerves all strung out and jangled. I don't feel like I'm in control of myself at all.

I step backward, with the intention, despite everything, to get to the road, to follow it down through the creepy darkness of the Heart-to-Heart Bridge, into town. But then I notice something else in the sky above Windale. A dark silhouette suspended in the misty curtain of clouds. I recognize the winged shape of it from two days ago, the worst kind of déjà vu.

The plane is on a downward trajectory, its nose pointed almost directly at me and my family's house. I turn and see the spot up on Dagger Hill that it's actually pointed at. The shaded gap in the trees where the clearing is, where my best friends and I were just eating our lunch, minding our own goddamn business, worrying about graduation and college and each other and what's going to happen to us when all of that hits.

And then something else hit. *Hard.*

It's a helpless feeling, standing underneath it as it's about to happen, knowing there's nothing I can do to stop it. Knowing there's nothing I can do now to help her.

So I just keep walking, up through the front yard, out onto the road. Without a clue as to why I'm doing it, I head for town.

27.

CHARLIE

YOUR FRIEND SLEEPS like you do. Sweet dreams, Charlie.

I'm staring at the note, seeing it and also not. It feels like a movie prop. Or a random line for some story idea I jotted down in a creative fever in the middle of the night. I do that sometimes. Photography isn't my only artistic passion. If I take a picture of something arbitrary—a kid riding his bike through the Triangle, maybe—I occasionally come up with a backstory to go with the photo. Who's the kid? Where's he going? What's his name? And oftentimes, that speculative, film-and-comic-book-loving part of my brain takes over, and the question becomes, *What is the kid riding away from so fast?*

That's why I was in Don Cranston's office Friday morning. I like to take pictures, and I like to tell stories, and so often the most frightening stories come from real life.

Cases in point: the note, the person who was in my room last night, the plane crash.

Absently, I rub at the inside of my elbow, where the docs injected me with that capsule thing. It doesn't hurt, but I can feel the node under my skin, a tiny bump about the size of a cherry pit. I thought it was supposed to dissolve.

"Hey, man."

I look up, startled, expecting to see a black form with big, goggled eyes, like a fly's, standing over me. But it's just Gabe, leaning in the doorway, hands in his pockets, glancing over his shoulder in a way that reminds me of Chet when he was here.

"Dude," I say. "Thank god you're here." Without thinking, I slide the note from last night under my blanket. *Sweet dreams, Charlie.* "I'm *sooooo* bored."

Gabe smiles and steps into the room, but not before sneaking one more anxious look up the hallway. "Sorry, man. At least you have Louise Engleton here to keep you company." He waggles his eyebrows.

"Oh, you're telling me." I stretch, putting my hands behind my head. "She kept me doped up half the night. There's no telling what she could have done to me. *This*," I say, gesturing to my body, specifically my stiff, cast-bound leg, "has to be hard to resist."

We both laugh, but it sounds manufactured.

"How is the leg?" Gabe asks.

"Hurts. They lowered the dose on my pain meds this morning, so it's kind of all I feel right now."

"Well, that's probably for the best. You were trashed last night."

"Wait, you were here last night?" I say.

Gabe laughs again. This time it sounds more genuine. "Sonya and I were both here, doofus. You don't remember?"

"Only a little bit."

"Do you remember . . . ?" Gabe asks, his expression going dark.

I know what he's going to say, so I spare him. "Kimberly?" I say. "Yeah. Unfortunately, that's one of the only pieces of info that I do remember. That and my mom being stuck outside the town line." I pause, clenching my teeth through a fresh pulse of misery from my hobbled leg. "They're kicking me out of this joint today. I don't know what I'm gonna do."

The idea of going home, where it'll be just me and Chet until the army reopens Windale, is my absolute worst nightmare. Especially when that length of time is the exact same amount that Chet has to wait before he gets his next fix. The more he goes through withdrawals, the worse he's going to get. I could be there to help him through it, hoping the whole time that he comes out of it sober on the other side. But who would be there to help *me* through it?

"Well, you know you always have a place at my house," Gabe says.

"Why don't you just come stay with us? I know my mom would be totally cool with it."

"What about your dad?" I ask.

"He'd be a little disgruntled, but he still likes *you*, as far as I know. So you should be okay." He says it with a sarcastic chuckle.

"What do you mean? He doesn't like Sonya?" As long as I can remember, none of our parents has ever had a problem with any of us. Some of them don't get along very well with each other, sure, but they've never held us kids accountable for that.

Gabe says, "I don't know. I haven't talked to him since last night, but the vibe he's been giving off is . . . not great."

"Because of her dad? And TerraCorp?"

He swallows, looking away. "Yeah. That's where the plane came from. We saw it land Friday morning while we were out at the Webber farm. Then it crashed later on that afternoon."

"*What?*" I say, hushing my voice, realizing that the army is still lurking around, maybe even listening.

Gabe nods. Whispering, he says, "But they're denying it. They flat-out lied to me and my dad about where the plane came from. I don't think they want anyone to know that they were at TerraCorp."

"But . . . *why*? They do, like, government stuff there, don't they? Have you talked to Sonya? She would probably know more than the two of us." My head feels heavy, weighed down by stress and morphine. It's hard to connect the dots, if there are any dots to connect at all.

"No, I haven't talked to her," Gabe says. "Not really, anyway. She's so focused on finding Kimberly that I think she'll believe whatever they tell her. But there's something else. Something I haven't told anyone . . ."

I ignore the throb in my leg as I sit up, watching Gabe pick at a loose thread in his jeans, stalling. I've seen him do the same thing with his parents—broken window with a baseball, failed test, whiskey bottle topped off with A-Treat cola. Name the trouble and I guarantee you Gabe has been in it, usually with me by his side.

"Oh . . . kay?" I say. "You're kind of scaring me, dude."

"I know. I'm scared myself. I don't know what the fuck is going on." His eyes are shiny, tears hanging on to his short lashes.

"Gabe." I grab his arm, squeeze it. I have a hazy recollection of him doing the same thing for me last night. "Just tell me, man. Whatever it is, we'll deal with it together."

He pauses, sniffles, brushes his knuckles across his cheeks. "What if there was something else on that plane?" he says. "Something other than the pilots and weird chemicals, or whatever bullshit they told us."

"Like what?" I ask slowly, carefully. Almost on its own, my hand slips under the blanket and lays flat on top of the note. *Your friend sleeps like you do.*

"Something . . . alive." Gabe looks me dead in the eyes as he says the last word. Then, in a rush, he starts pacing at the end of my bed, talking at the ceiling, waving his hands around as if he were conducting an orchestra. "I've thought about it over and over again, and it's the only thing that makes sense. He was already on the plane. Why else would he have been out there?"

"Gabe. Buddy," I say. My hand closes into a fist with the note crumpled inside. Gabe doesn't seem to notice the sound it makes. "I mean this in the nicest way possible—what the flying fuck are you talking about?"

He quits pacing. He looks at me again, maybe so I know he's being serious. His face is ashen under the cold light. "Somebody took Kimberly. I watched it happen."

"What?" My heart nose-dives into high velocity and keeps picking up speed from there. I can feel the pointed edges of the balled-up note in my hand. "You haven't told anybody *that*? What if that's exactly what they need to find her? What if they know something we don't?"

"Charlie, that's just it," Gabe says, talking with his hands again. "They know *everything* we don't. Something just isn't adding up, okay? That plane landed in Windale Friday morning, and then it crashed on Dagger Hill Friday afternoon. Higgins and her men turned up so fast that there's no way they weren't already here."

"Well, now you're just speculating—"

"Then why would they lie?" He's whisper-shouting at me from the end of the bed, his voice getting hoarse, his throat probably still scratchy and sore, like mine. "Sergeant Hollis told me that the plane came from the West Coast. That's what they're telling everyone at the police station. But we all saw it land at TerraCorp."

"How do you know it's the same plane?" I dare to ask. I've never seen Gabe so worked up before. I don't want to use the word *paranoid*, but it's the only one that fits.

He gives me a fuck-off look that I've seen a million times. "Dude. I watched that thing *smash* into the Hill, almost right where we stood. You did, too. If you had seen the plane that morning—" His voice cracks as more tears spring up in his eyes.

"Whoa, whoa, whoa," I say, putting my hands up in mock surrender. "Okay. Let's say it was the same plane. And let's say Higgins was on it when it landed at TerraCorp. Why wasn't she on it when it crashed?"

"Maybe they needed to make room for someone else."

"That whole big plane for one person?"

"Maybe they were dangerous."

I give him a look.

"Maybe they were *really* dangerous, okay?" he cries, throwing his hands in the air. "I don't know any of this for sure, but I know that Kimberly was kidnapped. He came out of the wreck, gave me a thumbs-up, made me think he was there to help—not that I could have fought him off if I'd wanted to—and then he took her. Right in front of my eyes, he took her. But I wasn't sure if it was real or if I'd just hit my head. I . . . I didn't know what to do, or who I should tell."

I swallow, scratching the ball of my thumb against a corner of the ruined note. That original warning thought has sprung up into a fully blossomed, nightmarish idea. "And you think this guy was on the plane when it crashed?"

"It's the only explanation that makes sense."

"Except it doesn't make any sense, Gabe, because if he'd been on the plane, then he would have died when it crashed." But my voice has gone monotone. I think about the figure from last night, flailing for me in the dark.

"I know how it sounds." He scrubs his hands over his face. He looks ragged, shoulders slouched, face knotted up in concentration.

After a moment, I say, "What did he look like?" And I'm already afraid of the answer.

Gabe describes a man in all black, arms and body coated in leather—hands, too. He tells me that the man emerged from the fire and smoke, his face hidden by a black gas mask, the canister sticking out ahead like insect mandibles, framed by wide, smoky lenses. Taking the concept right out of my head, Gabe absently refers to him as the Bug Man, and my skin tightens with goose bumps.

"Holy shit," I breathe.

"I know," he replies. "It sounds totally insane, but I swear—"

"No." I cut him off. My chest is heaving, trying to pull oxygen into my damaged lungs. "Gabe, I saw him, too."

"Wait, what? Charlie, man, that's not funny . . ." But he must see something in my face. "You're serious?"

I nod. "The Bug Man was here last night. In my room."

Gabe jolts back, as if I just leaped out from some hiding spot and scared him. His mouth is moving like he wants to say something, but no words are coming out.

I pull the note out from under the blanket, unfurl it, and smooth it as best I can. I hold it out for Gabe to see. "He left this."

He takes the slip of paper and stares at it, mouth gaping, breath quickening.

"Is that real enough for you?" I ask.

28.
SONYA

THE STREETS OF Windale are abandoned. I'm able to walk right down the middle, along the yellow dividing line between lanes. The windows of the houses crouched together along Hazleton Avenue stare down at me. Not all of them are empty and dark, as I might expect in a frozen, nightmare version of a small town. There are lights on in some, the curtains stilled in the act of swaying in the breeze. They're not all completely haunted-looking, but it's still unnerving.

My ears are full of the falling-stone sound of slow thunder, a perpetual rumble like a bass drum still booming from a particularly hard hit. If I make it out of this madness, I might not do so with all my hearing.

I wander the roads and tiny thruways of town, kicking rocks and beer cans along the way and watching them slow down and halt in midair without ever touching the ground. The air is mostly stagnant and stale, but every now and then I catch a whiff of freshly mowed grass, of hot dogs on a grill, of the sickly sweet scent of fabric softener wafting from a dryer vent.

"What are you doing?" I mumble to myself. "What the hell are you doing, Sonya?"

But I keep walking.

My first instinct is to head to the Triangle, to the place where all my comfort is, the place where Gabe and Kim and Charlie and I find ourselves most often when we're not up on Dagger Hill. The diner or the movie theater or even the police station. From where I stand on

Main Street, I can see the white rectangle of the Sunrise's marquee and the fountain in the middle of the intersection, with its arcs of water stopped midstream as if they were an ice sculpture. I can see one chrome-plated corner of the King Street Diner, and right next door, wedged between that and the theater, the Stuck Pig, the only bar in town and not always as friendly as the one on *Cheers*.

My head down, I watch my feet move me away from Main Street and toward the west side of town, where the new strip mall sits along with some of Windale's oldest relics.

That's where I'm headed, for some reason. Not to Dagger Hill or to the Triangle or to anywhere very familiar. The same silent certainty that dragged me out of my house is pulling me in this direction, which is somehow comforting because at least I *have* a direction.

My smile fades when I look up at the shadowy mass of the plane in the clouds. Still hurtling toward destruction.

I realize suddenly that I'm on Raspberry Street, passing right in front of the Windale Medical Center. Guilt squeezes around my heart like a fist. Poor Charlie is in there somewhere. Well, not in *there* exactly, not in the stark white building I'm staring at right now. But in the same version of this place that exists in my Windale, Charlie is there, either alone or alone with Chet—I don't know which would be worse. Probably worried sick about his mom, about Kimberly, maybe even about Gabe and me, because he was probably too doped up to remember we were there last night.

In the same way that I can still see the crash in my mind's eye, I can see Charlie on top of the boulder just before it happened. Making us promise to always be there for each other. I can see him tying the four of us here together forever, and sudden guilt squeezes me tight, fueled a little bit by anger, too. Hatred, even, for the secrets I force myself to keep and the things I'm too cowardly to talk about out loud. I promised Charlie I would always be there, but only because I couldn't bring myself to tell him that maybe I didn't want to.

I do my best to shake it all off and push onward, leaving the WMC behind. I make a right onto Allegheny Road, then a left onto Perkiomen Avenue and follow that for two blocks until it cuts off at Baker Street, along which sits the strip mall with Ricky's Video Rentals, a sleezy-looking adult bookstore, a Wag's, a Pizza Hut, and Duncan's Arcade.

Although I feel a certain unexplainable pull toward Ricky's Video Rentals, that's still not where I'm going. I take another right onto Baker Street and follow it north.

A few blocks up, I come to an expanse of cracked, buckled blacktop that used to be a parking lot. It's overgrown with weeds and littered with rocks and trash. There's a plastic grocery bag caught in a tangle of crabgrass, frozen in time, filled up with the unmoving breeze. It looks like a white flag of surrender.

At the other end of the forgotten parking lot is the forgotten structure to which the lot belongs—an L-shaped, two-story motel that was once called the Widow's Lodge. The wrought-iron staircases leading up to the second-floor walkway have flaked off all their paint and are rusted over, sagging away from the structure, only holding on by a few loose bolts. The roof has collapsed in on itself in places, punched through by years of rain and snow and ice. The room numbers on the crackling, splintered doors are oxidized barnacles, barely legible in the shadowy light of the storm. Windows are broken, puking up moth-eaten curtains. Walls are peeling paint and creeping with mold, covered up in spots by colorful graffiti. There's a neon VACANCY sign in the office window that's hanging on by a single chain, a crooked, confused grin on a place that's older than my parents.

The place is obviously haunted. That's what everyone says, anyway. It's another one of those spooky Windale stories that come with the small-town vibe. Monsters up on Dagger Hill, a haunted motel, some mysterious deaths over the years. Sometimes I wonder if other places around the world have taller tales than the ones I've heard in Windale.

Normally, if you stand in the parking lot of the Widow's Lodge, you can hear a howling sound as the wind cuts through the old iron bars of the railings. Even on the quietest days, there's at least a soft whistling. I'm a woman of science, yes, but I've heard the howling myself. Kimberly and the guys have been with me when I've heard it, too. We all know the stories about this place, and we always talked about spending the night in one of the rooms, just to see what might happen. Kim was most excited about that idea, I think. Maybe she was even the one who came up with it, I don't know. But we never went through with it, and I wish now that we had. I wish the four of us had done a lot of things together while we still had the chance.

Anyway, the rotted, decaying look of the Widow's Lodge got it its reputation. The howling is what earned it its nickname: the Banshee Palace.

"A little spooky, isn't it?"

The voice comes from right beside me, and I nearly jump out of my skin. I squeeze a hand over my mouth to stifle the gut-wrenching scream that erupts from my core. Nearly falling on my ass, I stumble backward, away from the sound. I haven't seen or heard anybody else the whole time I've been here. The sound of another person's voice is so foreign that it almost feels like a violation against nature, as if some unspoken rule has been broken, the one to literally *not* *speak*.

When I move away and have the person in full view, I realize that I recognize who it is. Her wispy puff of gray, almost white, hair is as recognizable as the fountain in the Triangle.

Mrs. Rapaport smiles at me from her spot on the sidewalk, hands folded neatly in front of her. "Hello, dear," she says.

"M-M-Mrs. Rapaport?" I stammer. My heart continues to gallop. "W-W-What the hell?"

The old woman chuckles. "What the hell, indeed. These are strange times, aren't they, Sonya? Very strange."

"I . . . I don't understand. Why are you here?" It seems like the appropriate question, but only in the sense that I can't figure out why June Rapaport would pop up in my nightmare. She's a little crotchety at times, sure, and *definitely* eccentric, but she's mostly a pleasant woman. She's always been kind to me and the others.

"That's a good question," Mrs. Rapaport replies. "I suppose I could ask the same of you, but I already have a pretty strong suspicion about that." Her eyes dart to the Banshee Palace, the moldering husk that it is. "I couldn't tell you why I'm here, dear. Only that I've been wandering around for a while, waiting for something to happen. I've opened a few doors, checked in on a few people. Done my snooping, let's say. But now that I'm ready to go home, I just can't seem to find a way out."

"A . . . a way *out*?"

"You don't really still think this is just a dream, do you, darling?" she asks sweetly.

To that, I can only swallow.

"Yes, well," Mrs. Rapaport continues with a wry smile, "I tried going back to my house, but it turns out that place is infested with those nasty thousand-leggers. *Blech!*"

I think about what happened at my own house, with my bed, and I wonder if Mrs. Rapaport has had a similar experience. But I don't say anything, can't quite find my voice.

"Something brought me here," she says. "My children have children and even some of *them* have children, but that old motherly instinct never goes away, I guess. Somehow I must have known you'd be here."

"But . . . *why* am I here?" I ask, directing the question not just at Mrs. Rapaport but at whatever force brought us together.

"Another good question," she replies. She doesn't add anything else, though. Turning back to the Banshee Palace, she nods at it. I'm glad that time is on pause, or whatever, because I don't think I'd be able to handle it if I could hear the howling right now. It would just be too much. "I think you need to go in there."

"In . . . *there*?" I say. "No way!"

Mrs. Rapaport laughs again. "What's the matter, dear? You afraid of a few ghosts?"

"No," I say, my voice carrying a defiant edge. "I'm afraid of needing a tetanus shot."

Up on the second floor of the motel, the door to room 6 makes a noise like someone's knocking on it. The same urgent, beckoning sound as the knock that rattled my front door. Goose bumps spring up across my arms and legs, up my back.

"Somebody's waiting," Mrs. Rapaport says. And even though her voice is as pleasant as ever, when she turns to me this time, I see something new in her eyes, something desperate. "Listen to me, dear. You have to be careful. It doesn't know we're here. Not yet, anyway. When it finds out, things are going to change, and not for the better."

She turns and looks over her shoulder then, as if she hears something—someone calling her name, maybe. A moment passes, then another. She looks at me again and says, "I have to go now. I think maybe this time I can get out. Be *careful*, Sonya. It *knows* your fear. Can smell it on you. Maybe that's what drew you here in the first place. Heaven knows what it'll do if it finds you."

Mrs. Rapaport turns and leaves. I reach out to try to stop her, but she's faster than I expect a woman her age to be. My hand swipes through empty air, and when I look up and down Baker Street, it's empty. As if Mrs. Rapaport was never there at all.

The knock sounds from room 6 again. My whole body tenses. It's time to check in at the Banshee Palace.

29.
GABE

"WHAT DO WE do?" I ask Charlie after I tell him, in more detail, about how the Bug Man took Kimberly. Over the course of my story, Charlie remembered something else: He saw a figure moving through the wreckage just after the crash, a shadow that might have been a person. *It could even have been a deer or something,* Charlie said, trying to reason with himself. *Maybe it got spooked by the crash, got confused, ran into it instead of away from it.* But his eyes told me that was bullshit, not the least of all because there are never any animals up on Dagger Hill. That place is apparently as spooky to the wildlife as it is to the adults of Windale.

"I don't know what we do," Charlie says, responding to my question. "We could talk to your dad?"

I scoff, flipping the note that someone (*the Bug Man*) left for Charlie over in my hand again, hoping this time when it turns, it will be blank. But the words are still there, letters scratched in haste. *Fucking asshole,* I think.

"My dad will never believe us," I say. "You know how he is. He's never bought in to our sci-fi fantasy comic book stuff." I put on my best impression of Dad and say, "Why can't you kids just go out to parties like regular teenagers?"

"Go make some more friends," Charlie adds, deepening his voice and putting a finger across his lip like a mustache. A completely stupid mockery of my father but also totally perfect. I can't help but laugh.

That lighthearted feeling is quickly strangled by panic. All I can do is try to organize my thoughts, get the story straight. "So what do we know so far?" I raise my hand, stick out my thumb, counting off the bullet points: "The cattle out at Clark Webber's farm all died in one night after they got so scared of something that they slaughtered each other just to get away. Dad, Mr. Webber, Rebecca, Mel, and I all saw a cargo plane land on what I can only assume is a landing strip inside the TerraCorp compound. A few hours later, that same plane—or what I'm almost ninety percent sure is the same plane—crashes into Dagger Hill, almost right into you, me, Sonya, and Kim. A few minutes later, while we're all scattered and afraid and hurt, someone—"

"Or some*thing*," Charlie says absently.

"Or something," I continue, nodding, "comes out of the wreckage, dressed in all black and a gas mask, and takes Kimberly. You, Sonya, and I wake up here at the medical center, assuming that the army is here to help, until they lie to our faces about where the plane came from and why it was here. They give us the mother of all injections and send us on our way. A few hours after *that*, *you* see the Bug Man here in your room and he leaves you this note."

"*Somebody* leaves the note," Charlie says, looking at me. "I'm still not totally convinced I really saw anything. It could have been a bad dream."

"Fine," I say, rolling my eyes. "Somebody left the note. Even though this whole thing could just be a bad dream, or you could still just be hopped up on morphine."

"I wish," Charlie mumbles.

"Did I miss anything?"

"Don't forget the man who parachuted into town just before the plane crash and hasn't been seen or heard from since. Oh, and that the army inexplicably closed Windale, blocking all roads in or out of town." His voice has a bitter snap to it.

"Which may or may not be to help find Kimberly."

"*May or may not* implies that it's either one thing or the other," Charlie says, rubbing his temples with shaky fingers. "The army probably is looking for Kimberly. But if they really did lose something or someone valuable to them, they're looking for that, too."

"Not to mention the pilot, or whatever he was, who jumped out of the plane. If he's alive, he's somewhere in town."

"And if he's not alive?"

I tilt my head, considering. "Well, then, he's still somewhere in town. But nobody knows where."

Silence yawns open between us, filled up by our grief and our fear.

"Sounds like you've got a lot to consider."

The voice behind me makes me jump. On instinct, I crush Charlie's note in my hand and turn toward the sound, hiding the paper ball behind my back. A blue-eyed doctor is standing in the doorway. Her face is a void, expressionless except for a slight smirk at the corners of her lips. It looks like a kind of satisfaction to me. The word *busted* blinks once, in big red letters, behind my eyes. That happens a lot whenever my dad walks into the room.

"Dr. Reed," Charlie says behind me, trying to sound casual even though I can hear the wobble in his voice. "What's shakin'?"

Reed steps into the room, hands behind her back. She eyes me first, then Charlie, assessing us.

"You know a lot, but you don't know enough," Reed says. Her head is turned slightly, as if she's talking to me and Charlie and looking over her shoulder at the same time. There's a new quality to her voice now. Urgency?

"Come again?" Charlie says.

"There's so much more to this than either of you boys know." The urgency, surprisingly, has melted into what sounds like genuine concern. Reed's tone is almost motherly now. "If your friend is alive, she won't be for much longer. We don't know enough about the cargo that plane was carrying, but from what I just heard, you've confirmed many of our greatest fears."

"Hey, whoa," I say. "Slow down, okay? Who are you, and what are you talking about?"

Reed steps closer, lowering her voice to a hushed murmur. "My name is Claudia Reed, and I work with Sonya's father. I'm trying to help you."

I swivel my head around to look at Charlie. We blink at each other.

"Wait," Charlie says, shaking his head as if to clear it. "Weren't you, like, an ice queen just yesterday? You injected us with these medicine . . . testicles or whatever the hell they are like it was no big deal. And now you're trying to help?"

"Dr. Gutierrez is in the unique position of having a little bit of leverage over Colonel Higgins and the army, and he insisted that I be here to supervise them. It didn't really end up going that way. Mostly, they wound up supervising *me*. But Dr. G promised them I'd remain impartial if they let someone from his team assist with the medical screening. He knew what was on that plane just like the rest of us, and he wanted to make sure it hadn't done any harm to you kids." Her voice is just above a whisper, and her eyes keep flicking to the door, scanning it for someone who might get the drop on her just like she did on us.

"Dr. Reed," I say, feeling my chest heave. "What was on the plane?"

Finally, she turns her whole face to me, looks me dead in the eyes. There's nothing short of genuine fear in hers. "Something terrible," she says. Her eyes drift away, along with her thoughts. "It was weak when they found it. Dr. G wanted to keep it as far away as possible, but Higgins, she . . . god, she brought it *here*. The closer it got to Windale, the stronger it became. And now . . ."

"You're talking about the Bug Man?" Charlie asks. "The thing that took Kimberly?"

Out in the hall, there's the faint *click-clack* of bootheels. "Listen, there's not a lot of time," she says, fishing for something in the pocket of her coat. "They found your Polaroid up on the Hill this morning, along with some of the pictures you took." She produces a stack of white squares and shoves them into my hand. "They're pictures of the pictures, because if the originals turned up missing, they'd know I was snooping. It's the best I could do. You need to find the pilot. He was the only one who had any common sense when they showed up at the lab. He knew they were carrying something dangerous even before Higgins refused to get back on the plane with it."

"Dr. Reed, I still don't understand—" I start.

She grabs me by the shoulders. "The pilot's name is Rinaldi. There's no way to know for sure where he came down, but those pictures should help. Higgins is already a day ahead of you, but your dad must know this town better than anyone."

"Doc, you gotta give us a sec here," Charlie says. "Why is the pilot so important?"

"Because he knows what *it* is," Reed says. "He's seen it up close."

"And you haven't?" I ask. "Or Sonya's dad, either?"

She shakes her head. "No," she whispers. "They never even got it off the plane. The pilot—Rinaldi—he knows. If we find him, then *he* can help us find *it*. And maybe we can save your friend. Maybe we can save this whole town."

The boot steps get louder, closer. Dr. Reed smooths out the front of her white coat, and composes herself. She gives Charlie and me each a long look, willing us to understand. I'm not sure I do. Not completely. But I understand that at least some of my fears weren't misplaced. One of my best friends is still missing, maybe even dying, and I might have a way to help her. Everything else, for now, is just noise.

"Oh, and one more thing," Reed says. "The capsules? They're not medicine; they're trackers. They made us agree to put them in. The army is watching your every move. So be careful."

She steps through the doorway just as a pair of soldiers comes strolling past, talking about basketball playoffs or something. "I'll be back to check those vitals in a few hours, Mr. Bencroft," she says, loud enough for anyone to hear. Then, more quietly, just for us: "Until then, nobody should be around to bother you." She gives us one last look, raising her eyebrows, then slips out for good.

A beat, then Charlie says, "Did you catch any of that?"

"Barely," I say, letting out a long breath. "But I heard enough." I rub the inside of my elbow where the "capsule" is lodged. *The army is watching your every move.* I glance around the room, then I start pulling open some of the drawers in the small cabinet built into the wall, not knowing what I'm looking for until I find it.

"Dude, what are you doing?" Charlie asks.

I spin around, holding a scalpel and a pair of tweezers, both individually wrapped. "You heard the doctor," I say. "We have to find that pilot. But first we have to bust you out of this joint."

30.
SONYA

THE RICKETY STEPS leading up to the second floor of the Banshee Palace nearly collapse under my weight. They creak and sway in protest. From the top, I can see out over the strip mall to the start of the tree line that creeps up the side of Sunrise Hill.

It's little comfort when I step off the iron steps and onto the motel walkway. The entire building feels unstable. Even caught in a time bubble the way it is now, I feel like it could collapse in on itself at any second.

All the same, I move along the balcony toward room 6. There's another, smaller knock from the other side of the door when I get there. The curtains in the window are drawn. Through the tattered holes, I can only see blackness. No movement, no other sounds. Instinctively, I curl my fingers into a fist and reach up to knock myself. But then I think better of it, reach out for the knob, turn it.

The door opens onto a dark abyss. I expect a swarm of bugs or a puff of dust. But there's nothing, and no one. In the shadows, I see the outline of the bed, the covers still draped over it, and a table and chair in the corner. A painting on the wall hangs at a crooked angle. I see slash marks in it, as if someone took a knife to the canvas.

"Hello?" I say into the room. I'm too afraid to step inside. My feet won't budge. "What do you want from me?"

I hear a small, helpless noise. A whimper. A girl's voice. From the back of the room, back in the little nook that leads to the bathroom.

I recognize that voice. When I hear it again, I know for sure.

"K-Kim?" I say, not believing it yet, not allowing myself to. "Kimberly?"

The whimper comes again, then again, more urgent this time.

I rush into the darkness, unafraid. My body moves around the furniture obstacles. I can feel the time-frozen flecks of dust clinging to my skin as I pass through them. None of it matters. The only thing that matters is her.

She's curled up in the farthest, darkest corner of the room. Almost in the same position she was in at the clearing, her knees pulled up to her chest. Except now she looks withered and pale, her cheeks sunken, eye sockets huge and purple. In the thin gray light spilling in from the open door, I can barely see her, only her emaciated outline.

I drop to my knees in front of her. "Kimberly. Oh my god, Kimberly. What . . . what happened to you? Why are you here?"

She stares at me, eyes wide and afraid. But she doesn't say anything. Her lips don't even move. Her hand does, though. It lifts, small and shaking, and points to her mouth. Then she shakes her head.

"You . . . you can't speak?" I ask, trying to understand.

She shakes her head again.

"Okay. Do . . . do you know why?"

Again.

Terrified, I take her hands in mine. I can't stop the tears from spilling over my cheeks. "Kim, you have to . . . you have to give me something. Anything. Do you know where you are? Do you know what happened after the plane crash?"

She shakes her head again and again, almost as if she doesn't know any other way to respond. She's confused, I realize. Maybe she doesn't even recognize me. My heart clenches painfully with that thought, but I push through it, focusing on something else.

I sit back, an awful realization dawning on me.

"Kim," I say. "Are you alive?"

Her eyes meet mine one more time, and for the briefest moment

I can see the old Kimberly in there, staring back at me. She shrugs. The movement is weak, but the message is clear.

I don't know.

Then the man in the gas mask comes bursting out of the bathroom door, and his darkness swallows all the other darkness.

His enormous, insectile eyes are the last thing I see.

SO KISS A LITTLE LONGER

DEPUTY MELVIN O'CONNELL leads June Rapaport into the first holding cell of the Windale police station. Mel, Rebecca, and the chief sometimes refer to this part of the station as "the dungeon" because it's in the basement. Poorly lit, mostly hidden from the outside world, it's the perfect place to put Mrs. Rapaport until Mel can talk to the chief and figure out what to do with her.

She was out in the Triangle courtyard, as usual, accompanied by that constant stream of static from the netherworld between radio stations. But today there was something strange about the way her eyes never really focused, not even when one of the MPs approached her and started asking questions about the plane crash. Mel saw the transaction just as he was leaving the police station for his midday patrol. When the MP gave up, Mel went over and tried to get Mrs. Rapaport's attention himself, but she was basically catatonic. Still is, in fact.

Normally, Mel would have just taken Mrs. Rapaport to the WMC. But that place is even less desirable than this one just now. All those soldiers and scientists. Everyone up in arms about the crash itself instead of the missing Dowd girl. Bunch of cowards, that's what Mel O'Connell thinks. So today, the old lady gets the luxury suite in the dungeon and a five-course lunch of snacks from the vending machine upstairs.

As she moves into the cell, Mel is carrying Mrs. Rapaport's boom box under one arm, careful not to bump it, and holds Mrs. Rapaport's hand with the other. She goes willingly enough, her face serene, her eyes glazed and distant. Her feet shuffle across the concrete a few inches at a time. Down here, the sound of it would be loud if not for the static still rushing out of the stereo speakers. Mel was afraid to turn it off.

"That's it," Mel says gently, as if he's talking to a child. "There you go. A little bit more. We're almost there, Mrs. Rapaport."

There's a cot set up in the cell that he intends to sit the old woman down on as soon as she's in there. And after that, Mel wants two things: a cold bottle of Coke and a Pall Mall. Rebecca doesn't know he's still smoking, but that's okay—he's good at hiding it. As long as she doesn't taste the nicotine on his breath when she kisses him, he's golden. In fact, Mel thinks, he's almost as good at hiding his smoking from Rebecca as they are at hiding their relationship from the chief.

It takes several exhausting minutes, but eventually Mrs. Rapaport is inside the holding cell with her ass parked on the edge of the cot. Mel sets the boom box down on the floor next to her and stands back to marvel at what a strange sight this is: a woman well into her eighties with a big, bitchin' portable stereo sitting in a jail cell.

"Talk about your jailhouse rock," Mel mumbles to himself. "All right, Mrs. Rapaport, I'm going to close you up, but if you wake up and need anything, Alice should be back from lunch soon. She'll be right upstairs. Do you understand me? Blink once for yes, twice for no."

He puts his hands on his knees and looks her right in the eyes. She doesn't blink once. Or twice for that matter.

"Alrighty then," he sighs, standing up straight. "Suit yourself."

As soon as Mel turns to step through the cell door, the steady stream of static coming from the boom box hitches. Just a little bit, as if the dial got knocked out of place when he carried it in. But then Mel realizes the static has stopped entirely. The hitch wasn't just a hitch, it was the whole set clicking off.

Mel whirls on his feet . . . and finds himself nose to nose with Mrs. Rapaport. She's standing a hair's breadth away from him. Her breath is hot and smells of black licorice. Her pupils are hyperfocused points of darkness.

"It knows," Mrs. Rapaport growls. Then her voice begins to rise. "It *knows! It knows! It knows! It KNOWS! IT KNOWS, IT KNOWS, IT KNOWS, ITKNOWSITKNOWSITKNOWSITKNOWSITKNOWS!"*

The words devolve into unintelligible shouts. She's screaming in Mel's face, launching flecks of spittle across his cheeks. He takes two steps back until he hits the bars of the cell. Mrs. Rapaport closes the distance, still screaming, repeating those same words over and over.

"Mrs. Rapaport. June," Mel says calmly. "Please relax. Please. Everything is okay, I promise, we'll just—"

He can't even get everything he wants to say out before the elderly woman cocks her head to the side, snapping her mouth shut. The boom box clicks back on (Mel can hear the distinct twick of the button, he knows he can), but instead of static, a man's deep, inhuman voice comes rumbling through the speakers. It speaks and, at the same time, Mrs. Rapaport does.

"The old hag should have minded her own business."

Mrs. Rapaport—if it even is her anymore—lunges, and Mel is too slow. She pins him against the bars of the cell with strength that doesn't seem like her own, strength that doesn't seem human at all. With one hand pressed hard against his chest, the other hand slips its long, gnarled fingers around his throat. The hand squeezes, and the edges of Mel's vision go wonky—first distorted like a fun-house mirror, then dark like the shadows of birds racing across the ground, away from danger.

The last thing Mel thinks to do is reach behind him, grab the sliding door to the cell, and push it shut, locking them both inside. Then the world fades, and he falls down the hole into whatever waits at the bottom.

31.

CHARLIE

"I CANNOT BELIEVE you fucking cut that thing out of me," I say, panting. We're making our great escape. Slipping out of the WMC was easy enough, even on a crutch. But now we're out in the heat, and I'm lurching up Raspberry Street, the heel of my crutch clacking against the sidewalk. I'm practically dragging my casted leg across the ground, and it hurts more than the original break did. I'm struggling to breathe, dripping with sweat. Higgins had left my tattered clothes from the wreck behind last night, so Gabe used the scalpel, after he'd used it on me, to cut the left leg off my jeans and help me into them.

"It wasn't that bad," Gabe says, looking over his shoulder for the hundredth time. "You'll get over it."

"Easy for you to say," I protest. "You got to leave yours in."

"Yeah, well, we had to make it look realistic. It made sense for us to leave your tracker back at the medical center and take mine with me. I'll let you cut it out later if it'll make you happy, honey." He blows me a kiss, and I'm tempted to trip him with my crutch.

"Nobody's following us," I say. "If the army suspected anything, Higgins would be on top of us already."

Gabe trudges onward, helping me along as best he can, pressing a wad of gauze to my arm to soak up the blood. "After everything Reed told us, it's not just the army I'm worried about."

"Yeah," I huff. "You're telling me. You didn't have that thing in your room with you." I shiver in the ninety-degree heat.

"No, but I'm pretty sure he was in the kitchen with me and my mom this morning," Gabe says.

"What?" I slow down, looking at him.

He nods. "I thought it was just my concussion, but . . . the army aren't the only ones watching our every move."

We keep going, despite the fear that sentence instills in me. The sun bakes off the concrete in soupy waves of heat. I wade through them, fighting against my bad leg the whole way.

"What do you think it wants with us?" I ask after a moment. When I look around, the medical center is out of sight, and some of the tension releases between my shoulders.

"I don't know," Gabe says. "Maybe nothing. The better question is what does he want with Kimberly."

I ignore the fact that Gabe has clearly decided this thing is a person, even though Dr. Reed never said that was the case. *Something terrible* is what she said. That doesn't conjure the image of a human being. To me, that sounds like a monster.

We shuffle the rest of the way in silence, occasionally glancing around to make sure no one's watching us, army or otherwise. At last, we cut down a familiar alley toward Gabe's street, ignoring Mrs. Beaumont's yappy terrier, George, who barks at us from behind her fence.

Gabe's Chevelle is parked in the driveway behind his mom's Oldsmobile. Gabe puts a finger to his lips, and we creep around either side of the Chevelle, watching the windows of his house to make sure Mrs. Albright isn't looking out at us. Carefully, we pull our doors open and slide in, which is a struggle for me. I wince when my busted leg bangs into the footwell and wince again when my crutch makes a metallic *crang* sound against the doorframe. Gabe drops his visor, catches the spare set of keys in his hand. He turns the ignition, but only so far. Before he starts the engine, he puts the Chevelle in neutral, lifts off the brake, and lets us coast backward out of the driveway in silence. I can see the muscles flexing in his arms as he struggles to spin the wheel. The tires make a rubbery squelch against the hot asphalt. When we start to drift forward again, Gabe straightens the wheel out, needing just as much force to do it, favoring his injured left arm.

When the car has rolled down the hill to the end of the block, Gabe finally twists the key and fires up the engine.

"That was incredibly smooth," I say.

"Why thank you," he says, doing a mock bow in the driver's seat.

"Now what?" I ask. We're both sweating, in obvious pain, and I can't speak for Gabe, but I'm also pretty terrified.

"Now . . . I don't know," Gabe says. He's navigating down side streets, avoiding the main roads, heading in the general direction of the Triangle but without any real conviction. "I wanted to go talk to my dad, but . . ."

"You're afraid."

He shrugs. "Not of getting in trouble for leaving the house. He can only ground me for so long. I'm just afraid he won't believe us."

"I'm almost more afraid of what will happen if he does," I say. "If he finds out the army put trackers in us, that they really are trying to cover up what happened . . ."

"He's gonna freak."

"What about Sonya? It sounds like her dad was maybe trying to help, and she doesn't know she's being tracked, either."

"We don't know that Sonya's dad told Reed to help us, though," Gabe argues. "She could have done that on her own."

"Yeah, but if there's even the slightest chance that Sonya knows something about what's going on, and she starts snooping . . ." I trail off, letting the implications hang there. Gabe doesn't know that I know how he feels about Sonya. It's not like he came right out and told me. The poor guy tries to act tough, but he wears his feelings way down on his sleeve like the rest of us. Maybe that's why he never really fit in with the jocks.

"She could already be in trouble," Gabe mutters, tapping his fingers against the steering wheel anxiously. "Shit."

At the last second, he makes a sharp turn onto Houghton Avenue, cuts across King Street, then heads south until Houghton connects with Route 24 and we're headed for the Heart-to-Heart Bridge.

"This is probably a bad idea," Gabe says after a while.

As we come to the old covered bridge, tattooed with graffiti and littered with beer cans and cigarette butts and condom wrappers, I say, "Probably. But she's our friend. We help her first, if we have to. Then maybe we can all help Kimberly."

32.
SONYA

WAKING UP DOESN'T feel like waking up at all. It's more like *emerging*. Like stepping through a doorway that leads back into my own body. I open my eyes and find my bedroom waiting for me. The sun is still burning hot and bright behind the curtains, and David Cassidy is smiling down at me from his poster on the wall. My limbs are cold and stiff, my back hurts, my head is thudding, my eyes burn. I'm on the floor, spread out across the purple area rug my mom thought would look nice in here but is actually atrocious.

How long was I out?

I reach up slowly, gingerly, and use the bed to haul myself up off the floor. There's no way I was asleep for less than twelve hours. I ache all over—in my joints, in my muscles—as if I've been unconscious for days. Who knows; maybe I have.

A digital clock on the nightstand says otherwise. According to that, I've only been out for fifteen minutes. Was any of what I saw real? I get goose bumps thinking about the man in the gas mask, tearing out of the bathroom in room 6 at the Banshee Palace and . . . what? What happened after that?

I don't remember, and my head feels light trying to think about it. In small, careful steps, I turn around, meaning to go downstairs for some water. But I catch my reflection in the white wicker vanity on the opposite side of the room. On the mirror, scribbled in lipstick I hardly ever use, are words I'm sure I didn't write:

DON'T LET THE BEDBUGS BITE

It scares me at first, staring at the message. My heart rate kicks back up, and a fresh batch of tears stings my eyes. But then I'm just angry. *Furious* that I was right there, that *she* was right there, her hands in mine, and he took me away from her. Whoever *he* is. The thing that Mrs. Rapaport was trying to warn me about, probably.

I don't even look back at the bed, because if I do, I know all I'll see are those hundreds of thousand-leggers creeping over the blankets, their tiny legs going *scritch-scratch* over each other. Instead, I yank a dirty bath towel out of my laundry hamper, stomp over to the vanity, and scrub the lipstick words into a scarlet smear. Then I keep scrubbing, pushing against the mirror, making more of a mess than anything, but I don't care. My reflection gets lost under gobs of red and streaks of pink, and none of it is coming off. But at least the words are gone.

Kimberly's still there, though, her pallid face watching me every time I blink. Her shoulders lifting and falling helplessly. *I don't know.*

I'm crying now. Sobbing. Angry and afraid and alone. With my hand still wrapped in the towel, I punch the mirror. Just once, but hard. A spiderweb of cracks appears with my fist at its center. My face splits in half, hidden by a blood-colored veil. I don't even recognize who that person is. I've never seen her before in my life, and I'm not quite sure if she's good or bad.

The computer is under me, the plastic casing dotted with teardrops that are still leaking off my chin. I wipe my face and stand back, hyperaware of how quiet the house is and how loud the Commodore sounds, some piece whirring inside it. Humming, like a low, distant whistle. It bites at my nerves, makes my ears itch. It makes me think of my father, and in one last furious movement, I bend down, wrap the orange extension cord around my hand once, and yank as hard as I can.

The cord pulls taut against the corner of my bedroom doorframe and snags. I grab it with both hands and tug, desperate to make that tinny moan go silent. The line catches again, this time with a deep *thunk* from down the hall. I lean back, putting all my weight into it. I realize that I'm screaming, the idea that I could just unplug the computer's power cable from the extension cord only just now occurring to me.

Then the cord finally gives, and I fall backward on the floor. There's a wooden crunch from down the hall, and the orange rope of the extension cord goes slack. My room is blessedly silent. My heart is smacking against the inside of my chest. My lungs and throat ache, still tender.

I feel a little more like myself, though. A little less like I'm being invaded.

I get up and follow the orange length of extension cord, winding across the floor like a route on a road map. It takes me to my door, then traces a path down the hall to Dad's office. *The secret lair*, I think. Except it might not be so secret anymore, because the bottom corner of the door is bent outward, veined with cracks. There's something wedged between the door and the frame, pushing it into an awkward angle, creating a gap.

Without taking my eyes off the door, I take a few deep breaths, then call out to the house. "Mom? Dad?"

No answer. Everyone's still gone.

I move down the hall. Every creak of the floor makes me nervous.

Closer to Dad's office door, I realize the thing that's forcing the door apart is the surge protector, with the extension cord barely still plugged in to it. The prongs on the plug are bent sideways. I must have been pulling harder than I thought. Enough to crack the door, wedge it open just enough for me to slide numb, shaking fingers into the gap and . . .

I don't even know what I'm going to do before I'm doing it. I plant a foot against the wall, slide my fingers as high up on the inside of the door as I can, and just like with the cord, I pull.

Our house, as far as I know, was very expensive. Mom and Dad had it built when they first moved to Windale years ago, and for as long as I can remember, Dad's been complaining about how cheap the materials they used are. *Flimsy* is the word he likes to use. The doors are no exception. Once, when Sophia was a toddler, she went running full force into her bedroom door and nearly broke all the way through it. There was a vaguely Sophia-shaped crater in the wood for weeks until Dad could have it replaced. I can't imagine why he wouldn't have wanted the door to his secret lair made out of tougher stuff. Maybe it's because he trusted us to trust him.

I don't think I do anymore.

The door splinters even further along the bottom, but the locking mechanism is still caught firm in the jamb. It knocks against it with every pull, reminding me of the Banshee Palace, room 6.

But the door is peeling away, slowly widening that gap into a hole. My arms are shaking I'm pulling so hard. The surge protector is set free and falls to the floor, and I'm worried if I lose my grip, the door will flip back, seal the gap, and I'll lose my chance.

Chance at what? What am I even doing?

Then something gives within the hollow space of the door. The tension releases, and I stumble back into the opposite wall, showered in splinters, holding chunks of wood in my hands.

I glance down the hall, toward the stairs, fully expecting to see my dad coming up them. But the house is still eerily silent, still empty except for me.

In front of me, there's a hole in Dad's office door about the width of a textbook and maybe six inches tall. It's not very big, but it's a foot or so above the bottom of the door. Before I can talk myself out of doing anything stupid (because I've already made a bunch of stupid choices at this point), I drop to my knees in front of the door and slip my hand into the hole. It's just wide enough for me to get most of my arm in. I can reach up. I can feel the lock on the inside of the door. It's the only room in the house that needs a key, and Dad's the only one who has it.

I have to pat around to find the knob. When I do, the lock turns easily, and the door opens when I twist the knob.

As I pull my arm back through the hole, something on the inside of my elbow catches on the ragged edges of the wood—the pill thing that Hollis injected into me at the WMC. When I put my hand over it, the tiny knot feels firm, tight beneath my skin. It also feels slightly warm to the touch. Weird.

Fumbling around for the light switch, I realize that I've never been inside my dad's office before. It's foreign territory, built smack in the middle of my own home. I finally hit the lights, and a single fluorescent bar clicks to life on the ceiling.

The room is as boring as a county records office. No windows, a single hulking metal desk in the center of the floor, a few bulky filing cabinets. The walls are bare; the carpet is flat and stiff. On a shelf behind the desk are a few pieces of technology I don't recognize and some that I do. Like a massive tape recorder that must have been cutting edge in the sixties or seventies, with huge reels that remind me of the gaping lenses on the gas mask the man was wearing in my nightmare. Or whatever it was.

On the desk is the only thing that looks like it belongs in this decade: a computer. A Macintosh IIcx, to be exact. It's a $6,000 computer, brand-new. And there are two wires coming off it and curling around the desk. One is the power cord, which is plugged directly into the wall instead of the surge protector. There are a few other plugs dangling off the shelf nearby that look like they might have been plugged into the protector at one point but aren't anymore. I wonder if Dad had to unplug all his stuff just to get my Commodore powered on Friday morning. It doesn't look like everything would have reached, even with the extra-long extension cord he used. He thought my technological education was more important than whatever work he was doing in here?

The other wire connected to the Macintosh looks thinner than the power cable. I follow it behind the desk to the wall, where it's snapped into a phone jack. A phone jack?

I check the door, standing open and destroyed, and remind myself for the hundredth time that there's nobody else here, then I sink into the desk chair. The keyboard's in front of me. I hit the ENTER key, and the monitor comes to life with a mild click. The base of the computer beneath it is amazingly quiet—I can hear a small fan whirring inside, but it's nothing compared to the Commodore. A soft, breezy shushing sound is all it is, like rain.

The monitor brings up a screen that I don't recognize. It's not built into the computer's operating system. At least, not as far as I know—it seems too outdated. The flat green cursor at the top left corner moves, materializing words as it scrolls: **welcome. login? y or n**.

Along the bottom of the screen, I notice another string of letters: **RLDS-TCI-001.5**.

I have no clue what *RLDS* stands for, but I'm almost positive that *TCI* means TerraCorp Industries. Dad's tapped in to the computer network at TerraCorp from home via the phone lines.

I press the *Y* key with a shaky finger, and the screen changes.

id?

I close my eyes and try to picture Dad's ID badge, dangling from his lab coat. A picture of him with a goofy grin, the TerraCorp logo, his name. I don't remember anything else. No specific numbers or letters. I take a chance and type a single word: *GUTIERREZ*.

The screen changes again.

password?

The cursor blinks at me, daring me to try. But this is where all those computer coding books I've been reading come in handy. For a moment, I forget that I broke into my dad's office and am now snooping in a government-run computer system. I forget to be afraid. My fingers move across the keyboard in swift strikes, typing a few lines of code instead of a password. The code redirects me to another part of the system, "behind" the login screen. In my mind, I'm flipping back a silky curtain, revealing the mechanisms of some great machine.

I have no idea what Dad's password is. I could guess, but if the system is advanced enough, it'll lock me out if I get it wrong too many times. Or the computer will self-destruct. I don't need to know the password, though, because the system already has it saved for me. It's embedded in the code so that it can recognize the password correctly when Dad types it in. The keyboard clacks as I navigate lines of data on the screen. I get swept up in the fact that I actually know how to do this, that everything I've been working on to get into MIT is paying off.

Then again, the whole reason I wanted to go to MIT in the first place was because of my dad, and it's his system I'm hacking into right now, his secrets that I'm trying to dig up. What does that mean for my future?

The password turns out to be an arbitrary string of gibberish—numbers, letters, symbols. I memorize it, circle back to the original login screen. When I hit ENTER this time, the screen gives me a message: **ACCESS GRANTED. WELCOME, DR. GUTIERREZ.**

33.
GABE

THERE ARE NO other cars in Sonya's driveway when I pull the Chevelle in, and I'm not sure if that's a good sign or a bad one. I get out, then give Charlie a hand on his side. He looks a little less pale, and his arm has stopped bleeding. He winces with every awkward step he takes with the crutch, but he's getting better at it. Charlie Bencroft is one of the most resilient people I know. If there's one thing he knows how to do, it's bounce back. His leg won't slow him down. I'm not sure anything could.

We get to the front door and stop.

"Do we knock?" Charlie asks. "We usually just let ourselves in."

"Yeah. I don't know. Things feel different now, I guess."

I settle for ringing the doorbell.

At first, it seems like there's no one home. Maybe Sonya went to the medical center to see Charlie, in which case we could all end up circling Windale looking for each other. But then I'm certain I hear movement inside. It's a big house, but not very solid—every noise echoes. A shadow appears behind the curtain in the sidelight. A second later, the door flies open and Sonya shoves me backward as hard as she can. I nearly go sprawling off the front stoop.

"Jesus, you guys scared the *shit* out of me!" she hisses.

"What the hell, Sone?" Charlie says. "What's going on?"

She rears on him. "Why are you out of the medical center? Your leg is not going to heal if you're out wandering around."

I put my hands up in surrender. "Sonya, we just came to make sure you're okay. We think . . . we think the whole town might be in danger."

"It is," she snaps, turning her glare on me again.

"It . . . it is?" I ask, suddenly confused. Not to mention worried that we made the wrong choice by coming here.

"Yes." Her face is flat, but her chest is heaving. Some of her curls are stuck to her face with sweat. She's panicked. "Kimberly didn't just wander off. I think she was taken."

I open my mouth, close it again. I can't hide the look on my face.

"You knew," Sonya says, folding her arms and tapping her foot. "I fucking knew it." She spins around and storms back inside the house, but she leaves the door open.

Charlie and I look at each other. "I don't think we should follow her," he says. "I'm scared of her."

I roll my eyes and follow Sonya's path. She's in the kitchen, filling a glass with tap water. She gulps three-quarters of it in one go, then slams the cup down on the island.

"Sonya," I say, "I don't know what you know or how, but I'm sorry. I didn't mean to hide anything from you. From either of you. I was just afraid. I wasn't sure about your dad, but I was pretty sure I couldn't trust Higgins."

"You can't," she replies, still fuming.

Then, at the same time, we say, "Because she brought the plane to Windale."

We gape at each other. Then, again, we say, "You knew?"

Charlie scrubs his face with his hands. "You guys should really start sharing more," he says.

There's a long pause.

"I want to know everything you know," Sonya says. "And then I'll tell you what I know. You can start with the man in the gas mask and what he did with Kimberly."

I look at her, startled, then to Charlie for help.

He puts his hands up and shakes his head. "I'm out. I need a snack." He goes to the fridge and starts digging around like he always does.

Sonya is still staring at me, waiting. "Talk," she says.

While Charlie makes himself a snack, that's exactly what I do. I tell the whole story over again, starting with the moment the Bug Man took Kimberly.

"The Bug Man?" Sonya says. She looks shaken. "Why did you call him the Bug Man?"

"It's the mask," Charlie says around a big bite. There's a glob of mayonnaise on the corner of his mouth.

Sonya shivers. "Okay. I get it. Go on."

I backtrack to Friday morning at the Webber farm and tell her about the mutilated herd and the cargo plane landing at TerraCorp. Then I tell her everything Dr. Reed told me and Charlie an hour ago: the trackers, the pilot, the pictures. I pull the shots out of my back pocket and lay them on the kitchen island for her to see.

"Wait. *Trackers?* Actually, that makes sense. And she told you her name was Claudia?" Sonya asks.

Charlie and I nod.

"My dad took a phone call Friday morning. With his office door open. It wasn't a big deal at the time, but he was talking to someone named Claudia about Higgins and the airstrip. That's how I knew the plane was coming from TerraCorp."

"I should have just told you the truth from the beginning," I say. "I'm sorry, Sone. I didn't know who to trust, and I didn't . . . I *couldn't* put you in danger if your dad is somehow involved."

"He is," she says, staring blankly at the floor. There's a crumb from Charlie's sandwich on the counter nearby. She rolls it around with her thumb, her eyes glassy. "In fact, I think this whole thing might be his fault."

"So we can't trust him?" I ask as gently as I can.

"I don't know. We can debate that in a minute. First, let me tell you about my experience with the . . . you know."

"Bug Man?" Charlie says casually. He flicks his tongue out and wipes the dab of mayo off his lips.

"Yeah. Him," Sonya says, her voice tight.

"It," Charlie corrects without taking his eyes off his food.

"You might be right about that," she mutters. Then: "Okay. I fell asleep earlier . . ."

She tells us about her nightmare, about wandering through some paused version of Windale, just before the plane crash. She tells us about the old motel on the west side of town, the run-down old fire hazard that everyone calls the Banshee Palace. She tells us about Mrs. Rapaport's warning and seeing Kimberly in room 6, the way she looked, the fact that she couldn't speak. Then the Bug Man, bursting in.

"He shut me out," she says. "I was riding the signal, but he cut me off."

"I'm not following," I say.

"Let me show you. But we have to be quick. My mom and sister could be home any minute. And we cannot be here when they are."

"Wait, why not?" Charlie asks.

"Just come with me."

She leads us upstairs—Charlie needs a second to work out how to manage the steps with his leg but catches up quickly enough. At the top, I have to pause and process what I'm seeing.

Charlie asks the question before I can: "Did . . . did you *break* into your dad's office?"

"Uh . . . yeah," Sonya replies. Her cheeks darken. "Not totally on purpose. At first."

She shrugs and heads down the hall, stepping over pieces of broken door and what looks like an orange industrial extension cord.

"Who *are* you?" Charlie asks. But he's grinning when he says it.

We follow Sonya into the secret lair, a place we've always joked about while harboring a certain intimidated respect for Dr. G's privacy. He could have been hiding dead bodies in here, and we would never know.

The room looks as if it were transplanted from some drab office building and tucked inside the Gutierrez house by mistake. It's a cold metal box, like a cubicle. There are a few machines and instruments, along with a sick computer on the desk. Other than that, you would never know this office belongs to a scientist. An accountant could work here.

"We definitely overestimated what your dad had going on in here," Charlie says.

"Tell me about it," Sonya says, tapping away at the keyboard.

"Please don't tell me you went through your dad's computer, too," I say. I take an involuntary step back, suddenly afraid to be in the room with her.

"I didn't," she replies.

I deflate, relieved. "Good. I thought—"

"I went through the computer system at TerraCorp."

"*What?*" Charlie and I cry together.

"Yeah." She smiles, proud of herself. She picks up a manila folder that's jammed with paperwork, almost two inches thick. She must have pulled it from one of the filing cabinets. "You guys want to hear about Project Breakpoint?" She waves the folder.

"Probably not," I say. "But go for it."

Sonya drops the folder onto the desk with a heady smack and flips it open, cross-checking the page she's on with something on the computer screen as she scrunches her nose. I can't fight the nervous energy that flutters through me while looking at her like this. Even under the hard fluorescent light, her hair is ablaze, and there's that lovely quirk of her lips when she's focused on something. I have to give my head a quick, strong shake to pull myself back down to reality.

"A lot of this stuff is redacted or just super vague," Sonya says, flipping the page. "Especially as you get closer to the present. But the early stuff is straightforward. It's the whole reason TerraCorp is here. Hell, it's the whole reason *I'm* here."

"Tell us," I say, glancing at the clock hanging over the door. "I'm

177

getting antsy. And if we're going to leave, we should probably get that tracker out of you."

"Oh," she says, rubbing that part of her arm. "Right. Okay, yeah. Project Breakpoint is the founding program for TerraCorp. As far as I can tell, the government hired my dad and a few of his scientist friends to do research on the climate."

"As in the weather?" Charlie asked.

"Essentially, but more complicated than that. Dad and his buddies created TerraCorp around their research in . . . 1969, I think? Two years in, they moved the whole operation here, to Windale."

"Okay," I say slowly. "But why here? This place is nowhere now and it was probably nowhere then, too."

Sonya grins, totally in her element now, and my heart does a backflip. "That's what I wanted to know," she says. "Most of that information is blacked out even in the database. You need, like, presidential-level security clearance to access it. But there's a lot of talk about an anomaly that was detected here. Something they thought had to do with the earth and a lot of meteorological mumbo jumbo that I don't understand."

"And this . . . anomaly. It's in Windale?" Charlie asks.

"Yes. Dagger Hill, specifically."

"Shit. No wonder our parents never wanted us to go up there," I say.

Sonya nods. "No kidding."

"So what is the anomaly?" Charlie asks.

"I don't know. That part is classified to the point of being erased from history."

"Okay. So what does any of this have to do with us and what's going on right now?" I'm scratching my head, trying to keep up.

"Well, lucky for us, my dad is obnoxiously organized. He keeps records of everything, including phone calls. And over the past few months, one of the people he's been talking to the most is Colonel Higgins."

"Oh boy," Charlie says. "Here we go."

Sonya looks at him, gravely calm. "Right. Dad's notes aren't very specific, but this log entry here is the one that scares me the most." She reads from one of the pages in the folder. " 'June sixth, 1989. Took another call from Colonel Higgins today. We spoke about her desire to bring the other anomaly here to Windale. I once again refused.' "

"The *other* anomaly?" Charlie asks.

"That's what Reed was talking about," I say. *The closer it got to Windale, the stronger it became.* "She said Higgins brought something terrible here. She made it sound like the town was part of it somehow. Like . . . like it was drawing power from Windale."

Charlie is nodding, his eyes ticking back and forth, probably trying to remember the conversation himself. "Higgins sent it away. But it was already too late."

"The two anomalies are connected," Sonya says, chewing her lip.

"And one of them took Kimberly," I say.

We all jump when a phone rings from somewhere inside Dr. G's desk. The desk hums with each chime of the bell, loud and feral, like an animal trying to get out of a trap.

"Jesus," Sonya breathes.

"Do we answer it?" Charlie asks.

"Hell no, we do not answer it," Sonya spits back.

"Maybe we should," I say. She looks at me like I just sprouted an extra head. "Think about it. Your dad's at TerraCorp now, right? If this is a private line, which I'm pretty sure it is because I don't hear any other phones ringing in the house, then why would someone call him here? Everyone at TerraCorp knows he's not going to pick up."

"He has a point," Charlie says, shrugging.

Sonya shifts back and forth on her feet. Meanwhile, the phone keeps buzzing against the metal sides of the desk. It brays with an urgency that crawls under my skin and festers there. Sonya's eyes are wild and darting, indecisive.

"*Shit,*" I say, and come around the desk. I yank open one of the top drawers—just a bunch of paper clips and memo pads. I try the next one down and pull it while the phone is midring. The sound goes from being a hollow, captured thing to filling the room like a tornado siren. The phone itself isn't anything exciting, not like the computer. It's a simple rotary-style phone without the dial. There's a single button in the center of its round face and a blinking light just above it, flashing red.

"Gabe, *no!*" Sonya yells.

I pluck the handset from the receiver and put it to my ear. "Hello?"

A stretch of silence follows that makes my blood go cold. A steady crackle-click on the other end of the line makes me think of insect legs ticking as they creep by. Beneath that: a low, shrill whine. It digs into my ear, then into my brain, and I feel my hand grow sweaty against the phone.

"Hello?" I say again.

I'm staring down at the receiver, waiting for it to ring again or for the line to go dead or for someone to speak up. Sonya nudges my arm, and I glance up at her. She's not looking, but she points at the computer screen. It's gone haywire. The green strings of code blip in and out, coming back in jagged formations, layered on top of each other, twitching and hitching. For a moment, they seem to form the image of a face. I can see distinct eyes and a nose and a mouth. Then the screen glitches again, and one of the eyes winks at us, I know it does. Then it goes dark.

A second later, four words appear in huge, radioactive letters:

THEY'RE COMING FOR YOU.

I forget that I still have the phone pressed to my ear until something screeches on the other end of the line, sharp and piercing. I yelp and drop the handset, jerking back into the shelf of Dr. G's electronic gizmos.

Somewhere outside, maybe a mile or so away, a big engine revs. The kind of engine that belongs in an army Humvee or jeep.

"Oh my god," Sonya says, her voice shaky.

"We have to go," I say. "We have to go right now."

Charlie is already out the door, wielding his crutch like a pro. I hear him hit the stairs as Sonya sweeps the Project Breakpoint paperwork back into the folder and scoops it up, clutching it close to her chest.

"They must have seen me in the system," she whimpers. "I screwed up."

"Sone, it's okay. Just move." I practically shove her through the splintered office door and down the hall. I don't look back. We race down the stairs. Charlie is at the front door, throwing it open.

"Got the keys!" he shouts over his shoulder.

"Start her up!" I yell, then grab Sonya by the arm and lead her into the kitchen.

"Gabe, we have to go," she says.

I'm digging through drawers, looking for a knife. "Your tracker," I say. "We have to cut it out. Mine too."

She blinks at me for a second, dazed. Then she reaches over to a block of cutlery near the stove. She snatches a paring knife and holds it up. The blade glints in the sunlight.

"Use this," she says.

34.

CHARLIE

GABE AND SONYA sprint out of the house with blood dribbling down their arms. Some of Sonya's speckles the folder she's carrying, chock-full of government research that isn't ours and could probably get us all thrown in jail for life.

The Chevelle's engine is purring. I'm in the passenger seat with my bad leg throbbing in front of me. I can feel bones grinding around in there every time I move now, and the pain is out of this world. But I have to keep going.

"Let's go!" I yell out the window. Up the road, the sound of engines—a caravan of them, it seems like—is getting louder, closer.

Gabe throws himself behind the wheel, and Sonya dives across the bench seat in the back. Gabe's sneaker slams the gas pedal into the floor. The engine roars, the back tires spin, launching gravel as the ass end of the car sways. Gabe turns the wheel, aims us at the end of the driveway, and when the tires finally get purchase, we blast off at full speed. I'm shoved backward into my seat, clinging to the edge of it.

The army engines sounded like they were coming from the south end of Sonya's street, so Gabe heads north, turning left out of the drive and rocketing for the Hill-to-Hill Bridge. I lean forward. In the rearview mirror, I see a big green Humvee take a sharp turn into Sonya's driveway, followed by a couple of jeeps.

"Do you think they saw us?" Sonya asks.

"I don't know," I say.

She's watching through the back window, still holding on to her sheaf of papers like it's a bible.

"It doesn't matter," Gabe says, watching the road, hands cemented around the steering wheel. There's a tiny, ragged hole on the inside of his elbow, oozing blood that's dripping onto his jeans. "There's nowhere for us to go. They'll tear this whole town apart looking for us. And anyone we have ties to . . ." He trails off.

"Our parents," Sonya says quietly. "My sister." She slumps back, finally loosening her grip on the files.

"We don't know what they're going to do," I say, trying to keep my voice steady. "But I don't think there's anyone we can trust right now."

Gabe takes a sharp, frenzied turn onto the Hill-to-Hill Bridge, his foot still pressed hard against the gas pedal, trying to get us far away from Sonya's house as quickly as possible.

"There might be one person we can trust," he says. He shifts, pulls the Polaroids Dr. Reed gave us out of his pocket, drops them into my lap. In one fuzzy shot, there's another picture that Gabe took from Dagger Hill, the man dangling in the air like a marionette, the ivy-green parachute billowed out above him, the streets of Windale still a couple thousand feet below.

I flip through the shots, none of them in focus, probably taken in a hurry. It would have been hard to tell where the pilot was drifting in the original photos, but a picture of a picture is even worse.

Sonya leans forward between the front seats. "We have no idea where he would have landed. Those shots are crap. Maybe if Charlie had been the one taking the photos to begin with . . ."

"Hey," Gabe says. "I was just goofing around. I didn't think they'd be the center of a life-or-death scenario, okay?"

"Yeah, well, maybe if you took things more seriously—"

"We were supposed to be having fun! Just hanging out. And I take lots of stuff seriously, all right?"

"Like what? Your hair?"

"My . . . ? Are you kidding?"

"*Guys!*" I yell, and they go quiet. "Listen. Nobody could have known. Okay? We have a lot of reasons to be afraid right now, but fighting is not going to fix any of them. And the thing we should be most afraid of is losing Kimberly."

They glance at each other, then at me, and nod.

"You're right, Charlie," Sonya says. "But I don't know what we're supposed to do. Reed gave you guys these pictures because she thought you'd take them to Gabe's dad and track down the pilot. After what just happened, that'll be the first place Higgins goes."

"Right," Gabe agrees. "The police station would have been the safest place, but now it's the most dangerous."

"And there's no way we'll find the pilot on our own. Even if we do, who knows if he'll be able to help us."

On the other side of the bridge, Gabe turns us north again, away from the Triangle. A couple of blocks later, he turns left, heading west, because if we go too far north, we'll hit the high school, where the army has set up its base of operations. Gabe's right—there's nowhere for us to go.

But maybe . . .

"I have a hunch about the pilot," I say, leaning forward, massaging the hip above my broken leg. "But I think we should split up."

"What? No way," Sonya says.

"Yeah, Charlie, that's not gonna happen. Get real. If we split up, we're as good as dead. Not only do we have the army hunting us down, but we've got that . . . *thing* on our tails, too."

"The Bug Man," I say. "Who warned us about the army showing up. Why would it do that? Why would it take Kimberly in the first place?"

"I . . . don't know," he says, sitting back, relaxing his grip on the steering wheel.

"Think about it," I argue. "If we're all together, and we get caught, the rest of the town is still in danger. Higgins is going to do whatever she can to track down the Bug Man and cover up her mistake. If we split up and one of us gets caught, at least the others can keep trying to blow this thing up." I raise one of the blurry images of the pilot floating over Windale. "I'm going to start with this. If I'm right, we might get a leg up on Higgins. Pun very much intended." I knock on the plaster of my cast for emphasis, and it actually puts a grin on both of their faces. "I think you guys should go to Kimberly's house."

"Why?" Sonya asks.

"Because the Bug Man took Kimberly for a reason. She was so off on Friday, before the crash. More off than usual. Right?"

Sonya's face tells me enough.

"Maybe she knew something," I say. "*Felt* something, I don't know."

"It was like she saw it coming," Gabe says.

Sonya nods, her eyes distant. "Yeah. Something was on her mind. Her parents might know something we don't. Maybe give us some clue about where to start looking for her."

"And if not them, then maybe Mr. Kunz at the diner?" Gabe says. "He would have been the last person to talk to her before she met up with us on Friday."

"Okay," I say. "Then that's the plan. You guys drop me off first, then head to Kimberly's house, talk to her parents. After that, we can meet back up at the diner and see what Harry Kunz knows. Good?"

Sonya dips her head once, chewing her lip.

"Good," Gabe replies. "But where are we dropping you off?"

"The newspaper office. If anybody has seen something out of the ordinary in Windale, it's Don Cranston."

35.

SONYA

THE DOWDS LIVE in a jigsaw puzzle of a house on the northeast side of town. It used to be a thousand-square-foot Cape Cod with two bedrooms and a single bathroom. Then Kimberly's parents added three separate additions, none of which quite match the original paint job. They're both writers for a couple of different magazines, and they like to keep to themselves. Charlie and Gabe and I have never had a bad experience at Kim's house, but none of us has spoken more than a handful of sentences to either of her parents.

I have to stop myself when I get to the front of the house. It used to be so easy for me to waltz right up to the front door and let myself in, find Kimberly lounging on the couch reading some book, something by Thomas Hardy or Charlotte Brontë, something dense and complicated that would put me to sleep in a second. She likes to scribble poetry in the margins of the pages—her shelves are filled with books that are both classic novels and her own journals.

Knowing that she's not in there waiting for one or all of us to come sweep her into some lame adventure . . .

The tears come before I know they're building, and I drop my chin to my chest. The concrete at my feet develops dark splotches where the teardrops hit and quickly evaporate into nothing. If I stand here long enough, maybe the heat can bake my grief away, too.

"What the hell did we get ourselves into?" Gabe asks beside me.

When I look at him, I'm surprised to see tears in his eyes, too. He's got the same fears weighing on his mind as I do, with Kimberly at the center. But he'll never understand my fear, the basis for wanting to believe that Kim is alive out there. I have to keep reminding myself that he's worried about our friend, same as I am, and that no matter what, he's on my side. Gabe's never been anything less than a friend to me. Maybe he's wanted more, and maybe I've pulled away from him because of that, but I know he'd never let anything happen to me. He didn't keep secrets because he didn't trust me—he kept them because he wanted me to be safe, and I'm grateful for that.

"Let's go," I say. "We don't know how much time we have."

Walking up to Kimberly's front porch feels like walking to the edge of a cliff. My feet are unreliable, my legs shaky and hollow. I'm a ceramic doll, a piece of porcelain that could tip and shatter with just a breath of wind.

There isn't any wind now, not even a breeze. Just the June sun, a perfect yellow circle driving beams of thick heat down on Windale. My forearms are sweating, my shirt clinging to my back. The old boards creak as we step across them to the front door. There's little escape from the heat under the shade of the awning, but I feel a chill anyway. I lift my fist to knock but hesitate.

"You do it," I whisper to Gabe. "Please?"

He swallows, nodding, then lifts his own fist. I can see it shaking. Then there's the sharp crack of Gabe's knuckles on the door, which cuts through me in an unpleasant way. I shut my eyes and see the slo-mo world of the Windale I explored in my dream (*nightmare?*) and the front door that was supposed to look like my own but definitely wasn't. I hear the knock. When the door opens this time, though, the man in the gas mask is waiting on the stoop, dressed from head to toe in black, the big lenses of the mask tinted a smoky shade of gray, hiding the eyes that watch me from behind them.

My eyes snap open, and I suck in a harsh breath, almost a gasp. Gabe leans over. "You all right?" he asks.

"Yeah," I lie. "Yeah. Just nervous."

"Me too."

I feel his hand slip into mine, his skin just as clammy as mine. My first instinct is to snatch my hand away, put it in my pocket, protect him from getting the wrong idea. But I get the feeling he's looking for comfort as much as he's trying to give some to me. And if I'm being really honest, it's good to have someone to hold on to, someone who's been there through practically every knee scrape and heartbreak of my childhood.

A few years ago, when our dog, Presto, died, Gabe held my hand just like this while Dad buried him in the soft ground near the canal. Charlie and Kim were there, too. Kimberly was holding my other hand, and Charlie was holding hers. We all cried together that day, and then we went to the diner and Harry brought us milkshakes and we took turns telling our favorite Presto stories. By the end of the night, those three had me laughing so hard that my tears were less grief and more joy.

Now, I squeeze Gabe's hand. For that memory and so many others like it.

When nobody answers the door, Gabe knocks again. This time we can hear footsteps moving through the house. We see the top of Mrs. Dowd's head poke up into the little window at the top of the front door. Then the locks click—the dead bolt and the doorknob—and the door swings open.

Mrs. Dowd stands in the dim foyer, dressed in wrinkled sweatpants and a sweatshirt that's too small for her. I recognize it as Kimberly's Flyers sweatshirt. It's old and faded, the elastic in the cuffs worn out so that the sleeves droop open like sagging jowls. I can smell Kim's perfume on it even from here, wouldn't be surprised if Mrs. Dowd had sprayed a little extra on the sweatshirt before squeezing herself into it. Her eyes are wide and puffy, the color drained from her cheeks.

"Hi, kids," she says, trying a tiny half-hearted smile.

"Hi, Mrs. Dowd," Gabe says. He has his empty hand buried in the pocket of his jeans, and his head is pulled down between his shoulders like a turtle trying to hide in its shell.

Mrs. Dowd lets out a single cluck of laughter. "Gabe, in all these years, no matter how many times I've told you, you still refuse to call me Sheila."

Gabe waggles his head back and forth, grinning a little himself. "Sorry. Force of habit, I guess."

"Yeah," Mrs. Dowd says, her expression souring. "I get that." She doesn't elaborate, but she tugs at the bottom of Kimberly's sweatshirt, rubbing the fabric between her fingers almost tenderly.

"Mrs. Dowd," I say, my voice croaking. "How are you doing? How's Mr. Dowd?"

"Bradley?" she says. "I have no idea how he's doing. I have no idea if he even . . . if he even knows . . ." She pauses, pulling in a shaky breath. "Bradley got caught outside the army barricade. He was driving back from Doylestown Friday afternoon when . . . he never made it back, and I haven't been able to get ahold of him."

"Wait," I say. "So you've been here by *yourself*?"

Mrs. Dowd nods, not looking directly at me or Gabe. But she seems to snap back into herself, her eyes clearing up a bit. "Why don't you kids come in out of the heat? We can talk. Tell me how *you're* doing."

"Yeah," I say. "Yeah, that sounds nice."

She pulls the door open all the way, and before we step in, Gabe and I both steal glances over our shoulders. We parked the Chevelle in an alley a block or so away, as out of sight as we could get it, but the MPs could already be patrolling the streets looking for us. If they find the car, they'll most likely find us here.

It's delightfully cold inside the house. No wonder Mrs. Dowd is dressed in sweats—the AC is on full blast, and it must be sixty degrees in here at most. I shiver when the cool air falls across my damp, sticky skin.

Mrs. Dowd ushers us into the living room, which is cluttered with stacks of books and notepads, newspapers and magazines. There's a small TV set in the corner, but the remote is resting on top and both are covered in a carpet of dust. Honestly, I don't think I've ever seen the TV switched on in this house.

"Can I get you something to drink?" Mrs. Dowd asks. She drops mechanically into one of the overstuffed chairs while Gabe and I sit down on the couch. "I think I have some Turkey Hill iced tea in the fridge?"

"I'm okay," Gabe says.

"Me too," I say. "We won't bother you for too long, Mrs. Dowd. We just wanted to ask you some things about Kimberly and—"

"You're not a bother," she says, cutting me off. "It's good to see you two. Where's Charlie?" Her eyes widen again as she realizes what kind of horrible responses we could have to a question like that.

"He's . . . uh, at the medical center," I say quickly. "He was . . . he was hurt pretty badly, but he's okay."

"We're trying to get some answers," Gabe says, glancing in my direction, looking for reassurance that I'm not equipped to provide. "I think . . . Mrs. Dowd, I think we might be in a lot of trouble here. And we could really use your help."

As Gabe talks, the Dowds' two cats—a snowy-white Ragdoll named Marshmallow and a striped mackerel tabby named Meatloaf—saunter into the living room. Meatloaf, a little thick around the edges, makes a lumbering leap up onto the armrest of Mrs. Dowd's chair. She scratches under his chin absently, as if she barely heard what Gabe said. Meanwhile, Marshmallow stretches her legs and scratches at the carpet inside a rectangle of sunlight. Her sky-blue eyes dart around anxiously. Both cats seem really on edge.

"I'm guessing you both have had experience with the colonel?" Mrs. Dowd asks, letting Meatloaf nudge his face into her fingers. "Lovely woman that she is."

"Higgins?" Gabe says. He squirms in his seat a bit. "Yeah. Unfortunately."

"She . . . uh . . . She put her boot in my door." All at once, there are tears in the eyes of my best friend's mom. I can't watch her cry, have to look away. My eyes fall on the cottony fluff of Marshmallow pacing in the sun. Except for the paws and the nose and quietly swishing tail, she could be a wad of pillow stuffing that someone forgot on the floor. I can't escape Mrs. Dowd's voice, though, thick with emotion. "She practically forced her way inside my house. Wouldn't leave me alone."

"Did she ask you any questions?" Gabe asks.

"Yes," Mrs. Dowd replies. "But none that seemed to have anything to do with . . . with finding Kimberly. They were so personal. So . . . *invasive*. She wanted to know when Kimberly's last period was. Can you believe that?"

Gabe makes an uncomfortable noise next to me and sits back.

"That's . . . obnoxious," I say, shooting Gabe a sideways glare. "Did it seem like she was getting at something?"

"I guess she was just trying to . . . I don't know . . . figure Kimberly out?" She sniffles. "She was trying to find out if Kimberly would have *wanted* to disappear. You kids didn't notice anything, did you?"

Her eyes, drowning in hope and grief, all but break my heart.

"We came here to ask you the same thing, Mrs. Dowd," I say softly. "Kimberly was . . . *off* on Friday." I look to Gabe now for confirmation—part of me still believes I could have made up her strange behavior, imagined it somehow.

But Gabe is nodding emphatically.

"Yeah," he says. "She's always been kind of . . ." He trails off, cringing, afraid to say the thing that I'm also thinking in my head.

Mrs. Dowd surprises me by saying it for us. "Rough around the edges?"

Gabe and I smile sheepishly. So does Kimberly's mom. It's strange to feel so guilty and relieved at the same time. I've never had this kind of conversation with one of my friends' parents. It's always hollow niceties and cheery clichés. Stupid, half-sarcastic jokes about school or the weather. I wonder, suddenly, if Gabe and Kimberly and Charlie and I have ever had to deal with anything truly serious. Our regular, everyday high school drama feels a lot less important than it always has. If it was ever important at all.

"It's okay," Mrs. Dowd goes on. "I'm her mother, remember? I know how she gets." For some reason, she glances at me with a look that's full of an emotion I can't place. "But maybe you kids know her better than I do." She inhales sharply. Something catches at the back of her throat. "Kimberly has these moments. These rare, spontaneous days of joy. Her laugh comes so easy, and it's like she's a little girl again. She's so . . . *untroubled* in those moments. You know what I mean."

Mrs. Dowd is looking at me when she says that, and I don't hear a question. I nod, because I *do* know what she means. Kimberly is so bright and full and vibrant on those days her mom is talking about. Her smile is this perfect, fragile thing. It makes you feel like you have to be delicate with her, otherwise it might shatter and she'll fold back into herself.

But those days aren't the reason we're all friends with Kimberly. And they're certainly not the reason I fell in love with her. If we were always holding out for Kimberly's good days—simply tolerating her through the bad ones—our friendship would never have lasted. Kim is our friend *because* of those days when she drags like an anchor at the bottom of the ocean, not despite them. She's the most brutally honest of us all, the most fearless. She stares *into* you, not at you or through you. Sometimes, when she's quiet and reserved and thoughtful, she just watches me, or Gabe, or Charlie, and she knows what we're thinking even before we say it. At school, she's an Almost Nobody because, according to bullshit high school stereotypes, she looks and sounds like she should be this bubbly, rich-kid, cheerleader type. But half the time you can find her in one of the rigid, uncomfortable chairs in the library, rolled into a ball with a book in one hand, the pages held open by her thumb. The other hand is busy fiddling with her hair, twirling and untwirling it— threads of soft gold wound around the slender spools of her fingers.

"Yeah," I say to Mrs. Dowd now. "I know what you mean. But Friday was different. We know what she's like when she's being herself, when she's . . . I don't know . . . tuned in to another station, one that only plays her own thoughts."

Mrs. Dowd grins at that, nodding thoughtfully. "I've never thought of it like that, but yes, that's a good way of putting it," she says.

I go on, leaning forward in my seat. "This wasn't her being herself. She was different. Bothered by something. Mrs. Dowd, do you have any idea what that might be?"

She puts a fist to her mouth and bites the knuckle of her index finger. Meatloaf is pressing his face against her wrist, looking for more love.

"I honestly don't know," she says finally, dropping her hands into her lap and looking ashamed. "I was busy with an article for the *Saturday Evening Post*. She was in the kitchen briefly. *Maybe* she said goodbye? I . . . I just don't remember. God, it was only two days ago, but I just wasn't paying enough attention."

She looks at Gabe and me with eyes that are round, wet saucers. She looks ready to cry again, but there might not be any tears left in her. This whole thing may have hollowed her out. I know it's done that to me.

"It's okay, Mrs. Dowd," Gabe says next to me. "Don't beat yourself up. We weren't paying attention, either. At least, not enough to really ask her about what might have been going on. You know how Charlie and I are. We were talking about stupid movie shi—stuff. Sonya was the only one who really . . ." He trails off, and I remember going to Kimberly while we were eating lunch on Friday, right before the storm came in, and the plane with it. *Maybe we can talk later?* she said. "Did she say anything to you, Sone?"

"No," I say, unable to look either of them in the eyes. "She didn't say anything. I asked her what was up, but she . . . she just said we'd talk later."

"Sounds about right," Mrs. Dowd says with a sigh. But she's still staring at me and Gabe, the gears turning behind her squinting eyes. "Why are you guys really here?" she asks. "Colonel Higgins is running the investigation. We all told her everything we could." Her eyes are flicking from me to Gabe and back. "Didn't we?"

"There are some . . . additional details," Gabe says cautiously. "Things that happened on Friday . . ."

"And since," I add.

". . . that we don't feel comfortable sharing with the colonel," Gabe finishes. "To be honest, we, uh . . . we don't think we can trust her."

Mrs. Dowd's stare falls on me again, her eyes suddenly alert and piercing. "And what about your father, Sonya?" she asks. "Does he trust the colonel?"

The implications behind what she's asking are clear. I can't do anything but shift uncomfortably on the couch cushion. "It's complicated, Mrs. Dowd," I say. It's the only thing I *can* say, the only thing that even comes close to the truth.

"Except it's not," she replies. There's a sharper edge to her voice now. "It's not complicated in the slightest. My daughter is missing. Vanished because an airplane, an *army* airplane, fell out of the sky." She leans forward now, uncoiling like a snake protecting its eggs. Meatloaf hops down, startled, and scares Marshmallow, and they both skitter into the kitchen. Mrs. Dowd's stare is focused into laser precision, aimed right at me. Behind the glare, I can see her putting together the obvious pieces of the puzzle. "If your father knows anything about why that plane crashed," she says to me, then looks at Gabe. "Or if *your* father knows anything about why that plane crashed, you two need to tell me. Right now."

Her tone has taken on that parental quality, full of empty menace. She's trying to play the Mom card on us, which might have worked when we were ten and we were jumping too high on Kimberly's bed, but not now. Now, it just dings off the hard shell I've grown, my defense against all the things that can hurt me here in Windale, all the things I fully intended to leave behind when I went off to college.

Gabe speaks first, slowly and carefully. "We don't know anything for sure right now, Mrs. Dowd." There's a gentleness in his voice that I've never heard before. "All we know is that something very strange is happening here. Something that might turn out to be really scary.

Not just for us, but for everyone in Windale. And we need your help to get as much information as we can."

My thoughts turn to the Banshee Palace, to Kimberly huddled in the dark throat of the hotel room, to the black shape of the man in the gas mask bounding out of the bathroom, falling over me like a heavy velvet curtain. Fresh goose bumps spring up across my arms, and I shiver.

Kimberly's mom sees this, and the anger that was prickling toward her surface dwindles. She slumps back into the plump cushions of the chair with fresh tears in her eyes.

"I just want my daughter back," she whispers, tugging at the hem of her too-tight sweatshirt.

I get up and cross the room, squat down in front of her, take her hand. It's freezing. "Us too," I say. "The important thing is that we find Kimberly. After that, we can worry about everything else."

There's a pause while Mrs. Dowd sniffles, her chin on her chest. When she breathes in, her nose sounds remarkably similar to the gurgling of the canal.

After a moment, she looks up, over my shoulder at Gabe. "And this . . . scary thing. Whatever it is that you say might be happening. Finding Kimberly might help you figure out what it is?"

"Or the other way around," Gabe replies. "If we can figure out what's going on, it might help us find Kim."

Mrs. Dowd looks down at me, thinking. Then she squeezes my hand. A single, light pulse is all it is, but it comforts me in a way I can't describe.

"Okay," she tells us. "Like I said, I don't know much. But the one thing Colonel Higgins asked me to do that I refused was look around in Kimberly's bedroom. She said she'd come back with a warrant if she had to. I told her good luck getting Judge Hanlon out of bed on a Saturday." I smile at that. Something tells me that Higgins doesn't really need a warrant from our local, usually inebriated judge to get what she wants, but I'm proud of Mrs. Dowd for standing up for herself, and for Kimberly.

"You kids were closer to my daughter than I ever was," she continues. "If there's anything up in her room that seems odd or out of place, you'll know what it is. Go ahead and take a look."

I nod, standing. Gabe rises with me. We thank her again and head up the steps to Kimberly's bedroom. On the way, I try to shake the fact that Mrs. Dowd used the past tense just then. But I can't do it.

36.
GABE

THE DOOR TO Kim's bedroom is sealed like a crime scene. Yellow police tape, which I got for her from the station when we were in middle school, covers the door in a big X from corner to corner. The words DO NOT CROSS repeat themselves against the wood. A warning. One that I'm almost tempted to heed. A cowardly part of me wants to run back down the steps and out the Dowds' front door and not stop until I am home.

Beside me, Sonya shudders. She reaches out, brushes her finger-tips against the tape. It's old and filthy, and her fingers come away with a gray coating of dust. It's as if Kimberly hasn't been back here in years.

"They really don't know how to clean, do they?" Sonya whispers through the corner of her mouth.

That forces a surprised laugh out of me. "Not even a little bit." I almost snort.

She sighs dramatically. "Writers." Then she places her hand on the knob, without bothering to wipe off the dust, and turns it.

Kimberly's room is one of the few places we've rarely visited as a group; Sonya's house is our usual hangout spot. We've been in Kimberly's house hundreds of times—in the living room, in the dining room, out back, pretending to be volcanoes in the mounds of crackly leaves that fall from the big oak tree every autumn. But we hardly ever migrate up to the sanctum of her bedroom. Standing here now, it feels almost like a holy place—the room bathed in dim pink light coming in through the sheer curtains; her bed a disastrous knot of sheets and blankets and old, ratty stuffed animals; one wall lined with bookshelves, crammed with cracked, broken spines, some of the books read and reread so many times the titles and authors aren't even legible anymore.

It's an almost-perfect representation of who Kimberly is—spunky, feminine, poetic.

And closed off, I think. *A lot like her best friend.*

I glance at Sonya. Her head is tilted back, the magenta sunlight glowing in red streamers through her hair. Her lips are parted, eyes kind of wide and stunned. She looks the way I feel—as if we're standing in the rainbow mosaic of stained-glass windows in an old stone church. We're invaders of the worst kind. We definitely shouldn't be in here.

And yet.

"Do we even know what we're looking for?" I ask. I do one sweep of the room, then another, hoping that my eyes will catch on something that stands out, something that doesn't make sense, something that isn't fundamentally *Kimberly*. But it's all here: the books, the mess, the silence. Even the pack of Big Red chewing gum on her nightstand—her breath always smells like cinnamon.

"No idea," Sonya says. "Something . . . totally bizarre? Something that's definitely not any of this stuff." She casts a long gaze around, her neck stretched as if she's trying to see up on top of the shelves, looking for something that might be hidden there. All I see are old board games—Operation, Pictionary, Ghost Castle—in a haphazard stack.

I step sideways, meaning to slip between Sonya and the mussed bed to the other side of the room—not that I'm eager to come farther into a place that feels, for reasons I can't explain, like it doesn't want us here. But as I move behind Sonya, she steps backward, right into me, and we almost topple together onto the bed. I grab her shoulders and plant my feet like I'm about to be tackled on the football field, and we manage to stay upright. We're close, though. Close enough that I can smell the fruity, flowery fragrance of her shampoo, can see the gentle slope of her neck down to her shoulder.

Before I have time to even process any of that, I realize that my hands are still on her shoulders, and so does she. She jerks away from me, shimmies past, back to the doorway, as if her first instinct was to run away.

"Oh, god . . . uh . . . I'm sorry," I say, drooping my head, trying to shrink down into myself, roll up like an armadillo and hide.

"It's fine," she says, hugging herself. Putting up her defenses. Sending the same message she's been sending for months, the one that I've been choosing to ignore.

I sit on the edge of the bed. The metal frame cries out a rusty screech.

"Gabe—" she starts.

"Please don't." I cut her off, staring into the palms of my hands, still scraped in places from Dagger Hill. My shoulder still hurts, but it's dull compared with the agony I feel in my chest. I shouldn't even be worrying about this. We told Mrs. Dowd the only important thing right now is finding Kimberly, which is true.

And yet.

"I get it," I continue. "You've been shutting me out for almost a year. It's not like I haven't noticed. I just . . . I guess I was still hoping that . . . that maybe there was something there. I . . . I get it, Sone."

"No," she says. She's squeezing herself even tighter now. "Gabe, you really *don't* get it."

"What is there not to get? I keep putting myself out there, and you keep shutting me down. I thought . . . at the winter formal, when we danced . . ." I close my eyes and pictures of that night swim up out of the darkness. The icicle lights dangling from the ceiling of the school gym, the bleachers draped in blue and white tissue paper streamers. Mannheim Steamroller's version of "Little Drummer Boy" playing through the PA system because the school can't afford decent speakers.

The four of us were sitting at a table, Charlie making eyes at Elizabeth Williamson across the room, Sonya and Kimberly sitting close so they could hear each other talking. And me, on the other side of the table, feeling a silk ribbon cinch tight around my heart every time Sonya smiled or laughed or glanced at me. School was out for the holidays, and we were full of nervous excitement for whatever the night had in store and for the days after, when we'd be huddled together in one of our houses, watching movies, reading comic books, playing Nintendo. I asked Sonya to dance, and she didn't hesitate, just took my hand and led me out to the dance floor, where we swayed together while Chip Davis sang, *"Pa-rum pum pum pum."*

"Gabe, the four of us went to that as friends, remember?" Sonya says, bringing me back to the lightless heat of now. "We were just having a good time." She says that last part so quietly that I almost can't hear her. She's hurting, but I can't help myself.

"But I *felt* something," I say. "I felt it then, and I feel it now. And I know you do, too. I can see it."

She's quiet for a moment before she says, "I don't know what you think you see, but you're right. I do feel something."

I look up at her, my throat tight with a hope that I haven't felt since that night in December. But then I see Sonya staring down at the Big Red gum on Kimberly's nightstand. She picks it up, holds it to her nose, inhales deeply. And even though there are tears leaking from the corners of her eyes, she smiles. Tiny and sweet and all to herself. The last of that hope dies in me then, and the hairline fractures that have been forming across the surface of my heart all year finally split, opening wide.

"I feel all the same things you feel," Sonya says, looking at me with such bravery that it makes me feel awful and proud at the same time. "I just don't feel them . . . for you."

The weight of her words pulls my shoulders down. My body feels like it's full of sand. But there's also a strange lightness forming in my chest, something bright and, somehow, happy. Something that I can't describe and don't fully understand yet.

I see the winter formal again. Sonya and Kimberly, leaning in to each other, smiling. For the first time, I really register the look that

Sonya is giving Kimberly. It's the same look I was giving Sonya all night.

"Oh my god," I whisper. I look at her, and I see her, *really* see her. That lightness inside me, I realize, is the sense that I've been needlessly forcing myself into these tense, awkward situations for months, dragging Sonya into them with me. I've been letting myself down and taking it out on her. And all this time if I'd just opened my eyes . . . "Sonya, I don't know what to say."

She comes over, sits down on the bed next to me. The frame squeals again, and we both cringe. "You don't have to say anything," she says. "Just be there for me, okay? Be my friend, no matter what."

"But how can I do that when . . . when I'm in love with you?" I say, knowing it sounds pathetic, knowing that those feelings are already collapsing, to be replaced by a whole slew of other emotions— sadness, embarrassment, joy.

Sonya sighs. "You're not in love with me, Gabe. You're in love with . . . I don't know . . . with the *idea* of being in love with me, I guess. You're the same as I am. Stuck in this town, waiting to graduate so you can move on to the parts of your life that feel like they're really happening." Her eyes shift to the window. The coming night has almost completely swallowed the light outside. "Windale, everything and everybody here . . . it's just a fantasy."

I try to hold the tremor in my voice still and keep the tears behind my eyes. "But what about this?" Gesturing wildly around me, trying to make her understand. "What about the four of us? You guys are . . . *everything* to me. Is that a fantasy, too?"

She thinks about it, chewing her lip. "I don't know. Maybe. I hope not."

We're quiet for a while, staring at the shadows of our feet on the tan carpet. I heave a long, heavy sigh. I've been tying myself into knots about this for months, and finally I begin to feel those tangles unclench.

"You know, I would have stood outside your house with a boom box over my head," I say. And, thank god, she laughs.

She puts her hand in mine, drops her head to my shoulder, giggling. "I know, buddy. I know."

I don't think there's anything left to say, so we just sit there in the dreary dark. My eyes circle the room again, still searching for whatever it was we came here to find. I let my gaze linger on the spot where Kimberly's chewing gum was, the gum that's now closed in Sonya's hand. It was resting on top of a book, *The Lion, the Witch, and the Wardrobe* by C. S. Lewis. A strange book for Kim. Her tastes usually lie in the complex, meaty volumes of old literary fiction, not in children's fantasies. But I don't think I've ever seen her without a book somewhere on her person—eventually, the options have to become limited, don't they?

It's not just the book I'm interested in, though. There's something tucked into its pages, pushing the paperback cover into an arching bulge. I can just make out the shape of it.

"What is that?" I ask to no one in particular. I lean across Sonya and flick the bedside lamp on, then grab the book off the nightstand.

"That's a book, Gabe," Sonya says. "I know you don't read much, but you should at least recognize one when you see it."

I shoot her a look, and she shrugs, grinning. I flip the book open to the place where there's a thick piece of paper stuck between the pages—about a third of the way in. It doesn't look like it was put in any particular place, just slipped inside the book in a hurry, maybe as Kimberly was heading out the door Friday morning. The card stock, or whatever it is, is folded into quarters. As I pull it open, Sonya leans in to see.

It's a drawing, done in big, sweeping strokes with a thick black marker. Kimberly has dabbled in art before, impressionist paintings that Charlie and I have to turn our heads in every direction to even begin to understand what they're supposed to look like, but this is something different. The sight of it sends a cold droplet racing down my spine.

Dagger Hill is on the page in front of us, a startlingly perfect copy of the trees and bushes and the boulder. The one that was once a make-believe pirate ship and the place where Charlie bound the four of us Almost Nobodies together with a promise. He's in the picture, too. Along with me and Sonya and Kimberly. But we're dead. Strewn around the boulder, our bodies mangled, black spatters that I'm sure are meant to look like blood painting the rounded face of the boulder. In the image, Charlie is lying on top of the rock, one arm dangling, his lower half gone entirely. I look into my own open eyes and wonder what my last thought was in this version of history, Kimberly's nightmare.

"What does it mean?" Sonya murmurs, taking the paper and holding it close to her face, as if testing to see if it's real.

"I don't know," I say. My voice is a frail whisper. "She must have drawn this before the plane crash."

All my notions about the plane crash—how it happened, *why* it happened—and Kimberly's being taken simply by chance disintegrate into nothing. Higgins and TerraCorp may have made a lot of mistakes that helped cause the plane to end up where it did, but it wasn't just a random, freak accident. Kimberly knew something the rest of us didn't. Maybe she even would have recognized the Bug Man if she'd been conscious. Maybe the Bug Man recognized her.

"We need to get to the diner," I say, standing. I toss the Narnia book back onto Kimberly's nightstand, glad to finally be leaving this place. "See if Charlie found anything out."

Sonya nods. "Okay. But first we have to make a stop."

"Where?"

"The Banshee Palace," she says.

"You really want to go there? After everything you saw?" I can't imagine what that nightmare was like—if it was a nightmare at all—but I know I wouldn't want to visit room 6 if it was me.

She shrugs. "Not really. But Kimberly could actually be there. I don't know why Mrs. Rapaport would have shown it to me if it wasn't important."

"I don't know, Sone . . ."

"Let's just check it off the list, okay? Please?"

I take a few seconds to think it over, staring down at Kimberly's drawing, the nape of my neck tingling. "Okay," I say.

We hurry through the bedroom door and down the stairs. Mrs. Dowd is in the kitchen, fiddling with a cantaloupe. She might be trying to cut it open, but she has no knife.

"Find anything?" she calls to us.

I open my mouth to say yes, but Sonya beats me to the punch.

"Nothing that stands out," she calls back to Kim's mom. "Sorry, Mrs. Dowd. We'll keep you posted, though, okay?"

Mrs. Dowd only nods, staring sadly down at her melon. With that, Sonya and I slip out into a humid summer evening. I look across the walkway to the road and halt in my tracks. Sonya walks right into my back and half trips around me.

"What the hell, Gabe?" she says. But then she sees what I see.

Parked against the sidewalk is the Crown Victoria patrol car I'd recognize anywhere. The bubble lights are dark, the word CHIEF printed in large, faded letters across the side. My dad is leaning against the passenger door, legs stretched out in front of him, arms crossed, examining his nails. His eyes flip up and catch onto mine, like fishhooks. And he's about to reel me in.

"Change of plans," I say.

37.

CHARLIE

THE BUILDING ON Perkiomen Avenue where the *Windale Press* keeps its offices looks the same as it did when I left there on Friday, but it *feels* different. It feels tall and dark and crooked in the waning daylight, like the Bates house in *Psycho*. That makes me think of the Sunrise Theater. Every October they have Flick or Freak nights when they play old horror movies from sundown to sunup. The Hitchcock ones are my favorite. Not because they're very scary, but because of the tension. You can feel something terrible coming in Hitchcock's movies. A lingering sense of dread that you can't quite figure out until it's too late.

That's what I feel now.

I glance up and down the street again, making sure I don't see any flashes of green coming toward me. Or black leather, for that matter. It's strange to think that I'm less afraid of the Bug Man than I am of Higgins, but there it is. So far, Higgins is still the one who's done the most damage here. The worst thing the Bug Man's done is kidnap Kimberly, and according to Sonya, there's a chance that Kim's still alive. Not to mention the Bug Man may have saved our asses at Sonya's house. Why would he do that?

It, I remind myself. *Why would* it *do that?*

The word *anomaly* keeps knocking around in my head, like the clapper in a church bell.

As I hobble up the steps to the *Press* office door, I wince with every small motion of my broken leg. The pain has reached an overwhelming peak—the whole thing is swollen, pressing painfully against the inside of my cast; that grinding-bone sensation is still there, maybe worse than ever; and I can feel it throbbing from thigh to ankle in time with my pulse. I'm starting to understand that I may be doing permanent damage to my leg.

It doesn't matter right now, though. There's not a lot I can do to help that situation. I'm about to find out if there's anything I *can* help.

The buzzer sounds when I press the button. When I was here Friday, Don answered almost immediately, because he was expecting me. This time, there's no response.

"C'mon," I mutter, pushing the button again. "Don! Don, are you in there?" I holler, leaning on my crutch and cupping my hands around my mouth. I realize I'm probably drawing attention to myself, but Higgins hasn't exactly posted WANTED signs around town. Besides, she probably doesn't want any more eyes on her than necessary, which means she can't put eyes on us. That's what the trackers were for, I imagine, so she could keep tabs on me and Sonya and Gabe without being too conspicuous. The people of Windale are gossip-hungry vultures, just like in any small town—if there's a lot of chatter and it's about you, then you're probably up to no good.

I press my whole palm against the door buzzer, as if applying more pressure will somehow make it louder. "Don! If you're in there, open up! It's Charlie! Charlie Bencroft!"

Behind the door, I hear movement—some rustling papers, hollow footsteps, angry muttering. Then Don's voice, saying, "Now is not a good time, Mr. Bencroft." His voice is wavering and pitchy.

"Don," I say through the door. I glance up at the half-circle window in the top of the door, expecting to see Don there, watching me through the sheer curtain. He's not, but I still feel like someone is looking. "Don, please. I really need your help. I'm . . . I'm in kind of a situation here—"

The door flies open then, so fast I hardly hear the knob turn. The hinges squeal.

"I know exactly what kind of *situation* you're in, Mr. Bencroft,"

Don says, his voice low and harsh. He's got his trench coat on, as if I caught him just as he was leaving. "My sources around town tell me the army is everywhere."

I have to scoff. "Your *sources*? You mean Maureen Newcomb at the hair salon?"

Don scowls. "Very funny, Bencroft. You have no idea what I know, okay? First, the army was looking for your friend, the Dowd girl. Supposedly, anyway. Mostly they were looking for . . . something else. And now? Now, they're looking for *you*." He jabs his pointer finger at me. "Along with the chief's son and Dr. Gutierrez's daughter."

Something in my expression must tell him he's right, because he folds his arms and leans against the doorframe with smug satisfaction. But then he looks me over—at my leg and my crutch and the way I must look, pale and sweaty and struggling to stand up straight—and his expression softens.

Mine doesn't. I haul myself up one more step, until I'm right under Don's chin. "Listen, McGruff the Crime Dog. You're right. Is that what you want to hear? I didn't come here because I want to put you in any danger—I think the whole town is deep enough into that already. I came here because you know what goes on in Windale better than anyone, and I *need your help*."

The tension goes out of his shoulders, and he looks away for a moment, chewing the inside of his cheek. Then his eyes swing back to me. "Go on," he says.

"We're looking for someone," I say, feeling a small tug of hope in my chest. I slip the Polaroids Dr. Reed gave us from my pocket and hold them up for Don to see. "Somebody jumped out of that plane right before it crashed," I tell him. "We think it might be the pilot, and we think he can help us prove that the army is trying to cover their tracks, make it seem like they were never in Windale at all—"

Don completes my thought for me: "Before the proverbial shit hits the proverbial fan." His face is slack with shock, and he stands upright, his eyes darting from side to side.

"Right," I say.

"Come inside, Mr. Bencroft," Don says. He turns on his heels and disappears into the office, leaving the door open. As he walks away, I see him chewing on a hangnail, mumbling to himself.

I follow him inside, where it's only a little cooler thanks to a box fan propped near his desk.

"You won't believe a word I tell you," Don says. He leans back against his desk, pushes off it, leans back again.

"Yeah, that's kind of going around today," I reply.

"Where did you get those photos?"

"Long story, but the original pictures were taken at Dagger Hill just as the storm rolled in on Friday. Just before . . . well, you know."

"Yes. Yes, I know." He looks at me again with what must be renewed clarity. "Charlie, you look awful. Sit down. Please." He drags over one of the stiff wooden chairs that I sat in a couple of days ago and helps me lower myself into it. The relief of pushing my leg out in front of me and taking some of the pressure off it is so great that I might cry.

"You were right about the army, Don," I say. "They are looking for us. Sonya may have opened a can of worms using her dad's personal computer."

His eyes widen. "You're kidding. What did she find out?"

"I'll tell you. But first I need to know that you can help me track down the pilot."

He nods grimly. "I think I can do you one better," he says.

I cock my head, confused. I open my mouth to ask him what he means, but then I look down at the desktop behind him, really taking it in for the first time. There are maps of Windale spread out across the entire surface, along with other papers—what look like old issues of the newspaper, typed letters with official seals, ancient photographs of grim-looking men in tweed coats. There are also two coffee mugs perched on the desk, both still steaming.

"Don . . . ?" I say slowly. "Who else is here?"

Don doesn't reply, but he glances up over the top of my head.

Right behind me, the floor creaks.

My first thought is of the Bug Man, looking down at me through the foggy lenses of its gas mask, the sound of its breathing thin and muffled through the rubber. If it breathes at all.

When I twist around in my chair, though, it's not the Bug Man standing there, but a regular man, dressed in clothes that are a little big for his lean frame and definitely in the style of Don Cranston. He's got a strong neck and a stern face, white skin, piercing blue eyes, and sandy blond hair (*like Kimberly's*, I think) that fades up to a high and tight military cut.

The blue eyes shift to the Polaroids still in my hand, the blurry green parachute plumped up like a rotten apple.

"Not my best picture," the guy says, looking kind of sheepish. "But I bet there are some from my West Point days that are much worse." He sticks his hand out, grinning awkwardly.

"Charlie," Don says behind me. "Meet Captain Jake Rinaldi. The pilot you're looking for."

"I . . ." The words get lost in transit. I open my mouth to try again but come up empty.

"C'mon, kid," Rinaldi says, his hand still hovering between us. "Shit or get off the pot. My arm's getting tired."

With what feels like a weightless arm, I take Rinaldi's hand and shake. His grip is firm but not intimidating. He comes around my chair and joins Don at the desk, picks up one of the mugs, takes a sip. He grimaces and glances at Don to make sure he's not looking before spitting the coffee back into the cup. As he sets the mug down, Rinaldi tips me a wink.

"I . . . don't understand," I finally manage.

"I said you wouldn't believe me," Don replies. "If I'd said I knew exactly where he was, you would've thought I was full of it. That whole entry there was just good timing."

"I was hiding in the basement," Rinaldi says, folding his arms and leaning casually on the desk's edge. His tone sounds sulky, as if he'd been put there as punishment.

"How long?" I ask, looking to Don.

"Since Friday," he says. "I was outside trying to get pictures of the storm when I noticed the parachute through the mist. It was hazy from down here. Only really visible to me because I was using a longer lens. Then the plane crashed and . . . well, if anyone was looking up at the clouds before, they weren't after that. All eyes were on Dagger Hill from that point forward."

"Except for yours," Rinaldi says, and nudges Don with his elbow. Don blushes and adjusts the collar of his shirt. "Yeah, well."

"I came down pretty hard," Rinaldi explains. "The storm wanted to throw me every which way. Don must have been watching me the whole time, because he knew right where to find me."

"He was unconscious when I got to him near the park."

"I *wish* I'd landed in the park," Rinaldi says, rolling his eyes.

"Tree," Don says, gesturing with his arms. "Big one."

"Somehow, this guy got me down," Rinaldi continues. "Untangled the chute and used it to drag me back to his car."

"It wasn't a big deal." Don waves his hand demurely. "The rain made it easy."

"Sure." Rinaldi lifts his eyebrows and bumps his elbow into Don again. "Anyway, Don brought me back here and nursed me back to health."

"All it took was a cup of hot tea," Don says. "I would have taken him to the medical center, but . . . I don't know. Some instinct told me to bring him here. And when Jake came to, he was . . . terrified. Told me we had to stay hidden. So that's what we did."

The whole time, my head swivels back and forth with the rhythm of their story, from one man to the other then back again as they speak. At that last part, though, my eyes land on Rinaldi, whose face is suddenly pale. The muscles in his jaw flex.

"Hold on," I say. "Can we go back and talk about why you jumped out of the plane in the first place? No offense, Captain, but that crash kind of fucked up my summer, and I'd really like to figure out what went wrong."

Rinaldi looks at me, his body very still. "Did you see it?" he asks.

My blood turns icy. I don't have to ask him what he means. I swallow, then nod once.

"Yeah," he says. "That's what happened." He looks away, choking back his emotions.

"Captain Rinaldi," I say, leaning forward. "Whatever that thing is, it has my friend. I could really use your help."

"Yeah, well, it has my friend, too," Rinaldi says, turning sharply back to me. "Or I guess the better way of saying it is that thing . . . *is* my friend. Or was. God, I don't know. This whole thing went to hell in a handbasket so quick. It's all goddamn Higgins's fault." He shoves himself away from the desk and takes a few angry strides to the window and looks out.

I glance at Don, trying to understand.

"His copilot," Don says. "Jake wasn't alone on the plane when it took off from TerraCorp."

"That's not even the half of it," Rinaldi clarifies. "Thompson and I weren't the only living things on board. Maybe we were the only *human* living things, but . . ." He shivers.

"The Bug Man," I mutter.

They both look at me and say, "*The Bug Man?*"

I shrug. "That's what Gabe calls him. I guess because of the mask?"

"Mask?" Rinaldi says. "Kid, I don't know what you and your friends have seen, but the thing I saw on the plane wasn't wearing a mask. It was . . . It was horrible."

"What happened to your friend, Captain? Thompson, I mean. Your copilot." I feel my stomach turn over at the thought of what his answer might be.

"It ate him," Rinaldi says. "That thing *ate* Thompson. Or . . . or it became him. I don't know for sure. All I remember is this dark . . . *thing* behind us. It filled up the whole cargo bay. The controls went haywire. We could hear this screeching through our headsets. Then Thompson wasn't Thompson anymore. It broke his body. Made it longer. Made it faster. Made it stronger. It ripped his jaw apart when it screamed through him. Oh god, I'll never forget that sound till the day I die." His voice cracks and he finally breaks, letting the tears come. "They told us it would stay contained, but they were wrong. They've been wrong about everything. Everyone except that scientist. Claudia. At TerraCorp. She's the only one who has any damn sense at that godforsaken place."

"Funny," I say. "She said the same thing about you. She's the one who got us those photos back after Higgins took them. Well, sort of."

Rinaldi grins, wiping his face. "Clever lady."

There's a stretch of silence. Outside, every car I hear is an army transport coming to haul us away, put us at the bottom of some hole where we'll never be found while Higgins tries to sweep her mess under the rug.

"Captain," I say when I think it's safe to speak. "Why did Higgins bring that thing here in the first place?"

Rinaldi shrugs. "It's a lot of science jargon. Usually, if it doesn't have anything to do with flying, football, or whiskey, it goes right over my head."

"It's all right, Jake," Don says. "Tell him what you told me."

The pilot hesitates, looking at me the way I'd look at myself if I were in his shoes: as a kid who has no business getting caught up in government-level problems like this one.

But then he says, "I didn't pick up on much. But what I did hear is that Higgins had one of these things, and TerraCorp was monitoring another."

The anomalies.

"I guess they're connected somehow, because when we left the West Coast, the thing was all but dead. By the time we were over Nebraska, Higgins was scared out of her wits, and the . . . what'd she-call it? The anomaly? It was the most active it's ever been. Wreaked havoc on my systems. We nearly crashed on our way here."

"The closer you got to Windale," I say, paraphrasing Dr. Reed's words, "the stronger it got."

Rinaldi dips his head. "Right. And I guess the thing that's here. The other anomaly. It was responding, too. The guy who runs the lab at TerraCorp was livid. Wouldn't let Higgins take hers off the runway. He must have some dirt on her, because she eventually backed down. But . . . she's a coward."

"She was afraid," I say.

"After she saw how strong it got, yeah," Rinaldi continues. "At first, though, she thought that bringing her anomaly closer to the Windale anomaly was the obvious thing to do. There was something about the way they were . . . I forget what she said exactly. Something about the way they were *talking* to each other. Can you believe that? A couple of anomalies, thousands of miles apart, communicating?"

"It's not the most outlandish thing I've heard in the past two days," I say, rubbing my temples.

"Listen, if there's one thing I know about Higgins, it's that she is one hundred percent prepared for everything. She'll do whatever she can to stay six moves ahead of her enemy. The anomalies were a threat. She wanted to know more about them, but the people at TerraCorp kept shutting her out. So she took the whole thing into her own hands."

"Shit," I say. "Shit, shit, shit."

"That about sums it up, kid."

"Where are Gabe and Sonya now, Charlie?" Don asks.

"At Kimberly's house," I reply. "Sonya saw something that makes her think that Kim is alive, so they went to try to figure out why the Bug Man would want to take her."

"Can you please stop calling it that?" Rinaldi says, squeezing his eyes shut. "If that thing looks like a man at all, it's only because it's wearing my friend's body."

"Sorry. It just kind of stuck." To Don, I say, "After they leave Kimberly's place, we're supposed to meet back up at the diner."

"Why haven't you kids gone to Chief Albright with any of this?" Don says.

"Because up until Sonya hacked into TerraCorp's database, the chief was Higgins's biggest problem. She would have been breathing down his neck."

Don nods, and we all fall quiet.

After a while, a thought occurs to me. "Don. How much do you know about the history of Dagger Hill?"

He grins, walks around to the other side of his desk, and pulls open a drawer. A second later he comes up with an overstuffed folder that's remarkably similar to the one Sonya found in her dad's office; Don even drops the folder onto the desk in a similar way.

"How much time do you have?" he asks.

WINDALE DESCENDING
(interlude)

38.

AROUND THE SAME time that June Rapaport is squeezing Mel O'Connell's windpipe shut with her bare hands, Rebecca Conner is pulling her patrol car into a spot directly in front of Ricky's Video Rentals on Baker Street. She comes out here practically every weekend to get a movie. She usually wants to pick something romantic, but Mel, who stays behind at the house because their relationship is still only for those on a need-to-know basis and nobody else needs to know, asks her to pick up some gory horror flick. Truth be told, she secretly enjoys those kinds of movies better than the romance ones, anyway.

Today, though, she's here on official police business—somebody called the station and asked if they could send an officer out to check on the owner of the video store, Ricky Montoya. Not only is Ricky the only name in home video rentals in Windale, PA, but he's also the only name in electronics. And he's handy with them, too. The display he put together for all those fancy TV sets he's selling is nothing short of magical to look at. But the caller said they'd spotted Ricky on the roof of the strip mall, assembling . . . well, they couldn't say exactly what it was he was building, just that something didn't feel right.

Rebecca gets out of the car and immediately notices something tall and metallic protruding from the roof of Ricky's shop. It looks like a cross between a radio antenna and a metal sculpture. She has no idea what to make of it other than maybe Montoya is trying his hand at ham radio. Though, Rebecca is pretty sure, you don't need an antenna that big.

Maybe—and this is far more unlikely—Ricky's figured out how to intercept the army's radio communications here in Windale. Maybe *he knows exactly what's going on behind the curtain that Colonel Higgins has drawn over the entire disaster and can give Rebecca an insider tip. Maybe this mess will be over before it gets worse.*

Don't hope too hard, Becky, *her mother would have said at a time like this.* Or you'll scare the miracle away.

She goes to the glass door at the front of Ricky's Video Rentals and stops when she sees that the neon OPEN *light in the window is dark and that there's a paper sign taped inside the door.* CLOSED FOR GOVERNMENT TAKEOVER, *the sign reads in black marker.*

"Well, that's just not funny at all," *Rebecca mumbles to herself.*

She tries the door. Locked. She raps her knuckles against the glass a few times. "Mr. Montoya, it's Deputy Conner! We received a call from someone concerned about your well-being. Can you open up please?"

There's nobody else around. The Wag's and the Pizza Hut are both open for business, but the parking spots in front of them are all empty. The arcade won't open again until Thursday night. And no one is ever really sure whether the adult bookstore is open. The midday sun is pressing down against the windows and doors of the entire strip mall, and it's like standing near an open oven. Rebecca is already sweating, wishing for the AC that's still running in her cruiser.

"Mr. Montoya!" *she yells again, louder this time. She knocks on the glass as hard as she can without breaking it.* "Mr. Montoya, I need you to open the door and let me in! This is the police!"

A minute passes, then another. Finally, someone pushes open the door to the Pizza Hut and sticks her head out. Rebecca recognizes her as one of the high school students—Hannah something. She's got a face spattered with dark freckles and a silly-looking visor on her head emblazoned with the Pizza Hut logo.

"Deputy Conner?" *Hannah says.*

"Hi, hon," *Rebecca replies, moving down the sidewalk a few steps to where Hannah is standing. The door is propped open behind her, and a divinely cool breeze wafts out from inside.* "I'm looking for the gentleman who owns the video store. You know him?"

"Ricky?" *Hannah says.* "Sure, I know him. But I don't think he's in there. *We haven't seen him in a couple of days. Not since . . ."* She nods toward Dagger Hill, where from here, Rebecca can just make out the nasty new beauty mark the plane gouged into its face.

"Really?" Rebecca replies. *"No offense, but Ricky seems like the kind of guy who'd be more inclined to hike up his prices right about now. I guess the technical term for someone like him is shrewd, but where I come from, we prefer the word* weasel.*"*

Hannah laughs. *"You're not wrong. But he's also the kind of guy who might skip town before things get really sketchy. We call that a 'poser.'"*

"An astute observation, my dear," Rebecca says, grinning. *"Thanks for your help. If you happen to see him, do you mind giving the police station a call?"*

"Not at all." Hannah smiles and ducks back into the chilly paradise of the Pizza Hut.

Rebecca almost gets into her car and leaves, but she decides a look around back, just to make sure, would be proper protocol. With only a tiny groan, she gives her belt a hearty tug and trudges around to the back of the strip mall.

There's a line of green dumpsters, all overflowing with heaps of trash and surrounded by huge, buzzing flies. More searing blacktop with chemical shimmers radiating off it. There's also a ladder, propped up against the back of the building, right where Ricky's place is. That's presumably how Ricky got his contraption onto the roof, but there's not a chance in hell Rebecca's climbing that thing. If the Montoya kid passed out on the roof and is baking in the sun, then he's just going to be a cooked chicken—Rebecca's terrified of heights.

But she notices a sliver of darkness beneath the ladder that gives her hope. The back door to Ricky's Video Rentals is ajar, which hopefully means that even though Ricky's business is closed, Ricky is still working.

Rebecca walks past the dumpsters and their vile stench, goes around the shaky-looking ladder, and presses her ear to the open door. She hears nothing. Not a good sign. She knocks, knuckles banging against metal. "Mr. Montoya! This is Deputy Conner! I'm here on official police business! The door is open, and I'm coming in!"

With that, she pulls open the hefty door. It groans loudly, echoing through the silent back lot. Rebecca steps inside with her hand instinctively resting on the butt of her sidearm.

The back office is completely dark except for the too-bright sunlight reflecting in from outside. The AC's been off for a couple of days, it feels like, and the air inside is stuffy and still, making it hard to breathe. From the front of the store, Rebecca can hear something clicking, over and over, a rapid ticktickticktickticktick. On the swatch of the bizarrely patterned carpet that she can see from back here, she can see lights flickering.

"Ricky?"

Rebecca doesn't want to go up to the front, not after the weekend she's already had. Between Clark Webber's cows and the plane crash and the chief going toe to toe with that vile colonel—

But she goes, because she's a good cop and, more important, a good person who cares about the people who live in this town with her, even the weasels and the posers. She moves through the inky dark of the back office to the door with a sign on it that says SALES FLOOR and nudges it open.

The "sales floor" is partially lit by sunlight filtering in through the tinted front windows. But the flickering light is coming from the collection of TV sets that used to be neatly arranged on one wall. Now, they're scattered across the store. Thrown there, it seems, by somebody. A few of the screens are broken, shattered inward to reveal the wires and circuits inside. The others are powered on, with their screens like frenzied snow globes, sputtering static and noise. One of them is making that god-awful ticking sound. There are huge craters in the walls, and most of the particleboard shelves have been knocked over, tipped into one another like dominoes. The cardboard sleeves that belong to the VHS tapes are torn and strewn about—Rebecca can see the grinning faces of famous actors watching her from every corner of the store.

And there, with his head stuffed inside the broken shell of a thirty-two-inch Sony TV, is Ricky. Jagged teeth of glass stab into his chest and neck. Rebecca can't even see his face—it's lost in the maw of the gray creature that ate it. There's a puddle of blood under Ricky's body, soaked into the psychedelic carpet. It looks like dark, toxic ooze in the cold blue light of the other televisions.

Rebecca swallows something that might have been a sob or a scream, and she takes a step toward Ricky. She has to check his pulse, but something about this place, about the way he's lying face-first in the shattered remains of a television, sends a shiver up her spine. She doesn't think she's seen so much carnage in just two days as she has this weekend.

As she gets closer, she notices something in Ricky's hand, pale and limp as it is, but still holding on. It's a black plastic rectangle, the very thing that Ricky Montoya lived and, apparently, died for: a VHS tape.

Rebecca reaches behind her and yanks the radio out of her belt to call the chief.

39.

CHET LANDRY DOES not refer to himself as Charlie Bencroft's stepfather. In the same way that Charlie thinks of Chet only as his mom's husband, Chet thinks of Charlie as the bitch's kid. And since the bitch got locked out of town, and the bitch's kid has gone AWOL, Chet is left to fend for himself. Not an easy task, considering Sammy was supposed to bring the goods home with her and not a single other person in town that Chet knows has anything that can help take away his shivers.

He's been alone in the trailer since Saturday afternoon, chewing his fingernails down to their quicks, knocking back can after can of beer, alternating between nibbling on some saltine crackers and puking his brains out. Every time he hears a noise outside, he's positive it's the army showing up to drag him out and toss him into a cell. Chet's been mumbling to himself, but he's also trying to keep quiet because maybe, just maybe, the army has already been there. They could have planted a bug in one of the ceiling fans, could be listening in on everything he's doing, which has mostly just been drinking.

Chet sits in his armchair, bobbing his knee up and down, watching himself in the dark TV screen on the other side of the living room. It's quiet and hot. The trailer sits at the northeastern edge of the mobile home park, close enough to Dagger Hill that in the stuffy silence, Chet can just hear the faint echoes of the volunteers combing the woods for the kid's friend, the Dowd girl.

"KIMBERLY!" They're yelling her name, over and over again. "KIMBERLY DOWD!"

Or maybe it's just Chet's hard-boiled brain making him hear things. Either way, it's driving him fucking batshit.

He snatches up the remote from the end table, almost knocking his can of PBR over in the process, and hits the POWER button. There aren't any lights on in the house, but as soon as Chet presses the button, every light bulb flickers. Just a quick, momentary stutter, like an electronic shiver runs through the house.

The TV does come to life, though, only it's not tuned to any channel he recognizes. A brief cloud of static snow fades into darkness, cut through every so often by a thin gray line rolling from the top of the screen to the bottom, like a bad reel in a VHS tape. But Chet doesn't own a VCR.

On the screen, he can just make out something moving around in the fuzzy, unfocused shadows. At first, Chet thinks it's an animal. But it has a humanlike face. And maybe those are arms and legs? They just don't look right. None of this is right. Someone is tampering with Chet's cable lines. Maybe it's the army. Subliminal messaging. They're trying to take advantage of his weakened state and brainwash him.

"I know what you're doing!" Chet shouts at the TV. He hits the POWER button on the remote again, but the TV stays on. He tries a second time. The hazy outline of that thing is still there, lingering in the gray-black square of the screen. Watching him. It's tall, so it has to lean to the side to keep its head in the shot, sort of drooping over, arms hanging limp. There are dark pits where the eyes should be, but they're watching Chet all the same. For a second, he's even sure that it winks at him—a bizarrely human gesture for something that looks like it tried to be a human and couldn't quite get it right.

Chet throws the remote at the screen, and it knocks against the glass with a deep, gonging crack. Then the TV's speakers emit a sound that stabs into Chet's already aching head like a nail. He puts his hands over his ears, but it's not enough to block out the noise. It's as if the sound is coming from inside his own head. That can't be right, though, can it? God, he could use a line right now. Just one, just enough to smooth him out around the edges and bring the bubbling in his brain down to a low simmer.

The noise persists. It jabs into his head, and he falls forward out of his chair, hits the floor on his knees. Chet Landry is crying, dripping snot and tears onto the dirty carpet.

"Please," he moans. "Please make it stop."

He doesn't see the man in the gas mask standing behind the armchair where he was sitting only moments ago, staring down at him. He doesn't realize what's happening as that noise coming from the TV begins to break Chet down and pull him out. Memories and ideas go first, drifting away like flotsam and jetsam on a choppy swath of open sea. Then his personality—his addictions and ailments and the small shred of joyousness that he's reserved for things like NASCAR and rebuilding motorcycle engines. Gone.

Much like it tried to do with Ricky Montoya and June Rapaport, the thing in the TV leaves only enough of Chet behind to retain his motor function and his ability to follow directions, and not much else. Maybe there's a little leftover hatred banging around in there somewhere, but that's all right. That might come in handy.

Chet's crying eventually stops, and he's lying on his side on the floor, drooling from the corner of his mouth. After a few minutes, he pulls his hollowed body up, walks in a straight line across the living room, takes his truck keys off the hook by the door.

It's time to get to work.

As he steps out into the bright June day, unaware that the sun no longer burns his sore eyes, the cavities in his mind where Chet Landry used to exist begin to fill up with a strange sort of song, an ancient nursery rhyme that uses new words to tell an old story:

A song sung one, the end of the line.
A song sung two, we'll be just fine.
A song sung three, dead is divine.
A song sung four, all outta time.

40.

AT ABOUT THE same time that Charlie Bencroft is meeting Captain Jake Rinaldi and Chet Landry is pulling his truck out of the Dagger Hill Mobile Home Park, headed for town, Alice Kemmerer, Chief Albright's secretary, is returning to the station after her lunch break at the diner. Harry Kunz said that Colonel Higgins was there this morning, questioning him about the chief's son and his friends, said that she implied the kids were somehow responsible for Kimberly Dowd's disappearance.

It was a casual conversation—just Harry gabbing away as usual—but Alice tucked the info into the front pocket of her memory and means to get ahold of the chief first thing, let him know what's going on.

As she goes into the office, though, she hears something odd. A woman's voice, floating up from the holding cells in the basement. The door to "the dungeon," as everyone likes to call it, is standing open, and the lights are on downstairs. Now that she thinks about it, Alice remembers seeing Mel's patrol car parked out front. Which is odd, because he's normally out on his afternoon rounds by now.

"Mel?" she calls lightly. She pokes her head into the main part of the office, where everyone's desks are standing unattended. From the basement, that voice keeps going. It's almost like the woman is singing, but the sound of it is faint and crackly. "Hello?" Alice says without much conviction.

She's shaking a little by the time she approaches the basement door, and she's not sure why. Maybe it's because of everything going on in town right now. Maybe it's because she's starting to make out some *of the words to the woman's song, and it doesn't sound like anything she's ever heard before.*

Alice almost gets on the dispatch radio and calls for the chief before going down to the basement. Almost.

But then she sets her shoulders square and marches down the steps to the dungeon. There's a line of three cells down here. The only time they've ever used them during Alice's tenure with the WPD is to let some of the rowdier drunks spilling from the Stuck Pig sleep it off for a night.

Today, two of the cell doors are open, as they usually are. The one in the middle, however, is sealed shut. There's a lump of something on the floor just inside, pressing up against the bars. Something blue and black and uncomfortably familiar. There's a radio playing in there, too. That's what Alice is hearing. A weird, singsong rhyme repeating itself through crackling speakers. Only the voice sounds just as familiar.

"A song sung one, end of the line. A song sung two, we'll be just fine . . ."

Alice is more afraid than ever. She doesn't want to go all the way into the basement, to see what that blue lump is or figure out where the voice is coming from or who it belongs to. There's already a strange undercurrent to that rhyme that's edging itself deeper inside her head. A curled, knobby finger poking at the soft tissue of her mind, probing for weak spots.

She shakes her head, rolls her hands into fists, and takes the last strides into the dungeon.

The first thing she recognizes is June Rapaport's boom box. It's sitting on the cot inside the cell, and the song or rhyme or whatever it is that Alice is hearing is coming from the speakers. But the thing that sets Alice's nerves on edge is that it's June Rapaport's voice singing the words in a weak, whispery falsetto.

". . . A song sung three, dead is divine. A song sung four, all outta time . . ."

June herself is sitting on the cot right beside her stereo. Her head is tilted forward, the thin locks of her gray hair falling across her face. Her mouth does not appear to be moving.

Then Alice's eyes drift away from the older woman and down to that lump on the ground. It's a blue uniform and a black gun belt and a pale face that almost certainly belongs to Mel O'Connell. Or at least, it did. Anyone can see that he's dead now. Alice can see the finger-shaped bruises, dark purple ringed with red, around Mel's throat.

Alice backs away from the cell door, her hand over her mouth. She runs into the cinder block wall and has to stop, can't bring herself to move in any other direction. She can't bring herself to move anywhere—her legs are too weak and shaky. "Oh my god," she whimpers.

After that, all she can do is scream.

41.

COLONEL AUDREY S. HIGGINS *stands at the edge of the newly created crater on the face of Dagger Hill. The earth is churned and charred, black with ash and peppered with debris. Gnarled lengths of metal jut from the softened ground like the limbs of half-buried robots. It's an apocalyptic sight, but nothing so strong as to haunt her dreams. Or at least, it shouldn't be. But ever since arriving in this shit-speck of a town two days ago, Colonel Higgins has had some trouble sleeping.*

Out in the woods, she can see the beams of flashlights bobbing in between the stiff lines of the trees. Some of the people out there are her own soldiers, some of them are volunteers from said shit-speck, which sits down in the valley, streetlights winking to life in the evening gloom. Regardless of whose people they are, everyone in the search party, wading through the damp heat, getting eaten alive by gnats and mosquitoes, they're all yelling the girl's name.

"Kimberly!" Over and over. "Kimberly Dowd!"

There's a ghostlike quality to the way their faceless voices float down from the top of the Hill. A song with no melody. Higgins wishes she had a way to drown out the sound. It's been a long weekend, and she's tired.

Around the crash site, big arc sodium spotlights run on generators, washing cold light across what's left of the wreckage. More of her crew are hustling hither and thither, like a colony of ants—she's had bugs on her brain recently—carrying away the remnants of a picnic.

They've hauled most of the smaller chunks of the plane out of the clearing already. They've had a harder time getting trucks back here to take care of the bigger pieces, like the back half of the fuselage, which rests near the tree line, looking like a crumpled tube of toothpaste. The air smells of grass and char and jet fuel.

The colonel is unbothered by the circumstances—the plane crash, the missing girl, the repercussions of both—which have left some people in the lovely town of Windale feeling angry and rebellious. The chief of police, for instance. His son, too. But Higgins has dealt with her share of overconfident men, and Chief Albright is just another one of them, reactive to his own vulnerable masculinity.

No, what really bothers her is that through all this, across every inch of the destruction that this disaster left behind, both literal and figurative, she has seen not a single dead body. Not one cadaver to be found among the ruins of the aircraft—no cargo, no pilots. Not even the Dowd girl has turned up, dead or otherwise.

What the hell happened up there? she wonders. Thinking, not for the first time, that it was the smartest decision she's ever made to send the plane away from Windale without her and her men on board. They almost didn't make it to TerraCorp to begin with. Captain Rinaldi was none too pleased. Called her a coward. But who else would have the balls to clean up this mess?

And why the hell can't I get a decent night's sleep? Higgins thinks, adding to her lengthening list of questions. Her dreams are filled with voices and the ticking scratch of insect legs across the inside of her skull. Sometimes there's a face, covered with a gas mask. It speaks to her, but not with words. More than once, she's seen a glove-coated fist giving her a thumbs-up.

"Colonel?" somebody says behind her, jarring her out of her thoughts.

Higgins stiffens but doesn't flinch. She never flinches. "Yes?" she says, not bothering to glance at who it is. It's the voice of one of her soldiers, the sound of it vaguely recognizable. It doesn't matter who he is. The information he has is more important to her than his name. Hopefully those damn teenagers have finally been spotted somewhere. She refuses to think about what happened at the Gutierrez house—the good doctor's private office broken into and ransacked, the trackers left sitting in little puddles of blood on the kitchen counter. Higgins's temper begins to flare.

"Uh, ma'am," the soldier says, stumbling. "We have some . . . strange reports coming in from town." He pauses.

"Are you going to elaborate?" Higgins says with a bite in her voice. "Or did you want to draw me a picture?"

"Yes, ma'am. Sorry, ma'am. Three MPs making rounds in town are seeing some odd activity. The chief—Albright—was spotted at Kimberly Dowd's home less than an hour ago."

This is not news. Of course the chief of police would follow up with the missing girl's family. Higgins is only surprised that it's taken him this long to get around to it.

"And?" she says.

"One of the MPs is certain he saw the chief's son and Dr. Gutierrez's daughter leaving there with Chief Albright," the private goes on. "There was something else happening over at the video-rental store, too. Ricky's Rentals or something like that. Our men couldn't get too close, but . . ."

"But what, Private?"

"It looks like the kid who owned the place might be dead." The private seems perplexed by his own story. "And there's one other thing. A senior resident was spotted in the town square—I guess they call it the Triangle—with one of the chief's other deputies. That deputy escorted the old lady to the police station for some reason."

Higgins whirls on the private, who takes a nervous step back. "Why do I care about what happens to some old woman, Private?"

"Because the sergeant who reported it says that only fifteen minutes after the deputy took the old lady into the station, the station's secretary came running out, screaming for someone to help her. There was no one else around, so the MP went in to investigate."

Higgins is losing interest in this part of the story. She's still hung up on the part about Albright and Gutierrez leaving with Albright's father.

But the private surprises her. "The MP found the police deputy dead

230

inside one of the holding cells in the basement," he says. "The old lady was in there with him. Just sitting there, listening to the radio. It . . . it looked like the woman choked the guy to death."

Here we go, *Higgins thinks, not without a little macabre satisfaction.* Now we'll get a handle on this thing. The dead don't know how to lie.

42.

IT'S 7:23 PM *on Sunday, June 18, 1989, in Windale, Pennsylvania. On the west side of town, Deputy Rebecca Conner stands by as the only paramedic for the Windale Medical Center, Dean Harris, pushes the stretcher carrying Ricky Montoya's body into the back of the ambulance. Rebecca refuses to go back into the video store by herself, but she is holding on to the one piece of evidence she found—the VHS tape that Ricky had in his hand when she discovered his body.*

On the other side of town, Chief of Police Jack Albright ushers Gabe and Sonya into the back of his patrol car. They slide in, already protesting, already trying to explain to Jack what they've seen, what they've found. But they don't have to explain anything, and they quit talking as soon as they realize that someone else is in the passenger seat of Jack's sputtering Crown Victoria.

"Dad?" Sonya says.

On Dagger Hill, Colonel Higgins climbs into a jeep, feeling more confident than she has all weekend. She's ready to swoop into town, find those three kids, find the anomaly that she lost when the plane crashed, and then get the fuck out of Dodge.

In the Triangle, at the police station, Alice Kemmerer sits at her desk, her knees pulled up against her narrow torso, weeping quietly into a tissue. A headache forms behind her eyes, and the pain gets worse with every blip and squawk of the dispatch radio—the chief communicating back and forth with Rebecca. Alice hasn't called either of them about Mel yet, just can't bring herself to do it.

Downstairs, in the dungeon, one of Higgins's soldiers stands watch over the holding cell that still contains Deputy Mel O'Connell's body and the elderly June Rapaport, who is not weeping but smiling. She stares up into a corner of the cell, where the painted bricks converge and form a little wedge of shadow. Her stereo is still on, spewing only fuzz now. Her eyes are wide, empty circles. A thin runner of drool dangles from the edge of her lips.

Across the street, Charlie Bencroft is making his way inside the King Street Diner, moving slowly but steadily with his crutch and his broken leg. Don Cranston and Captain Jake Rinaldi are with him. They keep looking around, expecting to be seen, expecting to be arrested. But so far, they're in the clear. They have a lot to tell.

A few blocks east of Windale High School, the shell that used to be Chet Landry is pulling into the parking lot of the old Army-Navy thrift store. He's just a marionette now, but flashes of anger still linger—the slamming of his truck door, the hard shove as he pushes into the store, irritated by the little bell that jingles over his head. He scratches behind his ear, like a dog with an itch, until the sound dwindles.

The kid behind the counter has seen Chet in here before, pays him no mind. Near the back of the store, inside a long, lit glass case, Chet finds what he's been told to get. He punches a hole through the top of the glass with a bare fist, takes what he needs. The kid yells something about calling the police, but Chet ignores him.

On his way out, he makes a quick stop in the apparel section to grab some extras—a black leather jacket, gloves, black jeans, a gas mask.

*   *   *

Back at the strip mall, the ambulance finally pulls away. Rebecca climbs into the driver's seat of her patrol car and tosses the VHS tape onto the seat beside her. The words scrawled in bright red marker on the white label of the tape send an icy ripple down her spine.

IT KNOWS YOUR FEAR

Rebecca drives away, heading back to the police station to meet up with the chief.

Inside the darkened hollow of Ricky's Video Rentals, all the electronics are switched off and silent. Rebecca made sure to power everything down before locking the business up with a set of keys she found in the back office. There wasn't much she could do about the scene inside—there was no way to cover up the windows. If anybody walks past the storefront later this evening or tomorrow, they'll get an eerie eyeful.

But now, in the unsettled stillness, a bluish light appears amid the collapsed wrecks of shelving units on the sales floor. A TV set has just come to life. The screen is projecting nothing but static. And just like on Saturday morning, when Ricky Montoya entered this place as himself for the last time, there's a face etched in the snowstorm. Its features are carved from subtle shadows in the lost-signal haze. The eyes have no pupils, and the mouth is turned up in a snarling grin.

Connected to the back of the television, a dense cable winds through the store, disappearing into the drywall and looping up along the side of a support beam to the roof, where it reemerges and makes S shapes across the gravel, eventually meeting up with the metal structure that Ricky erected not long before his death. From that strange antenna, a signal begins to pulse, echoing out across Windale in bursts. A terrible, unheard sound.

In every Windale home, people are clicking on TVs and radios, computers and video games, popping movies into VCRs, dancing to Mick

Hucknall singing, Just get yourself together or we might as well say goodbye. *Invisible tethers begin to latch themselves onto those electronic vibrations, feeding an undercurrent through them, a secondary sound that carries with it that strange little verse: A song sung one, a song sung two, a song sung three, a song sung four.*

All outta time.

THE BUG MAN

43.
SONYA

"DAD?" I SAY, just after Chief Albright shuts the door.

Dad's sitting in the passenger seat, glasses pushed up onto his brow, squeezing the bridge of his nose with his fingers.

"Hi, little one," he says. His voice is so tender, so fundamentally *him* that I almost weep. "Are you okay?"

"I . . . I guess," I say, not really sure how to respond. "Dad, what are you doing here?" I glance over at Gabe. He looks just as perplexed as I feel.

"It's kind of a long story," Dad replies. Beside him, Chief Albright settles in behind the wheel. "But basically, we were shut out of the database at the lab. Higgins locked down all the computers and put some of her people on to monitor the logins. Our system, as you saw, is pretty outdated. As soon as they noticed someone logging in remotely with my password, they knew something was wrong. Claudia told me they were raiding the house, and I . . . I just thought the worst."

Chief Albright pulls us away from Kimberly's house quietly, letting Dad talk. He exchanges a tense glance with Gabe in the rearview mirror, then refocuses on the road.

"When they didn't find you at the house, I needed to get to you myself. I needed to find a way to keep you out of this." Dad turns in his seat and looks at me through the metal barrier between the front and back of the car. "I thought letting them put the tracker in you and keeping you at home while I sorted everything out from the lab was the best thing to do. But you're too curious for your own good. Just like me."

He grins hopefully, but I don't have anything for him.

He goes on, undeterred. "When I ran out of places to look for you without being too conspicuous, I went to the only person in Windale I knew I could trust."

"My *dad*?" Gabe asks, voicing the surprise we both have on our faces.

"The doc came asking if I could help him find Sonya," Chief Albright explains. "And by then I'd heard from your mother that you were gone, Gabe. Not long after that, Charlie turned up missing, too. So we've been out looking for you three ever since. Meanwhile, the whole goddamn town is in an uproar."

We're all quiet.

"You've lied about so much, Dad," I say. My voice is small and fragile.

He nods. "I know. I never meant to keep secrets from you, sweetheart. I just wanted to protect you."

"Protect me by letting me go up to the place where one of your fucking anomalies is? Practically every day since we were kids?"

Chief Albright speaks up again, holding a finger in the air. "For the record, I was always against that. Don't want to say I told you so, but—"

"*Dad*," Gabe says.

The chief just shrugs and keeps driving.

"What was I supposed to say, Sonya?" Dad asks. "For all we knew, the anomaly was harmless. Sort of. We moved our facility here to research it. It never presented any danger. In fact, you and your friends always seemed to be sort of . . . *drawn* to the Hill. Like you couldn't stay away. I thought maybe it would create some interesting data."

"So I was a guinea pig," I snap, folding my arms.

"No, that's not what I meant, I . . ." Dad sighs. "I don't know what the right answer is. I can explain everything I know about the anomalies, but what you need to know right now is that I love you, and

240

I never, *ever* meant to put you in harm's way. As soon as Higgins had you in her sights, I came looking for you. Your safety is more important than finding the other anomaly. The one that Higgins brought here."

"That's what you've been doing?" I loosen up a bit, softening because I can tell he's being honest.

"Trying to, anyway." Dad closes his eyes, shakes his head. "It hasn't been easy with Higgins looking over my shoulder at every turn. The only reason I was finally able to get away from the lab is because you three distracted her."

"Speaking of which," Chief Albright says, "where's Charlie? We assumed he'd be with you."

"By now, with any luck, he's waiting for us at the diner," Gabe says.

"What did you kids find out?" the chief asks.

I'm the one who answers. "Not a lot. Kimberly saw . . . *something* coming. She drew a picture of us dead on Dagger Hill before Higgins even showed up in Windale with the Bug Man."

"She must have picked up on some of the outbursts the anomalies were giving off just before the second one arrived here," Dad says. "That's what happened to Clark Webber's herd. We believe, anyway. The cows just . . . lost their minds to it."

Chief Albright scrunches his brow together, confused. "*The Bug Man?*"

"That's what we've been calling the second anomaly. Gabe saw it take Kimberly."

"You *what?*" Gabe's dad says, looking at his son through the mirror again, eyebrows raised.

Gabe nods. "At first, I thought it was a hallucination or something. But when we found out Kimberly was actually missing, and Higgins's men started lying about where the plane came from, I . . . I don't know. Something just didn't feel right. He looked like a man dressed in black wearing a gas mask. It has big, bug-eyed lenses and a canister that sticks out front. So . . . Bug Man."

"Jesus," the chief breathes. "Are we all hearing ourselves right now?"

"We were going to meet up with Charlie," I tell them. "We left him at the newspaper office to see if Don Cranston had any leads on where to find the pilot of the plane."

"Dr. G, your friend Claudia told Charlie and me that the pilot might be able to help," Gabe says to my dad. "She said he was the only one who had any reservations about what they were doing here in the first place."

Dad nods. "She's right. When she told me that they had pictures of the pilot jumping from the plane and that he hadn't been found yet, I knew he might be able to undermine whatever story Higgins was going to tell about the crash. But I never expected Claudia to put that on you kids."

"I mean, technically, she gave us the photos to give to my dad so *he* could go looking for the pilot, but . . ." Gabe shrugs. "We kind of got sidetracked."

"So you sent Charlie to *Mr. Junior Detective*?" Chief Albright asks, incredulous.

"Charlie went to Cranston himself," I say. "He had a hunch that maybe Don would already be looking into it. I don't know."

"We trust Charlie," Gabe says.

After a moment, Gabe's dad sighs. "Okay. Then so do I. We'll hit the diner, pick up Charlie, and go back over to the station to figure out what our next move is. While we do that, we can follow up with any leads that Charlie got from Cranston, and the doc can tell us all about the . . . Bug Man."

"We can also assess the Montoya situation," Dad says, mostly to the chief.

"The Montoya situation?" I ask.

"As in *Ricky* Montoya?" Gabe says. "The guy who owns the video store?"

A vague image of Ricky's face comes together in my mind's eye, sitting behind the counter of his video-rental store, sliding VHS tapes into their cardboard sleeves and checking them out to customers. The librarian of Hollywood entertainment in Windale.

"Yes," Chief Albright says. "He's dead. In a very violent way that Rebecca says was similar to what we saw at the Webber farm Friday morning."

"This is getting worse," I say. I can't help but think of Kimberly, of what might be happening to her right this second and knowing that I can't do anything to stop it.

Chief Albright steps on the gas.

44.

CHARLIE

"DAGGER HILL HAS been a hot spot for mystery and murder pretty much since Windale was founded in 1694," Don explains. He's chewing on one of my fries, which makes his voice a little garbled, but I get the gist of it.

I ordered a triple cheeseburger with fries and a chocolate milkshake. My leg is in less agony thanks to some decent pain pills Don gave me back at the office, and I feel like I could eat half the menu in one sitting now that I've had a chance to cool down. Plus, if I'm going to eat a final meal before whatever happens next, it better be a good one.

"Give me some examples," I say, before practically unhinging my jaw to take a bite of my burger. Beside me, Captain Rinaldi is sipping at a tall glass of sweet tea. He's got a baseball cap on, the bill obscuring his face. "Everyone's always talking about the horrible history that place has, and why we shouldn't hang out up there, but no one ever really talks specifics."

"Hold on," Rinaldi says. "You mean you and your friends hang out on that hill even though everybody tells you not to?"

I shrug. "Teenagers. What're you gonna do?"

Don shuffles through some of his paperwork, ignoring us. "The Welsh Quakers who established Windale were pretty much par for the course when Pennsylvania was first being settled," he says. "Their religious ideals jibed with everyone else's in the Welsh Tract until around 1699, when things started to get weird."

"Weird how?" I ask. I haven't completely swallowed a bite of burger, but I'm jamming more fries into my mouth anyway. For some reason, I have this feeling that I have to rush, that something is already happening, and we have to get ahead of it before *it* swallows *us*.

"The people of Windale at the time began telling stories about how the land was trying to communicate with them." Don's eyes are lit up with a pure, geeky joy that I have to respect, even though history isn't really my thing. "They said something in the woods on Dagger Hill was trying to lure them up there. A kind of spirit, they thought."

"If they were Quakers, why didn't they just assume it was God talking to them?" I ask. History might not be my thing, but I still know stuff.

Don grins. "They did. At first. But then something changed." He flips through his notes and starts reading from one of the pages. "This is from the journal of Henry Foster, one of the founding immigrants of Windale: 'Today, the voice on the Hill told me that God has left us. The voice said that it has excised the light within each of us and that henceforth we shall carry the voice in its place. The voice has sacrificed its sanctuary so that we may be free of false belief. It told me to come and sleep in its place on the Hill and unburden myself of this mortal prison. Four of us will go tonight. Pleased be us who may not be forced to return.' "

"Jesus, man," I mutter. "That was almost three hundred years ago. You're telling me this town has been sitting on top of . . . whatever it is for that long?"

"Longer," Don says casually. "The evidence is less precise the further back you go, but there's a trail that stretches as far as human history. If all of it is true, then this thing you call an anomaly has been here a lot longer than we have."

"Which means *we're* the anomalies." I set the last third of my cheeseburger back on the plate. I'm suddenly not so hungry. "What happened to Foster?"

"That entry in his journal was the last," Don says, sounding almost sad. "According to other locals, Foster and his wife went up to

Dagger Hill with Benjamin Windham, the guy Windale was named after, and *his* wife that very same night."

"I'm going to assume that this story does not have a happy ending," Rinaldi says, knocking his knuckles against the tabletop.

"Charlie already knows I have a hard-and-fast rule against making assumptions," Don says, grinning. "But in this case, you'd be right. Three of the four bodies were found mutilated, pieces of them scattered in every direction for almost fifty yards. At least, that's what the records say."

"What about the fourth?" I ask, pushing my plate away.

"That one was Foster. He'd talked his friends into going up to the Hill, massacred them when they arrived, and then killed himself after."

"How'd he do that?"

"They found him with his own heart in his hand," Don says, nibbling on another one of my fries. "He'd cut it out of his chest."

"Good god almighty," Rinaldi murmurs. He pushes the hat back on his head, rubbing his temples. "You know, I would very much like to bid this town a serious fucking adieu as soon as possible."

I pick up another fry, set it down, rub my fingers together to get the salt off them. "Put your hat down, Rinaldi. Low profile, remember? What else is there, Don?"

"After the Windhams and the Fosters died, the activity goes dormant for another hundred years or so," Don explains. He rifles through his paperwork as if he were sorting mail. "Windale carries on, but when people read Foster's journal and discover his obsession with 'the voice on the Hill,' the story becomes something like legend. A lot of the original settlers of Windale form a new religion devoted to the voice and the quote-unquote *sacrifice* Foster made to quote-unquote *protect* them. In fact, that's how Dagger Hill got its name in the first place—after the weapon he'd used to murder his friends and cut out his own heart."

"How does a man get his whole heart out of his chest without dying the second he snips one of those arteries?" Rinaldi asks. He's taken over my plate, ripping chunks of the burger off the uneaten side and popping them into his mouth, like popcorn in a movie theater.

"Well," Don says. "Either the story's been exaggerated over the years, or there was something unexplainable involved. An *anomaly*, let's say." He waggles his eyebrows, but Rinaldi and I just blink at him. "Anyway, in 1799, there was another incident. By then, Windale had pretty much isolated itself from the rest of Pennsylvania. The state was founded on the idea of religious tolerance, so even though most of the other settlements surrounding Windale thought the people here were a bunch of lunatics, they left them alone to worship their rock in peace."

"Their rock?" I say.

"Apparently," Don says, "the primary symbol for this new religion was a boulder, the place where Foster's body was found over a hundred years earlier. I think it's still accessible from Whisper Trail."

I shudder at the idea that the boulder Don's talking about might be the same boulder I was standing on Friday morning, the same boulder we played on as kids.

Promise me we'll always be there.

"Anyway, 1799 was the year of the Handley twins, James and Joshua, and their two young sisters, Edie and Elizabeth," Don continues. My plate is littered with only scraps now, but both men are still nibbling at the crumbs. I take a drag on my milkshake and recoil from the sweetness. I put the glass in front of Don, who slurps from it happily.

"They were all siblings?"

"Correct. The only four kids the Handleys had. Edie, the youngest, was the one who liked to play on the Hill the most." Don sits back, abandoning his paperwork for the first time since we sat down. He's unsettled.

"So what happened?" Rinaldi asks.

"Basically the same thing that happened a hundred years prior.

Except this time it was a little girl who talked her siblings into playing with her on the Hill and something chewed open their throats."

We pause for a long stretch, fidgeting in our own respective ways, almost like an unconscious moment of silence for the little girl and her brothers and sister.

"Two boys," I say, mostly to myself. "And two girls."

Don hears me, nodding. "That's right. Four people. Two of them male, two of them female. Every time."

"There were more?" I ask, startled.

"Plenty more," he says. "After the Handley kids, the people of Windale couldn't make sense of the violence. Why would the voice on the Hill compel a little girl to do such a thing? They figured it was punishment for renouncing God in the first place. So this time, they renounced the Hill."

"Which is why nobody else has made these connections before. Right?" Rinaldi asks. "Without that central thread tying them all together, the killings would just look like pure coincidence."

"Did anyone ever tell you how smart you are?" Don says. To me: "He's right, though. This has happened repeatedly over the years, but every time it comes with a different story. In 1863, a couple of Union soldiers returning home from the Battle of Gettysburg with two of the battlefield nurses, all of whom hailed from Windale, never made it past Dagger Hill. The records state that the bodies were . . ." He consults his notes. " '. . . disemboweled and mutilated in the manner of sharp teeth, and in no way that is capable of another human man.' So for a while after that, people decided Dagger Hill was home to a monster."

Don keeps going, turning pages, following his index finger down lines of information, but the pattern is already obvious. I just can't seem to bring myself to face it yet.

The most recent occurrence was twenty-five years ago, in 1964. A lot of the same people who live in Windale now would have been around back then, including most of our parents. All except for Sonya's, who were bound for here less than a few years later, drawn by the very thing that killed all these people. Or convinced them to kill themselves. Something like that.

The 1964 round of killings was simple: Just four friends hiking Whisper Trail together, back when it was still a popular thing to do. All four of them wound up falling down one of the steep, rocky inclines at the higher end of the trail. Their bodies were found at the bottom, bruised and bloodied almost beyond recognition. It was labeled an accident, and Whisper Trail was closed. But just like all the others, there were two males and two females involved.

Rinaldi lets out a hiss between his teeth.

"You see where this is going. Right, Charlie?" Don asks as gently as he can.

At first, I can only nod. Then, with a tongue that feels like a glob of hot lead, I say, "We were supposed to die up there."

I guess there's no adequate response for that, because I get none from either of the guys. We sit in a shallow pool of background noise, including the jukebox Harry keeps around for "nostalgic flair."

"But what about the second anomaly?" Rinaldi says after a while. "The Bug Man. Which I still think is a pretty stupid name. *That* thing killed Thompson and crashed the plane. Not this . . . voice in the boulder, or whatever it is."

"Voice on the Hill," Don corrects him. "But yes. The pattern was broken with the plane crash. Up until now, only one of these things has been involved."

"We all would have died Friday," I say. "If the pattern had repeated itself, that thing would have killed us. Like some kind of twisted sacrifice or something."

"But the plane crash interrupted that," Don says. His eyes widen, as if an idea is occurring to him. "And the second anomaly, the Bug Man, took one of you out of the loop. Maybe . . ." He trails off.

"It's almost like the Bug Man was trying to stop it from happening."

"It *did* stop it from happening, Charlie," Don says. "You said it yourself. If all these stories are to be believed, and I don't see why they shouldn't be, then you and your friends were supposed to die at the hands of the voice on the Hill, the Dagger Hill monster, whatever you want to call it. And the Bug Man got in the way before it could happen."

I think of Gabe telling me that the Bug Man gave him a thumbs-up just before scooping Kimberly up in its arms and disappearing into the trees.

"So the Bug Man was . . . protecting us?"

There's another stretch of silence while I let that idea sink in.

"Okay . . . ," Rinaldi says slowly, carefully beside me. "That theory is all well and good, but if the second anomaly went out of its way to stop the four of you from dying, why did it kill my copilot?"

I have no good answer for him, so I look to Don, who thinks it over.

"Maybe . . . a necessary sacrifice for the greater good?" he offers. "I'm not much of a scientist, but it seems to me that the thing on Dagger Hill relies on humans to survive. Like a parasite. If the Bug Man is even a little bit similar, maybe it needed a host to accomplish the rescue."

Rinaldi sits back, smiling to himself. "Thompson would have liked that idea. I don't know if it's true, but it sounds a hell of a lot better than him dying so that thing could cause mass destruction and kidnap teenage girls."

"I mean, not to split hairs," I say, "but it did technically do both of those things."

I glance past Don, out through one of the big windows. We took a booth close to the back of the diner so that it would be harder to spot us from the Triangle. But through that window, I can see just about everything going on out there. I see cars passing by on King Street. One of them is the chief's patrol car, that miserable wreck of a vehicle. It pulls up in front of the diner.

At first, I'm only surprised to see Sonya's dad sitting in the front seat with Gabe's. Then Chief Albright comes around and opens both back doors. Sonya and Gabe emerge, talking emphatically with both of their fathers.

"*Shhhhiit,*" I hiss.

"What? What is it?" Don asks. He looks over both shoulders once, then again.

"Stop. Don't make a scene. Hats on, heads down," I say.

I don't know why Gabe and Sonya are with the chief and Dr. G, but that was not part of the plan. The diner isn't packed, but it's crowded enough that maybe Don, Rinaldi, and I won't be spotted if they come in looking for us. Sonya will spot me immediately. If she doesn't want her dad and Gabe's dad to know I'm here, she won't say anything, and maybe they'll move on.

I glance up. They're still standing on the sidewalk near the chief's car. Gabe and Sonya are talking; Chief Albright and Dr. G are listening. Maybe it's all right. Maybe they're here to help.

Before I get a chance to find out, the bulbs in the stained-glass lamps dangling above the tables begin to flicker. I can hear the filaments buzzing and clicking. The long bar fluorescents in the kitchen are flickering, too. People gasp. The jukebox starts blaring much louder. Mark Dinning sings "Teen Angel" in his high, wavering voice. The sound of it scratches through the old speakers like a buzzing guitar string.

"Jake?" Don's voice. I look over and see Rinaldi in the stuttering lights, looking wildly around, terrified. Whatever happened on that plane, it scared him more than he's been letting on.

The lights keep snapping on and off; the jukebox blares its dead music. People sitting closest to it get up from their seats, backing away from the chrome-plated relic as if it's a grenade with no pin. Someone is at the front doors, trying to open them. I can't even see, but I know they're not opening, because they're just rattling back and forth.

"What the hell?" someone says.

"What's going on?"

A toddler in a high chair at the corner booth starts wailing.

All around, people are standing, panicking. A few of them look disoriented, swaying like Weebles, wobbling in one direction when the lights go out, wobbling in another when they come back on.

One woman with big round glasses and her hair blown out into an atomic mushroom cloud looks excessively pale. Her mouth is open, throat working, *choking*. As if she's about to puke.

Then she does.

She vomits up a writhing swarm of black thousand-leggers. They come pouring out, legs wriggling, bodies squirming, inky strands of living confetti. Some of them catch onto the woman's cheeks and climb across her face. She doesn't seem to notice—she's too busy gagging, shooting globs of spit and mucus out along with the insects.

The bugs keep coming, hundreds of them. The woman's body convulses, her chest and throat tightening with violent, heaving wretches. A few bugs clamber down her neck, up into her frizzy hair. The rest fall to the floor, bouncing, squirming, righting themselves, scattering. For a second, the mass of them looks like a glob of dried motor oil. But then they separate, untangling their hair-thin legs from each other, and begin tracing serpentine paths across the linoleum, vanishing and reappearing over the black and white squares.

People all around the woman are losing it. Screaming, climbing on top of tables, stomping on the bugs, trying to crush as many as they can. One man smashes his foot on a churning puddle of them, and his shoe comes away covered in dozens more than what he killed. They crawl up his bare leg and disappear into his khaki shorts. He hops backward, smacking at himself to try to get the bugs off, hits a table, and goes sprawling.

"*The doors won't open!*" someone screams.

"*Break a window!*" someone else shrieks.

"Shit!" Rinaldi barks next to me. "What the fuck?!"

Don is simply looking around, horrified. All the blood has gone out of his face, but he calmly places the last set of pages from his notes in the folder and closes it.

I look around, wishing I could pull my legs up onto the seat with me, but my cast prohibits me from doing so. Strangely, I'm okay with the idea of the thousand-leggers coming this way. There's a part of me, after everything I've seen and heard, that already knows they're not real. They're a product of the anomaly on Dagger Hill, invading my mind, invading everyone's minds. Angry, perhaps, because it was denied something two days ago when the Bug Man came to town. Using bugs to make us afraid of the thing that might have actually saved me and my friends.

As I glance around the room, my eyes land on a familiar face, and my stomach drops.

Chet is glaring at me through the chaos. Diners all around him are stumbling over one another, banging their fists against the windows, hitching in and out of the flickering lights like images in a slide projector. The woman who puked up the bugs is nearby. She's done throwing up, doubled over, the last of her blackened, bloody saliva dribbling out of her mouth. I'm amazed she's still standing.

It takes a single shove for Chet to knock her over. She tumbles backward onto a table, landing on plates of food and salt and pepper shakers. The ketchup bottle rolls off onto the floor, shatters, and a swarm of the thousand-leggers engulf it in seconds.

"Guys," I say, watching Chet. He pushed the woman out of the way so he could move forward, heading right for me. "Guys, look," I say to Don and Rinaldi. They look where I'm pointing, and Don turns back to me, worried and confused.

"Isn't that your stepdad?" he asks, practically yelling over the din.

I nod, but already I know something is different. Even for Chet, the vacancy in his eyes, tinged ever so slightly with anger, isn't like him. He's almost always *on*. Bobbing his knees, tapping his fingers, clicking his tongue. Right now, I see none of that in his face. All I see is stone-cold *emptiness*, and I have the notion that maybe this is what Henry Foster looked like just before he killed his wife and their friends three hundred years ago.

That's when I see the dagger in Chet's hand.

It's long and slim and razor-sharp. It picks up the colorful arc of the jukebox's light as Chet advances toward me. Instinctively, I grip my crutch and try to stand, try to get away. Don and Rinaldi are already standing, flanking me.

"Back it up, buddy," Rinaldi says. "I won't tell you twice."

Chet doesn't seem to hear. While everyone else in the diner is moving toward the front, trying to find a way out and away from the hundreds of bugs still skittering across the floor, Chet is moving toward the back, where we are. He has the dagger gripped so tight in his hand that his knuckles are pale knobs. He's picking up the pace, closing the distance between him and us.

Rinaldi is the first to move. Army training embedded deep into his nervous system must take over, because between flashes of the lights, he catches Chet's wrist, the one below the dagger hand, and grips it tight. The other arm he presses against Chet's torso and *shoves*. The two men pedal back across the path that Chet took to get here and smash into the bar. Stools and glasses of water tip every which way. Harry Kunz has appeared from the kitchen, a towel thrown over one shoulder, and is trying to get everyone to calm down. But when Chet and Rinaldi hit the bar, Harry jumps at the sound.

"Hey!" he yells. "Hey! No fighting in my place, ya hear me?"

They don't hear him.

Rinaldi throws a punch that connects with Chet's jaw like a firecracker. Chet tries to lunge upward, aiming the dagger at Rinaldi's chest. But Chet's bent over backward against the bar, his feet scrambling. Under the soles of his work boots, thousand-leggers are roiling by the dozen.

Meanwhile, Don helps me up and gets my crutch under my arm. "Let's go, Mr. Bencroft," he says. "Into the kitchen. C'mon."

We start in that direction, but then Chet calls out in a voice that only kind of sounds like his own. It's deep and guttural and tainted with vicious agony.

"The nightmare has to run its course!" he yells. I stop to look at him, unable to help myself. His eyes are huge, halfway rolled up into his head, showing off the cracked eggshells of his sclera. *The nightmare has to run its course!*

I glance around, looking for help, looking for any sign that this is going to end. But everyone is crowded at the windows and doors, pushing against them, climbing over each other in the stammering lights, throwing each other out of the way. Panicking, utterly and completely. Mark Dinning is still hollering from the jukebox, but it sounds slow and warbling. Thousand-leggers crawl everywhere I look—across the floor, up the walls, over plates of food left sitting along the bar.

My breath is thin, my pulse is a drum in my ears. My vision goes hazy. The lights flash on, then off, then on again. The sound of the music devolves into a deep, mournful wail, like wind high up in the hills. The outlines of everyone in the diner melt into one another, then evaporate into the background of swirling colors. When I scan the room again, it's a smear of alternating blackness and smudged light. Over at the bar, I can just barely make out the shapes of Chet and Rinaldi, but they're not moving. They're like mannequins in department store windows, posed in the middle of a duel.

The lights go out again, plunging me into filthy darkness. The music cuts out with a heavy, metallic *clonk*. Everything goes still.

When the bulbs come back to life, my vision has refocused as best it can. Only the lights above the tables have power this time, and everyone who was here is gone. No Don or Harry, no Chet or Rinaldi. It's just me, standing alone in the middle of a bunch of empty tables . . . and the Bug Man.

He's standing two feet away. The dim light traces narrow lines across the sleek surface of his leather jacket and gloves and mask. The oblong shapes of the mask lenses reflect the diner back at me. The checkered floor looks like a chessboard, with me standing as a feeble pawn. And I swear, I *swear*, I can see others in that reflection. All the people who were here with me only seconds ago, scrambling to get out. I can see Chet splayed across the bar with Rinaldi pinning him there, caught in their struggle. I can see a handful of people from town banging against the glass of a window. I can even see Don, standing only a few inches away, watching with growing concern as Chet slashes the dagger near Rinaldi's rib cage in slow motion.

"What are you?" I whisper. My voice wavers on the verge of cracking.

The Bug Man doesn't move, doesn't say a word.

"Where is Kimberly?"

Nothing. He only stands there, arms at his sides, watching me from behind the mask.

"Can you help us?"

This time, the Bug Man lifts his shoulders, then drops them. A shrug. As if to say, *Maybe, maybe not.*

When I speak again, my voice is just a breath of air. "Can we trust you?"

For a minute that feels like it spans several, he doesn't respond. Then he lifts his hand, curling the four gloved fingers. In the quiet, empty diner, the creak of the leather sounds like a rope twisting tight. He leaves the thumb extended, pointing upward. Then his head swivels, his glassy eyes aimed at the thing that's trying to kill me right now: my stepdad.

The Bug Man is still giving me a thumbs-up when the lights snap off again.

They snap back on, and I flinch away, expecting the dark mass of the Bug Man to be rushing toward me. But nothing is there. Everything is too quiet.

I spin around, glancing at the floor to search for thousand-leggers that might be getting close. There are none. At the front of the diner, people are backing away from the windows, looking around, patting their clothes, looking for the bugs themselves. Someone pushes the front doors open without any problem. The little bell above them rings, and the crowd goes rushing out.

Chief Albright, Gabe, Dr. Gutierrez, and Sonya are all waiting on the other side of the entryway. The chief comes in with a hand on the butt of his gun.

"Harry, what the hell just happened?" he says.

Harry Kunz is still behind the bar, scratching his head. "I . . . I honestly don't know, Jack. There were . . . bugs. Hundreds of them. And now there just . . . aren't." The older man looks perplexed and scared.

Chief Albright looks around at Gabe and Sonya, a look on his face that tells me he knows about the Bug Man. But he doesn't *really* know about the Bug Man. None of them do.

"Jake?" Don says. I forgot he was next to me, and I start at the sound of his voice. He moves away from me as if he's forgotten I'm there. He steps toward the place at the bar where Chet and Rinaldi are still on top of each other. Neither man is moving.

"Jesus," Chief Albright says, looking at Don, then looking at me. "Charlie, are you okay?"

But I'm too hung up on what Don is seeing: The way Chet and Rinaldi are slumping, limp against the Formica countertop, a pool of blood spreading under them, dripping down to the floor in long, stringlike streams. Chet's eyes are open, staring up at the ceiling from under Rinaldi's shoulder. Jutting through Rinaldi's back: the sharp, crimson-coated tip of the dagger. The Bug Man murdered Chet somehow, but not before Chet got that blade into someone.

Don drops his folder of papers. It hits the linoleum just outside the growing lake of blood. It's a struggle, but I manage to tilt myself over enough that I can pick it up and tuck it under my arm. Don's forgotten all about it. He's standing near the dead men, his shaking hands hovering just above Rinaldi's still back.

Gabe and Sonya are by my side.

"Charlie, man," Gabe says. "What happened? Are you okay?"

I'm staring at Chet's lifeless face, and I'm surprised at the grief welling up in my chest. Not for me, necessarily—for my mom. Chet is dead; that much is clear. But I think he was dead before this thing wielding the dagger showed up at the diner. This wasn't Chet at all—just a puppet, sent by the *anomaly*. The voice. The monster on Dagger Hill.

And the Bug Man saved me from it. I'm sure he did.

A moment later, Rebecca Conner appears in the doorway of the diner, pushing past customers who are still filtering out into the warm night. She aims for the chief, looking ready to spew a bunch of information. *Join the club*, I think. But she's halted by the sight of Chet and Rinaldi.

"What in the hell happened here?" she asks. Her eyes are wide and tired. Her dark, tightly curled hair, which is usually pulled into a perfect bun, is springing out in different directions, coming loose from the tie holding it in place.

"Still trying to figure that out," Chief Albright says. "What's up?"

Gabe, Sonya, and I stand by, watching and waiting, unsure of what to do now that we're not on our own.

"Montoya's body is on ice at the WMC," Deputy Conner says, trying to be quiet but not doing a very good job. "But there's something I think we need to look at."

"Okay. Call Dean. Tell him to keep the ambulance engine running and get his ass over here." The chief looks at the three of us. "You three." Then at Don. "And you." Then at Dr. Gutierrez, who is standing at Don's side, comforting him. "And you. You're with us. Everyone over to the station. And be ready to talk. I want to know everything that everyone knows, and I want to know it now."

We all head outside. Dr. G is able to pull Don away from the bodies. I'm reluctant to leave them behind myself. Rinaldi was a good man, and our key to disproving the stories that Higgins is surely going to tell about how this all went down. It's her word against ours now. I take strange comfort in knowing that it's not over yet. Not even close.

Outside, in the Triangle courtyard, Gabe and Sonya and I pause to take a breath. I lean on my crutch, happy for the break. There are tears in Sonya's eyes.

"I don't know what happened in there," she says. "But I feel like we came close to losing you, Charlie."

I wave her off, trying on a grin. It's weak, but it'll do. "Nah. Not even close." The last word comes out caught up in a sob, and I burst into tears. Sonya and Gabe wrap their arms around me, and the three of us stand there, holding each other, until my eyes dry up.

"The Bug Man saved our lives," I tell them after I've gotten myself together. I drag my arm under my nose. "More than once."

"What?" Gabe says. "What the hell are you talking about?"

I hold up Don's folder of Dagger Hill info. "The anomaly on Dagger Hill was trying to kill us." They exchange a glance that worries me, but I keep going. "The second anomaly, the Bug Man, it . . . he . . . *whatever*, stopped it from happening. He was desperate to get to the Hill, so he crashed the plane and took Kimberly away. He broke a cycle that's been repeating itself for hundreds of years. And he saved my life just now when Chet tried to kill me."

"Oh my god," Sonya whispers.

Don, Dr. G, Chief Albright, and Deputy Conner all join us in the courtyard. The chief opens his mouth to say something, but he never gets the words out. In that moment, the Triangle is filled up by the sound of revving engines and screeching tires. A convoy of jeeps and Humvees materializes, coming from the east, from Dagger Hill. They spill into the Triangle and encircle the courtyard. I can smell burning rubber and exhaust.

Soldiers hop from the vehicles, weapons in hand, and create a perimeter around us, gun barrels pointed in our direction. Colonel Higgins is the last to appear, sauntering slowly across the grass to where the seven of us are standing, arms tucked neatly behind her back as always.

"Good evening, folks," she says. To me, Gabe, and Sonya: "You kids are in a lot of trouble. Kidnapping. Murder. You've been on an impressive crime spree this weekend." She tips her head toward the diner, where people are still gathered outside, talking in frightened tones about what happened. "Looks like you weren't quite finished. If I'd been just a few minutes sooner, I might have saved some more lives."

"These kids have done nothing wrong," Chief Albright says, stepping between us and the colonel.

"And yet," Higgins replies. "Shall we go into the police station and see what happened to your friend Mr. O'Connell?"

"Mel?" Deputy Conner says. Her voice hitches up an octave. "What do you mean?" She looks to the chief. "What happened?"

Chief Albright, possibly for the first time since I've known him, looks caught off guard. He shakes his head.

"Mr. O'Connell is dead," Higgins says lightly.

"You're lying," Chief Albright growls, edging toward Higgins. The soldiers closest to her grip their weapons tighter.

"Dad." Gabe grabs his father by the arm and holds him steady. "Don't."

Deputy Conner takes one quick look around, her eyes wide, and then she runs for the police station. "Mel!" she screams at the building. "*Mel!* You come out here right now! *MEL!*" She shoves her way past a couple of soldiers and sprints up the steps, through the doors.

Higgins smiles, her lips flat and her eyes cold. "Shall we?"

45.

GABE

EVERYBODY CROWDS INTO the main office of the police station—me, Sonya, Charlie, Dad, Dr. Gutierrez, Don Cranston, and Colonel Higgins and a gaggle of her men. Each of them has a rifle in their hands. For now, the barrels are aimed at the floor, but I'm afraid to move too quickly, breathe too loudly. I stand with my hands tucked into my pockets. My left arm feels stiff and uncomfortable like this. But then, that's the way all of me feels right now.

From downstairs in the basement, where the holding cells are, we can hear Rebecca wailing softly. Dad wouldn't let us down there, but from what I overheard Alice telling him, June Rapaport murdered Mel. Which doesn't make *any* goddamn sense.

"I don't get it," I murmur to Sonya. Dad and Dr. G are talking in low whispers on the other side of the office—Dad looks grief-stricken, his face on the verge of erupting with emotion. Higgins is quietly ordering her men near the front entrance, directing them to different parts of town. She already has men investigating the incident at the diner. Don and Alice are sitting together on either side of her desk, cups of coffee between them going untouched. They both look gaunt and overtired, like they've been awake for days but just can't find the will to sleep.

"What don't you get?" Sonya asks. "She's framing us. I hacked into TerraCorp's database. They have that data recorded somewhere. She'll find a way to make this whole thing our fault and . . . and our lives end right here, tonight."

"Whoa, easy does it, Sone," Charlie says. "We don't know what's going to happen, okay?"

"Exactly," I tell her. "And that's not what I was talking about. You said Mrs. Rapaport was the one who led you to Kimberly in your nightmare. Why would she . . ." I have to swallow a lump that forms unexpectedly in my throat. "Why would she murder Mel?"

"The same reason Chet tried to murder me," Charlie says. "He was an asshole, but he wasn't a killer. The guy that I saw back there at the diner . . ." He shivers, wraps his arms around himself. "That was just a ventriloquist dummy that somebody dressed up to look like Chet."

"You think the same thing happened to Mrs. Rapaport?" Sonya asks.

Charlie nods. "She may have opened up some kind of back door for you. Let you into the space where the Dagger Hill anomaly works, to try to help you find Kim. Maybe it figured out what she was up to."

"And then the Bug Man got me out of there before it could do the same thing to me." Sonya's eyes are round and red. "Which means that I probably led the anomaly right to her. It knows where she is now. She might already be—" She buries her face in her hands, her words cutting themselves off.

I wrap an arm around her, startled by how easy that is to do after we talked at Kimberly's house. *It'll only get easier from here as long as we survive this*, I think. I reach out and take Charlie's hand, squeeze it. He drops me a wink, and again I'm astounded by his fortitude. Charlie is full—I keep telling myself that. He has a reserve of strength that seems bottomless. I don't know what I'd do without him.

Colonel Higgins emerges from the entryway, her hands clasped behind her back in that cold, indifferent way.

"The Windale Police Department is officially closed until further notice. The United States government will be handling any and all incidents of criminal activity in this town until our investigation is closed. I am implementing a mandatory curfew, which you are all in violation of right now."

"You're talking about martial law," Charlie protests. "You can't do that."

"Correction, Mr. Bencroft," Higgins says icily. "I am exactly the person who *can* do that. And we were already most of the way there, anyway. Closing off the town was only the first step. I thought you people could cooperate, but obviously you are incapable of doing that. So here we are."

"You can't just snuff this out, Higgins," Dad says. "It's all of our words against yours."

"He's right, Audrey," Sonya's dad says. He nudges his glasses back up on his nose. "Just let this go. The further down this path you get, the harder it's going to be to keep your story straight. There are too many variables. Too many people to keep quiet. There's all of us, plus everything that Claudia has seen."

"Oh, I took care of Dr. Reed, Alvaro," Higgins says, and Dr. G's face spasms with shock. "Just like I've already taken care of anyone else in this town who thinks they know what happened better than I do. By the way, you all will have to get your burgers from someone else going forward—Clark Webber's farm is, uh . . . closed indefinitely."

"You're a fucking monster," Sonya says. Even from six inches away, I can feel Sonya's body seizing up like a rusty engine. She balls her fists at her sides and bites at her lower lip until tears show in her eyes.

"No, the monster is out there," Higgins says, jabbing a finger toward the front doors. "It's running around your town making people murder other people."

"You don't understand what's happening here," Charlie protests. "You have it wrong."

"*I want everyone to kindly shut the fuck up. Right. Now.*" Higgins's voice is as sharp as a razor's edge, and just as cold. "Here's what's going to happen first. We're going to watch the tape that Mr. Montoya left us." She took the tape from Rebecca right after we arrived, and she holds it up now. I give Dad a look, but I can't get his attention—he's watching Higgins, listening for once. Words scribbled on the tape's label send a cutting chill through me: *It knows your fear.*

"After we watch the tape," Higgins goes on, "everybody—and I mean *everybody*—is going to tell me what they know. Or so help me god I will throw every single one of you in jail until I get the truth. That is what you want, isn't it? The truth. To *know* what happened to your friend. Where she is, what she might be doing, if she's even alive."

Sonya tenses again, and I look at her. My heart still thuds an extra beat when our eyes meet—I can't help it—but I no longer see the future I wanted for us. All I see is a person I can't live without. Like Charlie and Kimberly, my parents, maybe even this whole town. So many places here are painted with the memories of our friendship, like stamps in a passport. I feel the need to protect that with a force equal to the one compelling me to find Kimberly.

"Yes," I say weakly. "That's what we want." I look around at my friends, my dad, Dr. Gutierrez. I focus on him as I say, "We want the truth. And we'll cooperate to get it." I ignore the looks of defeat on Sonya's and Charlie's faces and redirect my attention to Colonel Higgins. Nobody else protests, because they all know that the only way out of this is to let Higgins lead the way.

"Good," she says. "Someone get me a television and a VCR. Now."

A few minutes later, Dad and Dr. Gutierrez emerge from a storage room at the back of the police station. They're rolling a tall metal cart into the office. There's a TV on top, and on a shelf just below that, a VCR.

Once the pair are plugged in, Sonya has to show them how to eject an outdated training video that Dad ordered from a police academy in New York State years ago. The label on the tape reads FIREARMS: A PRIVILEGE, NOT A RIGHT as it pops out of the machine.

"Nobody says a word until it's finished," Higgins warns us. "After it's over, we'll talk about what information you all have that you've been keeping hidden. And what the phrase 'obstruction of justice' means."

Charlie opens his mouth to argue. But Higgins stifles him with a raised finger before he can utter a single syllable.

"Not a word," she says again.

We gather up, and Sonya positions Ricky's tape inside the mouth of the VCR. She glances at the words scribbled on the label, and I watch a shudder pass through her. Then she nudges the tape, and the VCR slurps it up, and this is what we see:

A brief haze of static that cuts to a black screen.

Except it's not just black. There are fuzzy shapes moving in the darkness.

The volume is up on the TV, and there's a muffled thudding sound: fingers brushing the camera mic.

Something pulls away from the camera, and what was an obscure shot of dark, blurry, indiscernible shapes becomes one big thing.

It's the unlit outline of someone's face. A person without a mask, because there are eyes and a nose and a mouth, and they're all moving.

The eyes especially. They keep blinking in a nervous, agitated way.

"*Where's the goddamn . . . ,*" a voice says quietly. Ricky's voice. All the ticks and liquid pops of his speech are enhanced by the camera's microphone.

The screen flashes white suddenly, then the light quickly begins to fade, leaving only a wide, brilliant spot in the center of the screen. It looks like an atomic explosion.

Instead of a mushroom cloud, what's left in the aftermath is the brightly lit profile of Ricky Montoya.

He's looking over his shoulder.

"*I don't have much time,*" Ricky says, still looking behind him. He's huddled somewhere dark, hiding in a closet or a crawl space, maybe.

Ricky looks full-on at the eye of the camera then, and we get the sight of a young man who has been terrorized so deeply that his body has aged in a single day.

Ricky Montoya's eyes are hollowed-out peach pits, with tiny, glimmering gems resting inside them. His cheeks are pale sheets hung

265

on the hooked corners of his cheekbones. His lips are chapped—he keeps licking them, over and over—and his hair is mussed. He blinks once, then again, then again, then again. Again, again, again. Twelve blinks in five seconds.

Sonya puts a quivering hand over her mouth.

Her father wraps his arm around her shoulders and squeezes her close.

"*I don't have time,*" Ricky says again on the TV. Static lines roll up and down the screen. "*It's going to know what we did. Mrs. Rapaport and I. We tried to help her. We—*"

A sharp bang can be heard from off-screen, and Ricky's head pivots. He gasps, his whole face clenching as he peers out into the unknown dark.

He breathes heavily. Rapidly. Waiting.

Then he looks back into the camera, making eye contact with all of us and none of us.

"*I don't know where she is. I wish I did, but I don't.*" His voice is harsh and ragged. "*It knew what we were doing right away, but it . . . it* wants *us to fail. It wants us to suffer. He . . . I mean, it, it,* it, goddamn it. *It knows what you're afraid of. It will use that against you. It* feeds *on every negative thing.*" Ricky pauses, short of breath. His face, huge and stark, filling up the screen, jittering back and forth, collapses into sobs. "*I don't know what he is,*" he whines. His mouth is a dreadful smile, his lips connected by wet strings of spittle. "*I don't know what I did to deserve what I'm going to get, but I'm leaving this so someone knows . . . so you know that I tried. I tried to help you. There's an antenna on top of the video store. He made me build it. It's broadcasting . . . I don't know. Him, I guess. It.*"

The anguish in his face spreads out, blasted into wide, terrified features by a new noise in the background.

It's a small, distant bang, like a door slamming. Except it sounds like a cheap sound effect, like something that isn't real.

Then it's a few steady thumps: footsteps, heavy ones.

Then it's something that sounds like wooden floorboards bowing under a person's weight. But the video store doesn't have wooden floorboards.

Ricky Montoya is still looking directly at the camera, his eyes staring out of the screen, pleading.

"He knows," he whispers, barely even speaking at all. *"It knows. It knows, and it's here. Run. Don't hide. Because you can't. Just run."*

A hand appears within the range of the camera's light, but not anything even close to a human hand. This is a mass of something gray and slick, with long, bony extensions that only kind of remind me of fingers. It reaches out of the darkness and curls around Ricky's face in less than a second.

In the next, Ricky is yanked backward, sucked into the black void beyond the reach of the light.

His scream is loud at first, but it fades quickly, as if the sound were dropped down a deep well.

There are more bangs and thuds in the background, glass shattering, a garbled cry that might be Ricky or might be something else.

Then there's quiet.

There's the sound of plastic crunching.

Then static.

It plays out for what feels like a long, long time. We're all staring. Charlie, Sonya, and I are breathing rapidly. Even Dad and Dr. Gutierrez seem shaken—I'm not sure I've ever seen my father look so pale. The only sound I hear is a steady, metallic rattle. I glance over at one of Higgins's soldiers with his big automatic rifle. The gun is shaking because the soldier's hands are shaking, and the clips on the gun strap keep clicking together.

It knows *your fear,* I think. *Just like it knows mine. And Sonya's. And Charlie's.*

And Kimberly's.

"Jesus," Sonya's dad mutters. "I've never seen something so awful in my life."

One of Higgins's soldiers says, in an unsteady voice, "What . . . what the hell did it do to him?"

"You don't want to know."

We all turn toward Rebecca's voice. I didn't hear her come up from the dungeon. She's standing with her arms crossed, leaning against the wall. Casual, except for the puffiness around her eyes and the drawn-out look to her face.

Across the office, Dad lets out a long huff, like a sigh and a sob combined. He's leaning back against a desk—the one that used to be Mel's—with his arms crossed. His right hand is fussing with the badge pinned to his shirt. The word CHIEF is emblazoned across it. Dad is staring down at the thing as if he might take it off, drop it down a garbage disposal somewhere, and flip the switch until there's nothing left but gold shavings.

The only person in the room who doesn't seem bothered is Colonel Higgins. "How did you get the tape?" she asks, aiming the question at Rebecca.

Rebecca's head tilts up mechanically. "What did you say?"

"How. Did. *You*. Get. The. Tape." Higgins stands fully upright, hands behind her back. A few days ago, watching these two square off might have been entertaining. Right now, it's just scary.

"Montoya had it on his person," Rebecca says slowly. Her eyes droop into a long blink, then reopen. "I pried it out of his cold, dead hand, if that helps paint a mental picture for you."

Higgins makes a sound that could almost be a laughing snort. She looks around, distracted. "The damn thing left the tape for us to find," she says. "It's fucking with us."

"Hey, asshole," I say. "Care to clue the rest of us in?" The words are sharp and pointy, like shark teeth, and come spilling out before I can think twice. The pain and grief have bubbled into a low-burning fury that I've never felt before. I suppose it's been there since I woke up in the medical center. I haven't known what to do with it until now—I've just been tossing it around in my head like a grenade, waiting for someone to lob it at.

"Watch your fucking mouth," one of the soldiers says. All at once, his gun is raised, the barrel lined up with my chest.

"*HEY!*" my dad roars.

Sonya puts her hands over her ears.

Charlie jerks and winces.

Dr. Gutierrez rises to his feet beside Dad, glaring at the soldier right with him, a strange, partnership-y thing for him to do.

"It's okay, Private," Higgins says. "Lower that weapon. Keep the safety on and your hands off for now." Her eyes flick to mine. "I have a lot of respect for you people. I didn't at first. This town seemed like nothing but a rathole when I first arrived. But you have spunk, I'll give you that."

I don't think any of us know how to respond, so we don't.

"But everyone in this room is going to prison if I don't get some good intel here in the next five minutes," Higgins finishes. She flashes a flat-line smile. "Who wants to go first?"

"What does it matter?" Charlie says. "Even if we tell you what we know, which isn't a whole hell of a lot, you can't give us any guarantees."

"Guarantees?" Higgins tilts her head back, as if in laughter. "Kid, you and your friends lost your *guarantees* a long time ago. Right around the time that TerraCorp Junior here was hacking into her father's computer."

Sonya's cheeks go red with heat. Nobody says a word.

"Nothing we tell you is going to help you find that thing," I say. "And nothing you tell us is going to help us find Kimberly."

Higgins levels a glare at me.

Before she can toss more threats at us, Sonya says, "Except . . . I think I know where we can find them both."

Everyone looks at her. Her eyes lock onto mine, pleading silently for me to understand. And I think I do.

"The Banshee Palace," I say. It's not a question.

"Of course," Charlie says. He stands up as straight as he can, his limbs jittery with excitement. "The Bug Man and the Dagger Hill monster move around in the same way. At least, that's the way it seems. The motel hasn't had electricity in years. It might be the only place in Windale that the anomaly can't get to."

"Manipulation of electronic frequencies." That voice belongs to Sonya's dad. He looks around at all of us. "The anomalies give off high-frequency audio signatures that allow them to . . . invade the brain, so to speak. The one on Dagger Hill drew our attention when we were at the height of our climate research. We thought . . ." He shrugs, looking a bit sheepish. "We thought the earth was trying to speak to us. It didn't take long for us to realize that it was something different. Over the last twenty years, we've continued collecting data on the damage humans are doing to the earth's atmosphere, but we've also been keeping tabs on the anomaly."

"Do you know what it is?" Don has finally lifted his head, joining the conversation. "The anomaly, I mean."

Dr. G shakes his head. "Something that never should have been meddled with." His glare finds Colonel Higgins and stays there. "A little over a year ago, the second anomaly was discovered frozen inside an ice shelf in Antarctica. Its audio signature was so similar to the one here in Windale that the army thought it would be best to bring it here so we could research them together. Something told me it was a bad idea, but . . ."

Higgins says nothing.

"Dad," Sonya says, "Charlie thinks that the Bug Man helped us. He took Kimberly to protect us from what the Dagger Hill monster wanted her to do to us. And then to herself." She looks to Charlie for confirmation.

He nods. "Don could give you the specifics another time, but let's just say that if there's ever been a serial killer in Windale, it's the monster on Dagger Hill. It's taken a lot of lives over a lot of years. Does that make any sense?"

Sonya's father is nodding along with him, processing. "The data from the Antarctic research team showed that the second anomaly's signature was being produced the same way, but the frequency was different. Almost in an opposite range. And when Colonel Higgins described the thing they pulled out of the ice to me, it didn't line up with any of the information we had on the Dagger Hill anomaly. In fact, we've never encountered a physical representation of the Dagger Hill anomaly." He gestures to the blank TV where Ricky's video just played. "Until now."

"You think the . . . the thing that killed Ricky is the actual monster?" Charlie asks. "As in, real flesh and bone? If it even has those things?" His voice is shaking slightly.

"I do," Dr. G says. "If what you're saying is true, then the anomaly and the Dagger Hill . . . creature . . . might be natural enemies. One predator, one prey."

"And if the monster couldn't get to Kim or the Bug Man through sound, then it's trying to get to them in person," I say, finding my voice again, attempting to process another load of new information. "And it was damn close at Ricky's video store."

Sonya turns to me, panic brimming in her eyes. Her lower lip is trembling.

"We have to go," she says. "We have to go right now."

"Nobody is going anywhere." Apparently, Higgins has found her voice again, too. "Do you hear yourselves? Banshee palaces and bug men and monsters? The anomaly we brought back from Antarctica was just a blob. And it stayed that way for as long as it was in our possession. Until we brought it to this godforsaken town."

"A reactive response to being confronted with its—" Dr. G starts, but he's cut off.

"I don't give a damn what kind of response it was, Doctor," Higgins growls. Her perfect rows of glistening teeth are pressed together in a snarling grimace. "It scared the shit out of us coming down. Then it crashed my plane going out."

"You mean the plane you were too afraid to get back on?" Sonya asks.

Higgins has no response to that, and I cheer in my head for Sonya's small victory.

"Can I ask what might seem like a dumb question?" my dad says, raising his hand like a schoolkid. *"Why?"*

I almost ask him what he means, but the rest is obvious. Why here? Why us? Why did one anomaly use this town as its hunting ground for so long, and why did we get caught in the middle when another of its kind came to hunt *it*?

It's Don Cranston who stands and speaks first. "There doesn't have to be a *why*, does there?" he says. "Some things are just evil because they are." His eyes flick to Higgins. "Kind of like you."

She flinches, her mask of indifference slipping. "I don't even know who you are."

"Exactly."

"We're wasting too much time," Sonya pleads. "Those things are going to square off eventually. If she's still alive, we might be able to pull Kimberly out of the middle of it."

"Not so fast," Higgins says, holding up her hand. "People are dead. Government property was destroyed, and more government property is missing. *Some*body has to go to prison."

"The Bug Man is not your *property*," Charlie argues.

Higgins goes on as if he hasn't spoken. "And if your *Bug Man* and your *monster* end up killing each other, then any good they might have done us goes right in the shitter. *Ergo*, somebody needs to answer for what happened here. And it is not going to be me. Any volunteers?"

"Me." Dad is fully on his feet, chest held high. He looks stronger and more capable than I've ever seen him. He also looks wearier and more broken, a man on the verge of collapse. All I want to do is go to him, put my arms around his shoulders, and help hold him steady.

"Dad, no," I say, feeling my heart kick up a notch.

"It's okay, son." He looks at me, smiles an exhausted smile. "I'm really proud of you, okay? I never thought I could be as proud of you as I am right now."

I fight back the pressure behind my eyes, but it's too strong. My eyes fill and overflow.

"You're a good choice, actually," Higgins says. Her voice drips with ice. "You too, Dr. Gutierrez. The chief of police and the local scientist teaming up to protect their town's deadliest secret, even if it means killing a few innocent people along the way. I can piece that puzzle together."

"Wait," Sonya says. *"No."*

Her father stands beside mine, looks at his daughter with tears in his eyes. "Don't worry, little one. You're going to be amazing. No matter what you do. No matter where you go. No matter who you love." Then he winks, and Sonya tries to run to him, but one of Higgins's soldiers catches her by the arm and holds her back. Two others are already wrapping black zip ties around Dad's and Dr. G's wrists, cinching them tight.

"Get them out of here," Higgins says to the privates detaining our parents. To me, Sonya, and Charlie, she says, "Go home, kids. Grieve for your friend. Grieve for your parents. Wait for those two . . . whatever the fuck they are to kill each other." She consults her watch. "In twelve hours, this whole town is going to be a crater, and you won't have to worry about it anymore." She smiles a sickly, twisted smile. "I understand this is difficult."

"What?" Dad hollers. "What are you saying?" He's jerking and fighting against the soldiers who are half pushing, half dragging him out of the police station. They go right past Rebecca, who just watches with dazed, absent eyes.

"You can't do this, Audrey," Dr. G says, fighting his restraints. "You're talking about two thousand innocent lives. *You can't do it!"*

Higgins ignores him, follows them out of the main office. They disappear behind the corner, out into the small lobby, and through the front doors to the Triangle.

A SONG SUNG FOUR

WINDALE, PENNSYLVANIA, IS *home to 1,894 people, to be exact. Dr. Alvaro Gutierrez is close. What he doesn't realize as he's being hauled out of the police station by army soldiers is that many of those people are in the process of leaving their homes.*

A lot of them are dressed. A majority of them even have shoes on. But some wander out of their homes barefoot, in their underwear, with food still caught in their mouths midchew, with forks and pens and TV remotes still in their hands. They stumble into the muggy night and meander up the road. Dozens of them to a street, hundreds of them to a neighborhood. Their eyes are glazed and distracted, focused on some invisible carrot dangling in front of them.

The largest portion of Windale sits to the west of the Triangle, so the largest portion of its population emerges into this strange evening and aims itself east. Those on the other side of the canal, clustered at the base of Dagger Hill, they go west. They move at a brisk, shambling pace. They drool, sing, chant. A singsong rhyme that rises over the still air in a whispery call. A choir of ghosts.

They march into the Triangle a few at a time, heading for the police station.

46.

SONYA

"I DON'T BELIEVE it," Charlie says.

"Neither do I," Gabe says. His voice is thick.

Alice is over at the coffee maker behind her desk, trying to pour herself a cup. But her hands are too shaky. The pot keeps clattering against the mug, and the coffee sloshes out all over the place. I go to her, feeling surprisingly steady, and take the warm carafe from her.

"Let me help," I say, and finish pouring.

"Thank you," Alice whispers. She offers me some version of a smile, and I give her my best in return.

"It's just too easy," Charlie goes on.

I turn away from the coffee and put my hands on Alice's desk, stiffening my elbows, holding myself up, because if I don't, I think I might collapse to the floor. Don Cranston is sitting on the other side, tracing a circle on the desktop with his finger. Deputy Conner is leaning against the wall, her face blank. There are two soldiers behind her in the entryway, watching us, making sure we don't try anything stupid until Higgins and her men have gotten far enough away with my dad and Gabe's.

"They aren't really just going to . . . blow us up, are they?" I say, chiming in.

"They could," Don says. "Charlie's right. It's easy, but it's perfect easy. Meaning it mops up the mess Higgins made pretty neatly and efficiently."

"No more witnesses," Gabe suggests.

"No more evidence," I add.

"No more monsters." Charlie completes the thought.

"If she's being serious," I say, "then there's nothing we can do but wait. Even if we go out to the Banshee Palace, there's a good chance the anomaly kills us before the bomb does."

"Yeah, but what if the Bug Man has already killed the Dagger Hill anomaly?" Gabe asks.

"Or the anomaly killed the Bug Man," Charlie says. "And then . . ." He doesn't have to say the rest. If the anomaly won against the Bug Man, then Kimberly is already dead.

"Sounds like there are no good options," Don says. He slides a hand inside his trench coat and removes a silver flask, pours a nip into his coffee mug, considers the taste, then adds more.

"And what about this antenna on top of the video store?" I ask. "If it's broadcasting the Dagger Hill anomaly's . . . what did my dad call it? Audio frequency? Then what is it broadcasting to?"

"Or *who* is it broadcasting to?" Charlie asks.

None of us has an answer. I come back around the desk and slump against a desk next to Charlie. I put my head on his shoulder. He takes my hand, squeezes it. Gabe shifts toward us. He gives me what might be intended as a reassuring smile, but it's all nerves.

I wish Kimberly were here. Desperately. But for now, it's enough to just be with the boys. *My* boys. Not that long ago, right after Gabe got his license, we were all in the Chevelle together, cruising across the Hill-to-Hill Bridge, and Gabe kept hitting the brake too hard and we all kept jerking forward in our seats. Charlie and I were in the back; Kim was up front with Gabe. We all had whiplash later, but we were laughing so hard. Charlie kept calling the Chevelle the Tucker Torpedo right before Gabe would slam the brake down and Charlie's face would splat against the back of the headrest again.

My memory doesn't feel all that reliable right now, but I remember that day through a film of sunshine and spiraling pollen, like it was raining glitter. That might be a little more romantic than the truth, but all my memories of the four of us are cast in a golden hue.

Even on the coldest days growing up, wherever we went, we always seemed to carry the sun around with us.

In my peripheral vision, I'm aware of Alice still standing there, watching us. When I look her way, I see tears in her eyes. She's muttering something under her breath. Some kind of song, maybe? A nursery rhyme? Her eyes are wide, vacant, staring down at the floor through the steam of her coffee.

"*A song sung one,*" she whispers. "*The end of the line. A song sung two, we'll be just fine. A song sung three, dead is divine.*" Her eyes shift up and meet mine. A rash of goose bumps breaks out at the nape of my neck.

"You okay, Alice?" I ask. I realize that I'm still holding on to Gabe's and Charlie's hands, squeezing them tighter than ever.

"*A song sung four,*" Alice goes on, "*all outta time.*"

Outside, I can suddenly hear gunfire and shouting.

Inside, Alice Kemmerer drops her mug of hot coffee, lets it shatter across the floor. She raises her hands to the sides of her head and begins to scream.

47.

CHARLIE

I SEE HER coming.

Two days ago, on Dagger Hill, I saw a plane just as it was about to burst from the heart of a vicious thunderstorm and squash the lit fuse of our summer. I didn't do anything. *Couldn't* have done anything. Superman stops planes, not some kid in a red puffer vest and bifocals.

Tonight, though, I could tell something was wrong with Alice. Sonya helped her get coffee, and she was fine. But when she turned back around with the hot mug in her hands, her face was all screwed up. Not just confused but *warped*. A totally bizarre look in her eyes, as if somebody else was staring out of them.

I heard Sonya ask, "You okay, Alice?" And I saw the mug slipping from Alice's fingers before it started to fall. She was whispering that rhyme, like something from an old fairy tale I've never heard before. *A song sung four.*

Now the mug is shattering on the linoleum, spraying droplets of coffee everywhere. I feel one hit my cheek and burn there for a second. Another smacks into my forehead.

Alice is screaming. Then she stops, and that knotted-up look that Alice has curdles into a hateful sneer, and before the last pieces of her broken coffee cup settle, she's pulling herself up onto her desk, shoving picture frames and brick-bracks out of the way. The smiling face of someone who must be her husband dives headfirst to the floor, and his grin is cut apart by a spiderweb of cracks.

I still have Sonya's hand—she's gripping mine so tight that my fingertips are going numb.

Don is directly in Alice's path as she comes across the desk. His coffee mug tips backward and spills down the front of his shirt, still steaming hot. He shouts and shoves himself out of the way, almost falling out of his chair. Deputy Conner looks on, her eyes widening, watching without reacting.

"Hey!" one of the soldiers behind her yells. "Hey, what the hell is—" He's cut off by the sound of more gunshots from outside. He turns to his comrade. "Go check it out. I'll deal with this. Hey, lady! What's your problem?"

Alice ignores him, coming at us with knobby claws, long nails coated in robin's egg polish. A slippery string of drool dangles from the corner of her mouth. Her teeth shine behind her peeled lips, gnashing together as if she's chewing on a gristly piece of steak—or fantasizing about it, anyway.

Beside me, Gabe's voice: "Alice? Alice! What's wrong? *Charlie, what are you doing?*"

I'm lifting my crutch, grabbing it by the bottom like a baseball bat, and taking a swing. The aluminum piping smashes into Alice's knee. She falls over, arms flailing, and smacks an open palm against my left thigh. I bite back a scream, can't hold it, let it out. My eyes fill with tears. I bend forward as Alice hits the floor, screaming in a guttural way that freaks me out. It doesn't sound like something her vocal cords can produce. Just like her eyes, it was like the noise was coming from somewhere other than Alice's body.

I stumble back, trying to get my crutch under my arm, and nearly lose my balance. But Gabe is behind me, holding me up. Sonya, too.

On the floor, Alice squirms, her arms jerking like pistons, as if she can't figure out how to get up. Her eyes are huge and angry, swiveling around in their sockets like the roller balls on an arcade game console.

"Kids!" That's Deputy Conner's voice. She's standing farther inside the office now, near a gun cage that's standing open, a set of keys dangling from the lock. There's a shotgun in her hands. She pulls back on the action and buries the stock in the crook of her shoulder, aiming the barrel at Alice. "Get out of here! I've got her covered!"

Out in the entryway, the remaining soldier sees Deputy Conner with the gun, takes another glance at Alice thrashing on the floor, then turns and runs out the door into a separate chaos that I can only imagine.

Me, Gabe, and Sonya don't hesitate—we follow in the soldier's footsteps, avoiding Alice's reaching, snatching hands as we dart past her. My leg is in a fury of pain, but I push past it, crutch-stepping alongside my friends.

As we run past Deputy Conner, Gabe reaches out and squeezes her arm. She nods at him, only taking her eyes off Alice for a second.

Sonya hurries ahead to the doors while Gabe stops again at what looks like a storage closet.

"Wait, wait, wait," he says.

I glance around and see Alice finally gaining purchase, getting her knees under her like a toddler learning to walk. Gabe opens the closet door and ducks inside. Sonya is at the mouth of the lobby, bobbing from foot to foot, like she has to pee.

"Uh, Gabe, buddy?" I say.

"Just a second," he says from inside the closet.

Alice has crawled back to her desk, very near where Don was a moment ago. Now, he's pressed himself against the wall behind Deputy Conner.

"I . . . uh . . . I'm gonna stay with her," he says, and points at the gun instead of the woman. "Good luck, Mr. Bencroft."

"*Gabe!*" Sonya yells. "Let's go!"

"Got 'em," Gabe mutters. He reappears. "Keys," he says, and tosses a set with a Magic 8 Ball key chain to Sonya. She catches them deftly. "Dad's patrol car. *Go!*"

We're off again, leaving Alice, Deputy Conner, and Don behind. We cut through the lobby, then through the front doors to a scene I can't really describe. It's the Triangle, as we've always known it, but it isn't.

A swarm of Windale residents has come from all directions. Hundreds of them with the same wild, possessed look in their eyes as Alice had. They're smashing storefront windows, tipping garbage cans over, leaping at soldiers and tackling them to the ground. Some of the soldiers are firing rounds into the air, but no one takes notice. The Dagger Hill anomaly has spread itself like a virus to these people, and they're here to do what it tells them. The voice on the Hill.

Higgins is standing beside a jeep, flanked by two of her men. In the back seat of the vehicle, Chief Albright and Dr. Gutierrez are sitting, strapped in, with their hands still tied in front of them. They're looking around as snarling, screeching members of our community descend on the army soldiers and the police station.

"What the hell?" Gabe says.

We slow down at the top of the steps, looking out at the madness unfolding. Soldiers are spilling off Humvees and jeeps, trying to keep order but colliding with town citizens, people I've seen here and there my whole life, people who are now tearing rifles from the hands of soldiers and using the butt ends to pulverize kneecaps. Mr. Henries, a mail carrier who used to leave bags of chocolate chip cookies in our mailbox, clocks an MP in the side of the head with double fists, then throws himself on top of the soldier and bites into the man's cheek like it's a raw apple. Blood spurts and the MP screams and Mr. Henries, with dripping red teeth, moves on to the next victim.

A group of townspeople led by none other than Maureen New-comb, owner of Miles of Styles hair salon, plows into Colonel Higgins. They funnel themselves between vehicles like a herd in a cattle chute, tramping over Higgins's bodyguards and the colonel herself. Everybody disappears in a tangle of limbs.

The Triangle fills up with the sounds of shattering glass and shrieking and gunfire and the hard, meaty sound of bodies smashing into other bodies. People are running, screaming, tearing at their clothes, looking panicked but sure of themselves, confident in the mission they've been given.

And, it seems, the mission is us. Because as soon as Gabe and Sonya and I are spotted at the top of the police station steps, almost all the faces darting back and forth across the courtyard and the adjacent streets look in our direction. Their eyes are feral, furious points of light swaying beneath the streetlamps.

"Guys," I say. "We need to get out of here."

Sonya is already hurrying down the steps, but Gabe is hesitating at the top.

Behind us, I hear the blast of a shotgun going off, followed by a shrill, animalistic scream. A few seconds later, there's the squeak-hiss of the station doors swinging open and the scuffling sound of Alice's flats on concrete.

I don't wait any longer—I stagger down the steps one at a time, *step-clack, step-clack, step-clack*. Gabe is a second behind me and catches up quickly, but he doesn't run past, doesn't leave me in his wake. He matches my pace and sticks with me. I squeeze the grip on my crutch, knuckles going white, gritting my teeth. I glance over my shoulder to see Alice still standing at the top, looking out at the scene. If the real Alice is in there somewhere, she must be petrified. Or maybe she's lucky. Fortunate enough to have her fear swallowed by the anomaly, used as fuel instead of fertilizer.

In the corner of my eye, I notice Higgins clambering to her feet between her jeep and another sedan. The colonel's perfect bun has come loose, and there are stray curls of hair dangling around her head. Her cheek and chin are purple and swelling. The bottom half of her face is canted at a weird angle. Somebody broke her jaw, I realize.

There's a woman in the street with her hands covering her face. She looks familiar, but with only her wide, petrified eyes showing through her splayed fingers, I can't be sure. She's screaming. No, *howling*. *"WHAT IS HAPPENING? SOMEBODY HELP ME! THIS ISN'T REAL! THIS CAN'T BE REAL! SOMEBODY PLEASE, GOD, HELP!"*

The butt of a rifle swings in behind her, cracks against her skull. She goes down and goes quiet. The soldier who knocked her out stands over her, his head angled down to look at her. Then he moves on, stepping over the woman's limp body.

Sonya is already waiting by the passenger side door. Gabe and

I move around either side of the Crown Vic when the chief yells for his son.

"Gabe!" he shouts over the noise. "*Gabe!* Where the hell are you going?!'"

"To try to stop this!" Gabe yells back.

Meanwhile, Alice stumbles down the station steps, moving with a slow caution that makes it seem like she's never used a flight of stairs before. She's got a swift enough pace, though, that in a few seconds, she'll be back on top of us. She screams coming off the last step, her mouth huge, opening so wide that the skin at the corners of her lips is splitting. She lurches forward, closing the distance from a few feet to maybe two.

Another gun blast sounds off, and a raw red hole materializes in Alice's forehead. Her eyes roll up, and her momentum carries her another few inches. Then she's tipping, smacking down on the asphalt with a fleshy slap.

Sonya stops in the act of getting into the passenger seat and stares with Gabe and me in the direction of the gunshot.

I look around for the soldier who fired and find Higgins instead. She has her sidearm drawn, the end of it smoldering. She drops her arm, as if the gun were suddenly too heavy for her to hold, and her eyes find me, Gabe, and Sonya.

Then three of the anomaly's new puppets circle her. In one moment, their faces are filled with hate, but they're at least recognizable. In the next, one of them turns, tracing Higgins's stare back to us, and its head is covered in thousand-leggers, creeping and writhing over the skin of his face and neck.

To my right, Sonya flinches back, nearly dropping the car keys.

"Sone!" I call. "Sonya! Look at me!"

She turns, finds me. Eyes wide and red.

"It's not real," I say. "That part isn't real. It can't hurt us." The words feel false, but I have to try to protect her, to ease the fear that the monster has gone to such lengths to incubate.

Sonya closes her fingers around the keys, pressing her lips into a firm, determined line. She slides into the passenger seat of the cruiser, leans over, starts the engine. It hiccups to life, then immediately dies.

"What the hell?" Sonya shouts, banging the heel of her hand against the dashboard.

"Gabe!" It's Chief Albright again, standing in the back of the jeep, kicking at the occasional soldier as they fight past the people who are fending them off. "Gabe, you have to hit the gas a few times when you start her up!" he yells. "Whatever you're going to do, go do it!"

Behind me, Gabe is frozen, watching the chaos unravel across the Triangle, glancing at his dad just long enough to nod at what he's saying. Feeling useless, I pull the back door open and toss my crutch inside. I take two deep breaths, grabbing the doorframe with both hands, and slide in. The pain in my leg flares, but it's dull compared with Alice's falling into it back inside the station. I slide backward across the bench seat, with my cast stretched out over the tattered leather. Gabe is still outside, stalled where he stands.

"Gabe!" Sonya and I shout at the same time.

That finally snaps him out of it.

Gabe slides into the driver's seat, twists the keys in the ignition, and revs the engine. The Crown Vic coughs, roars, chokes, purrs. Gabe slams the gearshift down and plants his foot on the gas pedal. The cruiser rockets back into the street. It smashes into the rear end of someone else's vehicle, sending it spinning. For one heart-stopping instant, I think there's someone standing near that other car when we hit it. But the road behind us is mostly clear.

Glancing outside, I see Deputy Conner on the opposite side of Higgins's jeep, helping Dr. Gutierrez get out. Colonel Higgins herself is nowhere in sight as Gabe cranks the shifter down to DRIVE and floors it again. He swerves around a group of our neighbors at the last second.

The chief's patrol car carries us up Main Street, away from the worst of the bedlam, into a whole separate kind.

48.

GABE

MY MIND IS working through a hundred scenarios at once while my body is operating on autopilot. Driving my dad's patrol car, navigating it in the direction of the west-side strip mall. I can hardly process everything I saw back in the Triangle, everything that happened. It's like a series of Charlie's photographs lined up inside my brain, all of them blurry and out of focus, all of them terrifying.

I grip the steering wheel as tight as I can until it hurts. I lean forward and scream, banging my open palm against the wheel over and over.

"Gabe," Sonya says. She puts her hand on my shoulder. When I don't stop, she says my name again. Then again, louder.

"Holy shit, Gabe, stop!" Charlie hollers from the back seat.

I pull myself together just in time to hear the dull boom of something exploding somewhere behind us, in the direction of the Triangle. Sonya gasps, her hand clamping down on my shoulder.

"What was that?" she asks.

"I think . . . maybe . . . the propane tanks at the diner?" Charlie says. I can't tell if he doesn't really know or if he just doesn't want to be right.

More gunfire accompanies the explosion, and as we drive, I see more people out on their porches, on their lawns. They watch us go by, heads pivoting in unison.

I keep driving, ignoring the blank, haunted faces of everyone lining the streets.

"Where are we going?" Charlie asks.

"The Banshee Palace," Sonya says.

At the same time, I say, "Ricky's video store."

We look at each other, both of us confused.

"Gabe, we have to get Kimberly," she says.

"Sone, we have no idea if she's even alive," I reply. "As much as I want her to be, I think getting to Ricky's store and dismantling the antenna is the only way we're going to survive this. That has to be the thing that's making everyone . . . well, you know."

I turn onto Raspberry Street, trying to focus on where we're headed, what we're supposed to do, hoping that it will put a stop to the literal madness that's infected Windale. But I'm only confronted by more madness: Ahead of us, the Windale Medical Center is in full view, and the entire building is on fire. Dark smoke blots out the stars, and every window is snapping with dragon tongues of flame.

"What the hell?" I breathe. "Where is everyone?" I ask. "Where's the fire department?" We're pulling in front of the WMC now, so close we can hear the flames crackling.

"I don't know," Sonya replies. "But I don't think they're coming."

"Shouldn't we stop?" Charlie asks.

"And do what?" I say. "Stand and watch? Unless your crutch comes with a fire hose, there's not a whole lot we *can* do, Chuck."

I only ever call him that when I'm being a dick, which is often. But tonight, he doesn't even try to hit me on the arm. Couldn't if he wanted to—there's a metal barrier separating us.

We leave the flickering orange glow behind and continue in the direction of Sunrise Hill and the strip mall.

"Take me over to the Widow's Lodge and drop me off," Sonya says suddenly. "Then you guys can double back to the video store." She's switched into Computation Sonya mode. This incredible ability she has to pancake her emotions beneath the weight of all the mental equipment it takes to solve a complex problem. She's basically a robot when she's like this, but I'm not sure how well she's going to be able to hold it together if she really does find Kimberly in that hotel room.

"No way," Charlie says from the back seat. "There's not a chance we're splitting up. Not tonight. Not with everything like this."

"Sone, I don't know . . ." I start.

"Oh, get real, Gabe," she huffs, crossing her arms. "You're not going to pull some macho bullshit and hold me hostage just for my protection. You can drag me to the video store all you want, but I'll just get out and walk to the Banshee Palace by myself."

It sounds like a normal argument we might have had over the course of any other summer. All I can do is sigh, though. I don't have a snappy comeback. Part of me feels like it's not even worth arguing—we're going to die anyway. Windale is about to be blown to pieces, and even if we stop the anomaly—or, and this would be an even stranger scenario, if we help the Bug Man stop the anomaly—we won't be able to stop that.

"Fine," I say. I turn the car onto Baker Street. The strip mall is in sight, and from here I can see the metal structure on top of the video store. It's pieced together with strips of metal, coils of wiring, what looks like a stop sign. There's nothing fancy or overly intricate about it. From this vantage point, it looks like a sixth-grade science project. Or an art installation.

I hit the brake, hesitating. Suddenly, I don't want any part of this.

Sonya's hand curls around my forearm. "It's okay," she says. "Let me out here. I can walk up the street. Look." She points to the place a few blocks north, where the shadowy hulk of the abandoned motel sits. "I did it before. When Mrs. Rapaport showed me the way. I'll be okay. Leave the car here. Leave it running."

"No," I say. The words that I really want to say—*Let's just forget this and go home*—are at the back of my throat. Instead, I say, "You take the car. Kimberly's going to be weak. You might have to carry her. Charlie and I can run if we have to."

"Uh, you mean *you* can run," Charlie corrects me, knocking on the metal divider. "You might have to carry me if it comes down to that."

"Which is no different than when you stand on the sled for me during football practice," I counter. "Except this time, I'll be running for our lives. Piece of cake."

"Sure," Charlie says, flopping back against the seat. "No sweat."

"Are you sure?" Sonya asks me.

"Of course not," I reply immediately. "But . . . yeah. I'm sure." I give her my best smile, even though I already feel clammy and shaky.

"It's up to us," she says. "It started with us; it has to end with us."

"A song sung four," Charlie mutters from the back seat.

"I know she's there," Sonya says quietly. "I have to go get her, Gabe. I have to."

"I know," I say, and I put my hand over hers. "Just promise us you'll be careful."

She nods, but she doesn't actually promise anything.

A minute later, we're standing beside the cruiser. From the east, there are a few lone pops of gunfire, mixed with a shrill sound that might be someone screaming. Nobody's on Baker Street tonight. It's after seven on a Sunday. The strip mall is dark. The few houses along this road are silent. Twin pillars of smoke rise up out of town—one nearby, underlit by the orange glow of the burning medical center, the other farther off, coiling up from the Triangle.

"See you soon," Sonya says, and gives Charlie and me a quick hug. She doesn't pause to consider what's about to happen. If she does that, she might back out. I feel the same way right about now. So I just turn away, feeling a wet heat in my eyes and a knot in my throat. The cruiser's engine revs, then fades as it pulls away. I steal a glance over my shoulder, hoping to catch a glimpse of Sonya before she disappears. But all I see is the word CHIEF emblazoned across the side of the car.

Already, gnats are starting to swarm. It's a hot night, and the roof of the strip mall seems very high.

"Okay," I say to Charlie. "Here goes nothing."

49.
SONYA

IT KNOWS YOUR *fear*.

That's what Mrs. Rapaport said to me in the other Windale. And it's the warning that Ricky Montoya wrote on the label of his tape. This thing, the Dagger Hill monster, whatever it is. Ricky said it knows what we're afraid of, knows how to use it against us. But this whole time, I've only really been afraid of one thing: losing Kimberly. What's going to happen now that I have to face that fear? Am I giving the anomaly exactly what it wants? Am I *feeding* it?

I pull Chief Albright's cruiser into the Widow's Lodge parking lot. The buckled slab of asphalt jostles the car around, and I can hear weeds scraping along the undercarriage. The dark mass of rotted, collapsed wood is behind me, taking up all the space in the rearview mirror. The old motel is earning its nickname tonight—even from inside the car, I can hear the wind whistling through the exposed eaves. The part that's freaking me out, though, is that there isn't any wind. Ahead of me, across the street, a tree stands perfectly still. Not a single leaf is twitching. It's like my nightmare all over again.

With a badly shaking hand, I open the door. The keys are still in the ignition, the engine is still running. If I have to make a quick getaway, I don't want the engine to die on me the way it did back at the Triangle. I leave the driver's door ajar, and I don't look directly at the Banshee Palace as I walk around the front of the car and pull the passenger door open, too. This way, all we have to do is get the hell out of there, hop in, and go.

We.

In my head, not only is Kimberly still alive, but she's also in good enough health that she can just jog out of the motel along with me. I can't help but laugh at myself. I feel so stupid and afraid and pathetic. How did I ever let any person, human or not, have that kind of power over me? To make me feel so small, so closed in . . . It isn't fair.

I set my shoulders, lift my head. Room 6 is up there on the second floor, where it's always been. The door is shut, the brass number 6 slightly askew. Dark burgundy curtains hang in the window, pocked with holes that reveal only black behind them.

This is it.

I take a step forward . . . And when my foot comes down, something crunches beneath it. I look down and scream, pull away, hop up onto the trunk of the cruiser and pull my legs up with me. The bottom of my shoe still has the crushed body of a thousand-legger glued to it.

The parking lot, from corner to corner, is covered in bugs.

50.

CHARLIE

THE FRONT OF the store is locked, naturally. But we peer in through the windows anyway, just to see what we might be in for . . . and to make sure the Dagger Hill anomaly (or even the Bug Man) isn't waiting inside. All I see is a mess. Shelves torn down, kicked apart, TVs trashed. One in particular looks like it might be covered in blood, and I can only imagine what happened, how afraid Ricky must have been.

"Don't let it get to you," Gabe says as we head around to the back of the building.

"How can I not?" I reply. And the awful punctuation to that state-ment is a scream that sounds like it's really close by. Gabe stops, and we both listen. "Was that . . . ?"

"No. No, I don't think so."

We're cut off from view of the Widow's Lodge by a curving slope of Sunrise Hill. So if it was Sonya, we'd have to go back down to the street to even try to see her.

"Let's hurry," I say. "We're supposed to be the distraction, remember?"

"You mean the bait," Gabe says.

"Same thing."

We come around to the back of the strip mall, pressed right up against the hill. There's an assortment of dumpsters and a terrible reek. Flies are buzzing everywhere.

"Look," Gabe whispers behind me. He's pointing ahead of us. "His ladder is still set up."

Sure enough, propped up against the back of Ricky's place is a metal ladder. The back door to the shop is closed, probably locked, but nobody ever took the ladder down.

We approach the ladder, then stop. Neither of us moves. It's dark and quiet back here. I feel like I can sense every little sound, every tiny movement. My heart is kicking along at double time.

"I don't think I can make it up there," I say, peering up the length of the ladder to the roof. "I could try, but . . ."

"It's okay, man," Gabe says. "Let me see something . . ." He grabs the door handle, presses the button. It unlatches with a perfunctory click, and Gabe is able to pull the door open. "That thing has to be hardwired in somewhere, right? Jacked into some of the electronic stuff inside the store? Maybe you can go in there and figure out where that is and disconnect it?"

I squint into the dense black shadows lingering inside that doorway and swallow hard.

"Sure," I squeak. That's all I can manage.

"Okay," Gabe says, sounding more unsure of himself than ever. "Here I go." He comes around me, takes hold of the ladder, shakes it to see if it's sturdy. It rattles loudly, and I jump.

"I don't even know what to look for," I say. "Are there going to be wires? Computers? Do I have to cut the power?"

"How the hell should I know?" he hisses. "This is some weird *Ghostbusters* shit we're dealing with. If it looks important, break it."

I nod. So does he, then he shakes out his hands, hops from one foot to the other, and starts to climb.

As he ascends, I look nervously through the crack in the door that leads into the smothering black. I glance up at Gabe, who's already halfway to the roof. The ladder creaks and cracks under him. I wish I had a flashlight. I wish I had a *weapon* that isn't also the thing I need to help me walk. A knife, a gun, a baseball bat, anything. Another look up top, and Gabe is hauling himself onto the ledge. I look down around Ricky's dumpster and take inventory of what's there—a couple of boxes full of dismantled electronics that Ricky might have had staged for the antenna; a tied trash bag; a ladder on its side, pushed up against the wall; some empty bottles . . .

I do a double take at the ladder. It's not just another ladder—it's the *same* ladder that Gabe just climbed. When I look up at the roof again, Gabe's foot is disappearing over the edge, but the ladder is gone, as if it were never there.

"It knows we're here," I mutter. *"Gabe!"*

There's the metallic whine of a door opening. I turn my head and see the back door to Ricky's Video Rentals opening farther now, that slit of darkness widening to a gap.

"Charlie?" somebody says from inside the door, the voice soft and sweet, and my breath catches.

It's my mom.

51.
SONYA

"IT'S NOT REAL," I whisper to myself. "It's not real. It can't hurt us because it's not real. That's what Charlie said."

My eyes are shut, and my breathing is loud, heavy. But it doesn't drown out the ticking, scratching noise of all those insect legs moving across the pavement. Each time I open my eyes, they're still there, a pulsing sea of black thousand-leggers, blocking my way to the motel. The sagging iron staircase is only ten or twelve feet away, but there are just so many bugs. I imagine putting my foot down, trying to walk across them, and having them swarm me, engulf my legs, creep up my body, smother me—

I can't do it. I'm frozen. Trapped on top of the police car. I could try to climb inside the car and back over the bugs, pull up to the stairs and find a way up to room 6 without ever having to set foot on the parking lot. But if the anomaly can put the bugs here, it can put them anywhere. They were on my mattress in the nightmare, weren't they? Proof that the version of Windale I was in was his, a mimeographed iteration of this town that it created based on . . . what? How did it really know anything about this place without . . . ?

It hits me like any other moment when I've solved a problem. It's like my head's been in a vise, and as soon as the solution dawns on me, the vise loosens, and there's nothing but relief along with a giddy pleasure that I can't quite describe. Only tonight, the pleasure melts into more anxiety.

The Dagger Hill monster needed somebody who knew this town,

who saw it for all its brightest spots and darkest corners, who was an *observer*.

Which means there's a good chance Kimberly's still alive.

I take ten long, deep breaths. I open my eyes, steel myself. Then I slide off the back of the car and put my feet down on the parking lot.

No crunching. No bugs. Because they were never really there.

I start for the staircase, and right when I do, somebody knocks on the door to room 6.

52.

GABE

I HEAR CHARLIE call for me, but it sounds far away from up here. I have a pretty good view of Windale as it burns. The fire at the medical center is bigger and brighter than before. And the smoke rising up from the Triangle looks thicker, stronger somehow. Things have mostly gone quiet, but from somewhere really far away, I can hear the hollow cry of a siren. Somebody wants to help. How much good it'll do, I have no idea.

The contraption that Ricky put together looks even more like a scrap-metal sculpture up close. Shards and strips of metal are either welded together or held in place by wads of electrical tape. There really is a stop sign, still attached to its post and everything. And there *is* wiring. Lots of it. Looping and swirling up the antenna, coiling around metal piping like black snakes. I'm able to trace most of it down to a bunch of cables that wind their way to a breaker box at one side of the rooftop.

It seems like I have two options: Either dismantle the antenna and toss the pieces off the roof, or cut off whatever connection the wires have to the antenna, hopefully breaking the signal.

I think I'll go with . . . both.

Stepping up to the antenna, I take hold of a long piece of metal tubing. When I look through the apparatus to the other side of the roof, intending to shove this whole goddamn thing over the edge, I see the Bug Man standing in my way.

The creases in his leather jacket and the oblong discs of the gas mask lenses are full of pale light from the stars and the growing flames in town. The rest of him is solid black. I don't hear any breathing, despite the canister screwed to the mouth of the mask, but I hear the creak of his jacket and gloves when he raises his hand.

I half expect a thumbs-up, just like the one he gave me on Dagger Hill the day he took Kimberly. But instead, he has his index finger pointed upward. He ticks it back and forth at me.

No, no, no.

53.

CHARLIE

"CHARLIE?" MOM SAYS from the shadows. "Baby? Are you there?"

"M-Mom?" My throat has gone dry; the word comes out as a dusty record scratch.

"I missed you, baby." Mom's from Louisiana. Her voice has a slight Southern lilt to it. The sound of it has always brought me comfort, even in the worst of her drug-induced fogs.

"I'm so scared, Mom," I say. My eyes fill and spill, tears dripping off my chin. I realize that I'm just talking to a black opening in a doorway and that the thing I'm talking to is most definitely not my mother. But I don't care. Her voice sounds perfect and genuine, and I want to fall asleep while she sings me "Folsom Prison Blues."

"I know, sweetie," Mom whispers in the dark. I almost, *almost,* think I can see a wink of light in her eyes, staring out at me. "Come here, Charlie." Something in her voice warps a little, and my name sounds deeper, rougher. "Come give me a hug."

Something slips inside my head and presses the go button on my legs. I take one of my lurching steps forward. Then another one.

"Wait," I say. "Wait, no. Stop. Gabe. *Gabe! Gabe, help me!*"

My body surges forward. I try to will myself to stop, but my arm lifts my crutch, sets it down, and I do the work to hobble ahead. I can feel it, the anomaly, squirming around along the nerve endings of my brain, pulling at wires and resetting gears, trying to change me, trying to empty me out. The closer I get to it, the wider the back door opens. There's still nothing but empty blackness on the inside, not even a faint glow from the front windows of the store.

"Jesus Christ, *somebody help me, please!*"

"It's okay, sweetie," Mom says. There's no body to go along with the voice. It sounds like the entire doorway is a mouth, and it's speaking to me in an almost perfect imitation of my mother. Almost, because every so often, her tone dips, and that beautiful singsong accent drops a few octaves, turns sour.

My legs, broken or not, keep pulling me closer. There's nothing I can do to stop it.

"You'll be safe in here with me, Charlie," the doorway says in my mom's voice.

54.

SONYA

THERE'S ANOTHER KNOCK. It's coming from inside room 6. And this time it's more of a bang. Three of them, to be exact.

Bang, bang, bang.

And I can see the door rattling in its frame.

"If you're in there, come out and show yourself!" I yell. Mrs. Rapaport isn't here to encourage me this time. I just have to keep moving. One step, then another. The staircase is barely clinging to the side of the building, but I'm less afraid of its collapsing than I am of confronting whatever's inside that motel room.

Bang, bang, bang.

The sound seems bigger, broader than it should be, as if a microphone is amplifying it. Each heavy knock echoes down the street.

"Don't be such a fucking coward!" I scream. "Get out here and stop me if that's what you're going to do!"

In response, every remaining window of the Banshee Palace explodes outward. The entire building exhales in a violent shower of glass, and I feel the ground rumble beneath me. I stumble forward, almost falling over, covering my head with my arms as pointed shards come down around me like hail.

"You won't stop me," I say, not bothering to yell because I know it can hear me. "Nothing will ever stop me." I continue moving for the staircase, my feet crushing glass now instead of bugs.

When I'm less than a foot from the bottom step, the door to room 6 opens.

55.

GABE

"YOU MIGHT SCARE everyone else," I say to the Bug Man, knowing somehow that it's not really him. I've been afraid of him this whole time, even after Charlie told us he was trying to help. The image of him lifting my friend up and carrying her through smoke and flames still nags at my brain. "But you don't scare me."

It's both true and not true. I'm so scared right now that my knees are wobbling. The only thing keeping me on my feet is my grip on Ricky's antenna. On the other side, the monster dressed as the Bug Man is just standing there. But my words must be true enough to cause some kind of reaction, because he tilts his head to the side, a silent question.

And that's when I shove.

The antenna is heavy, but not so heavy that it can't be pushed across the gravel rooftop. Its feet carve lines in the pebbles, dragging and scraping against bare concrete as I keep the momentum going, putting my whole weight into it, as if I'm charging toward a particularly intimidating linebacker. The assembly, though, seems to get lighter and lighter the more I push. It's because there's another set of hands on the antenna next to mine, gloved ones. Black leather stretching all the way up to a gas mask. It looks at me with those big, smoky lenses. One of the hands lifts and gives me a thumbs-up.

"Thank you," I say to the real Bug Man. And together we keep pushing.

I'm surprised—not to mention delighted—when the anomaly

takes a step back, putting itself even closer to the edge of the roof. I'm screaming now, pushing forward with everything I have. The antenna catches on its wires for a second, but then the wires snap, disconnecting from the box and wriggling away as the Bug Man and I charge forward.

The antenna slams into the anomaly, knocking it backward. One jutting piece of metal catches it in what's supposed to look like its shoulder. Another jabs into the right lens of the gas mask, cracking it. The monster teeters backward, its ankles catching on the ledge. I shove the antenna all the way up to it, until the base knocks against the concrete and the whole thing starts to tip.

At first glance, the anomaly is still there, stuck between the antenna and the open air behind it. Then, as the antenna starts to fall, it's just . . . gone. The whole hastily assembled network of steel and rubber topples off the roof. A ragged hunk of rebar digs into my forearm as it swings upward and over, slicing my skin open. I stumble back, bleeding, lose my balance, and hit the gravel.

I look up just in time to see the last extensions of the antenna vanish over the edge. The sound of it smashing into the ground below is like a hundred quarters dropping into the Pac-Man machine at the arcade. It's the most satisfying thing I've heard all weekend.

A second later, a stray piece of metal emerges from my chest, coated in a glossy layer of my blood.

I look down at it with something akin to curiosity. A burning sensation in my back spreads, and the ground is pooling with a warm crimson puddle. My vision goes hazy, and the skyline of Windale—if you can even call it that—tilts.

Somebody comes around in front of me. One Bug Man . . . then another, the one with the cracked lens in its mask. They're latched on to each other, sparring in such a weirdly human way. Except the anomaly, whose gloved hand is coated in my blood, begins to break free of its disguise, gray limbs shaking loose as the leather jacket peels away. Its flesh is stretched and sinewy, traced with bluish veins. Some kind of mouth droops down below the bottom of the gas mask, lined with mismatched teeth that look like they were collected from dozens of other mouths.

It lunges for the Bug Man, and the Bug Man ducks, catches the monster around the waist and lifts. He smashes the monster down into the gravel, hard, and stomps on it with one booted foot. But those gnarly hands come up, grab the Bug Man's foot, and twist. There's a dull cracking sound, and the Bug Man stumbles back.

Then he begins to sing.

It's a high, wavering sound that drives into my brain the way a dull fork might. The audio signature. This is what it must sound like up close. It's strangely beautiful. Mostly, I think, because I've never heard anything quite like it before, and probably won't ever again.

The anomaly hits back with a signature of its own, this one even higher and sharper, as if someone turned sound into a nail and was trying to hammer it into my skull. I press my hands over my ears, but it doesn't do a lot of good—the sound is as much in my head as it is outside it.

It builds and builds, each creature on either side of the rooftop, pushing their strength into these sounds. I think I might go deaf from it. Or lose my mind the way Clark Webber's cows did.

Then the monster takes a step back, and I can see its gray flesh growing black splotches, like mold. It's taller than the Bug Man, with vaguely human-shaped features that don't feel like they were fully formed. It's terrifying to be this close to it. Even more terrifying to think that my head might rupture before I get to see who wins this fight.

The Bug Man takes a step forward, then another. The sound he's creating is so powerful, and between that and the anomaly's, I think I might pass out.

All at once, the anomaly drops, hitting the gravel on pointed knees. The Bug Man takes his shot, closing the distance between them in a second. He grabs the monster by its face, one half of its asymmetrical jaw in each hand, and he yanks his arms apart. Meanwhile, he's still emitting that sound, focusing it somehow, *aiming* it right down the anomaly's throat.

Until the monster falls apart, breaking down into dry, clumpy particles that either fall and mingle with the rooftop pebbles or drift off on the warm summer air.

The Dagger Hill monster is gone.

And the Bug Man lives. Except he looks hurt. He's stumbling, and the leather jacket seems to droop from his shoulders in a way it never has before, as if it's too big for him. As if he's shrinking inside it. The leather gloves are flopping loosely. There's a crack in his gas mask now, too. He manages to get himself to the roof ledge, and he sits down hard on it, sagging sideways, as if he's in pain.

The closer it got to Windale, the stronger it became.

But it wasn't Windale that made the Bug Man stronger. It was the anomaly. *One predator, one prey.* The only catch is that without the latter, the former has to remain dormant. They may have been natural enemies, but they also fed off each other's energy. The Bug Man might be dying right in front of me.

In the one good lens of his mask, I see my reflection . . . and others. I see bugs and lightning flashing in the clouds and a plane, wings burning, plummeting out of the sky.

When I open my mouth, a little dribble of blood comes out, and it's almost impossible to breathe.

"Wha-What are you?" I ask.

He, it, whatever. There's no reply. And I don't think I need one. I did what I came to do, and so did he. I tip my head back, look up at the night sky as it shrinks away. I'm speeding backward across a field of darkness. It's nice. Cooler. Quieter.

I close my eyes and let it take me.

56.

SONYA

THE THING THAT looks like a man in a gas mask steps out of room 6 almost casually, with its hands behind its back. From down here, it looks shorter than it should be, the leather jacket it wears sagging on its frame. It stumbles and pauses, wavering. It looks injured somehow, off-balance. I take the span of a single breath to wonder if Gabe and Charlie succeeded. Maybe they weakened the Bug Man *and* the anomaly by destroying the antenna, cutting off its signal.

But then the Bug Man is moving along the upper balcony of the Banshee Palace, looking down at me. Or at least, in my direction. It doesn't seem able to focus. Its head is lolling around, its hands still held behind its back, almost in the same way that Colonel Higgins always has hers.

"Where's Kimberly?" I ask it, stepping back from the staircase, keeping my eyes on the Bug Man as it hobbles away from room 6. The door is still open, a deep, yawning darkness on the other side.

She's in there somewhere. I know she is.

"Sonya!" somebody yells behind me. "Get back!"

I turn and see a patrol car pulling into the parking lot. Chief Albright and my dad are in the front seats. My dad is calling to me from the open passenger window. The chief stops the car, opens his door. He pulls his gun from his belt and aims it over my head at the Bug Man.

When I look back at the motel, the Bug Man is still moving for the stairs. But it's so weak, so tired-looking. It seems small and wounded. A part of me feels triumphant, knowing that my friends must have succeeded. Another part of me feels ill. Cruel, even. The Bug Man was trying to help us. It saved our lives. And now it might be collateral damage in the destruction of the monstrous thing that used our town to feast on the anguish of others. The thing that turned us all into monsters so it could stave off its own hunger.

"Just give me a second, Dad," I say, raising a hand to Chief Albright, trying to make him lower his gun. He shakes his head at me.

"Sonya, sweetheart," Dad says. He opens his door, steps out. His eyes are shifting from me to the Bug Man, watching it advance toward the stairs, making sure it keeps its distance. "It's okay. It's over. Higgins and the soldiers, they're gone. Everyone else in town is . . . waking up, I guess. Deputy Conner is at the video store getting the boys right now."

I look to Chief Albright, who only nods. He doesn't even look me right in the eyes. He's focused on the Bug Man, keeping the gun leveled at it.

What am I supposed to do? We don't know enough about what the Bug Man is to just let it go. It's hurt, maybe even dying. And the more I wait, the more Kimberly is inside that motel room suffering.

I turn back to the Banshee Palace, to the Bug Man limping across the balcony, leaning one hip against the railing now. Without even realizing I'm doing it, I lower my arms to my sides, quietly clearing the way for Chief Albright to take his shot.

"Now, Jack," Dad says. "Do it now."

The Bug Man takes a few more tiny, pointless steps. Its hands are still behind its back for some reason, almost as if they're *tied* there. But why would that be? And why are its clothes so big? The Bug Man I saw in my nightmares seemed so much more immense. I squint at it.

I see the loose cuffs of the jacket, and the bare hands poking out of them. Slender and pale.

I see the bare feet at the bottom of the black jeans, dirty and rough with scabs and dried blood.

I see the gas mask bobbing all around its head, hardly staying in place at all. There's something that looks like a price tag dangling from it.

I see the stray curls of sandy blond hair poking out from the cap on its head, bouncing like loosely wound springs.

I see one last trap set by the monster on Dagger Hill, still trying to get what it wants.

"Oh god," I whisper. "Oh my god, Chief, wait. *WAIT! NO!*"

The gun goes off.

I flail my arms, jumping up and over, hoping to be somewhere in the vicinity of the chief's sight line. My ears still ring from all the gunfire I've heard tonight, but this shot sounds louder than all the others.

Up on the balcony, I watch Kimberly stumble backward. Her hands are bound behind her, and god only knows how weak she is. Her balance was gone already. The bullet brings her all the way down. She falls back against the grimy stucco wall. When she slides down it, she leaves a wide paint stroke of blood.

I'm running. My feet are pounding against the broken pavement. I'm at the stairs, up them, ignoring the way the whole rickety staircase wobbles under me. It shrieks beneath my weight, but I'm at the top in a few seconds. I don't think I've ever moved so fast in my life.

I drop to my knees beside her, pull her close to me. The leather jacket feels foreign, slimy. It's even stranger to feel the gas mask in my hand as I peel it off her. I throw the damn thing over the railing.

When I see her face, I burst into tears.

KIMBERLY

57.

TWO WEEKS AFTER "the Riot of 1989," I wake up in a hospital bed. I don't know which hospital; I just know that it's not the Windale Medical Center and that Sonya is there with me. She's asleep in a chair beside the bed, her legs curled under her, the sunlight sweeping through her hair in fiery strings.

I don't have a lot of strength—there are wires and tubes on every side of me, my chest aches, my stomach hurts, my head is pounding—but I have strength enough to lift my hand, reach across the distance separating me from my friend, and squeeze her fingers.

She opens her eyes and smiles, slips her hand fully into mine and doesn't let go. There are so many things she knows that I don't, and so many things I know that she doesn't. But it's a door better left shut for now.

She can tell me later, I think. And I can tell her.

58.

IT TAKES A long time for Sonya to explain everything to me. She tells me about Colonel Higgins, a person I never met and hope to never have to meet. She tells me about the twin anomalies, predator and prey, one of which tormented Windale for centuries. It was that thing that plagued my head before the crash. That thing that drove terrible, violent thoughts into my mind when I wasn't paying attention. It had gotten to all four of us, lured us up to the Hill day after day, year after year. But as it amped up to finish us off for good, I felt it the most, could see what it meant to do. I just couldn't make sense of it.

Mostly, I just tell Sonya about how gross the motel room was.

"The whole time I was there," I tell her, "it was like being underwater. I could only come up for air every now and then. And even when I did, I still didn't feel like I was really there. I was only ever awake through the . . . the Bug Man?"

By now, I can sit up in bed. The gunshot wound in my shoulder is healing. It was a straight in-and-out shot, but it made a mess on the way through. After a couple of minor surgeries and some hospital food that makes Fancy Feast Friday sound like a five-course meal, I've been mostly feeling like myself again.

Mostly.

It helps to have Sonya here. It's a kind of therapy, I guess, talking to her. She's curled up in the bed beside me. We've got some terrible daytime TV on, and we're sharing a bag of Munchos. It would feel like any other summer day except for the way she's looking at me. There's a darkness in her eyes that wasn't there before, a flicker of something that either got left behind by what happened . . . or something that got ripped out of her. Maybe it's both.

"That's what we called it, yeah," she says, staring at me gravely. "Stupid name for something that saved our lives."

59.

I START CLIPPING newspaper articles, pasting them into an album. Colonel Higgins and some of her team were picked up near the Pennsylvania-Ohio border a week after they nearly decimated Windale. The colonel herself was next to dead after some of the zombified townspeople beat her senseless. Not long after that, the army came in, this time led by some bigwig general, and shut down TerraCorp, making up some story about hallucinogenic toxins being released in the air. They put it all on Higgins.

It's like I wasn't even there. I fell asleep in the woods on Dagger Hill and woke up almost two weeks later in the hospital. Everything I know has changed.

But sometimes it doesn't feel that way. Especially when Gabe and Charlie and Sonya come to see me.

Of the four of us, Gabe came the closest to dying that night. He lost so much blood by the time Rebecca Conner found him on the rooftop of the video store. Charlie was also in shock when she found him. And honestly, I don't know if he'll ever be the same. He still carries that same joy he always has, but sometimes it feels like there's slightly less of it.

We're all a little more subdued now. We laugh and rag on each other and try to make light of some of the things that went on that weekend. It's just easy to get bogged down by the idea that Windale itself might not be a livable place right now if not for what we did, if not for Jack Albright and Sonya's dad, too. They're both retired now. They hang out. A lot.

Charlie gets a chance to finally let his broken leg heal, but it will never be totally right after the strain he put on it. Doctors told him he'll probably need to use a cane for the rest of his life.

"That's okay," Charlie says. "It'll make me seem worldly and intriguing." He winks, and we all laugh.

It's good to be together like this, the three of them sitting on the end of my hospital bed, sharing snacks, talking about some movie or TV show or comic book, cracking jokes at each other's expense. But that same inevitable dread that hung over us the day of the crash is still there. Our lives almost ending didn't change the average teenage drama we were going through. Now, we're the Almost Somebodies. Because dying would have made us infamous. Living is just more of the same complicated pain.

A song sung four, I think, watching my friends play Go Fish around my feet. It's a rhyme that isn't mine. The only thing the anomaly left behind instead of took was this stupid lyric that plays in my head on a loop, and I hate it.

All outta time.

60.

THE FIRST TIME Sonya kisses me, I don't see it coming.

We're at my place, curled up on the couch with Meatloaf napping on one armrest and Marshmallow dozing on the other. Dad's home, and Mom is gradually coming to terms with everything. She doesn't completely buy the story that most people are selling about how TerraCorp created these hallucinations with their experiments. Hallucinations that caused some people—June Rapaport and Chet Landry, to name a couple—to do some pretty awful things. But she has some trouble wrapping her head around the idea of the Bug Man, too. Neither story sounds truly believable. She's just glad to have me home, she says.

Sonya and I are alone. Talking about anything that isn't related to the trial or what happened in June, to Sonya's dad, to the investigation, to Charlie, who hasn't really come back to himself yet. We're just talking to fill up the silence and keep our minds off everything.

I turn away for a second to scratch at the back of Marshmallow's head. When I turn back, Sonya's waiting for me, and her lips are suddenly pressed against mine. I inhale sharply, but I don't pull away. Instead, I pull in her scent—hot metal, lavender soap, cinnamon from the Big Red chewing gum she stole from my room.

When she finally leans back, there's this vulnerable look in her eyes, a swelling tenderness that's been growing for who knows how long. This is the pivotal moment that those feelings have been building toward, and I realize that I've been reserving feelings of my own. Parts of myself that I just haven't had time to try to figure out, that maybe I don't need to figure out.

Right now, I know two things. The first is that I love Sonya. The second is that her lips felt good, felt *right*, when they were connected to mine.

The first time Sonya kisses me, she catches me off guard.

The second time she kisses me, I kiss her back.

61.

A YEAR LATER, nothing is the same as it was, but somehow it might be better. It's an entirely new decade. The four of us are high school graduates. Charlie takes photos for the *Windale Press* and loves every second of it. Gabe is training to be a deputy under Chief Rebecca Conner. Sonya and I are preparing to head for Massachusetts any day now.

The "riot" left a lot of people in Windale feeling lost and unsure of their own realities. The anomaly invaded so many people's minds and caused so much trauma in the process that half the population of the town moved away. Toward the end of our last year of high school, businesses started closing their doors, too. The diner, which burned to the ground that night, never reopened. In March and April, the Sunrise Theater and Sid's Comic Emporium went under. By the time graduation came around, most of the Triangle was plastered with OUT OF BUSINESS signs.

In August of 1990, Sonya and I meet Gabe and Charlie at the end of Whisper Trail, at the lookout spot. We're too afraid to go down the trail to the clearing. But this is close enough. This spot is sacred in its own right, not just for our friendship but for so many lives lost to senseless, selfish violence.

We pull each other in and hold each other tight for what feels like a long time and not nearly long enough. Sonya's hand slips into mine, fingers lacing together. The air is warm, but there's a cool breeze. The leaves whisper and shake. It won't be long before autumn makes them extra chattery. In the distance, the water tower is like a pale blue balloon, lingering over a quiet, fearful place. A place that feels like home, even after everything.

"I still promise," I say, looking around at the others, lastly at Charlie, who grins and blushes. I don't have to explain what promise I'm referring to. "I still promise if you guys do."

"I promise," Sonya says, resting her forehead against mine.

"Me too," Gabe says. He runs a hand through his hair, squinting against the sun.

"Wait," Charlie says. "What the hell are you guys talking about? I don't remember any promise." The rest of us groan while he cackles, holding his stomach, leaning on his cane. After a moment, he says, "You know I promise. Always."

We stay there a while longer, hesitating before whatever comes next. I glance around, listening to the trees rustle. Not far along Whisper Trail, near the boulder where we made our original promise, I spot something moving up a gnarled trunk. It's long and slithery, a bug, winding its way up the tree with a thousand legs, searching ahead of itself with arching antennae. It's as black as a night sky.

I close my eyes, my chest suddenly tight with panic. *It's not real, it's not real, it's not real.* I count to ten. When I open my eyes, the thousand-legger is gone. But I still feel an itch creeping up the center of my back, a sense that we're not alone.

Maybe we never will be.

ACKNOWLEDGMENTS

THIS IS THE kind of book I've always wanted to write. Small town, big cast of characters, a monster, a menace. The twelve-year-old version of me, reading *It* for the first time by flashlight into the small hours of the morning, had visions of a book like this with my name on the cover. The problem was that I didn't think I had it in me. In the midst of coffee-and-ice-cream-fueled midnight writing sessions, picking apart one draft to form another, I felt so sure that Gabe, Sonya, Charlie, and Kimberly would never see a world beyond my computer's hard drive. There's a long list of people who believed differently, and if you enjoyed this novel, you should thank them more than me.

First, my publisher, Swoon Reads, and the team there. Created by Jean Feiwel and led fearlessly by Lauren Scobell, I couldn't ask for a better group of people to be at the helm of taking this book to print.

My editor, Emily Settle, and Lauren Scobell co-edited this book with grace, wisdom, and a few swift kicks to my imagination. They helped me turn the story into something I'm immensely proud of, and for that I cannot thank them enough.

Heather Vaughan illustrated the cover for *Dagger Hill*, and it's perfect, plain and simple. She's hugely talented and a fellow Pennsylvanian, which is probably why those thousand-leggers are so accurate and creepy.

The Swoon Squad of fellow authors is a life raft floating on the choppy, uncertain waters of the publishing industry. Our mutual friendship and support have helped get some of us through the dreariest days of our respective careers. I'm very grateful to be a part of that group.

I'd like to give a big shout-out to all the local indie bookstores that have hosted events for me and have put my books at the forefront of their stores. Three of the standouts include Cupboard Maker Books in Enola, Pennsylvania; Let's Play Books in Emmaus, Pennsylvania; and Towne Book Center in Collegeville, Pennsylvania. Huge thanks to booksellers there who have put valuable time and effort into helping get my books into the hands of readers.

In the realm of friends and family, I'd like to thank my best friend, Cait Brittenburg, who understands the nature of being an adult and how it can sometimes affect friendships. Ours has gone undeterred for many years now, and we're always no more than a text message away from picking up right where we left off. She always has my back.

My siblings and siblings-in-law: Shane, Chloe, Morgan, and Michael. This book is dedicated to my brother, Shane, because even though I'm older, he knows way more about a lot of random stuff than I do. His veins flow with trivia and music, and I thought about him several times while writing this book. All four of them are constantly supportive, forever positive, and always willing to babysit. Thanks, guys.

My in-laws, Dynel and Eric, who took us in during a really difficult period in our life and my life personally. They bought me dinner the night my first book came out because we had spent our last fifteen dollars on gas so I could drive around and sign copies all day. Now that we're back on our feet, I'm more grateful than ever for them and for their support.

My parents, Mylinda and Jeff. They are such an important part of my life and my kids' lives. They hold me up when I'm feeling heavy and anchor me down when I feel like I might float away. The term "parents" has had a nontraditional meaning in my family for a long time, but let me tell you, these two are the real deal. I have no idea what I'd do without them.

My wife, Kelsey, and my daughters, Rylan and Norrie, come last because they hold the closest place to my heart. They *are* my heart. They see me at my worst and best depending on what day it is and choose to love me either way. They are my number one fans and my greatest support system, and no matter how many times they beat me at Uno, I still wake up every day thankful that I have them here with me. Ladies, I love you a whole bunch. Also, nose bop.

This book, if nothing else, is a love letter to the horror genre. I grew up hunting down the thrill of being afraid. I doubt that I did that sensation any justice here, but I gave it my best shot. Thank you all for reading.